GUNFIRE IN THE NIGHT

The long, hard drive to Papago Wells began to take its toll. A dozen times Gil was jolted awake, aware that he had dozed in the saddle. The harder he strove to remain awake, to be alert, the more surely his weary body betrayed him.

But nothing brought a frontiersman to full awareness as quickly as gunfire, and such was the case with Gil Austin and his companions.

The night riders came in from the north, shouting and shooting. Gil and the rest of the nighthawks kicked their mounts to a gallop, and by the time they reached the spring, the rest of the outfit was in the saddle. Amid the shouting, there was a scream of terror; a Bowie in the hand of one of the Indian riders had found a victim. The outlaws had stampeded at least some of the horses, but when Gil and his riders began throwing lead at the oncoming rustlers, a strange thing happened. The horse herd, with mounted, gun-wielding riders behind and in front of them, split. The horses ran east and west, and the surprised outlaws came face-to-face with the entire Texas outfit. . . .

St. Martin's Paperbacks Titles
by Ralph Compton

The Trail Drive Series

The Goodnight Trail

The Western Trail

The Chisholm Trail

The Bandera Trail

The California Trail

The Shawnee Trail

The Virginia City Trail

The Dodge City Trail

The Oregon Trail

The Santa Fe Trail

The Old Spanish Trail

The Green River Trail

The Deadwood Trail

The Sundown Riders Series

North to the Bitterroot

Across the Rio Colorado

The Winchester Run

THE
CALIFORNIA
TRAIL

Ralph Compton

St. Martin's Paperbacks

This is a work of fiction, based on actual trail drives of the Old West. Many of the characters appearing in the Trail Drive Series were very real, and some of the trail drives actually took place. But the reader should be aware that, in the developing of characters and events, some fictional literary license has been employed. While some of the characters and events herein are purely the creation of the author, every effort has been made to portray them with accuracy. However, the inherent dangers of the trail are real, sufficient unto themselves, and seldom has it been necessary to enhance their reality.

THE CALIFORNIA TRAIL

Copyright © 1994 by Ralph Compton.

Cover photograph by Getty Images/Nicolas Russell.

Map on p. vii by David Lindroth, based upon material supplied by the author.

For information address St. Martin's Press, 175 Fifth Avenue, New York, NY 10010.

EAN: 978-0-312-95169-6

Printed in the United States of America

St. Martin's Paperbacks edition / January 1994

15   14   13   12   11

"When you've been throwed and stomped, get up, dust yourself off, and get back in the saddle. The worst that can happen is you'll get throwed and stomped again."

—Ralph Compton, 1993

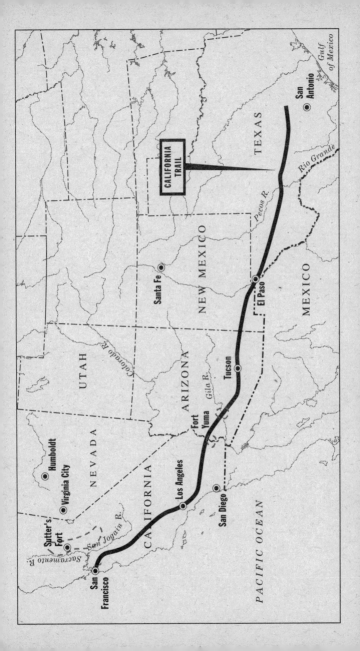

AUTHOR'S FOREWORD

*F*or nine long years, following the infamous battle at the Alamo, Texans lived under constant threat of invasion by Mexico. Not until 1845, when the Republic of Texas became part of the United States, did the threat cease. But the inevitable war between Mexico and the United States had yet to take place. Until 1848 Mexico still claimed the territories of New Mexico and California, and refused to recognize the Rio Grande as the border between Texas and Mexico. The war was brutal, bloody, and short. A treaty of peace was signed on February 2, 1848, in the presidential palace at Guadalupe Hidalgo, four miles north of Mexico City. The terms were brutal, but quite simple: The United States wanted only what it had already seized, which were the territories of New Mexico and California. And, of course, recognition of the Rio Grande as Mexico's border with Texas. The treaty was signed, the territories ceded to the United States, and the Rio Grande was recognized as the border. Mexico received a consolation payment of $15 million.

In California, in January 1848, gold was discovered at Sutter's Mill. Fearing the rush that eventually destroyed him, Sutter had tried to keep the discovery secret, and did for another year. But news leaked out, and by 1849 the rush was on. They came by the dozens, by the hundreds, by the thousands, and finally by the tens of thousands. Doctors, lawyers, preachers, farmers, scholars, illiterates, gamblers, dreamers, brave men, and cowards. By 1852 California's population had grown from .14,000 to more than 100,000, most of them tramping through the central valleys of the newly admitted state and up the slopes of the Sierra.

Mexico had relaxed many of the regulations the Spanish had imposed on California, allowing vessels under foreign flags to bring trade goods from England, China, France, and the United States. But the Californios needed something to trade, so they began slaughtering their longhorn cattle. Not for the meat, but for hides and tallow. Virtually overnight, the gold rush had created a need for the hundreds of thousands of longhorns that had been slaughtered for hides and tallow. In trade, the tallow brought six cents a pound, while the hides sold for as little as a dollar. Total profit from a cow might be as little as seven dollars, and no more than $8.50. The meat was left to rot, and there weren't enough scavengers to keep ahead of the terrible slaughter. A macabre joke was that vultures flew in, but were forced to walk away, being too gorged to fly. Sailing into the wind, a ship's crew could smell the stench hours before reaching port. Warehouses where hides had been stored were eventually abandoned. Nobody could stand the odor.

The beef that had rotted in the California sun was needed to feed the hungry miners. California had the gold, but Texas had the beef, and it was a one-time opportunity that some Texans were quick to recognize. Men with sand to attempt such a trail drive—those who lived to see the successful end of it—returned to Texas with the wealth that eluded most of the gold seekers.

This trail drive, with its Texas longhorns bound for the goldfields, would take the same perilous route the Butterfield Overland Express would follow a dozen years later. From South Texas to the Pecos River, across the plains of southern New Mexico and Arizona, to southern California. Eighteen hundred miles of treacherous rivers, hostile Indians, Comancheros, outlaws, stampedes, desert, sandstorms, and rattlesnakes the size of a man's leg. It was a poison-mean land where a man fought the elements and his own kind, and death was cloaked in so many forms, it staggered the imagination. It was a ride through Hell that few men lived to talk about. Those who did—mostly leather-tough Texans, handy with a Bowie and fast with a Colt—called it the "California Trail."

PROLOGUE

September 1, 1849

Gold had been discovered in California! Gil Austin rode out of San Antonio, bound for Bandera Range and the vast Box AA ranch he shared with his brother Van. Tucked into his saddlebag was a copy of the newspaper in which he had just read of the gold strike, and his heart leaped with excitement. Gil had not been smitten with "gold fever," a man's usual reaction to such news, but with the possibilities surrounding the discovery. It was the last two or three paragraphs of the newspaper account that had interested him. Miners were flocking to California by the thousands, and there was a critical shortage of beef. In Texas the problem facing them was exactly the reverse. There was a blessed plenty of beef, but a critical shortage of gold. A man didn't sell a cow, he was forced to swap it for something he could use.

According to the newspaper, a small herd of cattle driven from Oregon to the goldfields had sold for two hundred dollars a head. Other herds, even those less than prime, not a cow had gone for less than seventy-five dollars. For a thousand head, that was $75,000! Four thousand head would bring more than a quarter of a million dollars! Anxious to share the news with his brother Van, Gil kicked his horse into a slow gallop. As he rode, he allowed his mind to drift back over the years, recalling when he, Van, and their amigo, Clay Duval, had left Missouri to become part of the American Colony. Clay had been twenty-one, Gil nineteen, and Van a year younger.

The American Colony, after a disastrous beginning, was saved in 1825, when Stephen Austin—uncle to Gil and Van—had gone to Mexico City and received permission from the Mexican government to colonize millions of acres along the Brazos and Colorado rivers. Stephen had received 67,000 acres of land, and had managed to secure grants for his nephews next to his own. Gil and Van had taken their grants in 1833, and when Stephen had died in 1836, they had taken his grants too. In all, they had more than 75,000 acres, but the irony of it was, they had been lacking the cattle and horses necessary for the ranch they wanted.

In Mexico there had been an abundance of longhorn cows, valued only for hides and tallow. To the south of the State of Durango, Antonio Mendoza had raised fine blooded horses. Despite a conflict with Mexico that would lead to war, Clay Duval had been determined to ride south on a twofold mission. He planned to deal with Mendoza for breeding stock, and with Mexican ranchers for longhorn cattle. But when Clay reached the Mendoza ranch, he found that Mendoza had been ambushed, and that Victoria, his beautiful but conniving widow, was involved in a questionable relationship with Esteban Valverde, an unscrupulous neighbor. Victoria had wished to flee Mexico, and in return for safe passage back to Texas, had offered Clay Duval the horses and cattle he had wanted.

In the fall of 1842, Gil and Van Austin had received a letter from Clay, asking for their help. In December, Gil and Van had already ridden south. Barely across the border, they had been captured by Mexican soldiers. Facing prison, they had broken loose, making their way afoot to the Mendoza ranch. Gil and Van arrived to find

Clay Duval missing and Victoria Mendoza more eager than ever to escape Mexico. Her loyal riders—eight Mexican vaqueros, and three Mexican Indians—had joined Gil and Van in gathering five thousand longhorns. Angelina Ruiz, Victoria's young, rebellious sister, had believed she knew where Clay Duval was, and accompanied by the Indian, Solano, had ridden away in the night.

The first week of July 1843, the seemingly impossible trail drive had moved out, heading north. Victoria Mendoza had insisted on driving a wagon; a big, mysterious Conestoga. On the trail, in a final confrontation with Esteban Valverde, Victoria's teams had stampeded. The ill-fated wagon had gone over a canyon rim, taking Victoria Mendoza and Esteban Valverde with it. Thus Gil and Van had been left with the famous Mendoza horses, and a herd of almost five thousand longhorns, but the trail north had been fraught with danger. Mexican soldiers had been strung out for five hundred miles along the border, with military outposts at Meoqui, Monterrey, and Matamoros. Gil had found and taken in an orphaned, naked little Mexican girl they had known only as "Rosa." In a clash with Mexican soldiers, Gil and Van had been captured. Some of the soldiers had been left with the trail drive, instructed to take it to Matamoros, while the others had taken Gil and Van to the outpost at Monterrey. There they had been reunited with Long John Coons, a knife-wielding Cajun they had left in charge of their land grant on Bandera Range.

Gil, Van, and Long John had been taken to the outpost at Matamoros, a few miles south of the border. Unknown to Gil and Van, Angelina Ruiz and Solano had found and freed Clay Duval from a prison in Mexico City. The trio had then traveled north, toward the border, and had caught up to the soldier-escorted trail drive bound for Matamoros. Clay Duval had managed to rid the drive of the soldiers, and had devised a plan to free Gil and Van from the guardhouse at the Matamoros outpost. In a daring rescue, Clay had blown the roof off the guardhouse, freeing Gil, Van, Long John, and other captive Texans. But Mexican soldiers had gotten ahead of them and had gathered near the border. Gil, Van, and Clay had then stampeded the herd of long-horns and Mendoza horses, driving them through Mexican forces, and had reached the Texas side of the Rio Grande.*

But the danger hadn't been over. Rangers in South Texas had warned them of the infamous Torres gang, that the Torres brothers—Manuel and Miguel—might come after the Mendoza horses. But their fight with the Torres gang had taken place for an altogether different reason. Van and Mariposa—the Indian—had followed a mysterious trail that had proven to be that of the out-laws, and Van had caught Manuel Torres with a girl the gang had stolen from her home on the Atascosa River, south of San Antonio. Van had been forced to kill Manuel Torres, and eventually his brother Miguel, who had sought revenge. The hazardous trail drive from Durango, Mexico, to Bandera Range had been a journey bordering on the impossible, an adventure of a lifetime. Clay Duval and Van Austin, Gil decided, had been particularly blessed in a way that had eluded him.

The girl Van had rescued from the Torres gang—Dorinda Jabez—was now his wife, and young Van was almost two years old. Clay Duval, surprising nobody, had married Angelina Ruiz, and their daughter, Christabel, was the very image of Angelina. Clay was in full charge of their horse ranch—the Winged M—and he and Van had homes of their own. Gil sighed. He was now thirty-five years old, sleeping alone, with no other prospect in sight. His one salvation was that he didn't have to eat his own cooking. He was always welcome at Clay's or Van's table, and he was still the only man in young Rosa's life. Although unsure of her age, Rosa thought she was twelve, at least, and she spoke English like a Texan, born and bred. She was also an excellent cook, having been taught by Dorinda. Angelina set a good table, but Van, the lucky dog, had snared himself a farm girl from Kentucky. When Gil rode in, Rosa came running to meet him. Her dark hair curled neatly to her shoulders, and while she wore a dress when she absolutely had to, her usual garb was tight-legged vaquero breeches, loose-fitting shirt, and the moccasins the Indian riders were always making for her. She had retired the mule she had ridden from Mexico, and had her pick of the horses, loving them all. Gil had broken her from swearing in rapid-fire Spanish, only to find that she had developed it more eloquently in English. Now, he swung out of his saddle, grabbed Rosa, and kissed her on the cheek.

"Always on the cheek," she fussed. "When am I to receive a real kiss?"

"When you're thirty-six." Gil laughed. "Have you started supper?"

"No," she said, "I wish to eat with Van and Dorinda."

"Why not with Clay and Angelina?"

"I love Angelina like a sister," said Rosa, "but I am sick of the damn chili peppers."

"Rosa!"

"She puts them in everything except the coffee," said Rosa. "Tejano want Tejano grub."

"Every day you sound more like Long John Coons," said Gil. "Come on, I'll saddle you a horse."

Gil hoisted her up to the saddle and they rode on to the barn and the corrals. Gil had built a cookhouse and had hired a cook, a garrulous old man with a peg leg, known only as "Stump." He had been to sea, had scars from every waterfront dive from New Orleans to the West Indies, and could swear in five languages. Rosa adored him and his bloodthirsty tales. It was near suppertime, and the riders had gathered at the bunkhouse. Of the original Mendoza outfit, Gil still had eight riders. There was his segundo, Ramon Alcaraz, along with Juan Alamonte, Manuel Armijo, Domingo Chavez, Pedro Fagano, Vicente Gomez, Juan Padillo, and an Argentine known only as Bola, or "Bo." The Mexican Indian riders were unsurpassed as gentlers of horses, and the three—Solano, Mariposa, and Estanzio—were with Clay Duval at the horse ranch. Of course, there was the enigmatic Long John Coons. Gil wasn't sure why he had allowed the Cajun to stay, or why he had wanted to. Every rider—even the Indians—spoke English now, but only one man in the outfit seemed to consider Long John a friend. Bo, the Argentine who threw a three-headed bola like most men used a lariat, had found something to like about the Cajun. It had become a most unusual alliance, Long John a lanky giant of more than six feet, and Bola only an inch or two above five, even in his boots.

Van had seen Gil and Rosa coming, and when they rode in, he was waiting on the porch. Rosa dismounted and ran to scoop up little Van, who was about to fall off the porch trying to reach her.

"Light and come in," said Van. "We just happen to have a pair of extra places at the table, and you know Dorinda—she always cooks enough to feed everybody on the Bandera spread."

Gil took his time dismounting, allowing Rosa to go on into the house. What he was about to propose was going to create one hell of a furor, and he wanted to talk to Van without interruption from Rosa and Dorinda. From his saddlebag Gil took the newspaper, folded to the story about the discovery of gold in California, and without a word passed it to Van. His brother read it quickly, then read it again. With his half grin, he looked at Gil for a long moment before he spoke. When he did, it was to ask a question.

"How big a trail drive you got in mind, and how many riders?"

"Four thousand head," said Gil, "and all the riders except you, Clay, and Solano. You and Clay will have to hire some riders for the ranch. This is an opportunity that won't come again, and we have to make up for the lean years. God knows, if it hadn't been for the horse ranch, we'd have starved."

"There's just been a change in plans," said Van. "I'm going with you. Clay just got elected to hire some riders and segundo the Bandera spread."

1

Once Gil and Van Austin had agreed upon the trail drive to the California goldfields, they wasted no time in approaching Clay Duval with the proposal.

"You're right," said Clay, "this is somethin' we can't afford to pass up. If the kind of money they're talkin' about is for real, this one trail drive could set us up for life. We'd never have to sell another cow. Trouble is, I don't know if I should feel flattered that you're leavin' the Bandera spread in my hands, or insulted that you reckon you can take a herd of longhorns on such a drive without me."

"Take it as a compliment," said Gil. "Remember the last trail drive, when the both of us ended up in a Mexican *juzgado*? Next time, it may be a California *juzgado*. We may need you on the outside, with a keg of powder."*

"Don't laugh," said Van. "He may be more right than he knows. We're only lookin' at the potential reward of such a drive, without considering all we may have to survive to reach it. We could hire a segundo and the riders to look after the ranches, the longhorns, and the horses, but there's more at stake than that. I want to know that little Van and Dorinda are safe, all the time I'm away."

* Trail Drive #4, *The Bandera Trail*

"And there's Rosa," said Gil.

"Whoa," said Clay. "She's your *querida*.* She'll grab a horse and light out after you. You want me to rope her out of the saddle and hogtie her till you get back?"

"We still have some time," said Gil. "I'll talk to her." He looked forward to that with all the enthusiasm of a man about to be bucked off into a cactus patch and then stomped.

"You're only leavin' me Solano," said Clay, "but with Mariposa and Estanzio helping, we should be caught up on the gentling of horses before you're ready to move out. Now at your place, there'll be only the cook, old Stump. We'll need a good dozen riders while you're gone, and I don't mean just men with horse and cow savvy. Sooner or later the Comanches are goin' to come after us; if not for our hair, then for our horses. Same holds true for rustlers."

"Why don't you ride to San Antone tomorrow," said Gil, "and make known our need for hard-ridin', fast-shootin' men? While you're there, stop at the mercantile and have them order us new weapons. I want two dozen of the new Dragoon Colt six-shooters, with the seven and a half inch barrel, and a thousand rounds of ammunition for each. If possible, I'd like the same number of .50 caliber Hawken rifles, out of St. Louis. Get plenty of horseshoes too, along with an extra set of necessary tools. I'll want enough shoes for every horse on the trail drive to have an extra set. We'll be taking a sixty-horse remuda and five packhorses."

"My God," said Clay, "do we have that kind of credit in town?"

"We do," said Gil, "and more. Remember, we've been supplyin' beef to the town for nearly six years, gettin' only credit. Nobody's had any gold."

"That reminds me of something," said Van. "The outfit's been taking wages in cows. Do you aim to let that four thousand head include some or all of their stock?"

* Sweetheart.

"I'm inclined to," said Gil. "I think it's fair. We could allow every rider to take as many as fifty, without it hurtin' us."

"That's more than generous," said Clay. "All right, I'll ride to town tomorrow and get the word out that we're needin' riders, and I'll drop this list of needs off at the mercantile. I just hope *they* have credit enough to buy for *us*."

"So do I," said Gil.

For three days after she had learned of the impending trail drive, Rosa had sulked in silence. Not so much because she wouldn't be going, Gil felt, but because *he* would be. She had become so possessive, something had to be done. Thanks to Dorinda and Angelina, Rosa already had a better education than most frontier females, but Gil decided she was ready for something more formal. Such as a four-year girl's school, in New Orleans or St. Louis. If the trail drive to California proved even half as successful as they hoped, he would have the money for such an extravagance. But it soon became apparent that they wouldn't be able to begin the drive until after the first of the year, and that Rosa had ideas that exceeded Gil's wildest imagination.

She had always respected his privacy in the cabin they shared, and Gil had respected hers. It came as a shock when, one night, he awakened from a sound sleep and found Rosa in his room. She stood at the foot of his bed, and how long she had been there, he didn't know. While he wasn't sure why she was there, he had a terrifying suspicion. His first look at the girl dispelled forever his thoughts of her as a child. The light of a full moon shone through the window, and Rosa stood there stark naked, a woman in every sense of the word! Gil almost stopped breathing, but forced himself to continue slowly and evenly, lest she know that he was awake. But his years on the hazardous frontier had so conditioned him, that another's breathing could awaken him, and this Rosa knew. Still he played possum, fearing that she might actually get into bed with him, forcing him to acknowledge her presence. Finally she turned away and, like a pale ghost, swept slowly through the open door, out of his sight. He slept no more that night, discarding one idea after another, a vivid picture of the naked Rosa burned into his mind. When at last the eastern sky paled from gray to rose, Gil got up. He would say nothing of Rosa's nocturnal visit, covertly watching her. It came as no surprise when he found her in her usual garb, breakfast all but ready. He sat down and she poured his coffee. She returned the pot to the stove, and when she turned back to face him, the half smile on her lips was more terrifying than the frown she had worn for the past three days. Something in his expression told her what she wished to know, and she was glorying in it! She spoke not a word, but sat down across the table from him, sipping her own coffee. Her enigmatic smile remained, and in her eyes was the wisdom of a thousand years. Chill fingers caressed his spine, and he sat there looking into his half-empty cup. . . .

When Gil and Van Austin had departed, Clay Duval sat at the kitchen table so immersed in his own thoughts that Angelina had to speak to him twice before he heard her.

"They are going without you," she said. "Do you have regrets?"

"No," he said. "I was just wonderin' why Dorinda didn't come out breathin' fire and smoke when Van decided to go."

"Dorinda understands. Van is concerned about his brother."

Angelina had pulled out a chair and sat across the table from him. His eyebrows lifted, Clay looked at her, and she laughed.

"Gil is restless, lost, vulnerable," she said.

"So Van is goin' along to protect him," said Clay. *"Querida,* Gil Austin is about as vulnerable as a lobo wolf."

"I do not question his ability to physically defend himself against almost any odds," she said. "It is you and Van who are forcing him to face an enemy he fears, in a fight he is unsure of winning."

"Well, by God," said Clay, "thanks on behalf of Van and me."

She continued as though he hadn't spoken. "You have a home, a wife, and a daughter. Van has a home, a wife, and a son. Gil is lacking all this, and it is the contrast that is bothering him, making him vulnerable."

"So he's likely to go to California and bring back some female catamount that'll geld and brand him."

"Clay Duval, sometimes you are so crude, I—"

He grinned. "That ain't what you said, but it's what you meant."

"The problem does not lie in California, or at the end of any trail, but within Gil himself. Can you not see what is happening between him and Rosa?"

He kicked his chair back and got up, his palms flat on the table, just looking at her. His nostrils flared and his brown eyes had gone cold.

"Rosa can't be more than twelve," he said. "Thirteen at the most. Are you sayin' that Gil—"

"I did not accuse Gil of anything," she said. "While you think of Rosa as a child, she thinks of herself as a woman, and it is in that light that I see her. So does Dorinda. Rosa has the resources and the yearnings of a woman. A child of twelve, perhaps thirteen? I think not."

He sat down, allowing his temper to subside before he spoke. "So the trail drive to the goldfields ain't just the money," he said. "Gil's leavin' a situation here that he ain't sure he can handle. But a man can't run forever. What's going to keep this thing from gettin' back in the saddle and sinkin' the gut hooks in him again, when he returns?"

"A wife perhaps," said Angelina.

* * *

Oscar Stackmeier was a Missourian, a friend of Moses Austin, Stephen's late father. The potential of Texas's American Colony had excited Oscar, and he had given up his trading post in St. Joe for a larger one in San Antonio. Oscar had long been a friend to Gil and Van Austin, even when they were anything but flush, a condition that had plagued them since their arrival from Missouri. It had been Oscar Stackmeier's willingness to trade for beef that had been the salvation of the Bandera spread. He was a thin little man, with watery blue eyes and wire-rimmed spectacles, whose generosity was exceeded only by his bluntness. Having read the list Clay Duval had given him, he looked at Clay over the tops of his spectacles.

"Clay, you boys are a mite late. Two thousand years late. Jesus Christ could of turned longhorn beef into Hawken rifles and Colt revolvers, but I purely can't. I doubt the Hawken brothers make as many rifles in a year as you're wantin' right now. As for the Colt Dragoons, you'll have to get in line behind the Texas Rangers and the United States Army. Now horseshoes, I can get."

That had been setback enough, but the day wasn't over. Clay had made the rounds of the saloons, the stores, the barber shops and bathhouses, even the wagon yard, without finding even one potential rider for the Bandera ranch. Instead he heard story after story of men who had lit out for California in pursuit of gold. He had been about to ride out in total defeat, when he encountered "Big Foot" Wallace and several of his Rangers. In the fall of 1843, Gil, Van, and Clay had brought a herd of longhorns and a herd of blooded horses from Mexico, stampeding them across the Rio Grande, with the Mexican army in pursuit. Big Foot Wallace had been the first Texan they'd seen, and the big Ranger had taken a personal interest in them.*

* Trail Drive #4, *The Bandera Trail*

"Howdy," said Wallace. "Them Mex cows learnin' to eat Texas grass?"

"That's the easy part," Clay grinned. "We're aimin' to take a herd to California, to the goldfields, if we can find the guns, the ammunition, and the riders. We was hopin' for some of the new Colt Dragoon six-shooters, but I just learned the Rangers and the United States Army's ahead of us."

"You can thank Captain Jack Hays for that," said Wallace. "He's managed to order enough for every Ranger to have two Colts, plus an extra cylinder. The extra cylinder will interchange with either Colt, givin' a man eighteen shots without reloading."

"That's why we wanted our riders on the trail drive to California to have them," said Clay. "We hear there's hostile Injuns every jump of the way, and we come out of Mexico with all manner of foreign-made pistols. I reckon no two of 'em takes the same kind of ammunition, and I'd swap the whole bunch for one good Colt."

"Know what you mean," said Wallace. "How many Dragoons was you tryin' to get?"

"Two dozen," said Clay, "but we could make do with fifteen."

"Captain Ben McCulloch knows you and the Austins," said Wallace. "Ben's after Captain Jack Hays to order enough of the Dragoons so we'll have them to arm new men. You know, Colt went busted in 1842, and Ben thinks it could happen again. Let me talk to Ben McCulloch; if he can get Captain Jack to order a few dozen extra Dragoons, I might arrange for you to get the Colts you need. The Comanches are goin' to give us hell in the years to come, and I'd like to see every Texan armed with one of these Colt six-shooters."

"We'd be obliged," said Clay, "and the sooner the better. Now we need some riders. Ain't got a dozen Rangers, with horse and cow savvy, that you can spare for about a year, have you?"

Wallace laughed, not even dignifying that with a reply. Clay mounted and rode back to Bandera Range.

* * *

Gil had delayed his talk with Rosa as long as he could, and when he finally decided to be done with it, he found her every bit as adamant and unreasonable as he had expected.

"If I cannot go with you," she insisted, "then I will stay where I wish to stay, and I wish to stay here at our house. I am no longer a child, and I will not endure all the months you are gone, having Angelina and Dorinda threatening to spank me."

"I'd not mind you staying here," said Gil, "if our own riders were going to be in the bunkhouse. But they're going with me on the trail drive, and Clay will be hiring some new men to take over until we return. I am very much aware that you're no longer a child, Rosa, and I don't want you here alone, with strange riders in the bunkhouse."

"It would upset you, ah reckon," she said, imitating his drawl, "if these new riders had their way with me."

That half smile touched her lips. She was taunting him with the very thing he feared the most, throwing it in his face.

"Yes, damn it!" he shouted. "It would upset me. I didn't drag you out of Mexico to have you become a *puta* in my own house while I am away. Maybe I've been wrong, but I'd hoped that if you had no respect for your-self, that you'd have some for me!"

That got to her. Her face paled, the smile vanished, and she swallowed hard before she spoke.

"No man will ever use me against my will. I would kill him."

Their conversation ended, resolving nothing, but Gil discovered he had won a small victory. While she ada-mantly refused to stay with Angelina or Dorinda while he was gone, never again did she taunt him in a manner that opened her morality to question.

When Van and Clay again rode to Gil's place, their concern was for new riders. Or the lack of them. The three men seemed to fill a room, each of them over six feet without hat or boots. Gil and Van were towheaded and blue-eyed. Clay's hair was a faded brown, almost a sorrel. His eyes were soft brown, but when he was angry, they shot sparks of green fire.

"I've got just one possibility," said Gil, "and it's not my idea. Long John Coons claims if he could ride back to Louisiana for a few days, he could maybe bring us some old pards of his."

"For some reason I've never quite figured out," said Van, "I like Long John, but I'd think long and hard before hirin' any rider that's a friend of his. Remember in 'forty-two when we was tryin' to get a trail herd out of Mexico, and we ended up in a Mex *calabozo* in Monterrey? Who ends up right in there with us, but Long John Coons, big as life and twice as ugly? When we'd left him here with specific instructions to keep an eye on the ranch."*

"It was just a thought," said Gil. "We don't have that many prospects."

"Who wants to stay in Texas and nurse cows?" said Van. "Huntin' gold has to pay better."

"*Anything* pays better," said Clay. "Hell's fire, I hear a private in the army gets eight dollars a month. That's a regular bonanza, compared to what we've made in the cattle business."

"This is gettin' us nowhere," said Gil. "I'm going to ride into San Antone tomorrow and nose around some. Maybe I'll check with Big Foot Wallace and see if he's havin' any luck gettin' us some Colt Dragoons."

November 5, 1849. San Antonio, Texas

When Gil reached San Antonio, Wallace and his men were away. Captain Ben McCulloch was there, however, and that proved even more beneficial. Gil, Van, and Clay had fought under McCulloch's command at San

* Trail Drive #4, *The Bandera Trail*

Jacinto. Then, in 1843, when the trio had brought a miraculous trail drive from Mexico, they had so impressed Big Foot Wallace that the Ranger had arranged for them to tell their story to Sam Houston. The information Gil, Van, and Clay had supplied had been helpful in the eventual war with Mexico. As a result, Clay Duval and the Austins were well thought of by the Texas Rangers and by men at the reins of state government in Austin. When Gil saw Captain McCulloch go into a restaurant, he followed.

"I hear you're taking a trail drive to the goldfields," said McCulloch.

"I'm beginning to have some doubts," said Gil. "We've run headlong into a couple of problems, and haven't found a solution to either of them."

"I reckon I can solve one of them," said McCulloch. "The one you spoke to Wallace about. Eventually, I'll be forced to account for the, ah, items in question, and this is something you are not to speak of. Not to anybody."

"I understand," said Gil, "and I'm obliged, but I have to be honest. I purely don't have the money to pay for them, and won't until this trail drive is done. God knows, we've survived only by swappin' beef for everything from horseshoes to bacon on the hoof."

"I'll have a few months' grace," said McCulloch, "before I have to pay. We're a state, but Texas still ain't flush. Not by a jugful. Have you hired the riders Duval was lookin' for?"

"No," said Gil. "Looks like everybody's lit out for the goldfields."

"I can maybe get you some good men," said McCulloch. "That is, if you ain't opposed to Injuns."

"We brought three back from Mexico as part of our outfit," said Gil, "and I'd pay double wages for some more riders as good. We already have the riders for the trail drive, but I need some men on the spread I can trust. I agree with Big Foot—sooner or later the Comanches are going to try and run us out. I want some fighting men with cow savvy, but the longhorns can pretty well take care of themselves. The riders we leave behind will be working under Clay Duval, and he's responsible for the safety of all three of our homes and outbuildings on the Bandera spread."

"Then I think I may have the solution to your problem," said McCulloch. "You ever hear of the Lipan Apaches?"

"Yes," said Gil. "Captain Jack Hays has been using them as scouts against the Comanches."

"That he has," said McCulloch, "and a Lipan Apache will ride a hundred miles to fight Comanches. The tribes are bitter enemies. Otherwise, the Lipans are peaceful Injuns. There's a village south of here, on the San Antonio River. The Lipans catch a few cows, sometimes crossing into Mexico. They trade beef for goods at different villages, and are well thought of. They were friendly to the padres when the Spanish had missions here. The time's comin' when Texas will be cattle country, and these Lipan Apaches were the first cowboys, learning from the Spanish. They ride like they're part of the horse, they got cow savvy, they're hell on Comanches, and my God, they can follow a trail across solid rock. Someday—and you'll live to see it—there'll be many trail drives such as yours. Then I believe you'll see cattlemen turning to these Lipan Apaches as hard-ridin' cowboys, scouts, and Injun fighters."*

"They sound like our kind of people," said Gil. "Will there be a language problem?"

"Not if you speak Spanish," said McCulloch. "Most of them speak it well, but I'll ride down there with you, if you want."

"I'd take it as a favor," said Gil, "but can we do it tomorrow? Since Clay will be in charge of these riders, I'd like for him to go with us."

"Tomorrow, then," said McCulloch.

* * *

* Trail Drive #3, *The Chisholm Trail*

Returning to the Bandera spread, Gil rode immediately to Clay's, telling him of their good fortune and
setting a time for them to ride out the next morning.
When Gil returned to his own place, it was nearly suppertime, and Rosa had the meal ready for the table. She
seemed unusually contrite, and had a smile for him.
There had been a change, and he had no more than sat
down at the table when she told him what it was. Or
what she wished him to *believe* it was.

"While you are gone on the trail drive," she said, "I
will stay with Dorinda and little Van."

"Pardon me if I seem suspicious," said Gil, "but why
the sudden change?"

"I decided that I was being selfish, and that you would
worry about me. I remembered what you said about
bringing me out of Mexico, and I decided I was being
very ungrateful. You could have just left me where you
found me."

"You've done some growin' up since we talked last,"
said Gil, telling her what she wished to hear. His own
private conclusion was that she had decided what she
was going to do, and that staying with Dorinda was the
furthest thing from her mind.

Gil and Clay reached San Antonio an hour after first
light, and a few minutes later, when McCulloch led out,
they followed. They traveled south along the San Antonio River for a little more than three hours.

"Lipan Apaches aren't nomads," said McCulloch.
"They live in mud and log huts, and they have some
pretty decent farms. The women do, that is. The men
still hunt with bows and arrows."

"If they ride for us," said Gil, "I aim for 'em to have
guns. How do you feel about that?"

"If it was anybody but the Lipans," said McCulloch,
"I'd draw the line at guns. But for these Injuns, I'll have
to make an exception. I doubt they'll be a danger to
anybody but Comanches, and for every one they shoot,
it's one less we'll have to track down."

McCulloch knew the chief—Feurza—and when Gil had been introduced, McCulloch explained to Feurza what Gil wanted. Feurza called a meeting, and although he had excluded the women, they peeked from behind every bush and tree. Some of the men had seen at least seventy summers, and might not see another, while the youngest were only children of maybe nine or ten. Once Feurza had explained what Gil was seeking, there arose a clamor that would have drowned out a buffalo stampede. McCulloch spoke to Feurza, and the chief managed to restore order.

"He's telling them you want nobody younger than seventeen," said McCulloch.

"Ganos!" shouted a youth. *"Ganos!"*

He was muscular, a man by anybody's standard, and looked strong enough to throw a bull. But Feurza shook his head and spoke to McCulloch.

"His name is Goose," said McCulloch, "but he's not quite fifteen. By God, when he grows up, he'll be a man."*

One by one Feurza chose a dozen men, not a one older than twenty-one or -two. Much later Gil learned that the chief had honored him by choosing men that Feurza believed were a credit to the tribe. When it was all done, Gil was dismayed to learn that the dozen young Apaches would be riding with him that very day!

"We won't move out with the trail drive until sometime after Christmas," said Gil, "and until we do, there won't be room for them in the bunkhouse."

McCulloch chuckled. "No matter. You don't see a bunkhouse here, do you?"

Gil and Clay shook the hands of their new riders, and then Clay turned to McCulloch with a grin.

"Cap'n Mac, we owe you one. The Comanches come lookin' for a fight, I purely believe these hombres will see they get one."

* Trail Drive #1, *The Goodnight Trail*

McCulloch laughed. "I'm countin' on that. Why do you reckon I brought you here?"

Gil, Clay, and their new riders passed to the east of San Antonio, and it was there that Ben McCulloch left them, riding back to town. When they reached the Box AA, the new riders created a sensation. Rosa spoke to them in rapid Spanish and soon had them laughing. Ramon and the vaqueros greeted the Lipans in Spanish, and everybody was excited over their arrival except old Stump, the cook. Gil thought he swore in all five languages, and then slipped in a couple more of which nobody was aware.

"I got to bring Angelina over here to see these hombres," said Clay.

"Make it tomorrow, then," said Gil. "Bring Van and Dorinda too."

The following day was Sunday, and they made it a festive occasion. Rosa set a table for Van, Dorinda, Clay, and Angelina. Despite Stump's grousing, he rose to the occasion and fed the riders a meal they never forgot. While Dorinda was lacking in Spanish, she was readily accepted for her smile.

"They ain't a bit like the Indians we brought from Mexico," said Van. "But when we get back from California with our regular riders, what happens to our Lipan Apaches?"

"If this trail drive's the success we're lookin' for," said Gil, "we'll build another bunkhouse and keep them."

Suddenly there was a commotion outside, followed by a mad rush, as everybody in the house jumped up and headed for the door. The riders had finished eating and had gathered in a circle outside the bunkhouse. At the center of the circle, facing one another, was a grinning Long John Coons and one of the newly arrived Lipan Apaches. Each man grasped a deadly Bowie, and they circled each other warily, like a pair of lobo wolves.

"Dear God!" cried Dorinda. "Stop them!"

"No," said Van, "leave them be. Go back in the house."

But Dorinda didn't move. Her eyes were frozen in hypnotic horror on the two combatants. The lanky Long John was tall, gawky, seeming to loom over the Indian. Like a striking rattler, Long John's blade nicked the Apache's brawny forearm, drawing blood. The Indian laughed in savage glee, retaliating by slashing Long John's shirtsleeve from shoulder to elbow. Time after time they parried, until finally the Apache's blade struck Long John's with such force that the Bowie was torn from his grasp. The Indian then began what might have become a death thrust, slowing the drive until the point of his blade stopped just short of Long John's belly. Dorinda screamed, but nobody heard her except those on the porch. The riders, including Long John and his Indian adversary, were shouting and laughing. Angelina was pale and Dorinda was trembling. Only Rosa seemed at ease, dashing off the porch and joining the shouting riders.

"Don't swoon on us, ladies." Clay laughed. "They're just havin' themselves some frontier fun."

"Dear God," Dorinda cried, "if they call this fun, what happens when they get serious?"

"Somebody dies," said Clay.

2

Gil felt guilty, having no bunks for his new Indian riders, but it seemed not to bother them. They could have been comfortable in the barn, yet they chose to take their blankets and disappear into scrub oak and cottonwood thickets. But one of the white man's accommodations they readily accepted was the cookhouse. They made themselves at home at its long plank tables, and even won the grudging admiration of old Stump. The Apaches had voracious appetites, and whatever Stump put before them, they ate, accepting more if they could get it. There were times when Clay Duval took some of the Lipans to the Winged M, allowing them to become familiar with the horses and duties on the ranch. Thus the Lipan Apaches came to know the trio of Mexican Indians, Solano, Mariposa, and Estanzio.

It was a quiet time, those days before they began the trail drive to the goldfields. Gil Austin occupied himself with building bookshelves along one wall of his parlor. There he placed the many books left behind by his uncle, Stephen Austin. There was the worn family Bible, the works of Shakespeare, Chaucer, and others. But what interested Gil was the law books. It seemed a shame to him that Stephen Austin had spent months in New Orleans, studying the law, only to have his work go for naught. Stephen had taken over the colony at the dying request of Moses Austin, his father. Young Stephen had poured his strength, his knowledge—his very life—into a colony of men who had willfully cheated him of any compensation due him. The colony had survived because Austin had spent his own meager funds, fulfilling his father's wish. Once Gil had the books arranged along the wall, he began reading from them.

"There are so many," said Rosa, "how will you know when you have read enough of them to become a man of the law?"

"I don't know," said Gil.

"You are rich in land, horses, and cows. Why must you read them at all?"

He had no logical answer for her, and none for himself. While there had been lean times, he, Van, and Clay Duval had among them the beginning of an empire. What more could he, or any man, want? He took the old Bible from the shelf and opened it to the first pages, where the precise hand of Stephen Austin had carefully recorded the births and deaths over the years. The last entry—Stephen's death in 1836—Gil himself had written. Prior to that, Stephen had recorded Granny Austin's passing, in 1829. Gil had been just fifteen, and Van a year younger. How well he remembered the old woman reading from this very Bible, until her eyes had failed and even her spectacles no longer allowed her to see. Finally, on that day she had been laid to rest, when purple shadows had crept over the Ozarks, Stephen Austin had read over her from this same old Bible. Gil and Van had been orphaned while they were young, and Granny Austin had taken them in. She had forced them to sit quietly while she read to them from the scriptures. This day, Gil seemed to feel her presence, and from long ago and far away he heard her voice.

"Children, when you don't know what to do or where to turn, search the scriptures. When you're ready for the answers, you will find them there."

Gil opened the old Bible and began to read. . . .

* * *

After the melancholy days of fall, Gil felt the need of some merriment to lift everybody's spirits. Two weeks before Christmas, he shared his idea with Van and Clay.

"Let's dig a pit," said Gil, "kill a beef and roast it. Workin' around that, we'll put together a Christmas feed for all of us, our riders, and any friends who want to join us. Van, you can take a wagon and bring Dorinda's mama and daddy. We'll ask Big Foot Wallace, Captain Ben McCulloch, and their Rangers too."

Gil didn't say—nor did he need to say—that the next Christmas might find them far apart, or maybe dead. Three days before the holiday, Van returned with Eben and Matilda Jabez, Dorinda's parents. They brought food from their farm: live chickens, hams, many dozens of eggs, and vegetables. That same afternoon, Wallace and McCulloch rode in, accompanied by a dozen Rangers.

"Speakin' for us all," said McCulloch, "we're obliged. Rangers are as bad off as soldiers. Ours is a lonesome life, and our Christmas dinner may be a bit of beef jerky, if we're lucky. This is an unexpected and welcome treat for us."

There was a saying that if two Indians spent a day together, and each of them had a horse, there would be a horse race before the day's end. The Bandera spread's Apache riders proved that to be true, and they engaged in rough and tumble wrestling. But they had another sport that Gil feared would result in somebody being killed. The Apaches called it bull throwing, and Gil allowed it only after Ben McCulloch had explained it.

"You turn a bull loose and make the critter run," said McCulloch, "and a rider gallops after him. When the rider's alongside, he leaves his horse, grabs the bull by the horns and wrassles the varmint to the ground. It don't hurt the bull, and not much chance of the rider bein' hurt, unless he's still there when El Diablo gets on his feet. Once in a while some ornery old bull will turn and try to gore the horse before the rider can grab the bull's horns, but it's up to the rider to see that it don't happen. Usual way is to loose two bulls at the same time, and the rider that gets his bull down the quickest wins."

The holiday lasted five days and nights. Some of the Indians and vaqueros went hunting at first light, returning with deer and wild turkeys. Angelina, Dorinda, Rosa, and old Stump cooked until they were exhausted. It all ended amid laughter, backslapping, and handshaking. Before the Rangers rode out, Ben McCulloch spoke to Van.

"Ride in sometime after mid-January. We've been promised new arms on the fifteenth."

January 20, 1850. San Antonio, Texas

Clay Duval and Van Austin rode into town, dismounting near the jail. Since the Texas Rangers might be away for days and weeks at a time, they had no office, but could usually be found near the jail, or in the sheriff's office. That was where Ben McCulloch had been this day, but he had seen them coming and had stepped out onto the boardwalk.

"Stay around close," said McCulloch. "The sheriff goes home to dinner. When he leaves, ride down the alley behind the jail."

It was then almost two hours until noon, so Clay and Van had time on their hands. They had neither the money nor the desire to hang around the saloons, so they rode out far enough to find water and graze. There they picketed their mounts and the packhorse, and settled down to wait. They rode back to town a few minutes past noon, Van leading the packhorse. When they passed the sheriff's office, Ben McCulloch was out front, leaning on the hitch rail. He nodded to them. Clay and Van rode on to the end of the street and turned at the next cross street. From there they rode down the alley to the rear of the jail. McCulloch opened the back door and they went in. There in the corridor, near the back door, were the wooden gun cases from Colt.

"Two dozen?" McCulloch asked.

"Actually," said Clay, "twenty-six, for every rider to have one."

"Twenty-six, then," said McCulloch, "and there'll be an extra cylinder with each of them. But they shorted us on ammunition. Two hundred rounds for each piece. Best I can do."

"You've done more than enough, Cap'n," said Clay. "We're obliged, and we'll settle with you after the drive."

They wrapped the weapons carefully in blankets, and then, when the packhorse was loaded, covered the pack saddle with a piece of tarp. With final thanks to McCulloch, they rode out. When they reached Van's place, he took one of the Colt Dragoons for himself, and Clay took four: his own, and one each for Solano, Mariposa, and Estanzio. Van took the rest of the load to Gil's, and each of the riders was given one of the new Colts.

"We have plenty of pistol belts," said Gil, "but we'll have to cut some leather for new holsters to fit these new Colts."

That was of no concern to the Lipan Apaches. They wanted nothing restrictive around their middles. They wore buckskin breeches, and each man slipped his new Colt beneath the waistband, muzzle down. Some of them already carried a Bowie there, but most wore the big knife down their backs, secured to rawhide thongs around their necks. But the vaqueros set about altering their old holsters, or fashioning new ones.

"Now," said Van, "if we were as well-fixed for rifles, I'd feel better. You reckon we can salvage enough of that foreign-made artillery we brought from Mexico to arm every man with some kind of long gun?"

"We can try," said Gil. "The rifles are dependable enough. It's a lack of suitable ammunition that's the problem. For firepower we'll have to depend on the new

Colt six-shooters, with that extra cylinder. Our biggest concern is enough ammunition for them."

"We're ready, then," said Van. "When do you aim to start the drive?"

"Mid-February; that suit you?"

"I reckon," said Van. "Mixed herd?"

"No," said Gil. "Steers, two years old and up. Ramon says we can pull out that many without makin' a dent in the herd."

"Clay's got Solano, Mariposa, and Estanzio gettin' the remuda ready," said Van. "I told Clay to reshoe every horse, so they can start fresh. I'm figurin' six packhorses, with two carryin' extra horseshoes, necessary tools, and cookin' utensils. The others will carry grub. Every man packs his own extra ammunition and bedroll. Anything I've overlooked?"

"That sounds pretty complete," said Gil. "Big Foot Wallace promised to get us a new government map before we leave. It'll have New Mexico and California added. At least we'll have some idea where rivers and streams are."

February 16, 1850. Bandera Range

Gil was ready to move out at first light, but there were painful good-byes yet to be said. Clay, Angelina, and little Christabel were there, as were Dorinda, young Van, and Rosa. Gil hugged Rosa, and she seemed stiff as a corral post, saying nothing. Dorinda managed to restrain her tears until Van was gone.

"Move 'em out!" Gil shouted.

Mariposa and Estanzio led out with the horse remuda, which included the five packhorses. Ramon rode point, ahead of the longhorns. Van, Juan Alamonte, and Manuel Armijo were at right flank, with Domingo Chavez, Pedro Fagano, and Long John at the left. Vicente Gomez, Bo, Juan Padillo, and Gil rode drag. Mariposa and Estanzio would keep sharp eyes on the plains ahead of the horse remuda.

Some of the herd had come up the trail from Mexico in 1843, but they had retained none of their trail sense. They knew nothing except the old familiar range from which they had been driven, and to which every last one was determined to return. The outer perimeters of the herd were a mass of bunch quitters, and all that restrained the others was the fact that they were hemmed in. The brutes wanted to go anywhere except forward. One wild-eyed steer tried to gore Gil's horse, until he swung his doubled lariat and swatted the beast across his tender muzzle. Every rider wore a bandanna over nose and mouth, but it did little good. There were clouds of dust so dense, the drag riders couldn't see beyond the behinds of the steers right in front of them. Gil felt the grit on his teeth, and his eyes stung as rivulets of sweat streamed into them. Sweat darkened the shirts of riders and the flanks of their horses.

The sun was three hours above the western horizon, and Gil doubted they had traveled more than six or seven miles. Horses and riders were exhausted. Not a man had been able to break away long enough to change horses. First water they came to—granted they made it that far—Gil decided to halt the drive for the day. This bunch had yet to accept the idea they were a herd. Right now, after little more than half a day on the trail, some of them had, through their own frantic exertions, worked themselves into a thirst-crazed condition. Their tongues hung out and they bawled for water. There hadn't been a breath of wind all day, but that suddenly changed. A playful breeze from the west touched their sweaty bodies with a blessed coolness, but it brought with it the smell of water. For the first time that day, every steer in the herd lit out in the same direction, on the run. They split around the horse remuda and thundered on. Their insanity was contagious, and the horse remuda quickly joined the stampede. Not a rider pursued it. The cause was lost, and they knew it.

Their horses were exhausted; why kill good horses trying to head a stampede that could not be stopped?
They'd stop when they reached the water that had
started them running.

"That's somethin' I never expected to see," said Van
wearily. "Every one of the damn fools headed the same
direction, at the same time."

"Rein up!" shouted Gil. "Dismount and rest your
horses."

They found some shade and stepped tiredly from
their saddles.

"Reckon these gone be run lak hell bunch," said Juan
Padillo.

"Reckon you're right," Gil replied grimly. "Barely out
of sight of the ranch, and already we got a stampede.
Still, we may have time enough to gather them before
dark."

They rode what Gil judged to be three or four miles,
eventually coming to a willow-lined creek. Their longhorn herd and horse remuda had strung out, grazing.
Before attempting to round up the scattered herd, they
roped fresh horses, freeing their tired mounts.

"We'll nighthawk in two watches," said Gil.

Nothing disturbed the silence of the night except the
occasional yip of a coyote. They were up at first light. It
was Van's day to cook, and he got a fire going, reheating
leftover beans in a big iron pot. When there were
enough coals, he raked aside a bed of them for the coffeepot. When the pot of beans began to steam, he
moved the iron spider away and balanced a big iron
skillet on a trio of stones. He then hacked thick bacon
slabs into the skillet.

"Wish Stump come with us," said Juan Armijo.

"Any more ungrateful palaver," said Van, "and the
hombre spoutin' off will be cookin' his own grub."

There was some laughter, but not much. Gil reckoned
they were still irritable as a result of their first abysmal
day on the trail. But he was in no mood for daily bicker-
ing over who did or didn't do the cooking.

"Enough of that," he said. "There's thirteen of us, and that means we all have to cook just once every two weeks. Now, if there's one hombre here that thinks my cookin' is so god-awful bad he can't stand it every thirteen days, then he's welcome to take my turn as well as his own. I don't have many rules, but that's one."

They finished their breakfast in silence, loaded the packhorses, roped their mounts for the day, and got the herd moving. But the second day was only a little better than the first, and long before they reached water, every horse and rider was worn-out. While winter was seldom harsh in South Texas, this February day seemed unusually humid. The setting sun flared red behind a cloud bank, and there were faraway rumblings of thunder.

"Six men on the first watch," said Gil, "and seven—includin' me—on the second. Picket your horses and leave them saddled. When it's your turn to sleep, don't shuck anything but your hats. This bunch is so skittish, they may light out with the first clap of thunder."

Rosa watched the departing trail drive until it was swallowed by distance and the dust of its own passing. Dorinda had mounted and then reached for little Van, and Rosa handed him up to her. Rosa then mounted her own horse, following Dorinda back to the house. Rosa was silent, speaking only when Dorinda spoke to her. Although Rosa appeared serene, her mind was in a turmoil. Having secretly listened to Dorinda and Angelina talk, and having drawn her own conclusions from watching Gil, Rosa feared for him. Might he go to the faraway California and do some foolish thing that would change his life—and hers—forever? Fearful of Gil's wrath, but more fearful that she might be separated from him for all time, Rosa silently vowed to follow the trail drive. But she dared not move hastily. First, she must convince Dorinda, Angelina, and Clay that she intended to keep her promise to Gil by remaining at the ranch. Second, she must wait until the trail drive had traveled far enough that Gil couldn't bring her back.

Rosa knew the riders would have their hands full with bunch quitters for the first few days. The drive might not cover more than fifty miles the first week, and she must bridle her impatience, allowing two weeks to elapse before she caught up to them. There would be some risk. She had listened to the Texas Rangers speak of the Comanches who lurked along the Pecos River, ravaging West Texas. But she had a pistol. Once the riders had received the new Colt Dragoons, it had been no problem for her to sneak Ramon's old five-shot Colt out of the bunkhouse, along with some of the ammunition.

Rosa planned to ride at night, for several reasons. First, she wished to avoid the danger of discovery by the Comanches, and second, she must not be seen by Gil or the riders. With the Indian threat, Mariposa and Estanzio would be as concerned with the back trail as with what lay ahead. Their eagle eyes would not miss the dust of even one horse. But when she rode away, would Clay Duval come after her, or perhaps send one of the Lipan Apaches? It was just another chance she would have to take. . . .

"Be storm," said Ramon.

"I think so," Gil replied.

It was unseasonably warm for the time of year, and it was anybody's guess as to what the elements might conjure up to surprise them. They might get hailstones the size of horse apples, or spheres of ground lightning as big as wagon wheels.

"Reckon we'd better get supper behind us," said Van. "It'll be dark early, and we'll have a long night ahead of us."

"Who cook tomorrow?" Pedro Fagano wondered.

"Long John," Van replied with a grin.

There was a chorus of exaggerated groans, and Long John cackled wildly. The Cajun was fond of mixing a variety of ingredients in a huge iron pot, adding other things as he went along, until he had stew thick enough to eat with a fork. So far, it hadn't been all that bad, Gil thought.

"Jes' wait'll we git t' Californy," said Long John, "t' the big water. Lemme git the right stuff, an' I'll fix us a mess o' crab laig gumbo an' catfish eyeball stew."

Van got the supper ready, and they finished it in record time. Clouds to the west had wholly swallowed the sun, fading the sky from a brilliant rose to dusty gray. The wind was out of the northwest, beginning to rise. The riders began tying down their hats with piggin string. A steer bawled nervously, and some of his companions echoed his unease. Thunder rumbled, closer now, and far to the west lightning flickered gold behind the dirty gray of the clouds. Mariposa and Estanzio were already with the horses.

"She's gonna blow," said Gil. "Hold the herd if you can, but don't do anything foolish. I'd rather spend a week roundin' 'em up than a day buryin' some of you. Let's ride!"

They split up, riding clockwise and counterclockwise, circling the horse remuda and the herd of restless longhorns. Lightning—blue, green, and gold—swept from one horizon to the other. Then, bounding out of the northwest, came the fearsome spheres of ground lightning. They seemed borne on the wind, like giant tumbleweeds, glowing eerily in the gloom, throwing sparks as they came. Immediately there was a drumroll of thunder that seemed endless, shaking the very earth. The scenario couldn't have been more complete if Hell itself had opened up, spewing fire and brimstone. As one, the longhorns surged to their feet, creating a thunder of their own as they pounded away to the east. Unable to hold the longhorns, the riders rode like madmen, trying to head the horse remuda. The mane of Gil's horse became green fire, and the animal reared, nickering wildly.

Mariposa and Estanzio, anticipating the stampede, had gotten ahead of the lead horses, slowing them enough for the rest of the outfit to catch up. The wind had died to a cooling breeze, and the thunder had rumbled away, and through it all not a drop of rain had fallen. Mariposa and Estanzio moved swiftly through the nervous remuda, calming the animals with "horse talk."

"Bueno, amigos," said Gil. "No way we could have held the longhorns. You're a bueno bunch of Texas cowboys, savin' the horse remuda."

"By the Almighty," said Long John, "all that, an' not a drap o' rain."

"Two watches tonight," said Gil. "Keep the horses bunched, and at first light we'll go after the longhorns."

Gil sighed. Two days on the trail, and the herd, stampeding back the way they had come, had cost them one of those days. Now, if experience was worth anything, they would lose two more days gathering the scattered longhorns.

March 2, 1850. Bandera Range

For several days Rosa had been preparing for her escape. In her saddlebag was a change of clothes, extra moccasins, enough jerked beef for fifteen days, and the five-shot Colt revolver with its ammunition. Around her neck, on its thin chain, she wore the little golden locket that had belonged to her mother. Waiting until she was sure Dorinda was asleep, Rosa crept out of the house. Pausing on the back porch, she listened. Hearing nothing, she rounded the house and made her way to the barn. Swiftly she saddled her horse—one of the Mendoza blacks—and led the animal out into the night. Later there would be a moon, but now there was only dim starlight. Rosa led the horse until she was almost a mile from the house. She then swung into the saddle, kicked the horse into a slow gallop and headed west. She rested the horse at hourly intervals, and with the first light of the approaching dawn, concealed herself

and her mount in an arroyo lined with young cottonwoods.

Dorinda was up, as usual, at first light. Discovering
Rosa's horse was gone, Dorinda saddled her own, and
taking little Van, rode to the Winged M ranch. She
found Clay and Angelina at the breakfast table.

"Damn it," said Clay, "I was afraid of this."

"But she waited so long," said Dorinda, "I had
hoped—"

"She knows exactly what she's doing," said Clay. "She
waited for the drive to go far enough that Gil can't bring
her back."

"I feel responsible for her," said Dorinda. "Should
you—or one of the riders—go after her?"

"No," Clay replied. "She's sixty or seventy miles away
by now. I could ride a good horse to death and still not
catch up to her. Even if I did, and dragged her back,
we'd have to hogtie her, or she'd be gone again. Do you
want to spend every day and night watching Rosa?"

"No," she said slowly, "you are right. I suppose this is
Gil's problem, and I don't envy him."

"Stay for breakfast," said Angelina.

Rosa slept in snatches, often dreaming that she heard
horses. In the early afternoon she stood looking along
her back trail. If Clay—or anyone—was coming after
her, there ought to be some telltale dust soon. But there
was none, and she rode out at sundown, elated that she
was not being pursued.

Gil and the outfit arose before first light. Breakfast
was a hurried affair, and leaving Estanzio and Mariposa
with the horse remuda, the rest of them rode out in
search of the scattered longhorns.

"Storm not last long," said Juan Alamonte. "They not
run far."

That proved to be the case, and Gil sighed with relief.
By the time they had ridden half a dozen miles, it

seemed they might gather the scattered herd in a single day. Despite the initial unruliness of the brutes, they seemed to have acquired some sense of belonging to the trail drive. The riders got them bunched and headed west in time to bed them down along the creek from which they'd stampeded the night before.

"Is luck," said Ramon, "they run from storm. They thirst, run to water, it be hell."

"That's gospel," said Gil. "Give 'em a scare, and they'll tire quick. Let 'em be thirsty, smell water, and they'll run till they reach it, if it's twenty miles."

After their good fortune in gathering the herd, there was enough daylight for Gil to study the government map Big Foot Wallace had provided. It was the only complete map of the United States that included New Mexico and California, for not until February 1848 had Mexico ceded the two new territories.

"We owe Wallace a big one for this map," said Van. "It even shows the desert that reaches to Horsehead Crossing."

"Llano Estacado," said Gil, "but we'll pass to the south of it."

"Damn," said Long John, in mock despair, "had m' heart set on seein' the Staked Plains."

"You can ride across it on the way back," said Gil. "While we'll miss the Llano, we're swappin' it for maybe two hundred fifty miles of Comanche country. We'll be near enough to the border to be in danger from Mexican bandits too."

"By this map," said Van, "they claim El Paso is five hundred miles from San Antone. When we cross the Pecos, we'll still be three hundred miles east of El Paso. When we finally reach El Paso, we'll still be less than a third of the way to the goldfields. If we don't make better time, we won't get these brutes there until the middle of next year."

"The herd's settlin' down," said Gil, "and we ought to make better time. With this map, we know where the water is. We'll start early and quit late. I want these longhorn brutes so tired at night, they won't run from anything less than a prairie fire."

Rosa always concealed herself and her horse near water, but she knew better than to remain *too* near it. So foolish a habit invited discovery by anyone seeking the water. Once she and the horse drank, Rosa moved well away from the water, before settling down for the day. For days on end she had seen nobody. She believed it would take the trail drive three days, if not longer, to travel as far as she was riding in a single night. Surely she would catch them in another day. Rosa and her horse had spent the day some three hundred yards from a small creek. Near sundown, when it was time for them to be on their way, she led the horse to the creek so it could drink. When the animal had drunk its fill, she led it away, half-hitching the reins to a convenient limb.

Rosa then lay belly down, her head hung over the low bank, and satisfied her own thirst. Suddenly her horse nickered and she froze, her heart pounding. Behind her, reflected in the clear water of the creek, was a half circle of painted, grinning Indians!

3

Slowly Rosa got to her trembling knees, but she didn't have a chance. One of the Indians caught her by the hair and dragged her to her feet. He was a leathery old man who stank of grease and sweat, ancient enough to have been her grandfather, if she'd had one. There were seven of them, but the old one seemed to be the leader, the chief. He silenced the jabbering of the others with a wave of his hand. Rosa said nothing, trying not to seem afraid. The chief grabbed a fistful of her shirt front and ripped it open, popping off the buttons, and Rosa stood there naked to the waist. The old Indian was drooling, while his companions shouted their approval. Again he silenced them, and pointed to Rosa's horse. When it was led to him, he took the reins and nodded to Rosa to mount.

At the end of their tenth day on the trail, Gil signaled a halt near what their map called a river.

"God," said Long John, "after the hosses an' cows drink, they won't be 'nough fer us t' make coffee."

While it wasn't quite that bad, the water *was* low. It was Bola's day to cook, and while Gil waited for supper, he looked at the map again.

"If I'm readin' this map right," he said, "we have maybe a hundred miles behind us."

"Ten mile," said Vicente Gomez. "Bad day."

"Nothin' to get excited about," said Van. "If we can't beat that, we're still forty days out of El Paso, and God knows how many months away from California."

"I reckon I get the blame for our slow progress," said Gil. "While I'm glad we have this map, I've been dependin' on it too much. We've bedded down the herd accordin' to the water on the map. I've cut some days short, when we could have put in another two or three hours on the trail and *still* reached water. Startin' tomorrow, I aim to scout twenty miles ahead of the drive, like I did when we brought the herd from Mexico, back in 'forty-three."

"Is good," said Ramon, and the other riders nodded their agreement.

"We help," said Estanzio.

"I'm countin' on you and Mariposa," said Gil, "especially when we get into southern New Mexico and Arizona."

Rosa rode ahead, the old man holding the reins of her horse, while the rest of the Indians brought up the rear. It was soon dark, and she had no idea where they were, or where they were going. But they hadn't ridden far when she heard the barking of dogs. The Indian village was well-hidden, and even in the dim starlight Rosa counted at least ten tepees. The dogs broke into an excited frenzy, and it seemed there must be a hundred. Other Indians stood outside their tepees, and some of them managed to silence the dogs. Finally Rosa's captor reined up her horse and his before one of the tepees, which proved to be his own.

The old man dismounted and began shouting orders. Rosa slid out of her saddle and found that the other six Indians were no longer with them. The old one looped the reins of his horse and Rosa's to a lodge pole. He then drew open the flap and shoved her into the dark interior of the tepee. Hands seized her, tore at her hair and clawed at her face. Her assailants were screeching like magpies, and the old chief had to bellow like a bull to make himself heard above the din. Then he was inside, shoving them through the open flap of the tepee. Rosa could still hear them outside, but her captor closed the flap, and she was alone. She didn't have to wonder who the two furious women were, or why they had attacked her. Even in her inexperience, she recognized them as jealous wives who well knew why they were being run out. This old fool had plans for her, and he didn't want an audience!

The tepee smelled of wood smoke, sweat, and roasted meat. Rosa began feeling around for something that might serve as a weapon, and her moccasined foot touched a stone. Kneeling, she found a circle of them, still warm. It was a fire ring, and feeling the stones, she selected a large one. Prying it loose, she hefted it in both hands. It was a poor weapon, but better than nothing. There was a sliver of light where the tepee flap hadn't been fully closed, and when she put one eye to it, she could see her horse in the light of a rising moon. Her pistol was in the saddlebag! She had her hand on the tepee flap when an Indian spoke and a companion answered. While she couldn't see them, they were watching the tepee until her captor returned. With a sigh, she again took up the heavy stone.

The next voice Rosa heard was that of the old one in whose lodge she waited. She hoped he was dismissing the guards. He came in, closing the flap behind him, and Rosa heard the distinctive sound of leather against leather. He was getting undressed! In spite of herself, she jumped when she felt his rough hands on her bare skin. She waited until his fingers reached the waist of the breeches she wore, and then she brought up her right knee in a savage thrust, where it would get the most attention. His breath exploded in an agonized groan, and she felt his sagging head against her bare belly. Stepping back just enough to lift the heavy stone, she brought it crashing down on the back of his head. . . .

*   *   *

Gil rode out at first light the following morning. While he couldn't be sure, he felt the government map noted only the larger streams and rivers. While it was a help, and he was thankful for it, they needed the in-between streams and water holes too. Once the drive passed El Paso and was into the badlands and desert beyond, the map's river locations would be invaluable. But until then there would be lesser streams that didn't appear on the map, and these were essential. The herd had begun to settle down, and a day's drive could be stretched to fifteen miles or more, as long as there was water at the end of it. He had ridden well over ten miles when he came upon a substantial runoff that definitely wasn't on the government map. It would extend their day's drive, and if he could find another such water source for the following day, they might make up some lost time. The mountainous regions of southwest Texas would have lesser streams that, while not qualifying as rivers, would provide water enough to suit their purpose. Gil had ridden at least thirty miles before he found the second such source, again not evident on the government map. Elated, he rode back to meet the trail drive, bearing good news.

Her knees weak, sick to her stomach, Rosa dropped the stone. However justifiable the deed, it sickened her, and she wanted only to escape. She stepped over the inert old man and moved the tepee flap enough to see outside. Her horse was still there, and she sighed with relief. Quickly she stepped out, closing the tepee flap behind her. Apparently the rest of the camp respected the chief's privacy, for she saw or heard nobody. Loosing the reins of her horse, she crept away from the te-pee. She had to pass two others, and held her breath.

But for the dogs, she might have made it. One of them discovered her, and the others lent their voices, not knowing or caring if there was justification for the clamor. The need for stealth was gone, and Rosa sprang into her saddle, kicking the horse into a fast gallop. This time there would be no capture. When they discovered what she had done, if they caught her, death would be swift and certain. She found herself on the open plains, in the light of a full moon, with no cover in sight. Taking her direction from the stars, she rode west as hard as the horse could run. They must not catch her on the plains! She was momentarily annoyed with herself because she hadn't taken the time to get the Colt from her saddlebag, but common sense prevailed. Effective shooting from the back of a running horse, even in good light, was difficult. At night it would be impossible, and she had fired a pistol only once in her life. It would all depend on the valiant black horse with the Winged M on its left flank. On she rode, but even in the cool of the night, she dared not gallop the horse for more than a few minutes. Fearfully she looked back, and saw a mass of moving shadows emerge from the trees. They were coming!

Gil met the oncoming trail drive in the afternoon. They had already come far enough that they would reach water before sundown. On the trail by first light tomorrow, even with a long day's drive, they would reach the next water before dark. The riders shouted their approval when they were told of the longer drives and the assurance of water.

"If we can average fifteen miles a day," said Van, "that cuts our trail time by a third."

"Can't look at it that way," said Gil. "The fifteen-mile days will make up for the bad days when we don't quite make ten. Or the even worse days, following a stampede, when we work from daylight till dark, roundin' up the scattered herd."

"Well, hell," grumbled Van, "you can't fault a man for dreaming."

"No," Gil grinned, "long as he don't forget that's exactly what it is."

The herd was becoming trailwise. The rest of the day passed without incident, and the night proved equally peaceful. Gil's premonition began to claw at him, reminding him this was the calm before the storm, that when everything seemed right, all hell was about to break loose. But he fought down his misgivings and rode out at dawn, seeking water for this day and the next. When he found water, he found trouble. There were the tracks of twenty-four unshod horses. Tracks only hours old, and they led to the northeast . . .

Rosa could see the welcome shadow of trees ahead. She must lose her pursuers, and she must do it quickly. While they hadn't gained on her, neither had she gained on them. The woods she sought proved to be a scrub oak thicket, and the farther into it she went, the more dense it became. She dared not continue straight ahead. Dismounting, she led the tired horse and veered away to the north, deeper and deeper into the brush. If they searched for her, it would have to be on foot, and she moved as silently as possible. If they weren't sure which direction she had taken, they would have to split their forces so thin, they might overlook her entirely. Just by accident, Rosa found excellent cover for herself and her horse, simply by falling headlong into a tree-shrouded depression in the earth. The horse made a more graceful descent, and although Rosa didn't know its origin, they had taken cover in what had once been a buffalo wallow. Indian voices came close, and the girl held her hands over the muzzle of her horse. Finally there was only silence. But she must not linger. Having lost her in darkness, she had no assurance they wouldn't come looking for her again at first light. Removing her buttonless shirt, she replaced it with the one from her saddlebag. Then she climbed out of the depression in which she'd been hiding and stood there listening. But there was only the sleepy chirp of birds and the cry of a distant coyote. Unsure of her direction, she led her horse until the thicket thinned out enough for her to see the starry sky. Taking her direction, she mounted, kicking her horse into a slow gallop. Scarred by her experience, but the stronger for it, she again rode west.

Gil only took the time to rest his horse before starting back the way he had come. Unshod horses were bad news, and if the riders continued in the direction they'd ridden out, there was no way they could be unaware of the trail drive. They almost had to be Comanches, he thought grimly, and they could easily circle around and come at the drag riders from behind. He had traveled less than half the distance back to the drive when he heard the ominous rattle of gunfire. He soon began meeting remnants of the horse remuda and still-trotting longhorn steers. The Comanches had stampeded the herd, and whether or not they took any scalps, they would round up the scattered horses at their leisure. The firing ceased, adding to Gil's suspicion that the purpose of the daylight attack had been to stampede the herd and steal the horses. His immediate fear was that his drag riders—Vicente Gomez, Bo, and Juan Padillo —might have been hurt or killed.

The first riders Gil saw were Estanzio and Mariposa, coming hard. He didn't stop them, and they rode on. They had the right idea. Without swift action, they would lose their horse remuda. Van had the same idea. Following him came Long John, Ramon, Juan Alamonte, Manuel Armijo, Domingo Chavez, Pedro Fagano, and Bo. Vicente Gomez and Juan Padillo were missing.

"Vicente and Juan were wounded," said Van, "but they'll live. They can still shoot, but there's nothin' to shoot at. The attack's over, and if we don't do some fast ridin', we won't have a horse remuda."

"Ride, then," said Gil. "I'll be along."

He wanted to be sure his wounded men were able to ride. He found them shirtless, seeing to their wounds.

Juan Padillo had a bloody left arm, while Vicente Gomez had a nasty wound beneath his right arm, along his side.

"The others are goin' ahead," said Gil, "hopin' to save the horses. If you can ride, we'll see to your wounds at the next camp."

"Stop blood," said Padillo, "then we ride."

The three of them rode out, and within three or four miles they found most of the longhorns grazing.

"They want horse," said Vicente, "not cow."

"I reckon that's goin' to be a problem," said Gil. "They'll kill us and stampede the longhorns just to get the horses, but we'll have to watch for Comancheros and border outlaws too. They'll take the horses *and* the cattle."

Rosa rode until the eastern horizon paled with the first light of dawn. She had no idea how far she'd ridden; she only hoped it was far enough to discourage further pursuit. Reaching a small stream, she watered her horse and then found a secluded place for them to spend the day. No sooner had she settled down to doze than her horse nickered, jolting her awake. She was on her feet in an instant, dragging the Colt from her waistband. But the horse was riderless, and on its left hip was the familiar Winged M brand. She recognized it as one of the animals she had ridden on the ranch, and the horse came to her readily. Something was wrong; Estanzio and Mariposa would never allow even one of the horse remuda to simply wander away. Using her lariat, she picketed the stray horse, and, moving farther up the creek, was elated to discover where the herd had been bedded down. The horse and cow droppings were fresh, and she believed the drive had spent a night here within the past two days. If she rode hard, she might catch up to them today! She returned to the horses on the run. While her own horse was tired, it could travel on a lead rope, so she saddled the stray. The rising sun at her back, she rode out.

* * *

As they rode, Gil, Vicente, and Juan found two of the packhorses, and when they reached the creek where Gil had first seen the unshod tracks, they found the other three packhorses and two dozen of their horse remuda. Bo and Manual Armijo were there.

"Bo, you and Manuel help me," said Gil, "and let's unload the packs. I need to get at the medicine to patch up Vicente and Juan. We'll set up camp here. When the rest of the riders return, we'll see where we stand on the horses."

When the rest of the outfit showed up, they had only sixteen of the missing horses. They simply couldn't afford to lose a third of their horse remuda, and Mariposa and Estanzio didn't intend to.

"Our Injuns took to the trail like a pair of bloodhounds," said Van, "and I let 'em go. We can leave four men here, and the rest of us can join Mariposa and Estanzio. They'll outnumber us nearly three to one, but we can surprise the bastards like they surprised us."

"Git 'em after dark," said Long John.

"Bo, you and Manuel stay here," said Gil, "and Vicente, since you and Juan have been hurt, I want you to remain here too. The rest of us will go after our horses. No fire tonight in camp. Those of you goin' with me, grab a handful of jerked beef and let's ride."

An hour west of the creek, Rosa found where the Indians had attacked and where the herd had stampeded. While she was new to the frontier, the signs were obvious, including several Indian arrows. Nor did it take a trailwise frontiersman to know the difference between the tracks of a running cow and a walking cow. There was a bloody bandanna where Vicente and Juan had tended their wounds. She rode on, hoping nobody had been seriously wounded or killed, until vegetation ahead warned her she was approaching water. Ahead, a horse nickered; the one she rode and the one she led responded. She reined up, waiting, her hand on the pistol in her waistband. The first man she saw was Juan Padillo, minus his shirt, a bloody bandage around his upper left arm.

"Juan," she shouted, kicking her horse into a gallop. "Juan, it's Rosa!"

Juan Padillo relaxed and holstered his Colt. He caught Rosa as she all but fell out of the saddle. She hadn't fully realized how great had been her emotional strain, until she saw Juan Padillo's friendly face. Her eyes swiftly took in the four riders returning to the wounded Juan and Vicente.

"Oh," she cried, "you've been hurt. Is it . . . bad?"

"We not hurt bad." Juan grinned. "Reckon you be hurt more worse. Senor Gil, he be mad lak hell."

"I reckon he will," said Rosa, "but he'll get over it. Where is he, and the other riders?"

"Go after horse remuda," said Juan. "Injuns take 'em."

"Not all of them," said Rosa. "I brought one of them with me."

Juan grinned. "Senor Gil still be mad lak hell."

"Then maybe I be mad lak hell right along with him," Rosa replied.

Swift pursuit by Mariposa and Estanzio gave the cowboys a valuable edge. Knowing Gil and the outfit would follow, the Indian riders strove only to keep the quarry in sight. The night would come, and darkness would become the equalizer. Strangely enough, the Indians were driving the stolen horses in almost exactly the same direction the trail drive had been headed.

"They're on their way to Pecos River country," said Gil. "Accordin' to the map, it's maybe ninety miles to where we'll cross the Pecos."

"They stop with the night," said Ramon.

"I hope they do," Gil replied, "so we can end this chase."

"Be jus' like the red devils t' run all night," said Long John.

"I don't think so," said Van. "I doubt this bunch can teach Mariposa and Estanzio anything. All we got to do is stay back until our Injuns tell us where these Comanches are hunkered down for the night."

"They reckon we jus' a bunch o' dumb Tejano cowpunchers that can't foller a hoss if we got aholt of its tail," said Long John.

"That's exactly what we want them to think," Gil replied.

Sundown came and they still hadn't caught up to Mariposa and Estanzio.

"We'd as well settle down and wait for them to get back to us," said Gil. "If we go stumbling around in the dark, in unfamiliar country, we may lose ourselves until they can't find us. Where we are now, they can find us by following their back trail."

They drank creek water and chewed on jerked beef, and the full moon had been up for an hour when Mariposa found them.

"Them stop, watch hoss," said Mariposa. "Come."

They rode for almost two hours before the Indian reined up. Following his lead, they dismounted, half-hitching their reins to whatever limb or bush was convenient. They didn't know when Estanzio would join them, but suddenly he did. They covered the last mile or two on foot, and when they were near enough to hear the movement of the horses, Mariposa and Estanzio halted. It was time to silence the Indians who were watching the horses, and they waited as Mariposa and Estanzio faded into the shadows. There was not a sound, and when the Indians returned, they drove the blades of their Bowies into the soft earth. Then Estanzio drew his Colt from his waistband, raised it high for them to see, and pointed to himself. Once they were in position, he would fire first.

Gil was elated to discover the horses were well away from the Indian camp. Perhaps it was a forlorn hope, but they might be able to end this without stampeding

the herd. Mariposa and Estanzio guided them well beyond the horses, and they came at the Indian camp from
the other side. All the blanketed forms were strung out
along the far bank of a small stream, and overhanging
trees and vegetation left them in shadow. Mariposa took
his position at one end of the camp, while Estanzio
placed the rest of the riders. When Estanzio touched his
arm, Gil remained where he was, while the Indian
placed the next man, and the next. Estanzio then took
the last position down the creek. While they were outnumbered, they had every one of the Indian horse
thieves within range of a Colt six-shooter. It was strategy
worthy of a military field commander. Gil had his Colt
out and ready. When Estanzio fired, the rest of them
followed, and the roar was deafening. Justified as they
were, Gil felt a little guilty. It went against the grain,
shooting a sleeping man, even a horse-thieving Indian.
Once the firing had begun, Gil thought he had seen
some movement, but it seemed the slaughter had been
complete. Mariposa and Estanzio left nothing to
chance. After waiting a few minutes, they waded the
creek. When they returned, Mariposa held up two fingers.

"Them run," said Mariposa.

"They'll keep running," said Gil. "This is a mighty big
dose of bad medicine."

Nobody slept the rest of the night. They brought up
their own horses, and until first light kept watch on the
stolen portion of their horse remuda. In daylight they
found only nineteen of their horses.

"They missed one," said Gil. "Maybe it'll show up
before we move on."

"Some o' them Injun hosses ain't too poor," said
Long John. "Likely bin stole, jus' like they stole ours."

"We'll take the best ones," said Gil, "and turn the
others loose."

Ten of the Indian mounts looked as though they
might have been taken from somebody's barn or corral.

"Some o' these cayuses got brands," said Long John. "Yonder's a pitchfork, an' there's a Rockin' K."

"We'll take them with us," said Gil. "If any man claims them, he can have them. If nobody does, they're ours."

4

Gil and the outfit rode out early, pushing the horse herd. The drive would fall yet another day behind, because they still must round up the scattered cattle.

"The longhorns didn't seem scattered too bad," said Van. "Maybe we'll get lucky and round 'em up today. We lost half a day yesterday, and we'll lose all of today. I purely hate to lose another whole day tomorrow."

"Estanzio and Mariposa find hoss quick," said Pedro Fagano.

"They did," said Gil. "No way we could have recovered the horses any faster, without any risk to ourselves. We're fortunate that two of our riders were only hurt, instead of killed. Not often that Comanches attack in daylight, but we can't ever again take it for granted they won't. From now on, those of you riding flank and drag will have to be as watchful as the point rider. We dare not let them take us like that again. Next time, some of us may die."

The riders who had remained in camp shouted their enthusiasm when Gil and the rest of the outfit drove in the recovered horses. Gil dismounted to face a grinning Juan Padillo.

"Glad you and Vicente are doin' all right," said Gil. "I reckon you had no trouble while we were gone?"

"We have no trouble," said Juan. "Mayhap be some for you. Rosa come."

For a minute Gil said nothing, just leaning his head against his saddle. When he finally spoke, it was with a calmness he didn't feel.

"Where is she?"

"Down by creek," said Juan. "She bring remuda horse."

Gil unsaddled his horse, giving himself time to collect his thoughts. Suddenly he was aware that the rest of the outfit was watching him expectantly.

"Bo, Manuel, Vicente, and Juan will remain in camp," said Gil. "Van, you and the rest of the outfit start gatherin' the scattered longhorns. I may be here awhile. There's . . . somethin' I have to attend to."

"I know." Van grinned. "We saw her at the creek."

They saddled fresh horses and rode out. Suddenly Gil was exhausted, and it was more than just a long day in the saddle and a night without any sleep. That he could have endured, and often had. No, it was the bitter realization that, for the duration of this trail drive to California, and their return to Texas, his constant companion would be an impulsive, moody, temperamental female. While she was young enough to be his daughter, she had made it abundantly clear she had no intention of behaving like one. He grunted, slapped his Stetson against his thigh and started for the creek. He found her sitting with her back against an elm, calmly awaiting whatever punishment might be her fate. He made a silent vow not to lose his temper, lest he yield to temptation and strangle her.

"Ah reckon," she said, without remorse, "you are angry with me."

"Not so much angry," he said evenly, "as disappointed. Disappointed that I am unable to trust you out of my sight. Why did you lie to me?"

"Because I knew you would not let me come with you. Had I not promised to stay at the ranch, you would have had Clay chain me in the house."

"It crossed my mind," said Gil.

"Why do you punish me, when I only wish to be with you?"

"Because," he shouted, breaking his resolution, "a trail drive is no place for a female!"

"You brought me out of Mexico on a trail drive."

"That was different, and you know it. I couldn't just leave you there, homeless and alone."

"You cared so much for me then, why do you hate me now?"

"I don't hate you," he said desperately. "You were just a child when I found you, and you're not that much older now. You're still just a child."

"I am not a child," she said. "I am a woman."

She got to her feet and began unbuttoning her shirt.

"No!" he shouted, turning his back on her. "Rosa, there's more to bein' a woman than . . . that."

"I know," she said, enjoying his discomfort. "I have the rest of it too. I was little when you found me, but now I am like my *madre*. She was a small woman, but big where it matters. I am like her."

He turned back to her, trying not to notice that half the buttons on her shirt were undone.

"Rosa, when I found you, you were very little. Didn't your mama—your *madre*—ever tell you your age? How old you were?"

"She never spoke of it," said Rosa. "You said I was seven, and that was five years ago. It bothers you that I am young in years?"

"It bothers me that you claim to be twelve," said Gil, "while you have the . . . the . . ."

"The body of a woman," Rosa finished, "and it is you who say I am twelve. I am as much a woman as I will ever be, and you have no woman. Why do you not want me?"

Gil almost laughed, but thought better of it. With guns or knives, he would have faced another man in a fight to the death, but this female had disarmed him. It was a Mexican standoff, and the best he could expect was a truce, to allow himself time to think. He tried another approach.

"Rosa, I . . . it makes me uncomfortable, your feelings, when I am so much older than you. We'll be many months finishing this trail drive, and I don't need anything else on my mind. Especially a woman, and that includes you."

It was a small compromise, his alluding to her as a woman, but she was pleased and saw it as a major victory.

"Then you will allow me to finish the trail drive with you?" she asked.

"We're a hundred and fifty miles from the ranch; I have no choice."

"You have a choice," she said. "I know it is too far along the trail for you to take me back, and you won't have to. You took me when I was so little, and so afraid, and I will never forget you for that. But you do not have to keep me forever. If you do not want me with you on the trail drive, then you do not want me with you at the ranch. Give me a horse of my own and I will go. I will not stay where I am not wanted."

She turned away and stood looking into the creek. Gil forgot she had lied to him, that he was old enough and frustrated enough to be her father. He took her by the shoulders and turned her around to face him. Not since that long-ago day in Mexico when he had buried her parents, had he seen so much misery in her eyes. She had put her future in his hands.

"Rosa," he said, "I want you to stay."

There was no avoiding what followed next. She wept long and hard into the dusty front of his shirt, and until she became silent, he said nothing. Then he moved away, his hands on her shoulders, and looked at her.

"I'll have to agree with you," he said. "You're no longer a child, and there are few women on the frontier. A man has his hands full, just keepin' himself alive. Now I must look out for you as well. Disobeying an order on the trail could mean the difference between living and dying. The first damn time you go contrary to what I tell you, you'll be sorry. I'll remind you of this day by taking a strap to your backside. You have my promise that you'll ride standing in your stirrups for a week. *Comprender?*"

"*Comprender,*" she said. "I will obey."

Her calm acceptance threw him, causing him to question his own judgment. Gil had begun to realize that it was not so much Rosa's intention to irritate him as to gain his attention, to have him notice her, and that was as much the way of a woman as of a child. He had no other Mexican woman with whom to compare her, and being small in stature he had judged her young in years. But now he wondered. . . .

While the longhorns hadn't wandered far, they still weren't able to get the herd ready for the trail that same day. Instead of moving out at first light the next morning, they had to beat the brush for more than two hundred head of missing steers. But as unplanned as Rosa's arrival had been, it had made an immediate difference in the life of every rider in the outfit, for Rosa had offered to do the cooking.

"I can't imagine why you ever objected to her comin' along in the first place," said Van innocently.

"She cook more better than Stump," said Juan Padillo. "More pretty too."

"Some night in the dark o' the moon," said Long John, "ye gon' lose that little gal, 'cause I'm gon' grab 'er an' run off."

None of the flattery was lost on Rosa, and Gil took it as well as he could. At least he didn't have to fear for Rosa's safety insofar as the men were concerned, for any one of them would have fought to the death for her. But he knew not what awaited them in the weeks and months ahead on the long trail, for the hazards were many. But in the deep of the night, his head on his saddle, Gil Austin faced reality. No danger the frontier had to offer troubled him as much as this impossible relationship between himself and Rosa. For a long time he had known that her feeling for him went far beyond that of a little girl for a caring father, but he had told himself it was a one-sided thing, a feeling that he didn't share. But now he knew better. Unconsciously his feelings toward Rosa had begun to change, and that change had become all too evident to him. When she had offered to take a horse and ride out of his life, the very thought of it had torn him apart, and his grief had *not* been that of a father about to lose a daughter. His feelings for her went deeper, and were akin to her desire for him, and the whole damn affair was as ludicrous as it was impossible. He was too old for her, but if he rejected her, he was going to lose her. Somewhere along this twisted trail, or at the end of it, he had a decision to make. For one of the few times in his life, Gil was afraid. . . .

March 15, 1850. Southwest Texas, near the Pecos River

"Twenty-eight days on the trail," said Gil disgustedly, "and we've come only two hundred miles. That's a little more than seven miles a day!"

"Yes," said Van, "but trouble of one kind or another accounted for nine of those days."

"Not good enough," said Gil. "We're almost fifteen miles from the Pecos. I aim to reach it tonight, and we'll cross at dawn, when our backs are to the sun. Before we leave the river, I want those steers to drink all they can hold, because there'll be no water for another twenty miles. We're going to drive from the Pecos to that next water, without a break, even if we're on the trail till midnight."

"Why must we cross the river with the sun to our backs?" Rosa wondered.

"Longhorns won't cross with the sun in their eyes," said Gil. "They have to see the other bank, to know where they're going."

"Then why do they run at night, when they can see nothing?"

Long John chuckled. "Gal, if ye ever figger out why a longhorn does nor don't do *anything,* write it down. Ever' cowboy on the frontier'll pay good money fer it."

Even Gil laughed at that, and they pushed on. When they were within two hours of the Pecos, Gil rode ahead, seeking a place where they might safely water the stock. The Pecos was notorious for its treacherous quicksand, and its presence or the lack of it would determine their approach to the river. For a safe river crossing, Gil sought a point where east and west banks were low, without sudden drop-offs. Gil's riding ahead to scout the river served a twofold purpose. Finding a safe crossing for the herd the following morning assured them of easy access to the water, when the drive reached the river in late afternoon. Miles away from the water, the longhorns must be headed toward the proposed crossing. Thirsty cattle might stampede headlong over high banks, or even bluffs.*

Gil found what seemed an ideal crossing. East and west banks sloped to the water for three hundred yards, and there seemed leeway enough that even a stampeding herd could reach the water without danger. Gil rode his horse into the water, finding it shallow and without quicksand. He rode to the farthest bank and then back. Not only had he found the crossing he wanted, it would allow the longhorns easy access to the water to satisfy their thirst.

Gil rode a mile upriver, returned to the crossing, and continued for about the same distance to the south. Finding no tracks, no Indian sign, he rode back to meet the drive.

"Water's low," Gil told them. "Crossin' should be no trouble."

"Much water come," Mariposa remarked.

---

* Trail Drive #1, *The Goodnight Trail*

"They ain't a cloud in sight," said Long John dubiously.

Mariposa looked at the Cajun with what might have been contempt, and said no more. But Gil didn't dismiss Mariposa's prediction lightly. The Indian riders rarely spoke or offered advice, but when they did, he listened. In the west, in dry country, a man didn't have to see the rain to find himself over his head in what had been a shallow river only hours before. While the rain might fall fifty miles away, the river just ahead of them could become a raging torrent as the result of it. The sun was noon high, and Gil made a decision. He spoke to Ramon and some of the other riders who had ridden up from the flank.

"River's shallow, for now," he said. "If we can reach it after sundown, but before dark, I think we'll go ahead and cross. Rest of you keep the herd moving, and I'll ride back and tell the drag riders."

"It be hard drive," said Ramon.

"I don't blame him, though," said Van. "A storm somewhere upriver could flood the Pecos for three days, and if there's goin' to be spring rain, it'll come soon."

Gil remained with the drag, and they drove the steers to a faster gait. As Long John had pointed out, there were no clouds, but he hadn't caught the full significance of Mariposa's words. The Indian had said "much water," not "rain." As the sun sank lower, reaching for the western horizon, there was a dirty mass of gray clouds waiting to receive it. There was a tongue of lightning, so brief it might have been imagination. Within an hour of sundown the clouds had darkened and the mass had shifted to the northwest. A cooling breeze whispered through the cottonwoods, and had the steers been long without water, a stampede would have been inevitable. Rosa followed Gil as he rode around the herd, speaking to the riders. Reaching the drag position, Gil joined Juan Alamonte, Manuel Armijo, and Domingo Chavez. Rosa rode along with them, shaking out her lariat as Gil was doing.

"Storm's buildin' to the northwest," Gil shouted. "We're goin' to push on to the Pecos and try to cross tonight. There may be high water by morning. Let's hit 'em hard, keep 'em bunched, and keep 'em moving!"

They began swinging doubled lariats against dusty flanks, forcing the drag steers into a lope, and those steers began hooking the rumps of the animals ahead. It had the desired effect, and soon the entire herd rumbled along like a slow-moving stampede. Some of the steers bellowed in protest, but they were caught up in the movement and forced along with the rest.

"Keep them moving," shouted Gil. "We're going to run 'em on across!"

He rode at a fast gallop to warn the rest of the riders, and by the time he had reached the point position, Ramon already knew what Gil planned to do. Mariposa and Estanzio also knew, and the horse remuda and the packhorses were strung out well ahead of the longhorns. Gil slowed his horse and rode alongside Ramon, ahead of the loping longhorns.

"The leaders may try to drink, Ramon, soon as they hit the water. We got to keep 'em bunched, keep 'em moving. When they're all across, they can water from the other bank. We'll have to hit 'em hard, don't let 'em start to mill!"

Ramon nodded and they separated, Ramon taking his position at the right point, while Gil remained at the left. Both men knew the risk they were taking. Once the lead steers hit the water, they might balk and begin to mill. Worse, they might stampede up- or downstream. Either action might result in Gil and Ramon being caught up in a maelstrom of slashing horns and trampling hooves. Gil held his breath as the horse remuda neared the river. He knew that should the horses balk or even slow their gallop, he and Ramon might be trapped between the horse remuda and the oncoming longhorns. But the intrepid Indian riders didn't intend for that to happen. Mariposa and Estanzio were behind the horse remuda every step of the way, shouting, shoving, driving. They kept the horses bunched, and it was already dusky dark when the leaders hit the water of the Pecos. The horse remuda cleared the river, slowing only as they climbed out on the farthest bank.

Even above the thunder of the herd, Gil could hear the shouting of the riders as they kept the steers moving, kept them bunched. The first lead steer into the river tried to turn upstream, and Gil swung his doubled lariat, smashing the animal on its tender nose. The longhorn righted its course, and the others followed. Prodded from behind by the lethal horns of their trailing comrades, the leaders took the only unobstructed path available, stumbling out on the farthest bank and trotting away. The rest of the steers were right on their heels, as the drag riders kept them bunched and moving. When the last steer was out of the water, the drag riders trotted their horses across the river.

"They did it!" shouted Rosa. "It was magnificent!"

"You're a bueno Tejano outfit!" Gil cried.

Some of the longhorns had started back toward the river, and that ended their moment of jubilation.

"Come on," said Gil. "They still have to be watered, and they can't all go at once. Long John, Van, Manuel, Pedro, and Bola, you come with me. We will cut out maybe a third of them and let them drink. The rest of you, hold the others back until these are done."

Mariposa and Estanzio had the horse remuda under control. The horses would drink when the longhorns were out of the way. The outfit was two hours into darkness when the last horse and the last longhorn had drunk its fill.

"What of supper?" Rosa asked.

"Jerked beef and Pecos tea," said Gil. "I know it's been a long, hard day, but the night will be even tougher if we have to spend it fightin' the Comanches. So no fire. We'll have to wait till first light for our coffee. Two watches, as usual, and since I'm odd man, I'll work the second."

"There is no odd man," said Rosa. "There are four-

teen of us. I will take the first watch and do the cooking."

"You cook," said Juan Padillo. "We watch."

"That's fair," said Van. "The watch we can handle,
but we can't none of us cook worth a damn."

"No," said Rosa, "I am part of this trail drive, and I
do not wish to be treated as a child. I will take my
watch, and I will also cook."

Nobody objected to that. As long as Rosa did the
cooking, they didn't care what liberties she took. They
would be at Gil's expense, of course, but he said nothing. They would be together on the trail for months, and
he might as well make the best of it. Since he had taken
the second watch, he almost insisted she take the first,
but that would only aggravate an already touchy situation. She would raise hell, and after a fight, he'd end up
with her on his watch anyway. He had little doubt the
outfit already knew the perilous position he was in, but
he vowed not to fight with Rosa in their presence. Juan
Alamonte, Manuel Armijo, Domingo Chavez, Juan
Padillo, and Bola joined Gil and Rosa on the first watch.
Riders seldom spoke while they were on watch, but it
was a tradition that Rosa didn't intend to observe. "You
did not want me to ride with you," she said.

"I said nothing against you," he said defensively.

"You said nothing for me either."

"Why should I? Rosa, you're trying to force me into a
position where I will have to prove something to you, or
where you can prove something to yourself. Which is it,
and what do you hope to prove?"

"Perhaps I wish to know if you feel anything more for
me than the sympathy you expressed when you found
me in Mexico."

"Rosa, I am thirty-six years old, and I have no right to
any feelings toward you beyond what a father feels for a
daughter."

"You are not being honest with me. You say that you
have no right to any feelings for me, but you do not say
if the feelings are there. Do you feel nothing more for

me than the pity you would bestow on any little *bastardo,* or do you have the feeling for me that a man should have for a woman?"

She had a way of shredding his logic, of forcing him into a corner where only a brutal yes or no would suffice. He considered simply lying to her, telling her that above and beyond his sympathy, he didn't care. But something he had done or failed to do had convinced her otherwise, and the fact that she was so much aware of his thoughts and his feelings made him all the more uncomfortable. He had reached the point where the truth could hurt him no more than an unconvincing lie that she would see through immediately.

"Yes," he said, "I felt sorry for you, Rosa. I'd have felt the same toward any child so young and so alone. But you've asked for an honest answer, and I'm going to give you one, although both of us are going to be sorry for it. While you're young in years, you are very much a woman, and I am drawn to you. But that doesn't make it right, and it can never be right as long as I feel guilty for my very thoughts."

For a long time she said nothing, and when she finally spoke, it was in almost a whisper, as though she would be sure nobody heard but him.

"I believe you," she said, "and I understand a little, I think. I wanted only to know your feelings for me. I asked for nothing more. Someday, you will turn to me, and the years and the guilt will fall away. Until then, I only need to know that you care."

By dawn the Pecos River had overflowed its banks and continued to rise. Limbs, stumps, and even young trees were swept before the surging brown water. Attempting to cross, even by a rider on horseback, would have been sheer madness. Long John looked at the violent river, then at Mariposa.

"Hombre," said Long John, "nex' time ye say water's acomin', I swear t' take it as gospel."

"So do I," said Gil. "Might take three or four days for that to subside."

They watered the herd and the horse remuda, and then made up for the hot supper they had missed the night before. Mariposa and Estanzio already had the horse remuda moving out, and the longhorns were following, when Rosa looked back across the river.

"Look," cried the girl. "Indians!"

On the farthest bank of the swollen river, a large band of Indians sat their horses, viewing the high water with evident frustration. Van laughed.

"It's a mite early for that," said Gil. "That water level *will* drop, and that pack of war whoops can ride seventy miles a day. Our best day—and that was yesterday—has been fifteen, and our average is ten."

It was a sobering thought, and they pushed on, twenty miles away from the next water, unless the violent storm to the northwest had provided something closer. Only Rosa suggested the possibility.

"No," said Gil, "we can't count on anything as a result of yesterday's thunderstorm. Where there might be water this morning, there'll be only mud when we get there. Wet weather streams are good only for a few hours. We'll be able to depend only on the water we *know* is there."

On the government map Big Foot Wallace had provided, there were alarming stretches of plains where no water was indicated. Here, they must depend on their own scouting, and providential springs. These were dependable, year-round water sources where the runoff might continue for only a mile or two before being swallowed by the sandy plain. It was to just such a spring that Gil was taking his thirsty horses and longhorns, with full awareness of the risk. In dry country, where streams were few and far between, all living things were drawn to what water there was. And that included hostile Indians. A spring, with its limited runoff, was especially hazardous, because all who came for water were concentrated in that one small area.

"Ramon," said Gil, "I'm ridin' ahead to scout the spring for Indian sign. There's a short runoff, so we'll have to pitch camp right at the spring for the herd to have room enough to drink. Remind every rider, especially the drag, to keep their eyes open for possible attack. Remember that bunch of Indians at the river. The water level won't have to drop much before they'll be after us. I just hope we can reach the spring in time to dig in and be ready for them. Push the herd as hard as you can."

The Indians would know of the spring, and they would be aware that it was the destination of the trail drive. At best, Gil hoped they could make it to the spring. At worst, the Indians would cross the Pecos and force them to make a stand on the dry plain. Thirsty horses and cattle would be impossible to control, and the Indians would count on that as a distraction. Such an attack, miles from water, would force Gil and his riders to abandon the herd and fight for their lives. The sun was noon high when Gil reached the spring. There were deer and turkey tracks, a few coyote tracks, but no Indian sign. Gil allowed his horse to drink from the runoff. Then Gil, with caution, went belly down to satisfy his own thirst from the clear pool that surrounded the spring. The frightened nicker of his horse was all that saved him. Gil rolled to his left, drawing his Colt as an arrow plowed into the water where he had been drinking. He fired twice before the Indian could loose another arrow, but the brave wasn't alone. There were angry shouts from his comrades, and Gil could see them coming through the brush beyond the spring. His horse was already running when Gil hit the saddle. He could see Indians riding hard to cut him off, to trap him in a deadly cross fire. On he rode, kicking the valiant black horse into a fast gallop.

But their horses were fresher than his, and Gil's horse could stand only a few minutes of hard running. His pursuers were within range, and the arrows were coming fearfully close. One tore through Gil's shirt, cutting a gash across his ribs. Suddenly the horse screamed and stumbled, and Gil knew the animal had been hit. Despite his danger, he slowed the faithful black, allowing it to recover as best it could. He drew his Colt, reloading the two empty chambers as he rode. At best, he had but a few more minutes. . . .

5

Gil began looking for some cover, but there was nothing in sight that looked promising. He wasn't sure how many Indians were in pursuit, but there were more than enough to surround him, wherever he had to make a stand. He drew his Colt, turned in the saddle and fired three shots. While he'd hit none of his pursuers, and hadn't expected to, he had spaced his shots. It was a distress signal his outfit had used before. The wind was at his back, and he judged he was close enough for the sound to carry. He leaned forward on his horse's neck, praying he wouldn't hear the black heaving for air. Instead, faint but distinct, he heard a shot. A second later there was another, and finally a third. They knew he was in trouble! If only his horse could last a little longer. But time had run out. He felt the black horse falter, and riding it to death wouldn't save him. He could see a spire of rock ahead, and when the horse was near enough, Gil left the saddle. He rolled with the fall, scrambling behind the rock, which was only about waist high. He had hoped for a rock cluster, but it wasn't there. He had cover only from one side, and the Indians would quickly circle his position, pinning him down in a cross fire. He reloaded the empty chambers in his Colt, preparing to defend himself as best he could. There were eight Indians, shouting at one another, and he could see them splitting up to circle him.

Then, above the excited shouts of his pursuers, Gil heard something else. It at first seemed like the faraway rush of wind, perhaps the roar of an approaching storm. Or a stampede! The herd was coming, running hard! Within seconds, through rising clouds of dust, he could see them, fanned out like a vengeful horned avalanche. The Indians were now shouting in alarm, and those who had begun to circle his precarious position turned their horses and rode for their lives. Now Gil was facing a new danger, with only a slender finger of rock between him and sixteen thousand thundering hooves! If the herd failed to split around him, he was done. Then his heart leaped. A rider galloped madly alongside the stampeding longhorns, seeking to get ahead of them. The rider was hatless, his long hair streaming in the wind, a scarlet sash about his waist. Estanzio! Into the path of the herd he rode, and it seemed horse and rider couldn't possibly avoid the hooves and horns of the on-coming longhorns. Estanzio rode like he was part of the horse, and when he leaned forward on the black's neck, he might have been speaking in a language the horse understood. The black surged ahead, seeming to double its speed. They were forty yards ahead of the longhorns, then sixty, and finally a hundred! When Gil waved his hat, horse and rider swept across the plain toward him. Gil caught Estanzio's hand with the horse on the run, but with the black carrying double, they began losing ground to the stampede. But the longhorns had begun to tire. Flank riders had caught up to the lead steers, and when the herd began to slow, Estanzio slowed the black to a walk. Gil slid off Estanzio's horse, and the first rider he saw was Rosa. She had caught his horse, and he could see the fear in her eyes. It was no time for a show of concern from her, so he turned back to Estanzio, who was tending the arrow wound on the left flank of Gil's horse. Gil slapped Estanzio on the shoulder in affection and appreciation.

"Thanks, pard," he said.

Estanzio didn't acknowledge the thanks or change his

expression. He had taken a tin of sulfur salve from a knotted bandanna and was applying the salve to the horse's wound. Mariposa, Juan Padillo, and Bola had the horse remuda under control. The horses had been behind the longhorn herd, which meant the stampede had been for Gil's benefit.

"They've stopped the stampede!" Rosa cried.

The longhorns appeared to be moving at their usual gait. Van, Long John, and Ramon rode back to see how Gil was.

"We didn't know you was afoot when we started the stampede," said Van.

"Ye come outta it wi' yer hair an' yer hide," said Long John. "Cain't do no better'n that, when yer dealin' wi' Injuns."

"Speaking of Indians," said Gil, "is anybody botherin' to see where that bunch went that was after me?"

"Scattered seven ways from Sunday," said Van.

"They caught me at the spring," said Gil, "and they know damn well that's where we're headed now. With our luck, that bunch waitin' to cross the Pecos will show up before mornin'. No fire tonight, and there'll be just one watch. It'll begin at dusk, and it'll involve us all. Now let's ride."

They reached the spring without incident, and the body of the Indian Gil had shot was gone.

"Maybe we ought to just water the stock and keep the drive goin'," said Van. "Might confuse that bunch if we don't spend the night here."

"Not near as much as it'll confuse us," said Gil. "There won't be much of a moon tonight, and it'll rise late. Comanches kill as readily at night as they do in broad daylight, and us strung out with the herd, they'd pick us off in the dark, one at a time. Besides, I haven't had a chance to scout for the next water."

"All right!" said Van irritably. "All right!"

Rosa had been about to say something, but thought better of it. Instead, Long John asked the question.

"No fire tonight," he said, "but it ain't night yit. How 'bout supper?"

"Supper fire, then," said Gil, "but see that it's out before dark."

"Won't matter," said Van, "since they know we're here."

"By God," snapped Gil, *"I said put out the fire before dark!"*

"Is it not better," Rosa asked, "that we spend our anger on the Indians instead of each other?"

Long John laughed first, and the others joined in, relieving the tension. They built a cook fire, and Rosa hurried the supper. They all felt better after they had eaten, even with a sleepless night ahead of them.

"Tonight," said Gil, "listen for *anything* that doesn't sound right. Pay particular attention to the coyotes. Listen for the echo."

"Echo of what?" Rosa asked.

They all laughed except Gil, and Rosa thought he was about to lose patience with her. But he recovered and spoke calmly.

"There's no echo to an animal's cry, Rosa. When you hear a coyote with an echo, you know it's the two-legged kind."

When darkness came, Gil spread the riders out around the horse remuda and the longhorns in a huge circle, not to ride, but to watch.

"Keep your horses saddled and close by," said Gil, "but unless the herd gets restless, stay out of the saddle. Even in starlight they can pick us off from cover, so we'll find us a place and keep out of sight."

Far to the northwest there was lightning and the faint rumbling of thunder. The wind rose slightly, bringing a spring freshness that said rain was falling not too many miles distant. Rosa had settled down near Gil, and he had made no attempt to discourage her. But the girl had said little, either because she was aware of the need for silence or perhaps she hadn't forgotten his earlier flare of temper. When she eventually spoke, she did so quietly.

"There is more rain. Perhaps the river will continue to flood, and that other band of Indians will not be able to follow us."

"Maybe," said Gil, "but we can't depend on that. Anyway, I shot one of that bunch that jumped me at the spring. I look for the others to get even, if they can."

"What are we going to do if they come?"

"They can't attack the camp," said Gil, "because the way we're spread out, there is no camp. The way we're circlin' the herd, they can't come near the horses or cattle without bein' caught by some of us. So we wait for them to come to us, if they're fool enough to do it."

With the first cry of a coyote, Rosa caught her breath. She thought there was a slight echo, and when the cry came again, she was sure of it. Gil hadn't moved, but even in the starlight she could see he'd drawn his Colt. Rosa drew her own pistol, holding it with both hands to steady their trembling. Gil had gotten silently to his feet, and in a moment she knew why. A shadow had separated itself from the surrounding darkness. While Rosa thought it was Mariposa or Estanzio, she couldn't be sure. After an inaudible conversation with Gil, the shadow faded into the night. Rosa remained silent, waiting until Gil finally spoke.

"Mariposa killed a two-legged coyote," Gil said, "and Estanzio's on the trail of a second one. They've been sent to scout the camp, to find out just where we are. We'll sit tight for a while. If Estanzio gets another, the rest may decide we're bad medicine and ride on."

Rosa remained with Gil until Estanzio arrived. He still carried the big Bowie in his hand, and the starlight reflected off its long blade.

"Coyote dead," said Estanzio. "Others run."

"Then we have nothing more to fear?" Rosa asked.

"Depends on that bunch of Indians we left at the Pecos," said Gil. "But I think we'll continue this watch, with the entire outfit, at least for tonight."

Gil made the rounds, talking to each of the riders. When he returned, Rosa said nothing more. For the past several days their relationship had become strained, and each of them had been painfully polite to the other. Rosa was sure Gil's sharp tongue and short temper were a result of his frustration toward her.

"Rosa," Gil said, "you can get some sleep, if you like. I'll wake you, if there's any need."

"I wish to do my part," said Rosa. "I will watch with the rest of you."

She half expected that to anger him, and in a way she hoped it did. Gil had been ignoring her, while shouting at Van and the other riders, and she was ready to see that justice was done. They had the rest of the night, and she would reach some kind of understanding with him before the dawn. With full responsibility for the trail drive, and with all the dangers of the trail, just keeping them all alive needed his undivided attention. Rosa walked around the circle of riders, speaking to them all. But when she returned, she said nothing to Gil. It was he who had a burr under his tail, and it was he who would make the first move. By the stars, it was well past midnight before he finally spoke.

"Rosa?"

"Yes," she replied.

"I reckon you know why I . . . I've been such a bastard the last day or two."

"No," she said innocently. "Why?" She wouldn't make it easy for him.

He felt the need to talk, to air his frustration, but the very thought of it only added to his discomfort. Rosa was cutting him no slack, offering no encouragement, and that didn't help.

"Damn it," he finally blurted, "I ain't a man to live with loose ends, with somethin' unsettled. We've got to resolve this . . . thing . . . between us."

"I want you," said Rosa, "and you want me. This 'thing' between us is a thing you have placed there, and only you can remove it. It is you who chooses to think of me as a daughter when I am not."

"It's more than that," said Gil. "It's . . . you're so young, and I'm so old. . . ."

"I am perhaps young in years, but I am old in my feelings, and I have the body of a woman. Should I live a hundred years, I will never become more complete than that."

"So it's all up to me," Gil said.

"It is all up to you," Rosa replied. "Would it be easier for you if I just cocked this pistol and shot myself?"

"Oh, for God's sake," he growled. "Don't be a damn fool."

"Then stop shouting at the other riders," she said, "when it is me who bothers you. You accuse me of being a child, and it is you who behaves as one."

"Are you done with the tongue-lashing, mama?"

"For tonight," she said. "Now that the Indians are gone, I am going to take a bath."

"Where, in the spring? The runoff's just about deep enough to cover your ankles."

"It is enough. I do not have to be up to my ears in water," she said.

"It don't bother you that there's thirteen men who might see you?"

"In the dark? There is as much light from the moon as from a firefly. You do not look at me, but you are fearful that other men will."

Without another word Rosa started back toward the spring and the runoff beyond. Eventually she was far enough from the spring that even one of the riders coming for water wouldn't have known she was there. She kicked off her moccasins, peeled off her shirt, and stepped out of the tight vaquero trousers. She was about to kneel in the little stream when she heard a footstep. She froze.

"Gil, is that you?"

"Why, hell yes, it's me," he growled. "Are you expectin' somebody else?"

She only laughed, and he didn't know if that was good or bad.

Gil scouted the area at first light. As expected, the bodies of the two Indians Mariposa and Estanzio had knifed were gone. The survivors had ridden north. They still could veer to the west, with the intention of laying an ambush, but Gil didn't think so. Waylaying a party of white men was one thing, but when that party included a pair of lobo wolves like Mariposa and Estanzio, that was something else. Once the horse remuda had been led out, the herd following, Gil began his daily search for water. Few streams had been worthy of the map makers' mention, and the trail drive would have to depend entirely on Gil's daily quest for springs and lesser water holes. That day, they were forced to travel almost twenty miles to water, and a good fifteen the next day. For three weeks they saw no Indian sign. On April seventh they crossed the Salt River, 150 miles southeast of El Paso. Thirteen days later they crossed into southern New Mexico. They bedded down the herd on the Rio Grande, twenty miles north of El Paso. Near sundown two riders out of the west paused, looked at the herd, and rode on without stopping.

April 21, 1850. El Paso, Texas

"My God," said Van, "we've been on the trail sixty-three days, and we've come only five hundred miles. That's barely eight miles a day."

"Be thankful for the last three weeks of good weather, no storms, and no stampedes," said Gil. "We could have done worse."

"Are we going to El Paso?" Rosa asked.

"I want to talk to the sheriff," said Gil, "and see if there's anything he can tell us about the territory through New Mexico and Arizona. I'll ride in tomorrow morning. Some of you can ride along if you like."

* * *

The following morning, Gil, Van, Long John, and Rosa rode into the salty border town of El Paso. There was a wagon yard with a freight shed from which a freight line operated, a blacksmith, a livery, several mercantiles, and nine saloons. Shifty-eyed men watched Gil and his companions suspiciously.

"Some o' these hombres," said Long John, "looks like they could have their necks stretched on either side o' the border."

"I expect they could," said Gil. "That's all the more reason for us to take care of our business, get back to the herd, and move on."

"I'm goin' to the store," said Van, "while you talk to the sheriff."

"We got no money," said Gil. "What's the use in looking?"

"We'll have money on the way back," said Van. "You comin', Long John?"

Long John followed, and Rosa looked at Gil.

"Oh, all right," said Gil, "but stay close to Van and Long John."

The sheriff's office and jail was across the dirt street from the wagon yard.

"Sheriff Weatherford," said the lawman.

"I'm Gil Austin," said Gil, taking Weatherford's hand.

Gil explained their destination, and then asked for advice and information.

"You'd best beware of old man Clanton's gang," said the sheriff. "He's called 'old man,' but he can't be more'n twenty-five. Married this widder woman, an' she already had four sons, near grown. There's Isaac, Pete, Phin, and Billy."*

"Rustlers?" Gil asked.

"Rustlers, killers, and God knows what else," said

---

* Billy Clanton died October 26, 1881, during the gunfight at the OK Corral.

Weatherford. "Clanton claims land in southern New Mexico, as well as southern Arizona. Not that he owns it; he just squats there, and nobody can make him move. He steals and sells stock on both sides of the border. The Rangers ran Clanton out of South Texas, thank God. I've heard the scutter's got as many as four hundred gunslingers and border riffraff workin' for him. There's a pair of his rattlers, Morgan Pinder and Verd Connor, that's in town. Rode in last night."

Suddenly there was a shot. Sheriff Weatherford kicked the chair back from his scarred desk and got up. He was a big man, gone mostly to fat, but he wore a thonged-down Colt that looked well-used.

"Here we go again," he sighed.

He hitched up his pistol belt, and Gil followed him out to the street. Men, some of them mounted, had gathered outside the mercantile, the one to which Van, Long John, and Rosa had gone.

By the time Gil and the sheriff arrived, somebody was shouting for a rope. Van and Long John stood with their backs to the log wall of the store, and both men had their Colts in their hands.

"Break it up, gents," bawled Sheriff Weatherford, "and if it ain't expectin' too much, somebody tell me what started this ruckus."

"Hoss thieves," shouted a man, pointing to Van and Long John.

"Sheriff," said Gil, "these men are my riders, one of them my brother."

"Mebbe we oughta hang you too!" somebody shouted.

"I'll shoot the first man that uncoils a rope," said Sheriff Weatherford. "Now who's accusin' who, and why?"

"I'm claimin' that lanky jasper is forkin' a hoss belongin' to my outfit," said a hard-eyed, bearded man, his hand on the butt of his pistol.

"Gil," said Van, "he's claiming the horse Long John's ridin'—the sorrel with the pitchfork brand—is his."

"Pinder," said the sheriff, "you don't accuse a man without proof. What proof have you got? You Clanton riders ain't even got brands on the horses you ride. Since when has a brand—any brand—meant anything to you?"

"Sheriff," said Gil, "let me talk to him, and you listen. Pinder, we took that horse from Indians, more than three hundred miles east of here, when we recovered horses the Comanches had stolen from us. Now, you show some proof the pitchfork is your brand, and maybe we'll give you the horse. Show me just one of your horses with a brand like the sorrel's."

"You got my word!" snarled Pinder.

"Sorry," said Gil. "I wouldn't take your word it was rainin' till I was neck deep in it."

Some of the other men looked at Pinder and laughed.

"That's it, Pinder," said the sheriff. "I'd suggest you mount up and ride. You done wore out your welcome."

"I'll ride when I'm ready," shouted Pinder, "and I ain't ready!"

Pinder had lost his support, mostly a saloon crowd, and he backed away. But he still had his eyes on Gil when he spoke.

"Nobody calls Morg Pinder a liar an' goes on breathin'. This ain't over."

"It is in this town," snapped Sheriff Weatherford.

"Anytime you're ready, Pinder," said Gil, "and I'll have somebody watching my back."

Van and Long John holstered their Colts.

"Get our horses," said Gil, "and let's get out of here. Where's Rosa?"

"She was in the store," said Van, "when we come out here to see what this Pinder was shoutin' about."

But there was no sign of Rosa in the store. The store-keeper was a thin little man in a white apron that might never have been washed.

"There was a girl in here," said Gil. "Where is she?"

"I . . . I dunno," stammered the little man. "One of

them Clanton riders took her out the back way. She was kickin', fightin', an' cussin', an' I—"

"And you *let* him take her?" snarled Gil, grabbing a fistful of the man's dirty apron.

"I— He said she . . . was his gal. I—I couldn't do nothin'."

Gil was out the back door on the run. There was an alley with nothing but run-down, uninhabited store buildings. Gil heard what would have been a scream if it hadn't been shut off. He ran to the first door, but the building had been closed, the door barricaded from inside.

"Rosa!" he shouted, "where are you?"

She did not—perhaps could not—cry out. Her response was a choked-off sob, but it was enough. A sagging door stood partially open, and Gil kicked it the rest of the way. Rosa's shirt lay on the dirty floor, and her breeches were down around her ankles. Her captor stood behind her, his right arm circling her middle, his other hand over her mouth.

"Let her go," said Gil, "and back away."

"Who'n hell are you, her daddy?"

"Close enough," said Gil grimly. "Now let her go, and pull your iron."

Rosa looked dazed. Blood oozed from a cut above her left eye. But she suddenly became a fighting fury. She bit the hand that covered her mouth, and unable to free herself by struggling, she went limp and slid to the floor. The big man went for his pistol, but he was off balance and died with the gun in his hand. Gil shot him just above his fancy belt buckle, and he fell on his back, raising a cloud of dust.

Rosa sat on the floor, trying to get her arms into the sleeves of the shirt, but making a poor showing. Gil holstered his Colt, got her on her feet, and Rosa gave up. She threw her arms around him, sobbing wildly. Gil took her by the shoulders and shook her till her teeth rattled.

"Damn it," he snapped, "save that for later! Did he do . . . anything . . . ?"

"No," she sobbed, "but he . . . he was going to."

"Let's get your clothes on; I'd as soon all of El Paso didn't see you jaybird naked. We've got to get out of here, and out of this town."

He got the shirt on her, found it was inside out, and had to start over. Rosa bent down to pull up her trousers and almost fell on her face. Gil got them up and buttoned, barely in time. Sheriff Weatherford stepped through the open door, and other men followed. Among them was Morgan Pinder, and beyond him, Van and Long John.

"The bastard shot my pard!" bawled Pinder. "Verd's dead!"

"Sheriff," said Gil, "he took Rosa, and if there's any doubt in your mind as to what he aimed to do, then we'll let her tell it to the court."

The evidence was damning. The dead man still gripped his pistol, and Rosa had a bloody gash above her left eye. Not a man on the frontier would condemn Gil for the shooting, and Pinder knew it. Just for a moment he let his hate-filled eyes bore into Gil. Then, without another word, he pushed through the other men and was gone.

"By God, Austin," said Sheriff Weatherford, "you purely know how to raise hell and prop it up on the edge. You just shot Verd Connor, one of the Clanton gunslingers."

"And I'd do it again," said Gil. "What do you aim to do?"

"Give you some good advice, my friend. Get your outfit together and ride, and it ain't a good idea to close your eyes till you're in California."

6

"I reckon," said Van as they rode out of El Paso, "we ain't made the trail ahead any easier, gettin' on the outs with this Clanton bunch."

"Wal, hell," growled Long John, "ye cain't own up t' hoss-stealin' an' git yerself strung up jus' t' keep a bunch o' owlhoots happy. Me, I ain't about t' take the rap fer somethin' I ain't done."

"That puts you right alongside me, Long John," said Gil.

"I seen a gent pull that rustlin' trick oncet b'fore," said Long John. "Feller that was called a thief went ahead an' give up the hoss, tryin' t' head off trouble. They wasn't no proof agin him, but when he give up the hoss 'thout a fight, he got the name of a hoss thief. After that, he was robbed blind, and they wasn't nothin' he could do. Nobody looks fer one hoss thief t' steal from another."

"I can understand that," said Gil. "Take the name of a thief, and when your own stock's stolen, nobody believes you."

"It'll be near noon when we get back to the herd," said Van. "Do we move out and go as far as we can, or wait until morning?"

"We'll wait till morning," said Gil. "This may be the last chance we'll have to wash our clothes and blankets for a while. Besides, I'll have to use the rest of today, ridin' as far ahead as I can, lookin' for water. This map shows almost no water in southern New Mexico. We're going to have to depend more and more on our own scouting."

When they reached the herd, Gil saddled a fresh horse. For the first time since leaving El Paso, Rosa spoke to him.

"I'd like to ride with you," she said.

Gil nodded, saddled her another horse, and they rode west. When they had ridden an hour, they stopped to rest the horses.

"This country is very dry," said Rosa. "What will we do when there's more than a day's drive from one stream to the next?"

"Unless there's Indian sign," said Gil, "we may just push on, and not stop for the night until we reach water. A thirsty herd won't bed down or graze, so keepin' the drive moving won't be any worse than tryin' to hold 'em in dry camp."

Rosa unbuttoned her shirtsleeves and rolled them up to her elbows.

"I expected you to stay in camp and wash clothes," said Gil.

"I have none to wash except what I am wearing," said Rosa. "I will have to wait for the night to wash, and then cover myself with a blanket until my clothes are dry."

"Why in tarnation did you light out for California with only the clothes you were wearing?"

"I brought other clothes," said Rosa. "I find that I have grown around the middle since I last wore the other pants, and now I cannot button them. My other shirt has no buttons."

He laughed, and she found it a pleasant alternative to his usual moods.

"It amuses you that I am so fat I have no pants that will fit, and that my only other shirt has no buttons?"

"It amuses me that you're so damn perfect in some ways," he said, "and so far from it in others. At the risk of soundin' like a fool, why would you bring an extra shirt that has no buttons?"

"It had buttons," she said, "but Indians caught me, and one of them tore my shirt open."

That got his attention, with the near disaster in El Paso still fresh on his mind. Laughter forgotten, he seemed as grim as ever.

"But he did . . . nothing else?"

"That is all," she said. "I killed him."

"Why didn't you put up that kind of fight in El Paso, before that owlhoot stripped you naked?"

He had given her no credit for saving herself from the Indians, only condemning her for not having accomplished the same feat a second time, when a burly man had knocked her senseless with a pistol barrel. His remark had been cruel and insensitive, and he was immediately sorry. Rosa turned from him, leaning against her horse, her chin on her saddle. He took her by the shoulders and turned her to face him. Her eyes were closed, but that didn't hinder the big silent tears that rolled down her cheeks. He held her close, unable to think of anything to say, and it was a long while before she spoke.

"He hit me . . . with his pistol," she said, "and I was not aware that he was . . . was taking off my clothes. When you called, I . . . I barely heard you. I fought him when he first took me, but he was too strong for me. I . . . I am sorry you had to shoot him because of me. Now we will have his friends after us."

"We were already in trouble with that bunch," said Gil, "before I shot Connor. Van and Long John had already had words with Morgan Pinder."

It was a poor excuse for an apology, and Gil felt like a skunk. There was dried blood in her hair, above her left ear, where she had been slugged with a pistol barrel, and he hadn't even noticed. Worse, he hadn't even asked how she felt. All he had done was criticize her for her inadequate defense against a brute with a pistol.

"Then you are not angry with me?" she asked.

"No," he said, and he touched the bruise above her ear. "I'm sorry that I didn't notice that you'd been hurt. Most of all, I'm sorry about what I . . . what I said. This Verd Connor was big as a mountain, and looked bull-strong. With his fists, he might have beaten me, so I had no right to criticize you. Has your head stopped hurting?"

"Yes," she said. "But it is very sore."

Despite the fact that he felt like an insensitive brute, inadequate in all he said and did, he made up his mind to be honest with her about something he had discovered about himself. Gathering his courage, he spoke.

"Rosa, bad as this thing was—him taking you—it forced me to admit somethin' I just couldn't seem to accept before. When I saw this Verd Connor forcing himself on you, I knew that I wanted you. I wanted you for myself. Right or wrong, however damn old I am, or however young you are . . ."

Her smile was worth all his painful admission had cost him.

"When you are ready," said Rosa, "you will not have to hit me with a gun."

"I'll keep that in mind." He grinned. "But for now, we're up to our ears in this trail drive, with all those horses and cows needin' water. Let's ride."

It was well they had waited until the next morning to resume the trail drive. Gil and Rosa rode at least thirty miles to the Potrillo Mountains before they found water.

"This will be the first test," he said. "We'll have to drive straight through to water, even if it takes all night. We'll water and graze the herd in daylight and drive them at night, if that's what it takes to avoid dry camps."

By the time they had returned to their camp on the Rio Grande, the sun was only a rosy memory on the horizon, and purple shadows were awaiting their opportunity to swallow the plains in the coming night.

"Long as you've been gone," said Van, "I reckon we'll have one hell of a drive gettin' to the next water."

"Thirty miles or more," said Gil, "and we don't stop until we get there."

"Is good," said Ramon, and the other riders agreed. Anything was better than trying to hold thirsty, bawling, stampede-prone longhorns in a dry camp.

After supper Gil gathered his dirty clothes. There was just about enough time before dark to do his wash, but it would likely still be damp at first light, when he had to pack it in. Rosa followed, bringing a folded blanket, and they headed upstream.

"Rosa," he said, grinning at her, "you purely are a caution. You aim to strip, wash your clothes, and spend the night with nothing but a blanket? Suppose the herd stampedes, and we all have to hit the saddle and ride?"

"You are the trail boss," she said. "Do you wish me to ride that way?"

"Tarnation, I don't even want you naked in this river, with the rest of the riders too close. We'll go upstream a pretty good ways, and I'll watch, while you wash."

"Will you watch me, or the plains?"

"I'll sneak a look at the plains once in a while," said Gil.

Gil had the trail drive moving at first light, the horse remuda leading out.

"We'll use the same precautions for outlaws that we use for Indians," he told them. "You drag riders keep a sharp eye to the back trail. This Clanton bunch will be after the horses *and* the longhorns, so a stampede will be their style. But remember, they're killers too, so once they're in range, we'll be dodgin' lead."

Gil had considered remaining with the drive until it reached the water he and Rosa had already found, and then riding from there. But he rejected the idea. If he rode out today, he must cover thirty miles and then ride the length of a day's drive beyond. Suppose there was no water for *another* thirty miles? It was a risk he had to take, because he remembered what El Paso's sheriff Weatherford had told him. Old man Clanton had a hardcase outfit claiming land in New Mexico and Arizona. A man didn't have to be too bright to figure the possibilities of such an arrangement. Eventually the trail drive would have to cross the land on which the outlaws squatted. That, or the drive must turn north, with plans to continue west somewhere beyond the outlaw holdings. But if this bunch could claim any land on which they chose to squat, their "boundary" could extend as far north as they needed to take it. Gil quickly decided that boundary would be extended far enough that the trail drive couldn't get around it.

So he decided he must stay two days ahead of the drive, when it came to seeking water. If the Clanton bunch of owlhoots were as resourceful as they seemed, they would be claiming water rights at some point where their own water became essential. It was Gil's intention of finding this trouble before the absolute necessity of water made his position intolerable. If such an unconscionable shakedown had been planned, Gil looked for it at least four days' drive west of El Paso. That would lessen the possibility of word leaking back to warn the unwary.

Once he reached the Potrillo Mountains, he rested and watered his horse before riding on. While the government map showed little water, it faithfully accounted for the various mountains. The new map had taught him one thing: the chain of mountains he and Van had once seen from Mexico—mountains west of the Sierra Madres—were part of the continental divide. Once across the divide, streams and rivers ran from east to west, flowing toward the Pacific Ocean. They would see the great water once they reached California.

Many of the mountains on Gil's map were not named. They were marked with lines of inverted V's, like Indian tepees, but that was all. It was in the foothills of some unnamed mountains that he found a second day's water. It began with a spring, flowed down a rock face in a waterfall, then formed a large pool with a runoff. Here, Gil found tracks of horses. Shod horses. There had been five riders, and they had ridden in from the north before turning west. It was time to return to the trail drive. The spring, Gil figured, was a little more than twenty miles west of where they would bed down the herd tonight.

He decided this would be his last time to ride out alone. Somewhere west of this spring, he would be looking for a confrontation with the Clanton outlaws, and he had no intention of stumbling on them unexpectedly. The skills of Mariposa and Estanzio were too valuable to go unused, and from now on he would have one of the Indians riding with him. Mariposa and Estanzio could stalk and silence Comanches in the darkest of night, and Gil thought there might be some unpleasant surprises in store for the Clanton thieves and killers. He rode back and met the trail drive.

"It's gonna be almighty late when we get these brutes to water," said Van, his eyes on the sun.

"We'll keep them moving till they get there," Gil replied, "if it takes all night. The next day's drive will be short; only twenty miles."

Long John, Ramon, and the other riders laughed at that.

Come sundown, the longhorns began bawling their discontent. It was time to water, to graze, to rest. But none of these comforts were in sight, and the drive went on. . . .

"By God," growled Long John, "it's jist our luck t' git a bunch o' longhorns what knows the diff'rence betwixt day an' night. I never knowed they was that smart."

"Might as well get used to the bawling and bunch quitting," said Gil. "We're still a good fifteen miles from water, but there'll be a moon, and it's just flat prairie till we reach the foothills. That's where the water is."

Without the moonlight, their cause would have been lost. Every steer in the bunch remembered the water they had left behind, and with no assurance of any ahead, every one of the troublesome brutes tried to take to the back trail. Even in the cool of the night, Gil felt the sweat soaking the back of his shirt, and he sleeved it out of his eyes. His bandanna over his nose and mouth did little good, and his tongue felt like he'd been licking the dusty prairie.

"Why do these cows never become tired?" Rosa asked.

"They are tired," said Gil. "That's why they're so damn cantankerous, but they're never too tired to light out along the back trail, toward the last water they remember. They want to drink, to graze, to rest."

"But without water," Van said, "they won't graze or rest. Why can't they at least be smart enough to know we're takin' 'em to water?"

"You expect a powerful lot from a cow," said Long John.

The riders wearily pursued one bunch quitter after another, until the longhorns finally saw the futility of it and gave up. They plodded on, bawling in protest as they went, but they kept moving ahead. Finally the riders and their horses got some relief, and the choking clouds of dust diminished. When Gil next looked at the stars, the Big Dipper said it was past midnight. The herd had been on the trail eighteen hours.

"I figure another two hours," said Gil.

"Let's whop their flanks," Van said, "and cut that to an hour."

"No," said Gil, "we'll leave well enough alone. They're tired. Try to push 'em any harder, and they'll just get ornery again. Then we'll be fighting them another four hours instead of just two."

In just a little more than twenty hours, they had covered thirty miles. When every horse and cow had drunk its fill, first light was little more than two hours away. The horse remuda and the longhorns settled down gladly, not even attempting to graze.

"Now," said Gil, "I need six volunteers to join me until first light. A short watch, but it would be a good time for somebody to hit us, while we're all ready to fall on our faces."

Exhausted as they were, every rider—including Rosa —offered to join the short watch. Gil chose Long John, Ramon, Van, Juan Padillo, Vicente, and Bola.

"Come first light," said Gil, "the rest of you can take over, and we'll sleep a couple of hours before we move out again. We'll have a fifteen-hour day ahead of us, but it won't be anything like the one we've just had."

Nobody complained. This was a trail drive, and the long, hard hours went with the territory. Rosa slept less than an hour, getting breakfast started so they could all eat together. By the time the sun was three hours high, they were again ready for the trail. Before they moved out, Gil told them of his suspicions, insofar as the Clanton gang was concerned, and then stressed the need for Mariposa or Estanzio to accompany him as he rode ahead in search of water.

"When Mariposa or Estanzio is with me," said Gil, "that'll leave just one rider with the horse remuda. Ramon, during these times, you'll need to help with the horses. The next closest riders will be Van and Juan Padillo. Call for them if you need them. I'll take Mariposa with me today, and Estanzio, you'll go tomorrow."

Gil and Mariposa rode out well ahead of the herd. To the north Gil could see mountains, and for a change his map had a name for them. They were the Guadalupes, towering over a wilderness through which there would someday be a trail to Colorado.*

Gil immediately found the tracks he had seen the day before; tracks of the five riders who had ridden in from the north and then turned westward. Mariposa dismounted and followed the tracks a few yards, studying them.

"Two day," said Mariposa.

That meant the riders had arrived at the spring the day before Gil had gotten there. As Gil saw it, there had

---

* Trail Drive #1, *The Goodnight Trail*

been plenty of time for Morgan Pinder to ride back and alert his owlhoot companions to the trail drive. The very afternoon the trail drive had bedded down on the Rio Grande, north of El Paso, two riders had come in from the west, apparently on their way to the border town. The men had paused, too far away to be identified, and had ridden on. This pair fitted Gil's suspicions as Morgan Pinder and Verd Connor. Why else would Pinder have provoked trouble by hurling an impossible-to-prove charge of horse stealing at Long John and Van? These five riders, whose tracks Gil and Mariposa were following, could have been following up Pinder's report, spying on the trail drive. They had returned by a northerly direction to avoid leaving an obvious trail back to their camp. Watering their horses at the spring, they had then ridden west. Gil had little doubt these tracks would lead him and Mariposa to where this faction of the Clanton gang was holed up. Gil decided if he reached water before these tracks played out or changed direction, he and Mariposa would follow this trail to its end. The sooner he had some idea where the gang planned to jump the trail drive, the sooner an offensive could be planned.

"Water close by," said Mariposa, pointing skyward.

The honeybees were tiny specks in the morning sun, but Gil could see them, returning the way he and Mariposa had just come. Gil and Mariposa rode on, traveling less than a mile to reach a shallow creek. The water didn't seem substantial enough for a permanent camp, or for what the Clanton bunch likely had in mind, but it would temporarily serve the needs of the oncoming trail drive. The tracks of the five riders crossed the creek and continued westward.

"We'll stay with this trail, Mariposa," said Gil.

Gil suspected the next water would be claimed by the outlaws, and that it might be a good thirty miles distant. Beyond that, the next water would be so far away, the trail drive couldn't possibly reach it without water in between. If that were the case, it would put them at the

mercy of the outlaws. When Mariposa reined up, Gil
estimated they had ridden twenty-five miles west of the
shallow creek. Gil moved up beside him. While the Indian said nothing, he didn't need to. Gil smelled the
smoke too. Mariposa dismounted, Gil following, and
they half-hitched their reins to a low-hanging limb. Mariposa leading, they climbed to the crest of the hill,
where they could see without being seen. A crude log
cabin stood in the bend of a wide, deep-running creek.
There was a barn, crude as the cabin, with an adjoining
corral. Gil counted two dozen horses in the corral, and
there was room for many more. Was there a man for
every horse, or were most of these animals stolen, awaiting delivery to new owners?

"Mariposa," said Gil, "I'll go back and hold our
horses so they don't break loose and run. When I've had
time to get to them, do your cougar cry. That ought to
empty the cabin pronto, and when the coyotes come
runnin' out, count them. Then get back here as quick as
you can, and we'll ride."

Mariposa nodded, and Gil hurried back to the horses.
He loosed the reins and took a firm grip. Mariposa
sounded so much like a cougar, Gil's hair wanted to
stand on end, even when he knew it was only the Indian
creating the fearful sound. Sure enough, when Mariposa
cut loose with his cougar song, both horses reared, and
Gil had a time calming them. Almost before the cry
faded, Mariposa was there, swinging into the saddle. Gil
mounted and they galloped away. Mariposa turned to
Gil, raising five fingers and then one more. That told Gil
there had been six men in the cabin, but he had no
assurance there wouldn't be more.

When Gil and Mariposa met the trail drive, it had
covered less than half the fifteen miles to the creek
where they would spend the night. Gil told them only
that there was water ahead. It would be soon enough,
once this hard day was done, for them to learn that
tomorrow they would be within a day's drive of the outlaw camp. Gil had suspicions as to what lay ahead, and

in his mind a plan was taking shape. It would depend heavily on Mariposa and Estanzio.

The last two hours of the day's drive, they were in the dark. They had traveled forty-five miles in two days, and as exhausted as they were, every rider was jubilant. They deserved a good meal, and Gil found a stump hole they used for a fire pit. There was no wind to carry the smoke, to reveal their presence. Riders who would take the second watch relieved those who were already on watch, so they could eat. Gil had intended to wait until the morning before he said anything about the nearness of the outlaw cabin, but Rosa was on the second watch with him, and full of curiosity.

"You have discovered something you haven't told us," she said.

He laughed. "If you're that smart, what have I discovered?"

"You have discovered where the outlaws are."

"Then where are they?" he asked.

"Just ahead of us," said Rosa, "and they have stolen all the water in New Mexico. Each time we water the herd, we will have to shoot outlaws."

"It ain't quite that bad," Gil said, "but you're close."

She had always listened patiently, rarely critical of his plans, so he had become more comfortable with her. But for now he told her only that there were six men in the cabin, and that there would be only tomorrow night's camp between them and where he expected trouble.

"What are we to do?" she asked. "If they claim the land we must cross, what can we do?"

"Their claim to it is only as strong as their gun muscle," Gil said, "and they've been watching us. They might demand money for us crossing their land, but I doubt it. I think they'll just take the horses and the herd, if they can. Tonight or tomorrow night, I look for one or more of them to come here to take our measure. Mariposa and Estanzio will be staked out to welcome them, and once we have our hands on one of the bastards, he'll tell us what they have in mind. Then we'll make some plans of our own."

The night passed without incident. Mariposa and Estanzio had seen or heard nothing out of the ordinary. If the Clanton outlaws lived up to Gil's suspicions, it would have to be tonight. After their bone-breaking drives of the past several days, the comparatively short drive—about twelve miles, to the next water—seemed short indeed. They reached the little creek well before sundown. Gil had ridden ahead, but found no new tracks.

"Tonight," said Gil, "I want Mariposa and Estanzio out in the night again, circling the camp. I look for this Clanton bunch to scout us out one more time before they come after us. If Mariposa and Estanzio can grab one of the coyotes, we'll drag him up to the fire, have a look at him, and then he can tell us everything he knows."

"Ye know wher' the cabin is," said Long John. "Why don't we jus' be ther' at daylight, an' gun down the lot of 'em?"

"Ten of us *are* going to be there at daylight," said Gil, "but you're getting ahead of me. While there were just six men at the cabin, there were more than two dozen horses in the corral. I'd like to know for dead certain how many men we're up against. Sheriff Weatherford told me this old man Clanton has more than four hundred outlaws scattered around New Mexico and Arizona. If we can force one of the gang to talk, we can learn how strong they are. If they don't show tonight, then we'll just have to take our chances."

"If they do or don't show tonight," said Van, "you aim for us to go after them in the morning?"

"We ride at two o'clock," said Gil, "one way or the other. It's twenty-five miles to the cabin. If there's six or sixty, we'll hit them before first light, and we'll be shooting to kill."

7

Come dark, and time for the first watch, Gil sent six men to circle the herd. Mariposa and Estanzio were to remain afoot, circling the camp. A few minutes before midnight, the Indians captured one of the outlaws. Gil punched up the fire as Mariposa and Estanzio forced the captive ahead of them and into the light. Morgan Pinder had his hands bound behind his back. Estanzio carried the outlaw's gun rig.

"Well, Pinder," Gil said, "we ain't seen you since El Paso. Considerate of you to drop by. We know where you owlhoots are holed up, and we got a fair to middlin' idea what you aim to do. But we want to hear it in your own words."

"Go to hell," grunted Pinder.

"It's you that'll be goin' to Hell," said Gil, "and a lot sooner than you expect, if you don't talk. Now spill your guts, or I'll have Estanzio or Mariposa spill them for you."

Pinder said nothing. Most of the other riders had gathered around, including Rosa. The next move was Gil's. He merely nodded to Mariposa. The Indian didn't bother unbuttoning Pinder's shirt, but with his Bowie slit the garment from the collar down. While Mariposa ripped the shirt away, Estanzio loosed Pinder's belt, dropping his trousers. Except for boots and hat, the outlaw stood there possum naked. Rosa gasped, but she didn't turn away.

"Now, Pinder," said Gil, "maybe we can't *make* you talk, but we can purely make you wish you had."

Pinder swallowed hard, but kept his silence. Mariposa moved behind the outlaw so he couldn't retreat, while Estanzio drew his Bowie. He touched the tip of the huge blade to the hollow of Pinder's throat, and as the knife moved down Pinder's chest, it left a trail of blood. Pinder began to whine, fighting to free himself. Behind the outlaw, Mariposa applied some pressure, and Pinder screamed. Estanzio paused with the tip of his blade just above Pinder's belly button.

"Pinder," said Gil, "that Bowie's goin' to keep travelin' south. When it's gone as far as it can go, it's goin' to slice off some parts you don't hanker to lose. Even if you don't bleed to death, you'll have to squat when you go to the bushes."

Pinder knew it was no bluff when the tip of the Bowie's blade again started to move, going deeper. He screamed.

"That'll do, Estanzio," said Gil. "I believe the man's goin' to become more sociable."

"Damn you!" sobbed Pinder. "Damn you!"

Again Estanzio stepped forward with the Bowie.

"There's six of . . . us," Pinder gasped, "but Clanton's sending . . . more."

"How many more?" Gil demanded.

"I don't know!" cried Pinder. "He never tells us nothin' until the last minute. The others are ridin' in tomorrow."

"For what purpose?"

"We aimed for you to pay, before crossin' our land and usin' our water," said Pinder.

"Then you'd have let us go in peace," said Gil.

"Yes," said Pinder.

"You're lying," said Gil. "You've scouted us before, and you're here tonight to see how well-prepared we are. You aim to gun us down from ambush, to take our horses and cattle."

"No!" shouted Pinder, but the look on his face gave truth to Gil's words.

"Estanzio," said Gil, "hogtie this coyote so he can't get loose. We'll be riding in two hours, so nobody sleeps tonight. Four riders will stay with the herd, but the rest of us are going to be at that outlaw cabin before first light. Mr. Pinder will be going with us."

Estanzio had shoved Pinder down with his back against a small tree. The outlaw's arms were passed around the tree, and his hands securely bound. Gil and the other riders saddled their horses and rode out to join the nighthawks already with the herd. Rosa rode close to Gil, and she was silent longer than he had expected. Finally she spoke.

"I have never seen such cruelty since the *soldados* murdered my *padre* and *madre*. They were mutilated— cut—like you would have cut this Morgan Pinder. Would you truly have allowed Estanzio to do that, to cut off this man's . . . private parts? It would be more merciful to kill him."

"A bluff's only good till somebody calls it," said Gil. "If Pinder had not talked, Estanzio would have convinced him it was no bluff."

"Madre de Dios," she cried, "suppose someone did that to you . . . cut off your private parts?"

"I reckon I'd be squattin' in the bushes too." He chuckled. "Would that bother you?"

"No," she sighed, and he thought it was a little exaggerated. "You are of no use to me in that way. The good times, like tonight, we talk. The bad times, we shout and swear. I do not think we will ever go beyond that."

He almost laughed, but decided it wasn't funny, and since he was unable to think of a suitable response, he said nothing.

It was time to ride, and time to choose the four riders who would remain with the herd.

"I want Rosa, Juan Padillo, Bola, and Vicente to stay with the longhorns and the horse remuda," said Gil. "That's every bit as important as what the rest of us are about to do. Actually, I'm leaving you short-handed, because I don't know how many men we may find at this outlaw cabin. So I'm asking the four of you to take some risk, so that I can take a larger force with me. Are there any questions before we move out?"

Gil had half expected some protest from Rosa, but there was none. She could hold her own with the trail drive itself, but this planned man-killing was something else, where hesitation went hand in hand with death. Had it not been for Rosa, Gil might have simply left the horse remuda and the herd unattended, taking the entire outfit. Perhaps Rosa and the riders left behind suspected this, but there had been no protest. They had respected Gil's wishes. Gil led out. Van followed, with Morgan Pinder's horse on a lead rope. Pinder's hands were securely bound behind his back, and he was bare to the middle.

Phin Clanton, never very pleasant, was in an especially vile mood. With ten men he had ridden all the way from Apache Creek, to join forces with the men far to the south. The large horse remuda and the huge herd of longhorns would have been motivation enough for what the gang was about to do, but there was another, stronger reason. Verd Connor had been one of old man Clanton's most trusted lieutenants, and now Verd was dead. According to the one-sided story Morgan Pinder had told, Verd Connor had been needlessly gunned down by some Texas bastard who was trail-bossing a herd of Texas longhorns. Phin's bloodthirsty daddy, N. H. Clanton, lived by his own perverted concept of Old Testament law, and this Texas outfit was going to pay for Verd's death. Phin Clanton and his men had ridden in after dark, to find that Morgan Pinder, the damn fool, had gone gunning for the Texan who had killed Verd Connor. There were fifteen men in the small

cabin, drinking and playing cards. Phin Clanton stood
on the porch, leaning against an upright that supported
the shake roof. Trig Rudolph, one of the men who had
ridden in with Clanton, stepped out on the porch.

"Why are you standin' out here?" Rudolph asked.

"Maybe I just like to breathe," said Clanton, who
didn't smoke. "This damn shack could be afire, and
there not be that much smoke."

"It's near midnight," said Rudolph. "Suppose Pinder
don't come back; you still aim to hit that trail herd at
first light?"

"What else can we do? Give Pinder another two
hours; if he ain't here, that'll mean they got him. Without aimin' to, he's made it easier for us. Once they get
Pinder and find out he's alone, it'll look like just what it
is. Pinder's pard was gunned down, so he went after the
hombre that done it. If we was plannin' anything else,
why would we of let Pinder go stompin' in and get the
whole damn outfit on the prod?"

Rudolph chuckled. "Smart. With Pinder out of the
way, they won't be lookin' for nobody else. We're ridin'
at two?"

"Yeah," said Clanton, "not quite two hours."

"What if Pinder shows up between now and then?"

"That'll mean he's shot somebody, and the rest of the
bunch will come foggin' after him, and the fight will
come to us. But Pinder won't be here, so get ready to
ride."

Gil called a halt to rest the horses. He judged it was
three o'clock, and that they had ridden not quite half
the distance to the outlaw cabin. As they mounted their
horses and rode on, Gil became uneasy. There had been
little wind. Now it had risen, turned treacherous, and
was at their backs. Small sounds, even the creaking of a
saddle, carried far in the still of the night. A sentry
ahead, only half listening, might become aware of the
riders well in advance of their arrival. Gil reined up,

halting the column. He couldn't ignore that premonition of danger that had served him so well in the past. Turning in his saddle, he spoke to Van, almost in a whisper.

"Estanzio and Mariposa. Pass the word."

He would use the Indian riders as advance scouts. It was a smart move, but it came too late. Gil's horse nickered, and it was all the warning they had. Every rider rolled out of the saddle, as the night erupted into a Hell of gunfire and a hail of lead. There was no time to even think of restraining the horses, and they galloped madly back the way they had come. Morgan Pinder's horse was among them, Pinder hunched low in the saddle. Following the first deadly volley, but for the diminishing sound of the running horses, there was only silence. Not a man moved. The wind was against them, and the slightest sound might invite swift and certain death. The moon was down, and it was the kind of standoff that might continue until dawn, with neither side gaining an advantage. But the Texas outfit had an edge of which the outlaws were unaware. While Mariposa and Estanzio were unable to make Gil aware of their intentions, it didn't hinder them doing what they knew must be done. Quietly, swiftly, Estanzio slipped to the south, while Mariposa crept northward, flanking the outlaws. While lead was unable to find its mark in the darkness, a deadly Bowie in the sure hand of an Indian had no such limitation.

Suddenly, somewhere beyond Gil's position, there was a scream of mortal terror, and then silence. Within seconds there was another scream, from yet another position. There was a chilling finality, a supernatural aura, about it all. Estanzio and Mariposa were perfectly capable of silent killing, but there was a time when fear itself became a weapon, and this was such a time. This was a tactic calculated to strike fear into the hearts of the outlaws, and it had the desired effect. The Clanton men began firing, not at the Texans, but at shadows. There was a yowl of pain as at least one of the outlaws was shot by a comrade. Gil and his riders held their fire, lest they hit Estanzio or Mariposa.

"Damn it," bawled Phin Clanton, "hold your fire!"

No sooner had the frantic firing ceased, when Mariposa or Estanzio took another victim. Again the man was allowed a single terrified shriek before he was silenced forever. That was enough. The rest of the outlaws lit out for their horses, throwing caution to the winds. Gil and his riders didn't move until Mariposa and Estanzio stepped out of the shadows.

"Coyotes run," said Estanzio. "We hunt?"

"No," said Gil, "we'd never catch them in the dark. Besides, you hombres handled it just right. They had us outnumbered, and were shooting from cover probably. Did anybody get hit when they cut down on us?"

When nobody responded, Gil again spoke.

"We'll ride on back to the herd, then, granted that we can find and catch our horses."

"Morgan Pinder's out there somewhere," said Van, "unless he's managed to get loose. I didn't consider him important enough to get myself shot."

"I doubt he'll be a problem to us," Gil replied. "I'm wondering if maybe he didn't come after us—or me—on his own. If he did, he won't be on good terms with the rest of the gang. By the time we reach the camp, it'll be time to eat and get the herd on the trail. Mariposa, I want you and Estanzio to trail that bunch of owlhoots, at least far enough to be sure we're rid of them. I doubt they'll still be at the cabin, but if they are, get the word to us pronto. If they rode out, trail them far enough to be sure they don't circle and double back. The whole thieving bunch could be laying for us somewhere farther west."

This was the darkest hour before dawn, when the stars seemed anxious to recede to that faraway realm where they spent their daylight hours. It was a poor time for Texas cowboys to be afoot in search of their horses.

"Damnation," Long John groaned wearily, "I hope them hosses don't run all the way back t' camp."

"They won't," said Gil. "Not with loose reins. Most western horses are trained to ground-tie. You didn't take the time to loop your reins around the horn, did you?"

"Reckon I did," said Long John sarcastically. "I allus see that m' hoss is took care of proper. 'Specially when a bunch o' owlhoot bastards is busy throwin' lead at me."

"Long John don't ride Mendoza horse," said Juan Alamonte. "Sorrel Long John ride, he be on his way to camp."

"That's right," said Van, with a laugh. "Long John's ridin' that stray with a pitchfork brand that nearly got us hung in El Paso. That cayuse may not stop runnin' till he hits the Pecos."

Despite their predicament, they laughed, but Long John had the last laugh. Before it was light enough to see more than a few feet, they heard a horse cropping grass. It was the sorrel with the pitchfork brand.

"Wal," chuckled Long John, as he mounted, "be seein' ya'll in camp."

The rest of the riders hunkered wearily where they were and waited for Long John. When he returned leading three horses, Mariposa, Estanzio, and Pedro Fagano had mounts. The four men rode out, and within a few minutes had returned with the rest of the horses. Long John had found the twisted rawhide thong that had bound Morgan Pinder's hands. The Cajun dismounted, dropped the rawhide at Estanzio's feet and grinned at the Indian.

"Somebody," said Long John, "dint tie that jaybird none too tight."

"Mebbe you no like?" Estanzio's tone was mild, but his eyes had narrowed to slits. He was border-shifting his Bowie from one hand to the other.

Long John whipped out his own Bowie, matching Estanzio's movements and grinning at the Indian.

"Enough of that," Gil snapped. "Have your fun some other time. Mount up and let's ride. Unless you find something we need to know, Mariposa, you and Estanzio wait for us at the outlaw cabin."

They reached camp to find that Rosa had breakfast waiting. When they had eaten, Gil spoke to them.

"It's twenty-five miles to the next water, and that's where the outlaw cabin is. I know it's another long drive, but there's no help for it. We'll be in the dark a good part of the way, because we're gettin' a late start. We don't know where that bunch of outlaws went. We don't know if they've given up on us, or if we'll have to fight at some other time and place. On the frontier, when there's any doubt, be ready to fight. Estanzio and Mariposa are following the owlhoots, so that we don't ride into an ambush. Unless the outlaws have returned to that cabin, I don't look for any trouble out of them. Ramon, I'll help you with the horse remuda. Let's ride!"

Gil pushed the herd as hard as he could, and although they had taken the trail three hours late, by two o'clock in the afternoon the drive had traveled more than ten miles. But the outfit was thirty-four hours without sleep, and it began to tell. Rosa dozed in the saddle, and other riders had taken to slapping themselves in the face with their hats. At the present pace, it would be midnight before they reached the creek where the outlaw cabin was. Without Mariposa and Estanzio, Gil and Ramon had their hands full with the packhorses and remuda.

"Outlaws be gone," said Ramon. "Mariposa and Estanzio not return."

"Yeah," said Gil, "and so far, that's the only good news. That, and the fact the herd ain't havin' one of its ornery days."

"Maybe we push 'em harder," said Ramon.

"Maybe," said Gil, "and maybe they'd just get cantankerous and take up their old bunch-quitting habits. Let's leave well enough alone."

"Soon be rain," said Ramon. "Longhorns trail better without so much sun."

It was true. Clouds had begun rolling in at mid-morning, and the sky was overcast. There were signs that the rain might come without the thunder and lightning that raised hell with a trail drive. They were moving due west, and it was from the west that most of their storms came. Longhorns tried to run away from thunder and lightning. A stampede would cost them as much as two days gathering the scattered herd, and a third day making up the wasted miles the spooked longhorns had run in the opposite direction.

"Rain's comin'," said Van, who had ridden up from the flank. "Bad news for Mariposa and Estanzio. Even they can't follow that outlaw trail after a good gully washer."

"Maybe they won't have to follow it any farther," said Gil. "All I want is that those owlhoots are going to keep riding. I'm hoping our hombres will know for sure before the trail's rained out."

"We got one thing in our favor," Van said, "that makes me think that outlaw bunch will leave us alone. Thanks to our Injun riders, they lost four men, while none of us got a scratch. Clanton—or whoever was the boss—lost control of them, and they started shootin' at one another in the dark. We could of burnt powder and throwed lead until daylight and not even touched those coyotes. Their own fear and superstition did what we couldn't have done in the dark, or even in daylight."

Gil laughed. "Can't fault them for running. Wouldn't you, if your pards were dying all around you, and there was nothin' for you to shoot at?"

"Damn right," said Van. "I wouldn't of stayed as long as they did. We purely got ourselves a pair of thinkin' Injuns. Every outlaw they cut, they let him squall just enough to scare hell out of the others."

With an overcast sky, darkness came early. When it became obvious the trail drive was going to continue without water or graze, the longhorns again expressed their discontent, bawling disconsolately as they plodded on.

"Cows not dry enough to run," said Juan Padillo.

"Hope you be right," said Vicente Gomez. "Wind come before rain."

Soon there was a light breeze out of the west, heavy with the smell of rain, but the longhorns kept on. They were tired, maybe hungry, but not yet stampede-thirsty.

"Thank God," Gil said, "the rain will solve our water problem until we're able to reach the creek."

"Ye sure?" asked the ever pessimistic Long John. "Texas longhorns is got t' be standin' in water up to their noses 'fore they knows it's there, an' I don't look fer it t' rain that deep."

The rain came, slow and steady for a change, rather than in windswept torrents. To the dusty, weary riders it was a welcome relief. Rosa rode with her hat under her arm, allowing the cooling rain to wash over her head and face. The longhorns ceased their restless bawling, and the drive continued through the darkness.

"If this wasn't open plains," Van said, "we'd be in trouble, with no moon and no stars."

"We'll be in trouble later on," said Gil, "because there's hill country the last four or five miles. We'll all be ridin' headlong into trees."

"Then we won't make the creek tonight," Van said, "unless it clears up."

"I doubt it'll clear up in time to help us," said Gil. "We'll soon be forced to call it a day, and wait for first light. But the grass is wet, and there's some water on the ground. That'll satisfy the cattle and horses until we reach the creek in the morning."

The rain continued, and as the open plain gave way to wooded hills and valleys, Gil halted the drive.

"We're all dead tired," Gil said, "but we'll have to keep watch. I'll be the first, but I'll need volunteers to join me."

"Wal, hell," said Long John, "I'll stick wi' ye. Who can sleep in all this rain?"

"I can," said Rosa.

"When we reach water in the morning," said Gil, "we'll take a day of rest."

They spent the rest of the long night in the saddle, most of the riders preferring to nighthawk instead of attempting to sleep. They would wait for the morning. The rain ceased before first light, and the sun announced its arrival with a rosy glow across the eastern sky. Soon as it was light enough to see, Gil and the riders were pushing the herd toward the creek ahead. Even with the rain, they had spent the night in dry camp, and there was no water. They couldn't eat or rest until they reached the creek and the outlaw cabin. When they finally topped a ridge overlooking their destination, the outfit had been in the saddle more than fifty hours. There was no sign of life at the cabin below, but as they watched, Estanzio came out of the barn. Raising his hand, he beckoned them on.

"All right," shouted Gil, "let's take 'em down to the creek!"

The sun had quickly erased all evidence of last night's rain. Longhorns and horse remuda trotted gladly toward the deep-running creek, while Gil and the riders reined up at the barn. The Indian riders were waiting, and Estanzio gave their report in a few words.

"Coyotes run," said Estanzio. "Ride nort'. Rain come, trail go to hell."

Gil nodded his thanks. It was about as he had expected. Rain had wiped out the trail, but Mariposa and Estanzio had gotten an early start. They'd had time to observe some pattern to the outlaws' flight.

"One more thing, Estanzio," said Gil. "What about Morgan Pinder? After he got loose, did he join the rest of the gang?"

"Him ride 'lone," said Estanzio, pointing west.

It confirmed Gil's suspicion that Pinder was acting on his own, likely seeking revenge for Verd Connor's death.

Pinder wouldn't be eager to get back with the Clanton gang.

"We'll lay over here for the rest of the day and to-night," said Gil. "We all need rest and sleep. Mariposa, you and Estanzio are rested. Ride on ahead and look for water, and for any sign of trouble."

8

*T*he riders took turns sleeping. Gil was up and about
after two hours, looking westward for some sign of
Estanzio and Mariposa. The longer they were gone, the
farther the herd would have to go in search of the next
water. Rosa had slept little, spending her time in the
abandoned cabin, searching through the debris the outlaws had left behind. The door was open, and when Gil
stepped into the cabin, the stink almost floored him.
Overriding everything else was the distinctive smell of a
cigar. Rosa knelt at the hearth, picking at the stones
with a horseshoe nail. She stood up when Gil came in.

"My God," he said, holding his nose, "how can you
stand it in here?"

"I left the door open," she said.

"You're wasting your time," said Gil. "That bunch
wouldn't leave anything of any use to us."

"I did not expect them to," said Rosa, "but this was
not their cabin. It was built by someone else, a man who
took pride in his work. See how carefully the stones in
the hearth and the fireplace have been laid? See how
the logs have been fitted to one another? There is almost no chinking. It is a house that was not built by
outlaws, I think."

"I think you're right," said Gil. "They likely rode in
and murdered the man who built the place. What are
you doing?"

Rosa again knelt at the stone hearth. "There is a stone loose," she said, "and I am wondering why."

"You'll never find out with that nail," said Gil. "Let me try it with the Bowie."

So well had the stones been fitted, he wondered how she had found this loose one. He had a time raising the flat stone enough that he could grip it with his fingers. In the small space beneath the stone was what looked to be nothing more than wadded paper. It was brittle with age, and when Gil brought it out, it broke up in his hands. It had once been a page from a newspaper, and amid the remains, there was the dull gleam of gold! Gil placed the double handful of crumbling newsprint and gold on the hearth, and Rosa knelt beside him. There were eleven thick, eight-sided gold pieces!

"Tarnation!" Gil exclaimed. "These are fifty-dollar gold pieces! Five hundred and fifty dollars' worth!"

"It is someone's treasure," said Rosa. "Perhaps we should not disturb it."

Gil was piecing some of the newsprint together, and finally he came up with a readable date.

"This paper was dated April second, 1834," he said. "Rosa, this gold's been here more than fifteen years, and the paper in which it was wrapped was printed in San Francisco. The man who left this gold here won't be comin' after it. He's long dead. This money is yours."

"But what am I to do with it? It saddens me to take it."

"If you don't," said Gil, "it'll just lay here until somebody else takes it. The man who left it here may have stolen it. I've heard of these eight-sided pieces, but these are the first I've ever seen. They were first minted by the Spanish, I think, when California was under Spanish rule. Here, take them. Tie them up in a bandanna, and tell nobody you have them. There may come a time when you'll need them."

He spoke more truth than he realized. The time would come when his very future would depend upon that handful of Spanish gold.

* * *

Mariposa and Estanzio returned with disturbing news. Once they left the plentiful water near what had been the outlaw camp, they faced a twenty-mile drive. While none of them knew what lay ahead, Gil had his suspicions, and he shared them with the outfit after they'd finished supper.

"It's goin' to be more mountainous," he said, "and I look for us to have to drive for miles along deep canyons before we find a way across. There'll be dry camps, because the distance between water will be too great for us to make it in a single day's drive. I look for canyons and dropoffs that'll make it impossible for us to trail the herd in the dark."

"If longhorns get thirsty and stampede in the night," said Ramon, "these same canyons and dropoffs still be there."

"You're damn right they will be," said Gil, "and one bad run over some canyon rim could cost us the herd *and* the horse remuda."

"We push lak hell in daylight," said Juan Padillo.

"We may have a dry camp ahead of us tomorrow night," said Van.

"No like dry camp," said Mariposa. "Make cow run."

"It may come to that," Gil said. "We may have to choose between running them in daylight when we can see where we're going, or having them become thirst-crazy and run at night. Maybe over a canyon rim. We'll move out in the morning the moment it's light enough to see, and drive them as hard as we can."

"Reckon ye can spare me an' Bola fer two er three hours in the mornin'?" Long John asked. "We seen deer tracks up the creek a while ago. We git there 'fore daylight, with an extry hoss fer the carcass, an' it's venison steaks fer supper."

"Long John," said Gil irritably, "this is a trail drive, not a deer hunt. Besides, in the early dawn, a shot can be heard for miles."

"They won't be no shot," said Long John. "We'll use the bola."

Long John's affable grin was missing, and he had fixed his cold blue eyes on Gil in a manner that suggested there might be trouble in the making.

"I would like some fresh venison," said Rosa.

"So would I," Van said.

Gil didn't fault Van or Rosa for attempting to avoid an ugly scene, but it angered him that they felt a need to interfere. If the time ever came when Gil Austin couldn't stand up to Long John Coons—or any man— he'd as well get on a fast horse and head back to Texas. Rosa's eyes wouldn't meet Gil's, but Van didn't flinch. There was an unmistakable coldness in Gil's voice when he again spoke to Long John.

"Go on, then," said Gil, "but if there's any trouble— Indian or otherwise—I'm holding you responsible. And don't waste any time catching up to the drive. We have a hard day ahead of us."

Rosa had always spread her blankets near Gil's, and sometimes they would talk before they slept. But tonight she turned in well ahead of him, and he suspected it was to avoid anything he might say about her interfering in his confrontation with Long John. She fooled him. By the time Gil had shucked his boots and hat, and was settling down with his head on his saddle, the girl was sitting on her blankets looking at him in the moonlight.

"I know you are angry with me," she said, "but must you always prove you are the boss, even when it gains you nothing?"

"Rosa," he said, and his voice was dangerously low, "when a man can no longer *prove* he's the boss, he's done. Like it or not, that's how it is on the frontier."

"Long John did not question your authority," said Rosa. "He only asked your permission to hunt deer. You could have simply granted him permission or refused it. Only you saw his request as a challenge to your authority."

Gil kicked out of his blankets, got up and hunkered down face-to-face with her. Rosa didn't cringe, even when he spoke to her through gritted teeth.

"I'm almighty damn tired of you talkin' down to me like I'm five years old and you're my mama," he said. "Worse, I feel like I'm stuck with all the miseries of a wife, with none of the benefits."

"Are those all my faults, or have you not finished?"

"I have not finished," he growled. "I don't like this . . . this obsession with Long John Coons. What'n hell do you see in him?"

"I see a lonely man who would be your friend, if you could stop being the boss long enough to allow it. And there is the little man, Bola, the Argentine. You have orders for him, but never a kind word."

"Well, by God," said Gil, "it's no wonder we've had so many problems. This is no trail drive, it's a tea social. Are you done tearin' me down?"

"I am not tearing you down. I am trying to stop you from tearing yourself down. Can you not be the boss without being hated?"

"I'm trail boss, and this is a trail drive," said Gil. "It's my job to keep these men alive. How I do it is my business, and whether or not they choose to hate me is theirs. You reckon I'd be more popular if I stopped the drive and let all the men ride back to El Paso for a Saturday night in town?"

"You are making fun of me, and I will speak to you no more."

Rosa emphasized that by stretching out on one blanket and covering herself—including her head—with a second one. Gil returned to his own bed, not to sleep, but to think. What irked him the most was the fact that Rosa seemed to see, to feel, to understand things he did not. Why had the girl used Long John and Bola to antagonize him? None of the riders—Mexican or Indian—who had joined him for that near-disastrous trail drive from Mexico in 1843 had ever caused him a minute's trouble or questioned his authority.* Bola had been part of that outfit, yet he had sought the friendship of the lanky Long John. The men were as different as daylight and dark. Bola was neither Mexican or Texan, but an Argentine. Long John was a man of the gun, the knife, and the saddle, but he was a Cajun from the Louisiana bayous, the son of a conjuring woman. While each man was part of the outfit, they were outcasts, drawn together by the very differences that set them apart. Gil was sorry for some of the things he had said to Rosa, and he sat up, tempted to speak to her. But she seemed asleep, and he again stretched out, his head on his saddle. Sleep was long in coming.

Well before daylight, Long John and Bola rode out, paralleling the creek, to the northeast. Gil and the rest of the outfit had the herd on the trail at the very first gray light of dawn. Mariposa and Estanzio were well ahead of the trail drive, beginning their quest for water for the next day. Gil and Ramon again had charge of the horse remuda and the packhorses. Rosa was riding drag, with Pedro Fagano and Juan Alamonte. More than once Gil had been moved to speak to the girl, but Rosa had been cool and unresponsive. Gil began to resent her aloofness, and for the first time began asking himself some troubling questions. Even if he accepted the differences in his age and hers, did he really wish to tie himself to a female who never seemed to see anything but his faults, and was damnably swift in pointing them out?

Long John and Bola had reached their chosen place along the creek well before daylight. The bola was a clever device the Argentine used as other cowboys used a lariat, except that the thing left his hand entirely, wrapping itself around the hind legs of cow, horse, or deer. The bola consisted of three long, braided strands

* Trail Drive Series #4, *The Bandera Trail*

of rawhide, joined at one end and loose at the other. At each of the loose ends was a leather pocket, and in that pocket an iron ball the size of a man's fist. A rider who threw the bola must be strong of arm and shoulder. Taking a grip on the butt, where the three leathers joined, the rider began swinging the bola over his head, much the way a cowboy swung a lariat. Judging he was close enough to a fleeing quarry, the rider released the bola, allowing it to entangle itself around the hind legs of the animal being pursued.

Long John had watched in silent admiration as Bo had captured horses, cows, and deer with the strange device. The Cajun had made up his mind that he would learn to throw the bola, and unknown to the rest of the outfit, the Argentine had tried to help Long John. But try as he might, Long John hadn't been able to master the damn thing. Time after time he tried, and couldn't twist the bola around a tree trunk often enough for it to be more than just accidental. Long John wasn't accustomed to failure, and his ego suffered mightily. He had half expected the Argentine to laugh at his clumsy efforts, but Bola had not. Thus had begun their strange friendship. The two men had reined up their horses behind a clump of brush where they could observe the stretch of creek the deer seemed to favor.

"Bo," said Long John, "s'pose ye lef' the hoss here, an' slunk up on 'em clost as ye can, an' made yer throw? They goin' t' light out an' run like hell, oncet we ride outta here."

"One cannot creep close enough without being heard, Long John," said Bo. "It is for sure the deer will run before I am close enough to throw, but with a horse, I can pursue. A deer's movements are swift, and a standing animal would have to move only a little to evade my throw. It is far easier to catch an animal on the run, using lariat or bola, because the prey is not attempting to avoid your throw. A standing animal may simply dodge your throw, while a running animal seeks only to escape."

"Reckon that's why I ain't had much luck with yer bola," Long John said. "That tree I was throwin' at should of been runnin'."

Bo grinned, appreciating Long John's laconic sense of humor. Bo had the bola ready, and no more was said until the deer appeared. There were three, one of them a young buck. Once they decided it was safe to drink and their heads were down, the two riders kicked their horses into a gallop. Long John was in the lead, seeking to flank the buck until Bola could get a clear throw. The trio of deer bounded through the creek and were scrambling up the farthest bank when the buck slipped. It was but a slight delay, just what the Argentine needed. The bola went true, entangled the buck's hind legs, and the animal fell with its hind quarters in the creek. Long John was out of his saddle in an instant, in water above his knees, the Bowie in his hand. So intent was the Cajun on cutting the captive buck's throat, he saw or heard nothing, until Bola spoke.

"Long John," he said quietly, "Indians."

Long John stood up, the bloody Bowie in his hand, and found himself facing no less than two dozen Indians. Long John drove the Bowie's big blade into the creek bank and then returned the knife to his waistband. As calmly as he could, he untangled the leather tails of the bola from the buck's hind legs and climbed out of the creek to face the Indians. They were afoot, which accounted for the fact he hadn't heard them approach. Long John chose an Indian who looked like a chief, and spoke to him in Spanish.

"*Jefe?*"

"*Jefe Tresosos,*" the Indian replied. "Apache."

Chief Three Bears, and he spoke at least some Spanish. Long John sighed, and raised his right hand in a sign of peace. Three Bears returned the sign, only to have a brave rush forward, his lance aimed at Long John's throat.

"*Gallo!*" bawled the chief. "*Ninguno!*"

The arrogant brave backed away, disappointed. Three

Bears had turned his attention to the dead buck. Raising his eyebrows, he pointed first to the deer and then to Long John. The Cajun shook his head, held up the three-headed bola in his left hand, and pointed to Bo. The Argentine appeared to relax in the saddle, but his right thumb was hooked in his pistol belt, just above the butt of his Colt. Long John shook his head, motioning Bola across the creek. When the Argentine reined up, Long John handed him the bola.

"Bo," said Long John, "Three Bears wants t' know how ye caught the buck. I'll see kin I git ye a runnin' hoss, so's ye kin show 'im."

It was a bold move, and it might mean the difference between living and dying. Long John pointed to the brave who had been so quick with his spear, and then the Cajun spoke to Three Bears.

"*Caballo,*" said Long John.

"*Caballo,*" Three Bears repeated, turning to the spear-toting brave.

When the surly brave had returned with the horse, Long John pointed to the Indian, then to the horse. This arrogant young fool's Apache name was Rooster, but when Long John was done with him, he wouldn't have anything to crow about. An Indian had a bizarre sense of humor. If Long John could make them laugh, he and Bo might yet ride away with their hair still in place. Rooster had brought the horse, but he refused to mount. He clearly did not intend to take orders from Long John, but when Three Bears repeated the order, he quickly reconsidered. When he was astride the horse, Long John spoke again.

"*Galope. Rapido.*"

This time the Indian obeyed. He kicked the horse into a fast gallop, Bo a few yards behind. The Argentine whirled the iron-balled device above his head a few times, and once released, it wrapped itself neatly around the hind legs of the running horse. The horse went down, and young Gallo took an ignominious tumble in the dirt. The rest of the Indians, including Three Bears, slapped their thighs and roared. But Gallo did not laugh. Around his neck, on a leather thong, he carried a Bowie. Whipping the big knife free, he came after Long John, his intentions clear. Nobody spoke, nobody attempted to stop him. Knowing the odds, Long John drew his own Bowie. If he refused to fight, he and Bo were as good as dead. While Indians revered a brave man and might allow him to go free, a coward was shown no mercy. But Long John faced a dilemma. He had a gut feeling that if he won this battle, killing this brash young fool, he would lose the war. The rest of the Apaches would leave him and Bo for the buzzards and coyotes. There was but one way Long John could win, yet sparing young Gallo a death thrust. He must disarm his opponent and count coup.

Gallo paused. Long John was perfectly at ease, the Bowie rock-steady in his right hand, his gaunt face alight with a malevolent grin. He had been not quite twelve when he'd gutted his first man on the New Orleans waterfront, and Long John Coons had learned a trick or two since then. Gallo made his first thrust, and Long John slammed the flat of his blade against the Indian's wrist. The Bowie fell to the ground, and Long John stood there grinning, waiting for Gallo to recover his weapon. There were grunts of approval from the rest of the Indians. The Apache snatched the Bowie with his left hand, proof enough that he had no grip in the other. Long John waited for his opponent to come to him, but Gallo clearly was not quite as confident with the Bowie in his left hand. He went through the motions, making some halfhearted thrusts and drawing some disapproving grunts from his companions. Finally he shifted the Bowie to his right hand and returned to the fight in earnest. Long John didn't move quite fast enough, and one of Gallo's thrusts nicked the Cajun's right thigh, drawing blood. Flushed with that small success, the Apache tried again, and Long John was ready for him. When Gallo tried to split Long John's belly with a sideways swipe, the Cajun seemed to fold in the middle, away from the Bowie. The Apache's blade missed, but Long John's didn't. The flat of Long John's blade slammed against Gallo's head just above his left ear, and the Indian went down like he'd been slugged with a singletree. Long John returned the Bowie to his waistband, turned to Three Bears and raised his right hand in the sign of peace. The Apache chief looked at the fallen brave, then at Long John.

"*Gallo hijo,*" he said, raising his right hand. "*Partir pronto.*"

Bo was already splashing across the creek, leading Long John's mount and the extra horse they'd brought for the deer carcass. The slain deer the farthest thing from their minds, Long John and Bo wasted no time mounting. But their elation was short-lived. Three Bears wasn't quite ready for them to go. Looking at Long John, he shook his head. He then turned to two of his braves and pointed to the deer carcass. While Long John and Bo looked on in amazement, two of the Indians lifted the deer carcass out of the creek and lashed it to the back of the nervous packhorse. Three Bears raised his right hand and spoke to Long John and Bo.

"*Partir en paz,*" he said.*

They needed no urging. Bo leading the horse bearing the deer, they rode out at a slow gallop. Gallo was on his knees, glaring at them. Once they were safely away and sure there was no pursuit, they slowed their horses.

"You did not know Gallo was the son of Chief Three Bears?" Bola asked.

"Wal, hell no." Long John grinned. "How could I of knowed that? My ma is a conjurin' woman, an' she allus said fer me t' shy away from cards an' wimen. She should of included Injuns, I reckon."

Despite the twenty-mile drive facing them, Gil was feeling good about the progress they were making. He

_____
* Depart in peace.

had given the order to move the herd at a faster pace, and the longhorns had responded.

"Is good," said Ramon. "Good water, good grass las' night, and they run better today."

"I reckon we've got the hang of it, Ramon," said Gil exultantly. "The only way we can make a longer drive to water is to begin each day's drive after a night of good water and good graze. We don't know this country, and it's lookin' more and more like we'll have to figure at least twenty miles a day from one waterin' hole to the next."

The herd had been on the trail three hours when Long John and Bo caught up. When they had stopped to rest their horses, they'd taken the time to bleed and gut the deer. The carcass had then been covered with a piece of canvas they'd taken for that purpose. Expecting them, Gil had ridden back to drag, and was there when Long John and Bo caught up. Gil raised his hand in greeting, grinning at them. It was an apology of sorts, for his sour response the day before.

"No trouble, I reckon," said Gil.

"None t' speak of," said Long John. "We went fer a deer, an' we got one."

Bo said nothing, matching Long John's good nature.

"The herd's behavin' itself and movin' at a good lope," said Gil. "Me and Ramon's got things under control up front. Bo, I expect you'd best keep that led horse back here. We can't risk havin' that deer carcass spook the horse remuda. Long John, you stay with the drag too. That'll make us a mite heavy at this end, but we'll need more riders here. With these longer drives to water, we'll be pushing 'em harder. When they begin to tire, don't let 'em lag. Keep 'em bunched, the ranks tight, so they don't slow down."

Gil rode ahead to the horse remuda, and Rosa trotted her horse alongside Long John's. Her eyes were on the three-inch slash in Long John's trousers and the dried blood on his thigh.

"You have been cut," she said.

"It do look like it," said Long John, "but they's thorn bushes in these parts what can rip a man like a knife."

Rosa dropped back until she was riding next to Bo, and when she didn't speak, neither did he. He rode with his eyes straight ahead, apparently fascinated by the ears of his horse. His face told her nothing.

9

May 2, 1850. Southwestern New Mexico Territory

$\mathcal{F}$rom El Paso west to the continental divide, southern New Mexico had been much like the Texas
plains. In fact, the eastern two-thirds of the territory had
once *been* part of Texas, until Mexico had ceded the
western portion to the United States in 1848. As the
trail drive moved farther west, the air became clear and
dry, and as Gil had expected, the plains gave way to
wooded, mountainous terrain. The longhorns, driven
hard since first light, had begun to tire. By the sun, it
was near noon.

"They're startin' to lag on us, Ramon," said Gil. "I'm
goin' to ride back and talk to the riders. From now to
sundown we'll have to fight the herd for every mile."

Gil found the drag riders doing their best, swinging
doubled lariats against dusty flanks. The longhorns
bawled their discontent, but they kept bunched and kept
moving.

"That's the way," Gil said. "We're pushin' 'em harder
than they're used to, and they're tired. But not near as
tired as they're going to be. We'll have to do as well
from now to sundown as we've done so far. If we don't,
it's dry camp."

Gil rode ahead to the horse remuda to find that Mariposa and Estanzio had returned.

"Find water," said Mariposa. "Fi'teen mile, mebbe."

Ramon and Gil dropped back, allowing Mariposa and Estanzio to again take control of the horse remuda and the packhorses.

"Ramon," said Gil, "you take the left flank and I'll take the right. The herd's so strung out, the flank riders have more than they can handle. We'll ride the length of the herd and back again, taking up the slack. It's the cows in the middle ranks that are draggin' their feet. Let's get in there and burn some backsides."

Lower and lower the sun slipped toward the western horizon, until finally, in a burst of crimson, it was gone. Bats and swallows flashed across a graying sky, and the cry of a night bird was melancholy in the twilight. Blue shadows crept over the land, and awakening stars blinked sleepily from far away. One of the horses in the remuda nickered. Tired as they were, the lead steers lurched into a trot, and the rest of the herd followed. There were triumphant cowboy yells from some of the riders. There was water ahead!

"It ain't as plentiful as yesterday," said Van, "but by the Eternal, it's enough."

"Gon' be dark 'fore we kin git supper," said Long John. "We still goin' t' have them venison steaks?"

"Damn right," said Gil, "even if we have to dig a fire pit. My hat's off to every one of you, for proving we *can* drive twenty miles in a day, and to Bo and Long John for gettin' the deer. Let's unload the packhorses and get on with the grub."

It became the most memorable day they'd had on the trail. Their camp was in a secluded valley, and at some time in the distant past, a rock slide had created an enormous fire pit that shielded their supper fire. They roasted and ate huge amounts of the venison, and Rosa vowed to cook the rest of it before it spoiled. By the light of the fire, over cups of hot, black coffee, they studied the government map.

"If this map's even close to bein' right," Gil said, "we'll soon be in Arizona. I figure it at no more than fifty miles."

"There be more water in Arizona?" Ramon asked.

"More rivers," said Gil. "The San Simon flows almost along the border between New Mexico and Arizona. West of there, maybe fifty miles, we'll cross the San Pedro, and beyond that, I'd say twenty-five miles, is Cienega Creek."

"How'd a creek git in there?" Long John asked. "Thought they wasn't countin' nothin' but rivers."

"I don't know," said Gil, "but it's on here as a creek. Just a few miles east of Tucson."*

"There is a town?" Rosa asked.

"Mining town, I expect," said Gil. "There's been some silver strikes in that part of the territory. If we continue the way we're headed, we'll go within hollerin' distance of Tucson."

"If it's a mining town," said Van, "they should have money. Why don't we sell 'em a few steers? We still have forty-one hundred."

"We'll stop there," Gil said, "and ask about the country ahead. I'd not object to selling them some beef, if they don't want too much. Our best market is still the goldfields, but it might be to our advantage not to reach California broke. We'll be mighty low on grub by then, and I don't aim to be pushed into selling the herd until we've made our best deal. It just might be worth our while to sell a few head in Tucson, if the price is right."

"Many horse need shoe," said Estanzio. "Need stop, fix."

"Good Lord, yes," Van said. "All our horses are overdue, and we have only enough shoes to reshoe them all once. We purely can't make it from Tucson to the goldfields without extra shoes. That's reason enough to sell some beef. We'll almost have to."

---

* Tucson was established by the Spanish, in 1560.

"Mebbe there be no shoes to buy," said Vicente Gomez.

"It be mining town," said Juan Padillo, "there be horses."

"Mules," said Long John. "Hosses ain't wuth a damn in a minin' camp, 'cept fer ridin'. Silver minin', that's mule work."

"We're wasting time talking about it," said Gil. "We'll just have to see what we can or can't do, once we get there. Right now, we need a first and second watch for the night."

Gil and Rosa were on the second watch, and for a change they weren't at odds with one another.

"If there is no sale of beef at Tucson," said Rosa, "I have the gold. It is almost for certain the horses will have to be shod again before we reach the goldfields."

"I know that," said Gil. "But for the extra weight, I'd have brought more shoes."

"Why did you not bring a wagon?"

"Two good reasons," said Gil. "First, we had plenty of horses, no money, and the wagon yard don't sell on credit. Second, I didn't know how rough the country would be, or if a wagon could even make the journey. You've ridden the trail all the way from Bandera; how would you have gotten a wagon over some of the rough country we've had to cross?"

"I suppose it would have been difficult."

"Difficult, hell," said Gil. "Impossible."

"I have the gold, then, if you need it."

"Keep it," said Gil, "and keep quiet about it. Bein' a mining town, you can count on Tucson havin' outlaws. The very last thing you want to do is go flashing a fifty-dollar gold piece."

Mariposa and Estanzio rode out at first light, again seeking water.

"If that map's right," said Van, "and we're fifty miles out of Arizona, we may have to go all the way to the San Simon tomorrow, before we reach water."

"We'll make our fifteen miles today," said Gil, "and see what Mariposa and Estanzio come up with for tomorrow."

Gil had the herd moving at first light, and again the riders pushed the longhorns hard. When Mariposa and Estanzio had not returned at noon, it looked like bad news for the next day. The longer the Indian riders were gone, the farther they'd had to ride for water. It was well into the afternoon when Mariposa and Estanzio returned.

"Find river," said Estanzio. "It be far, much miles."

There it was. The San Simon was thirty, perhaps thirty-five, miles west, a near impossible one-day drive. But what choice did they have? After their twenty miles the day before, the fifteen they must travel this day seemed short. They pushed on, reaching the small stream before sundown. They had barely finished supper when Mariposa pointed to the west.

"Riders come," said the Indian.

There were two of them, and their horses were heaving, totally spent. The men wore range clothes and sweat-stained flop hats. They were Mexican, and so much alike that Gil immediately suspected they were brothers. But what set this pair apart was their buscadera gun rigs. On a frontier where most men were armed with one pistol and maybe an extra cylinder, these hombres wore a tied-down pistol on each hip. The lead rider had a lawman's star pinned to the left pocket of his shirt, and it was he who spoke.

"I am Neomo Zouave," he said, "and this is Alfredo, my deputy. We are in pursuit of robbers who murdered a man in Tucson, and we are in need of fresh horses."

While the man wore a badge, nothing he had said rang true. No frontiersman—especially a lawman—rode his horse to death. Not only had these horses been ridden to exhaustion, they had been stolen and mounted hurriedly, for the stirrups needed letting down. Gil cut his eyes to Estanzio, and while the Indian said nothing, his expression said much. He and Mariposa had just

returned from a thirty-mile westward ride, and they had
seen no riders and no tracks. If anybody was running
from the law, it was this pair of Mexican gun throwers.
Gil had his thumb hooked in his belt, just above the butt
of his Colt. Coldly, deliberately, he spoke to the Mexican wearing the star.

"Whatever these robbers did in Tucson," he said, "I
think they also bushwhacked a sheriff and his deputy
along the trail. Now, just usin' a thumb and finger, you
coyotes lift your pistols free and let 'em drop."

Both men went for their guns. Gil shot Neomo twice
before he cleared leather. Three other riders cut down
Alfredo. The pair sprawled backward over the rumps of
their horses and slid to the ground. Disregarding the
fallen riders, Ramon and Van began unsaddling the exhausted horses. They would be given a little water when
they were able to handle it.

"Drag this pair of rattlers away from camp," said Gil,
"and take them far enough so the smell can't spook our
horses or the longhorns. I won't be much surprised if we
find some real lawmen—dead ones—between here and
Tucson. Once we get there, we can let the town know
these coyotes didn't escape."

While the sun lost none of the splendor of its depar-
ture, it set red beyond a massive bank of gray clouds.

"Rain come," said Mariposa. *"Mañana."*

First light came with a haze of clouds lessening the
usual bite of the sun, and Gil viewed that as a mixed
blessing. Without the sun burning down, they could
push the herd harder, longer. On the other hand, a wind
from the west, with a cooling breath of rain, could drive
the longhorns crazy. They would run till hell wouldn't
have it, without regard for canyon rims or other dangers.

"Rain come late," said Ramon. "We push lak hell all
day."

Gil, expecting a hard day, had kept Mariposa and Estanzio with the herd. Once they reached the San Simon,

the map accounted for water for the next several days.
They'd been on the trail about four hours when they
saw the buzzards. They circled lazily in the gray western
sky, harbingers of death.

"Come on, Mariposa," said Gil. "I reckon I know
what they're after."

The two men had been shot down from ambush, and
it was a grisly scene. Going through their pockets, Gil
identified them as the sheriff and a deputy. He took
their wallets and a few other personal belongings, which
he would take to Tucson. There was no sign of the outlaws' horses. Apparently they had recovered sufficiently
to wander away, perhaps back to Tucson. Having no
tools for digging, Gil did the best he could. He and
Mariposa carried the bodies to a small coulee and managed to cover them by caving in the sandy banks. It
wasn't much of a grave, but it would protect the remains
from the buzzards and coyotes. On the brutal frontier,
many a man's mortal remains were left at the mercy of
predators and the elements. Having done their duty as
best they could, Gil and Mariposa returned to the trail
drive.

"They're trailin' great," said Van. "Without the sun,
they'll trot. Like Ramon says, we got to just run the hell
out of them, and get as far as we can before the rain
comes."

By late afternoon they knew there was going to be
more than rain. While the sun withheld its fury, there
was no wind. The flanks of the horses and longhorns
were dark with sweat, and every rider's shirt was soaked.
With no wind to carry it away, dust hung in the air like
smoke, seeping through their bandannas to nose and
mouth, becoming instant mud when it touched a rider's
bare skin. Lightning danced across the western horizon,
and thunder grumbled its accompaniment. The longhorns began bawling, as if sensing the coming of the
storm. That was a bad sign. It seemed they were preparing themselves, and at the peak of some unknown but
anticipated fury, they would run. They could stampede

toward water, or they could flee from thunder and lightning, running back the way they had come. While there were no deep canyons between here and the San Simon, Mariposa and Estanzio had reported rough, broken land. If they were going to run, a stampede toward water would favor the riders. Gil rode back to the drag, taking Ramon with him. Rosa, Vicente, Juan Padillo, Bo, and Long John were already there.

"If they run toward water," said Gil, "we'll come out of this all right. But if they run from the storm, it's goin' to be hell with the lid off. If we can, we'll head them, but if you see they're goin' to overrun us, ride for your lives. Don't risk yourself or your horse."

"This bunch ain't thirsty enough t' run fer water," said Long John.

"You'd better hope they are," said Gil. "We've got a good twenty miles behind us. If they get spooked and backtrack, we'll have to make that twenty miles all over again."

"Mebbe they be too tired," said Juan Padillo.

"Maybe," said Gil, "but if they are, it'll be the first time in the history of the world. Shake the ground with enough thunder, blind 'em with lots of lightning, and they'd run with four busted legs."

It soon became obvious that although they would eventually get some rain, the thunder and lightning would reach them first. The thunder escalated into an almost continuous roll, and while the lightning flamed blue, green, and gold, it wasn't striking. But when it finally did, it came at the worst possible time and place. A hundred yards ahead of the horse remuda and the lead steers stood an old dead pine. Lightning struck, traveling the length of the tree, turning its resinous corpse into a flaming, sixty-foot torch. The horse remuda was nearest this fiery apparition, and the best efforts of Mariposa and Estanzio were in vain. The horses wheeled, nickering their fear, and broke into a fast gallop. The horses, running headlong toward the lead steers, would have been enough, but the leaders could see the flaming pine for themselves. The herd being bunched, the longhorns couldn't just turn and run, so they did the next worst thing. The herd split. Roughly half the lead steers took a horseshoe turn to the left, while the rest of the leaders took a similar turn to the right. The rest of the herd split behind the leaders, and the horse remuda, running hell-for-leather, split in the same manner. The flank riders didn't stand a chance, and had to run for their lives. Gil and the drag riders were safe enough. The longhorns were running away toward the west, and by the time they doubled back to the east, they had separated into two columns. Gil had never seen anything quite like it. While the horse remuda and longhorns all thundered back toward the east, it was actually two stampedes. Ironically, before the sound of the stampedes had died, the thunder and lightning began to diminish. The wind rose, coming out of the southwest, bringing with it a cooling rain.

"Wal," said Long John, "they's one thing fer shore. We ain't goin' t' make camp on the San Simon t'night."

"Mebbe not tomorrow night also," Juan Padillo added.

"Perhaps we will just remain here forever," said Rosa, "hunting stampeded cows and horses."

"Anybody wantin' to say the hell with it and ride back to Texas, light out," said Gil. "Me, I'm ridin' after the herd."

Gil's sense of humor had slipped again. He rode out, and the others followed, grinning at one another. They soon began finding bunches of longhorns and horses. Soon as they had turned away from the flaming, lightning-struck tree, the herd had slowed, stopped, and begun to graze.

"Well," said Van, "we didn't make it to the river, but when we take the trail tomorrow, it won't be with a thirsty herd. That is, if this bunch is smart enough to drink from puddles."

"We've got a while before dark," said Gil. "Let's start gettin' these brutes back together. Once the rain lets up, these puddles won't last. Then we'll still be stuck with a thirsty herd, fifteen miles from water."

But some of the stubborn longhorns chose to remain where they were, and no sooner had they been driven in with the slowly growing gather, when they became bunch quitters. It was during a mad chase after one of these brutes that Ramon's horse threw a left rear shoe. Within minutes Gil's horse threw a right front shoe, and threw Gil. He came down flat on his back in a depression half full of muddy water.

"I went t' the circus oncet," said Long John, "an' I never seen nothin' half as good as that."

The other riders had tried not to laugh, but Long John spoiled their act. Everybody howled. Gil got up, killing mad at first, but forced to see the humor in the situation.

"Many horse need shoe," said Mariposa.

"Tomorrow, then," said Gil, "we'll replace the shoes of those most in need of it, and we'll see to all the others once we reach Tucson. A thrown shoe can cripple a horse, as well as the rider."

By the time it was light enough to see, Gil had every rider in the saddle, rounding up the horse remuda and the scattered longhorns. Once the horses had been gathered, he withdrew Mariposa and Estanzio from the roundup.

"Check out every horse," said Gil, "and those in danger of throwing a shoe, see that they're reshod before we leave here. But unless they're just about barefooted and in real need, let's try to hold off until we reach Tucson."

The sun rose in a clear sky, determined to compensate for its absence the day before. Every drop of standing water was swallowed up, and the last night's rain might never have fallen. Mariposa and Estanzio found all of the horses needing new shoes, but only nine seemed in immediate danger of throwing a shoe. Those,

and the horses Ramon and Gil had ridden the day before, would be reshod. The others could wait until they
reached Tucson, or at least a camp where there was
water. The gather was going far better than Gil expected, and he was elated.

"Better when cows run from storm than run to water," said Ramon.

"That's gospel," said Van. "When they're dry and
smell water, they'll run till they find it, if it's twenty
miles. When the storm lets up, a storm scare wears off
quick. This storm caused 'em to run, but it done us a
favor. Thanks to the rain, there was water most of the
night."

"Reckon I'd be ongrateful," said Long John, "was I t'
say that won't do us no good t'night."

"Ungrateful," said Gil, "but truthful."

"There be moon," said Pedro Fagana. "Mebbe go at
night."

"Rough lak hell," said Estanzio, shaking his head.

"I've been over this with Mariposa and Estanzio,"
said Gil, "and I'm convinced we don't want to take a
herd through such country at night. There is broken
land, drop-offs, and rock slides. Cow or horse could
break a leg in the dark. From here to the San Simon,
and probably through all of Arizona, I think we'll need a
point rider far enough ahead of the herd to warn us as
to change of direction. There may be some deep canyons ahead of us, and one good, hell-for-leather stampede could ruin us. Not only are we unable to travel at
night, we'll have to be especially watchful in the daylight."

Try as they might, the horses and longhorns could not
be gathered in time to salvage any of the daylight hours,
and they were stuck in a dry camp for the night. Mariposa and Estanzio had replaced one or more shoes on
eleven horses. As usual, Gil split the outfit into two
watches for the night. After a day in the hot sun, thirst
had caught up with the longhorns. Restless, they milled
aimlessly about, bawling and hooking at one another in

their frustration. When Gil and the second watch took over at midnight, the brutes still hadn't settled down.

"If they wander around all night," said Rosa, "tomorrow they will be too tired to run."

"Haw, haw," Long John cackled, "the cow ain't been borned that was too tired t' run."

"I'd have to agree," said Gil, "but there's one thing in our favor. Sometime before dawn there'll be dew fall, and it'll wet the grass enough to take the edge off their thirst. But give 'em two hours in the morning sun, and they'll be thirsty as ever, and cantankerous as sore-tailed grizzlies."

"Meanin' they ain't goin' t' take kindly t' bein' drove hard," said Long John.

"They won't like it," said Gil, "but they'll take it. I promise you, we'll reach the San Simon tomorrow, if every cow in this bunch ends up with a black-and-blue backside. Now let's get out there and swing those lariats, and show 'em what hard driving really is."

There was no water for coffee, so the outfit made do with a breakfast of jerked beef. Before it was good daylight, Gil had the herd on the trail, pushing them hard. The dew-wet grass had settled the longhorns down, and Gil thought they'd travel well for maybe two hours. By then the sun would be well on its way to sucking the last drop of moisture out of man and beast. The next water —the San Simon River—was more than fifteen miles away. Gil wanted to see for himself what the broken country was like, since there was a possibility they'd be facing it most of the way across Arizona. Mariposa and Estanzio would remain with the herd until they reached the San Simon. That would be soon enough to scout ahead for the next water. Gil soon understood the caution of his Indian riders. There were gullies whose banks weren't steep but were shale, shifting beneath his horse's hooves. Gil had to find a way around such obstacles and then get back to the herd in time to turn them. He had to grin at Rosa's suggestion that he should have brought a wagon. He doubted a man would live enough years to get a wagon through such desolate, broken country as this.*

By the time the sun was noon high the longhorns had given a whole new meaning to the term "ornery." While they had no assurance there was water ahead, their bovine memories reminded them of water they had left behind. How far it was didn't matter. They knew it was there, and every steer in the bunch was hell-bent on returning to it. Bunch quitters became so numerous that riders were forced to desert the main herd entirely, chasing those who had broken away and hightailed it down the back trail. Rosa had pursued one big steer who had decided to simply gore her and her horse. In a dangerous move that would have made Gil furious, Rosa swung her doubled lariat hard, laying it full force across the steer's tender muzzle. Only then did he wheel and run bawling back to the herd.

Gil found Mariposa and Estanzio had distanced the horse remuda considerably ahead of the longhorns. It was a smart move, preventing the horses from picking up on the skittishness of the longhorns. While the big Texas steers were unruly, they could be handled. The test would come in late afternoon. For now, there was no wind, but later there might be. A treacherous wind out of the west, bringing with it the maddening promise of water . . .

* This was to eventually become the Butterfield Overland Mail Route. From September 15, 1858, until March 1, 1861, Butterfield operated a semiweekly stage mail and passenger service extending from St. Louis to San Francisco, a distance of 2795 miles.

10

*T*he graze in southern New Mexico had been exceptionally good, consisting of blue grama or buffalo grass, and sometimes a mix of the two. There was juniper, pinion pine, and an occasional ponderosa. Gil continued to push the herd as hard as he dared. Theirs was a race with the westering sun, and for all their efforts, the sun was winning. It was Van who mentioned something Gil had thought of a time or two.

"Sometimes," Van said, "I wonder if we didn't lean too heavy on the map Big Foot Wallace got for us. We could have crossed the Rio south of El Paso, and kind of straddled the line between the United States and Mexico all the way to southern California."

"I thought you'd had a bellyful of Mexico," said Gil.

"I have," said Van, "but I can't help wonderin' if that would have made any difference in the water situation."

"Except for springs and occasional water holes, how could it? Mexico's rivers and creeks flow into the Gulf of Mexico to the east, or into the Gulf of California to the west. I think if we were too near or below the border, we'd only increase our chances of being ambushed by Mexican bandits."

In the late afternoon, riding ahead of the horse remuda, Estanzio and Mariposa flushed some javelina.

They shot two of the wild pigs, wrapped them in a piece of tarp, and lashed them to one of the extra horses.

While the thirsty longhorns plodded on, they slowed continually, bawling their objections when prodded to a faster pace. There was an interval, between sundown and dark, when nature made her own decision. Would there or would there not be wind, and if there was, from which of the four corners would it come? In the western territories it often came from the west or the southwest, and this day was no exception. It was a west wind so gentle, it might have gone unnoticed had it not been for a hint of moisture.

"This is it," shouted Gil. "They're gonna run!"

And run they did! Estanzio and Mariposa fought to control the horse remuda, but it had no effect on the longhorns. The herd split, running on both sides of the remuda, taking some of the horses with them. Gil, Van, Ramon, and Long John tried in vain to get ahead of the longhorns. As it became a lost cause, the riders fell back, helping Mariposa and Estanzio hold the rest of the remuda.

"Now," shouted Gil, "let's move 'em ahead!"

It began orderly enough, but the horses had scented water and were in no mood to lag. They charged ahead and soon were in a mad gallop, defying all attempts to slow them. Mariposa and Estanzio, followed by the rest of the riders, went after the packhorses. At least they would avoid having their grub and supplies scattered from hell to breakfast. Before the riders reached the scene, the frantic bawling of longhorns told them there was trouble ahead. Three of the brutes had lost their footing in a shale slide and had tumbled into a gulley. One had died with a broken neck, while the others suffered broken legs. Gil shot the two injured animals, and they rode on, every man silently hoping they wouldn't find any of the horses in a similar condition. Miraculously, they reached the river without finding any more injured or dead animals.

"We're lucky to have lost only three steers," said Gil.

"Had we been any farther from the river, we might have lost a lot more, and some of the horses too."

Having watered, the rest of the horses and longhorns began to graze.

"Still a little while before dark," said Van. "Some of us ought to ride back and save some of that beef. I can't see lettin' the coyotes and buzzards have it all."

"Good thinking," said Gil. "Take a couple of men and save what you can."

Van rode out, taking Vicente and Pedro with him. The others unloaded the packhorses and went about setting up the camp.

"Kin we have a cook fire t'night?" Long John asked. "We got them two wild pigs an' all that beef, an' I'm hongry enough t' eat the lot of it."

"Yes," said Gil, "I think we'll risk a fire, but conceal it as best you can. I'd as soon not have any visitors."

It was a celebration of sorts, the trail drive reaching the San Simon. Exhausted as they all were, they stuffed themselves with fresh beef and pork, washing it down with plenty of strong, black coffee. As usual, Gil divided the night into two watches, but they were not disturbed. There was nothing more sinister than the yipping of coyotes. They had discovered the remains of the three steers and were spreading the news.

"It purely gripes me," said Van, "to bring 'em this far and then end up feedin' 'em to coyotes."

"Do not dwell on what you have lost," said Rosa, "but on all that you have left. And did you not have fresh steak for supper?"

"The most expensive damn steak a man ever laid tongue to," said Van.

"Ye git tired of steak," said Long John, "me an' Bo can always git us another deer."

"I'm satisfied," said Gil. "Like Rosa put it, let's not complain about the three we lost, but be thankful for the many we didn't lose. Remember how hopeless it all seemed, us racing with the sun, trying to reach water before dark? Well, we lost in one respect, but won big in another. The ground we covered in the daylight was ground that was behind us, when the herd stampeded. We were close enough to the river that the run was short. In a way, a trail drive is like a high stakes poker game, and sometimes the only way you can win is to cut your losses."

As though in applause, the coyote chorus chimed in, and they all had to laugh at the irony. Later, when they were into the second watch, Gil had a surprise awaiting him.

"Tonight," Rosa told him, "I was proud of what you said. You spoke like a man."

"It's not a thing I customarily do, then," he said.

"No," she replied. "In the ways you most needed to, you are growing up."

She was less than half his age, telling him he needed to grow up! He laughed, and the suddenness of it startled his horse. When he spoke, it was with none of the anger she had half expected.

"Maybe I took your advice," said Gil, "and done some thinkin' on the little we lost, compared to all that we might have lost. I reckon it ain't the nature of a cattleman to think that way."

"Remember that day in Mexico, after my *madre* and *padre* were murdered? When you found me, I was stark naked. Have you ever wondered why?"*

"No," he said. "You were doin' your damnedest to shove a pitchfork into my gut, and that kind of took my mind off everything else."

"My *madre* had washed the only dress I owned, and it had not had time to dry. So when it comes to being thankful for what I have, instead of crying for what I do not have, or have lost, it is a lesson I learned early. You have not been so fortunate."

She was young in years, but in the ways that mattered, older than time. So profound were her words, he could think of nothing to say, and they rode on in silence.

* Trail Drive Series #4, *The Bandera Trail*

* * *

May 7, 1850. San Simon River, Arizona Territory

Gil spoke to the outfit before breakfast.

"I think we'll take a day of rest here. Accordin' to this government map, the next river is the San Pedro, and it's a good fifty miles. There has to be water between here and there, even if it's only a spring, but I don't aim to go chargin' out of here until I know how far it is to the next water. So we'll spend today cookin' and preserving some of this extra meat, while Mariposa and Estanzio ride ahead. From here on, we'll have to concern ourselves with more than just water. I want to know where the potential danger lies—the drop-offs, the canyons, and how we are to get around them."

Mariposa and Estanzio were less than an hour out of camp when they reined up in a stand of pinion. Six riders passed, and there was no way they could miss the trail drive on the San Simon. Mariposa looked at his companion, and Estanzio shook his head.

"Town hombres," said Estanzio. "Hunt lawmen."

It would not be necessary for them to warn the camp, and when the party was out of sight, Estanzio and Mariposa rode west. This land—Arizona—seemed as strange to them as anything they had seen since leaving Mexico. Amid creosote bushes and greasewood, there was mesquite, pinion, and oak. Except for scattered sagebrush, one entire slope was dominated by giant cacti. These were multiarmed saguaros, most of them standing taller than a man on a horse. The Indians rode on in silent wonder. Cacti they had seen before, but nothing like these.

When the six riders reined up, Gil was waiting to greet them. But he wasn't alone. Van, Ramon, Bo, Long John, and some of the other riders were ready if they were needed.

"Step down," said Gil, "if you're of a mind to."

All the men wore Colts, and several carried rifles in saddle boots. But they didn't have the look or the sweat of working cowboys, and from their dress, Gil decided they were town men. A tall, thin-faced man, apparently the leader, spoke.

"I'm Vento Henneagar," he said, "and we're from Tucson. Our sheriff and his deputy lit out after a pair of greaser killers. One way or t'other, it's time our boys was comin' back, if they're comin'."

"They won't be comin'," said Gil. "We buried them. I have some of their personal things in my saddlebag."

He removed from his saddlebag a pair of small leather pokes, which he passed to Henneagar. The tall man opened each, looked at the contents, and passed them to the other men. He then turned his attention back to Gil.

"This pair of Mex gun throwers rode in at sundown," said Gil. "Two-gun men. Neomo Zouave and a gent called Alfredo, which I'd guess was his brother. These coyotes had rode their horses to death, and tried to use a lawman's star to wrangle fresh horses from us. When I challenged them, they drew on me, and we salted 'em down. Next morning we found your men and buried them. They'd been ambushed, shot in the back."

"We're obliged," said Henneagar. "I'd pin a medal on you, if I had one. It's a pleasure to meet up with an outfit that knows what to do with thievin', back-shootin' killers. Texans?"

"Texans," said Gil. "While you gents see to your horses, we'll put the coffeepot on the fire. We have fresh beef, and wild pig too."

Despite the grim news Gil had for the men from Tucson, they remained for a meal and passed on some valuable information about the trail ahead, and about the town of Tucson. Henneagar's brother owned the livery. He also sold horses, mules, and when he could get them, cattle. There was a smithy who could supply horseshoes, and a pair of general stores to see to their other needs.

"You're maybe seventy miles from Cienega Creek,"

said Henneagar, "and from there, maybe twenty miles from Tucson. True, you'll have a fifty-mile run to the San Pedro, but there's springs in between. Just come on, and I'll spread the word there's beef on the way."

Two hours after the riders from Tucson had departed, Mariposa and Estanzio returned.

"Did you see the men from Tucson?" Gil asked.

"We see them, they no see us," said Estanzio.

"They say we'll find water twice between here and the San Pedro River."

"Find spring," said Mariposa. "Mebbe not twenty mile."

"That's good news," said Gil. "For the next four days, the very worst we can expect is twenty miles."

"I wish we'd asked those gents from Tucson about the Indian situation," said Van. "This is Apache country."

Gil turned to Mariposa and Estanzio.

"No Injun sign," said Mariposa. "No Injun pony track."

"All Apaches ain't bloodthirsty killers," said Long John. "Find ye a tribe what ain't a fanatical bunch o' war whoops, an' they ain't any better scouts in the world. Apaches is notorious fer not gettin' along wi' one another. Tribes has been knowed to join whites, fightin' other tribes."

"You know all about Apaches, Long John?" Ramon asked.

"Wal, not all," said Long John, "but I know they's some good'uns an' some bad'uns. Me'n some other jaybirds was trapped by Apaches oncet. We was total surrounded, down t' our las' two er three loads."

"And they spared you?" Ramon asked.

"Wal, no," said Long John, with a straight face and a twinkle in his eyes. "Turned out t' be a bad bunch, an' they scalped ever' damn one o' us."

Everybody laughed, including Ramon. The vaqueros still didn't fully understand Long John's macabre sense of humor, and still fell victim to it. In the afternoon, Bo and Long John rode off up the San Simon a ways to try their luck fishing. To their own delight, and everybody else's surprise, they came back with enough trout for supper. After they had eaten, Gil got out his logbook.

"We've been on the trail eighty-one days," said Gil, "and we've come a little less than seven hundred miles. That's about eight and a half miles a day."

"Is not bad," said Juan Alamonte.

"A month ago," Van said, "I'd have disagreed with you, but everything considered, I reckon we ain't done too bad."

"We lose many days," said Pedro Fagano.

"We did," said Gil, "but we've lost hardly any stock."

"Whilst me an' Bo was upriver fishin'," said Long John, "we seen a rattlesnake was wider'n m' leg. Rest o' ye do as ye like, but me, I'm wearin' my chaps an' stuffin' m' britches legs into m' boots from here on."

Everybody laughed dubiously. So adept was Long John, none of them could be sure when the lanky Cajun was being truthful or just running another sandy at their expense.

"Bo," Ramon asked, "is this Long John's snake, or do you see it as well?"

"It was as he says," said Bo. "This time, Long John tells the truth."

"This time?" yelped Long John. "Ye implyin' that I usually don't?"

When the laughter subsided, Bo continued. "Only on the Amazon have I seen a reptile so large. This one, this rattlesnake, I would judge to be twenty feet in length."

Bo was shy, rarely speaking, and his eloquence seemed strange. While he was every inch a cowboy, Gil Austin suspected the little man was much more than that. Most of the outfit laughed at the strange friendship that had developed between Bo and Long John Coons. The two men were opposites in every sense of the word. Bo, shy and quiet, was well-liked. Long John, loud, arrogant, often hostile, was only tolerated, and by at least one of the riders, not even that. Estanzio purely didn't like Long John, and had been trying for months to en-

gage the Cajun in a knife fight. Certainly Long John
hadn't discouraged it, but Gil had. Gil had an uneasy
suspicion that if he left the two of them alone for any
length of time, he'd return to find them cut to ribbons,
one or both bleeding and dying.

"It's purely hard to believe there's snakes as big as
that," said Van, "but I reckon in this wild country, anything's possible. It's just goin' to be almighty hot,
wearin' leather chaps."

"Hot temporary," said Juan Padillo. "Dead permanent."

Juan had begun to develop a cowboy sense of humor
like a Tejano. He even got a laugh out of Long John.

One thing a man learned quickly on the frontier, if he
wanted to go on living, was that peace was never more
than temporary. While this camp on the San Simon
seemed secure, and they had seen no Indian sign, Gil
remained as cautious as ever. He believed that when
everything seemed the most tranquil, it was most prone
to go to hell at any moment. That was why Gil always
took the midnight-to-dawn watch. Nine times out of ten,
when trouble came, it would be in the dark, small hours
of the morning, when men were least prepared. Gil had
made a change in the nighthawking, which some of the
riders, including Van, didn't like. While the rest of the
outfit still split up into two watches, Mariposa and Estanzio spent the entire night with the horse remuda.
Gil's purpose was twofold. First, with the Indian riders
securing the horse remuda, the rest of the nighthawks
were free to devote their full attention to longhorns.
Second, the horse remuda and the longhorns could be
separated. On nights when the longhorns were skittish
and troublesome, refusing to bed down, the horses
picked up on it and acted accordingly. Gil believed that
if the herds were separated, they'd be easier to control,
that if one stampeded, it might not involve the other.

"Suppose we got hit by horse thieves?" Van had
asked. "There'll never be more than two riders with the
horses."

"Suppose you had cows and horses bunched to-gether," Gil had argued, "and with every nighthawk cir-cling the combined herds. They'll all be at different positions. How often will you have any two riders close enough to the horses to help in case of attack? Thieves would just wait until most of the nighthawks were far-thest from the horses."

In Indian country they were more in danger of losing the horses than the longhorns. Gil believed they would soon vindicate his theory, or totally discredit it. The thing that made his plan so effective was the ability of Mariposa and Estanzio to virtually disappear in the darkness. However, that might be considered a flaw, in-viting an attack, since the horse herd seemed unpro-tected. Gil dismissed that possibility, because horse thieves didn't actually attempt to take the herd from under the noses of the nighthawks. That was suicide. It was less risky to just stampede the horses, and when the outfit rode in pursuit at first light, gun them down from ambush. That allowed the thieves to gather the horses at their leisure. That is, if the outfit was green enough to allow itself to be ambushed.

This night, the horse remuda was three-quarters of a mile downriver from the longhorns. Far enough, Gil be-lieved, so that a disturbance among one herd might not affect the other. There was one point on which not a man in the outfit disagreed. If night riders spooked the horses, it took far less time to recover the horses than to gather the longhorns. But let the longhorns stampede with the horses, and it meant at least two days shot to hell. Maybe longer, depending on what direction the brutes decided to run.

The moon had already set, and the stars had begun to distance themselves from the coming dawn. It was that darkest hour when a man's night vision simply was not enough, and it was at that moment the night riders hit the horse herd. There were shots, shouts, and a clatter of hoofs. But there were cries of anguish too. Sudden as the attack had been, Mariposa and Estanzio hadn't al-

lowed the thieves to escape without payment. Every
rider followed Gil's prior orders, remaining where he
was. Gil found it difficult to follow his own orders, wanting to ride to the aid of Estanzio and Mariposa. It was
the most deadly, the most effective means of countering
a surprise attack. Keep your own forces stationary, de-
ploy a few good men, and let them kill anything that
moved. Some of the longhorns had lumbered to their
feet, but for a change the wind was friendly. It carried
the sound away from the cattle, and after a few anxious
moments, they settled down. Gil sensed rather than saw
one of the Indian riders.

"Some horse run," said Estanzio. "Third, mebbe.
Mejicano thieves. Two die."

It was the facts, simply stated, but every man recognized the accomplishment. Long John acknowledged it.

"Wal, we got t' give our segundo credit fer knowin'
what he's doin'. If we all had a gone skalleyhootin' after
them thieves in the dark, we wouldn't of got a one.
Likely, we'd of ended up shootin' at one another."

"Cows no run," said Ramon. "Is biggest blessing of
all."

"Soon as it's light enough," said Gil, "we'll go after
our horses."

He said no more, nor did he need to. Every man had
a lariat on his saddle, and every man knew how to tie a
thirteen-knot noose.

The outfit waited impatiently for first light, riding the
moment the Indian riders could pick up the trail. There
had been eleven rustlers, the swift action of Mariposa
and Estanzio having reduced their number to nine. Gil
had taken Mariposa, Estanzio, Long John, Bo, and Vicente Gomez. There would be no pitched battle, where
they would have to face all the rustlers at once. The
thieves couldn't gather the scattered horses in the dark,
and working from first light, there simply wouldn't be
enough time. There had to be an ambush, calculated to
slow the pursuers, lest they ride blindly into it. Gil Aus-

tin welcomed the ambush. The sooner they eliminated it, the sooner they could recover their horses and bring this chase to a close. His instructions to Mariposa and Estanzio were simple.

"Once you know where the ambush is, circle them and come in from the south. I doubt they'll leave more than three or four men. Once you're near enough, cut down on them, and we'll advance. I'll call them out once; after that, it's shoot to kill."

The first shots came quickly, perhaps not seeking a target, but to warn Gil the ambush had been located. It also was calculated to shake the confidence of the outlaws. Caught in a cross fire, they could no longer devote all their attention to the back trail. The outlaws had holed up behind some rocks, and once they were within rifle range, Gil reined up. While all his men had rifles, the reloading time made them impractical for close fighting.

"Long John," said Gil, "you and Bo take your rifles and put some lead in amongst those coyotes. While you're reloading, Vicente and me will give 'em another dose."

There was return fire from three rifles, and that told Gil what he most wanted to know. They faced three men, and they also had to reload. Gil and Vicente fired their rifles into the outlaw stronghold, but there was no return fire. Gil dismounted, the others following.

"This is gettin' us nowhere," said Gil. "They know we're out here, and that'll give Mariposa and Estanzio an edge. Boot your rifles, fan out, and we'll advance on foot. If we can't overrun them, we can draw their attention, givin' Mariposa and Estanzio a chance."

The four riders spread out, using what cover there was. The slope was dotted with greasewood and yucca. Gil had drawn his Colt, and when he thought he saw some movement, he sent lead screaming in among the rocks. His three companions followed, and the outlaws behind the rocks returned the fire. It was time for a challenge.

"You hombres in the rocks," shouted Gil, "drop your guns and come out. You're finished."

It drew exactly the response Gil had expected. They were now within pistol range, and the three rustlers concentrated their fire on the scant cover that concealed Gil. There had been no more firing from beyond the outlaws' position, and Gil thought he knew why. Mariposa and Estanzio were using each burst of gunfire as a means of creeping closer. Suddenly there was a screech of mortal agony, two frantic shots, and after sounds of a struggle, silence. The next sound they heard was Mariposa speaking.

"Ambush is finish."

"Bueno, hombres," said Gil. "Now let's go after our horses."

Within an hour the six of them were within sight of their horses and the six Mexican horse thieves. One of the rustlers looked back and saw the hard-riding cowboys in pursuit. Gil heard his shout of alarm, saw the other five riders turn in their saddles. They had lost two men when they had stampeded the horses, their ambush had been wiped out, and they now had a decision to make. Were they to live or to die? They abandoned the stolen horses and rode for their lives.

"Lookit 'em run!" shouted Long John. "The yellow coyotes."

"We got five of them," said Gil, "and recovered the horses. The rest of them ought to have their necks stretched, but they'll scatter like quail, and we have a trail drive waitin' for us. Let's turn this bunch of cayuses around and take 'em home."

❧⟨∾⟩❧

*E*ven with the time it took to chase the border outlaws and recover the horses, Gil and his riders were back with the outfit by mid-morning.

"You've done well," Van said, "but we're more than three hours into the day, with a twenty-mile drive to water. Do we risk it?"

"We do," said Gil. "The longhorns have had a day of rest. We'll delay just long enough for these twenty-one cayuses we just drove in to catch their wind. Then we'll water them and move out."

When the sun was noon high, they topped a ridge and beheld a scene of broken, desolate beauty. On the downward slope ahead, and on the rising slope beyond, there wasn't a single tree or bush. Instead, there was an army of giant saguaros, in some strange formation of their own choosing, their arms raised heavenward as though in surrender. Not to be outdone, yucca shot spires a dozen feet high, each topped with a cluster of white blooms, like tall old men with silvery hair.

Rosa sighed. "Never have I seen anything so beautiful."

Even Long John, not given to sentiment, was impressed.

"It do kind of git a man down wher' he lives," said the Cajun.

"No got water," said Mariposa, less impressed. *"Desierto."*

"All the more reason we can't travel at night," said Gil. "Imagine ridin' headlong into a cactus as big as a tree trunk."

"They grow so big," said Ramon. "How can there be no water below?"

"It's far below," said Gil, "if at all. From what I know, there's just one tree that's a sure sign of water, and that's the Joshua."

"I want the cactus with two arms," said Rosa. "I wish to take one back to Texas with me."

"A leetle one," teased Long John, "er one that's full-growed, an' tall as a house?"

"A full-growed one," Rosa replied, imitating him, "and when you're digging it up, just be careful that you do not harm any of the roots."

"You start now, Long John," said Juan Padillo, "and you be just about done when we ride back from California."

Gil pushed the longhorns hard, and despite their late start, he believed they would yet reach the water Mariposa and Estanzio had found, before darkness forced them into dry camp. Gil rode well ahead of the horse remuda, concerned with the rough terrain over which they would travel. Some of the slopes had thin ledges of rock, and a sudden crumbling of slate or sandstone might cripple a horse or cow. The trouble with broken country, Gil quickly learned, was that in avoiding one trail that appeared treacherous, you often were faced with another just as dangerous, if not more so. Time after time he found himself choosing a way not because it suited him, but because it was the best of a poor lot.

Finally, Gil reached a barren stretch that, with a little improvement, could have become a desert. It was a barren valley several miles wide, and except for an occasional saguaro, nothing grew there. The land was littered with rock in varying sizes, up to and including huge boulders higher than a man's head. In ages past,

Gil thought, it looked as though God had flung them in this valley and forgotten them. Ahead, among the gray of the stones and seeming out of place, was something white. Gil dismounted, and leading his horse, discovered he was looking at the smooth top of a human skull. The rest of the skeleton was there too, but the bones had become scattered by coyotes and buzzards. While the arm and leg bones had been separated, the bony hands and feet were still in a position that no frontiersman could overlook. The man had been spread-eagled, maybe over an anthill. Or he might have had a fire built in his crotch. When it came to inflicting pain, Indians were creative. While the eye sockets of the skull were empty, the bleached jaws were sprung in a silent scream of agony that time and the elements could not quell. The shafts of nine Indian arrows, feathers long gone, bristled out of the skeleton's rib cage and pelvic area. His captors had stood over this poor bastard and had shot arrows through his dead or dying body, literally spiking him to the ground. There was no way of knowing who he was, or how many months and years he had been claimed by this lonely, desolate land. The handiwork of Apaches? Probably, and if you accepted Long John's good Apache and bad Apache thinking, then this unknown pilgrim had had the misfortune to run into a bunch of "bad'uns."

Gil was about to turn back, to check on the herd, when a breath of west wind brought a stench that almost gagged him. Something was dead enough to stink, yet there wasn't a sign of a buzzard. It was a mystery that bore some looking into. Gil went on, determined to at least reach the farthest side of this desolate valley before he returned to the drive. Suddenly his horse shied and reared, and Gil drew his Colt. But the horse balked, unwilling to go a step farther. However dead the smell, whatever evil that was ahead was very much alive. Concluding that the horse was the more intelligent of the two of them, Gil looped the reins around a stone as big as a Dutch oven and went ahead alone. He cocked the

Colt, trying to see into the jumble of rock ahead. In less than a heartbeat the hidden enemy struck. The ugly brown head was larger than Gil's own, the lethal fangs like curved sabers. The snake's strike fell short, but Gil backed away a dozen paces before he felt safe. It was the biggest rattler he'd ever seen, big enough that Long John could have described it truthfully. Why had the snake struck at him without sounding a warning? They did that at shedding time, of course, but this was much too early. In Texas, "dog days" came in August. Gil backtracked, then advanced ahead about as far as he had when the snake had struck. He must reach a point where he could see this monster without it being able to get at him. For sure, he had to kill it or drive it away. Otherwise, no horse or cow would ever set foot in this bleak valley. This damn snake, he thought grimly, had managed to obstruct the only decent trail. If they were unable to cross here, they might be forced to travel many extra miles, and that meant a dry camp for tonight. If it was snake or dry camp, he decided, the snake had to go.

Gil found a series of boulders that stair-stepped him high enough to see over the jumble of stones behind which the rattler was concealed. He caught his breath when he saw the size of the reptile. If Bo's estimate of twenty feet was accurate, his and Long John's snake would have to grow some to match this one! This rattler was writhing constantly, but going nowhere. Something or somebody had dealt the snake a fearful body blow, and its spine was broken. There had been no warning rattle because the rattler had lost control of the tail. Its strikes were clumsy, and it struck at everything in mad fury, even the nearby boulders. Finally it twisted around until Gil had a better look at the body wound. Where the spine was broken, the flesh had begun to rot away toward head and tail, and that accounted for the dead smell. The snake was dying, but for now the coyotes and buzzards seemed to have business elsewhere. Gil made his way back to his horse and got his rifle from the saddle boot. Climbing back up his rocky stairs, he returned to his previous position. His rifle was a .50 caliber Sharps, heavy but accurate, given a decent target. He had shot snakes before, but never from so great a distance that he needed a rifle. And never at a crazy-mad target that was not still for a second. Gil followed the snake's erratic movements until the big Sharps had his arms numb with strain and his patience had hit bottom. He fired, watching in disgust as the lead struck a rock and whanged off in ricochet. But that gave him an idea. If he couldn't draw a bead on the big bastard, maybe he could ricochet lead off the rocks like shrapnel, killing him a little at a time. Even if he dared get close enough, he wasn't sure he could hit this plunging, writhing target with his Colt. His first two shots with the Sharps didn't seem to accomplish anything, but when he was reloaded and ready for a third shot, he could tell the big rattler was slowing down. On the rusty hide there were patches of blood. His lead was taking its toll. He was frozen in the very act of firing when a voice behind him spoke.

"Ease that cannon down, an' turn around."

Gil didn't know whether to laugh or to cry. He had to restrain himself from the overwhelming temptation to just turn and shoot Long John through the head. A man needed a sense of humor, but by God, this Cajun fool made a joke of everything, up to and including death. Taking the Sharps by its muzzle, he rested it butt down on the rock on which he stood. Controlling himself, he turned to face the grinning Long John. Bo was with him.

"T'was yer brother what sent us to see 'bout ye," said Long John. "Ye startin' whangin' away wi' yer rifle 'bout the time we foun' yer hoss. Is they somethin' er somebody out ther', er ye jus' feel the need fer practice?"

"Long John," said Gil as calmly as he could, "don't you ever again come on me from behind. If I hadn't recognized your voice, I might have dropped the Sharps, drawn my Colt and killed you."

"Ye might of tried." Long John chuckled, his good

humor not diminished in the slightest. "I've seen ye draw, an' yer fast. Keep at it, son, an' in a few years ye may be nearly as good as me. What'n hell ye shootin' at that ye plugged twice an' still ain't kilt?"

"Walk back there a ways," said Gil, "and climb up that chain of rocks. I'll let you have that third shot, mister dead eye, and see if you can do any better."

When Bo and Long John reached the point from which Gil had been firing, Gil said nothing, allowing them to see for themselves.

"It is much larger than the snake we saw," said Bo. "Can we not take another way and avoid it?"

"We could," said Gil, "but there'll be more miles, and a dry camp tonight."

"Wal, hell," growled Long John, "we ain't goin' t' lose a day over some damn snake hoggin' the trail, even if the varmint's sixty times bigger'n any son o' Satan's got any right t' be. Gimme that Sharps an' stand back."

"That snake's had its spine busted," said Gil, "and the wound's started to putrefy. I'd say he's been hit by a rock slide."

"We smelt that," said Long John, "an' reckoned maybe ye an' yer hoss had come down wi' loose bowels, all at oncet. Then ye started shootin', an' we figgered things had done got all complicated."

Long John raised the Sharps, not allowing it to waver in the slightest, and fired. To Gil's amazement, and probably Long John's, he scored a direct hit. The thrashing reptile's movements slowed markedly.

"One more shot," said Long John, "onless ye want t' wait an' let him cash in on his own."

"If we were goin' to do that," said Gil, "we might as well have found another way across this valley and left him where he is. Let's reload and finish the job. This part of it, anyway. We'll have to drag the carcass a ways off, or the herds still won't cross."

Gil reloaded the Sharps, offered it to Long John, but the Cajun shook his head. Raising the big rifle, Gil fired, and the slug caught the snake just below its head. Long

John had the grace not to mention that the big rattler's movements had been slowed drastically or that Gil's marksmanship had improved. It had been a well-placed shot. The trio climbed down from the rocky abutment, making their way back to Gil's horse, where Long John and Bo had also left their mounts.

"Some curious," said Long John, "as t' how that snake got its backbone busted. Was I able t' git to the bastard, I'd fight the devil hisself, wi' guns, knives, er pitchforks. But whatever er whoever it was that was big enough an' mean enough t' bust that rattler's back an' git away alive, I'd be scairt t' face that varmint."

"Snakes may be the least of our problems," said Gil. "I reckon you saw the bones of the gent the Apaches used to entertain themselves."

"Yeah," said Long John, "but like I tol' you, they's good Apaches an' they's bad Apaches. He jus' fell in with a bad lot."

"And you," said Gil dryly, "know the difference between good and bad Apaches. Is it an old Cajun family secret, or will you share it?"

"Nothin' to it," said Long John, with his usual laconic grin. "Anytime ye come away from Apaches forked end down, an' wi' yer hair in place, now them's good Apaches. But when they treats ye like they done this unfortunate bastard here in the valley, now that's a bad lot."

"Long John," said Bo, "when you can tell me how to know these savages are evil without having them first shoot me full of arrows, I will listen to you more closely."

"Amen to that," said Gil. He took the lariat from his saddle.

By the time they reached the snake, it was dead, or seemed so. Up close, the odor was really bad. Nose and mouth covered with their bandannas, they got on with the grisly task. The snake had died with its head flung over a boulder, so Gil was able to stay a few feet away, catching it with an underhand throw. None of them relished getting close to the monster, even after it apparently was dead. They got their shoulders under the rope and started dragging.

"By the Almighty," groaned Long John, "this thing mus' weigh a good three. hunnert pounds. Ever' man wi' a good, strong hoss, an' we ends up draggin' this overgrowed bastard by hand."

Gil said nothing, nor did Bo. None of them, Long John included, could have gotten a horse anywhere within sight of the giant rattler. They began dragging the carcass up the valley, over broken rock that made passage more and more difficult. Finally they reached what Gil judged was three hundred yards north of where they would cross the valley.

"This is as far as he goes," said Gil. "He still may have left enough stink, blood, and hide to make it tough on us."

"Yeah," said Long John. "Fust hoss er cow that gits a whiff o' that, they gon' light out, hell-fer-election, t'other way."

"Once they go so far," said Gil, "that jumbled rock becomes walls. They can't go anywhere but straight ahead. It'll be our job to get 'em to the point they can't break and run, where there's rock on both sides, and other horns digging into their backsides. They'll be well-committed before they reach the place we had to kill the snake. We'll push hard from behind, and if they get. spooked, the only way they can run is straight ahead."

They started back to meet the trail drive, aware of the sun moving ever toward the western horizon. On rare occasions, even Long John became serious, and this was one of the times.

"Makes ye wonder," said the Cajun, "what the rest o' the world mus' be like, them parts we ain't been to. Me, I'd purely hate t' go back t' the bayou country an' try t' convince anybody I'd seen a rattler big enough t' swallow a man."

"On the Amazon, in South America," said Bo, "there

are reptiles capable of doing just that. Of course, this is wild country where man has never lived, and perhaps never will. Reptiles grow large, because they have gone undisturbed for centuries, and I believe that is the case on your western frontier. In the old days, when much of this territory was claimed by the Spanish, it remained unsettled. The Spanish—and they are not alone, of course—acquired vast holdings wherever they could, with the intention of taking silver and gold from the new territory."

"And they learned damned pronto," said Gil, "that most of the territory they'd grabbed on the western frontier didn't have enough gold or silver for a good poker stake."

"An excellent summation," said Bo. "It is ironic that kings from the old world, in their haste to seize the wealth of other lands, got so little for their efforts. In less than thirty years, the Spanish lost their frontier holdings to Mexico, and Mexico, through a foolish war, was forced to cede these same territories to the United States."

Long John chuckled. "Jus' nine days 'fore Sutter made the big strike in Californy."

"Exactly," said Bo. "They could not see, or chose not to see the real potential. Here, they saw only the sagebrush and rattlesnakes."

"I won't fault 'em none fer that," said Long John. "I *still* ain't seein' nothin' but sagebrush an' rattlesnakes."

They rode on in silence. In Gil Austin's eyes, Bo had become more of an enigma than ever, speaking casually of kings and of foreign lands. Yet he seemed content, with only his horse and saddle, on a trail drive across a mostly uncharted western frontier. Comparing himself to Bo, Gil felt woefully inadequate. There was guilt too, as he recalled his uncle Stephen's library, long unused. Gil had many questions about Bo, and he strove to put them out of his mind. The questions to which he most needed answers had to do with himself, and he sus-

pected that when he came face-to-face with those answers, he wasn't going to like them.

"Well, thank God," said Van when the trio met the
trail drive. "I was already three riders short, or I'd have
sent somebody to look for the three of you."

"We could of used the help," said Long John with a
straight face. "Me an' Bo comes up on our segundo, an'
he's been treed by a rattler half as big as Texas. Took the
three o' us t' cash the bastard in."

The drive had slowed to a crawl, and some of the
other riders had come forward to see what was causing
the delay.

"Listen," said Gil, addressing them all, "before we get
too far from here, I aim for every one of you to have a
look at this snake Long John's talkin' about, because
there may be others. For right now, we may have a problem. There's a rock-cluttered valley ahead, maybe two
miles across, and there's only one good path to the
other side. Now maybe a hundred yards into this head-
high jumble of rocks and boulders, there'll be enough
hide, blood, and snake smell to stampede every horse
and every longhorn steer all the way back to Bandera
Range."

"They go through on the run," said Ramon.

"Not totally," said Gil. "We don't want a stampede
once they're out of the rocks. We do want 'em moving
fast enough that they're past this trouble spot before
they've had a chance to do anything foolish. Mostly, we
want them bunched, horns to rump, so they can't go
anywhere except straight ahead. Any questions?"

There were none, and they headed for the valley. Gil
thought of something he should already have considered. Since the horse remuda could move much faster
than the longhorns, why not push the horses ahead,
crossing them before the longhorns arrived? Gil spoke
to Van, to Ramon, and finally, to Mariposa and Estanzio, who were with the remuda. Van would keep the
longhorns moving, while Gil, Ramon, Mariposa, and Estanzio took the remuda ahead.

"Lead them into it," Gil told Estanzio and Mariposa once they approached the valley. "Ramon and me will be at the drag, keeping them bunched. While we don't want a stampede, if everything goes to hell and they decide to run, let's just be sure it's straight ahead."

Gil allowed Estanzio and Mariposa to choose the gait, and by the time the horse remuda entered the confines of the rock abutments, they were moving at a slow gallop. Each of them would pass the trouble spot within a matter of seconds. On the negative side, however, they were but a gait away from a stampede. Once the leaders broke free of the barricaded valley, it would depend entirely on Mariposa and Estanzio. If the leaders emerged in a fast gallop, there would be no stopping those that followed. Gil could tell when the leaders reached the point where the huge snake had died. One of the leaders nickered, and the horses at the tag end seemed to pause. Gil and Ramon laid on their doubled lariats, keeping them bunched, lest the trailing horses attempt to wheel and bolt back the way they had come. When the last few horses picked up on the snake smell, they tried to balk, to turn, but they could not. Gil and Ramon were there, shouting, shoving, and slapping rumps. To Gil's relief, the herd began to slow. Mariposa and Estanzio had calmed the leaders. Gil and Ramon stayed with the drag until the remuda was out of the valley and under control. Gil waved his hat, and the Indian riders responded with raised hands. They would slow the horse remuda until the longhorns caught up.

"Ramon," said Gil, "I'm goin' to take Rosa, Juan Padillo, and Bo, and cover the drag. I want the rest of you ahead of the herd, slowing the lead steers once they're past the snake scare. When they break free on the other side of the valley, the flank riders can fall back. We won't allow them any slack at the drag, so they'll have nowhere to go, except straight ahead. Once they're past the snake smell, slow the leaders, and the others should settle down before they're free to run."

As he rode to drag, Gil sent the extra riders forward to join Ramon. A look at the sun told him they had to make up some time, or spend the night in a dry camp. His companions at drag were having the same thoughts. Rosa rode her horse alongside his.

"Do you think we can reach water before darkness comes?" she asked.

"I think we don't have a choice," said Gil. "A dry camp could ruin us. Once we get the longhorns across this valley, I aim to ride on to the water, no matter how far it is. It'll be a hard drive the rest of the way, and we have to know what's ahead of us."

He rode on, passing the word to Bo and Juan Padillo, and when the herd picked up the pace, the four drag riders had to fight to keep the stragglers bunched. They hit the valley floor in a lope, the herd narrowing down to accommodate itself to the limited passage through the field of broken and scattered boulders.

"Keep 'em tight," Gil shouted. "The leaders may try to balk."

The lead steers would have balked, had they been able. Within seconds of Gil's warning, the leaders picked up the snake smell and began bawling their fear. A shudder seemed to run through the herd from front to back, and while his companions swung their lariats at longhorn rumps, Gil fired his Colt. While the resistance among the front ranks slowed the herd, it was forced ahead by the shouting, shooting, flank-popping drag riders. The farthest slope was reached by the lead steers, and the eight riders were there ahead of them, moving them in a widening stream as they again spread out. Gil, Rosa, Juan, and Bo brought up the rear, keeping the steers close, allowing them little opportunity to quit the bunch. But the scare was past, and the longhorns lumbered along, still at a faster than normal trot. Once the herd was trailing well, riders began dropping back to flank and drag positions, and Gil rode to the head of the drive.

"Keep them moving at this pace," he told Ramon and Van. "I'm riding on to the water. After this snake killing, I want to know what's ahead of us. If I run into trouble of any kind, I'll warn you as quickly as I can. If you don't hear warning shots, or if I don't ride back, just keep rolling. I'll be looking for anything that might slow us down, or for some better way. I aim to be back before you reach water. Don't slow or halt the drive unless you hear warning shots."

"I ain't doubtin' your word," said Van, "but I still want to see that snake. I've heard too many of Long John's windies."

"Get Long John or Bo to ride back with you," said Gil, "but just a pair of you at a time. Don't slow down the drive; we may already be in trouble."

Gil rode out, pushing his horse to a slow gallop. He wanted to reach water and return to the trail drive as quickly as he could. Once he was sure there was no potential trouble ahead, they could step up the pace even more. There was a chance, once the sun was down, that the wind would bring the scent of water. The herd would run the rest of the way, and every rider would be needed. He passed within sight of another rattler sunning itself on a flat rock. The reptile was nothing like the one they had just killed, and it slithered quickly away well before Gil reached it.

Much to Gil's relief, he reached the water they were seeking in less than an hour. He figured it at eight miles. The large year-round spring flowed out from a patch of rocks. Shaded by willows and undergrowth, the substantial runoff formed a series of pools for maybe a mile before the stream disappeared into the dry earth. Gil scouted the area for Indian sign and found none. He watered his horse and rode back to meet the trail drive.

On a distant ridge, concealed by brush and pinion oak, a lone rider sat his horse. He watched until Gil was lost to distance, then wheeled his pony and kicked it into a run. His words would cause much talk in the lodges. The old ones would speak bitterly of the iron hats who had come across the great water seeking *plata* and *oro*, and, their greed unsatisfied, had tortured and killed. His people, the Chiricahuas, knew and hated the white man.*

---

* The Spanish came to the American southwest seeking silver and gold, but found little or none. Convinced the tribes claimed and worked mines secretly, the Spanish tortured and murdered the Indians, seeking treasure that did not exist. They accomplished nothing except to earn an undying hatred for the white man that spanned centuries.

12

❧

"*I*t looks good the rest of the way," Gil said when he
returned to the drive. "No bluffs, bad canyons, and
no Indian sign. We'll push on, even if we wind it up in
the dark."

"Bueno," said Ramon. "Is better than dry camp."

Nobody disagreed with that. They redoubled their efforts, secure in the knowledge they wouldn't go over an
unexpected bluff or canyon rim in their haste. The sun
left them in purple shadow and then in twilight as the
night birds began tuning up. Gil heard a shout from
somewhere far ahead, and before he had time to ponder
the reason, he knew. The longhorns, already in a lope,
surged ahead. The water was near! The drag riders were
galloping their horses. Gil tugged his hat brim lower,
trying to protect his eyes. Dust filtered through his bandanna, tickling his nose and lying gritty on his tongue.
Rosa galloped her horse next to his, and she seemed
oblivious to the dust. Her old hat rode her shoulders,
secured by a leather thong under her chin. Her dark
hair had grown long, and streamed in the wind. She
laughed, her face a muddy mask; she hadn't even bothered with her bandanna. Gil had scarcely thought of her
all day, but he did now. She seemed more the woman
than ever, more beautiful than the last time he'd looked
at her, and his feelings surged anew. The tag end of the
herd began to slow, a sure sign the leaders had reached

water. There would be little for the riders to do, except, as the animals drank, moving them away so that the rest could water. Mariposa and Estanzio had wisely guided the horse remuda far enough from the spring to avoid the expected rush by the longhorns. While the horses watered from the very end of the runoff, the steers fought each other for access to what was left. The riders wouldn't even dismount until the last thirsty animal had drunk its fill and settled down to graze.

"It's already dark," said Van, "but after the day we've had, we purely need some hot coffee and hot grub. Do we risk a supper fire?"

"Only if it's well-concealed," Gil replied, "and we douse it soon as the grub's done. I didn't see any Injun sign, but that's when they're the most dangerous."

Nobody wasted any time. Once they had eaten, the first watch rode out to circle the herd. Gil and the rest of the second watch rolled into their blankets for what sleep they could get. As usual, Mariposa and Estanzio were with the horse remuda. When the second watch took over at midnight, there had been no sign of trouble, not even the mournful cry of a coyote.

"I reckon I ought to of taken first watch," said Van. "I been layin' there awake listenin' for two-legged coyotes."

"Perhaps you are not hearing them because they are not there," said Rosa.

"With Indians," said Gil, "it works almost exactly the opposite. Think. We've had no real Indian trouble since crossing the Pecos, before we reached El Paso. Those were Comanches. Here, we have not only the Chiricahua Apaches, but the Papago as well, and there may be others I'm not aware of. The truth is, we're overdue for a visit from one of these tribes, and if we don't hear from them tonight, it'll increase the possibility of 'em showing up tomorrow night, or the night after."

"I purely hate sittin' around waitin' for somebody to come after my hair," Van said. "I'd as soon they come on and be done with it."

"When they come," Rosa asked, "will it be for the cows, the horses, or us? The poor man whose bones are back there in the valley, we know he had no cows, and he might not have had a horse either."

"I doubt Indians will be concerned with the longhorns," Gil said, "unless they're in cahoots with Comancheros from below the border. If we have anything they want, it'll be the horses or our scalps, I reckon."

"I am thankful we have Mariposa and Estanzio with the horses," Rosa said. "Now we must only be concerned with them getting the longhorns or us."

"They may stampede the horses and the longhorns first," said Gil, "and take advantage of the confusion to pick off some of us. Remember, the horse remuda we leave alone. Mariposa and Estanzio will do what can be done, and if they can't hold them, then neither could the rest of us, even if we could get there in time. Besides, it's our job to try and hold the longhorns, even if the horses stampede. We may not even be able to do that if they hit both herds at once. If we can't hold the herd, it'll be impossible to head them in the dark. Don't endanger yourself or your horse."

The moon set in the small hours of the morning, and the stars attempted to follow its example, as they receded into the purple vastness of the heavens. The attack came totally without warning, riders hitting the horse remuda and the longhorn herd simultaneously. Indians, screeching like demons, rode with a left leg across the pony's back, a left arm around its neck. There simply were no targets at which to shoot.

Rosa's horse began to pitch, and then lit out running. She thought Van was behind her, and as she turned to look, a powerful arm swept her out of the saddle. There was the mingled smells of buckskin, sweat, wood smoke, and stale grease. She fought to free herself, and her struggle brought a mighty blow to the side of her head. Van had drawn his Colt, but so concerned was he with Rosa's danger, he wasn't aware of his own. A heavy war club crashed against the back of his head, and he would have been flung headlong out of the saddle had a brawny arm not caught him. The Indian riders continued to ride with the running herd for another hundred yards. Then they swung away into the night, taking their silent captives with them.

The first two riders Gil encountered in the darkness were Mariposa and Estanzio. Mariposa had taken a blow to the head, and both had taken severe blows to their pride. This time they hadn't accounted for any of their attackers, and they'd lost a big chunk of the horse remuda.

"We ride," said Estanzio grimly. "We kill. Find horse."

"Soon as it's light enough to see," said Gil.

Slowly the outfit came together. Nobody had been seriously hurt, but Van and Rosa were gone. Had they been taken prisoner, or did they lie wounded or dead somewhere in the darkness? Gil found one prospect just as unacceptable as the other, and the time that remained until first light seemed forever. In the first gray light of dawn, they found Van's hat and Colt, and a confusion of different trails. The stampede had run south.

"We'll follow the stampede for a while," said Gil. "These coyotes split up after the attack, but I'm gambling they'll come together somewhere to the south."

Following the unshod horses wasn't difficult, and it was Estanzio and Mariposa who came up with the grim news.

"Two horse," said Estanzio, pointing to the tracks. "Each carry double."

None of the attackers had been unhorsed, and with two Indian mounts carrying double, there was but one obvious conclusion.

"The bastards took Van and Rosa," said Gil. "Let's ride!"

                    *   *   *

When Van came to his senses, he had no trouble deciding where he was. When he moved his head, it brushed against the rough hide of a tepee. He at first thought a war dance was going on outside, and then decided the drum was in his head. His hands were bound behind him, and his shoulders ached from the strain. He opened his eyes, and in the gloom he could see a very disheveled Rosa.

"Why'n hell didn't you stay at Bandera Ranch?" he growled.

"What does it matter?" she replied. "Are you blaming the attack on me?"

"No," he responded grudgingly, "but without you here, I might be able to escape."

"Because I am a woman you are quick to weigh me and find me wanting," she said. "As I rode to catch up to the trail drive, I was captured by Indians, and I took care of myself."

"How did you escape?"

"I killed one and outrode the others," she said.

"This time you won't," he said.

"What do you think they will do with us?"

"Right now," said Van, "I reckon they're rounding up as many horses as they can. We're their insurance against attack. They don't doubt the rest of the outfit will come looking for us, but they don't dare try anything in daylight. They'll be forced to wait for darkness."

"So we are safe until then?"

"No," said Van. "I look for them to have some fun with us. They could strip us, stake us out, and do some things best left unsaid. Or they could just beat us half to death. Not just for their pleasure, of course. They can't be sure we're not part of a foolish outfit that will come galloping to save us in broad daylight. Don't you reckon Gil would come stormin' in here, his Colt blazing, if he saw some Indian about to have his way with you?"

"I do not know," she said in a small voice.

"Well, I know," said Van. "When it comes to a woman, a man's a fool."

"Does that include you? You fought a dozen outlaws for Dorinda."

"Yeah," he said, "that includes me."

As Gil had expected, the various trails began to converge a dozen miles south of the spring. The Apaches had a camp somewhere, and they were bound for it. While the attackers had separated, once they came together, they made no effort to conceal their trail. Gil didn't see that as a good sign. Was this band so large that they had no fear of whatever retribution the Texans might attempt? Once the individual trails had begun coming together, Mariposa and Estanzio had counted more than twenty riders. There might be twice or three times that number in the camp, Gil thought grimly. The Texans, fewer in number, would be forced to wait for darkness before attempting any rescue. In the interval, Gil didn't like to think about what might be done to Van and Rosa. Within several miles after leaving camp, the riders had begun seeing groups of grazing longhorns, but few horses.

"The varmints is after the hosses," said Long John.

That appeared to be the case. It would buy some time for Van and Rosa, Gil hoped. Eventually they met a bunch of more than a hundred longhorns, plodding along, bawling dismally.

"They be returning to water," said Ramon.

It was true. Following a stampede, the longhorns sought the nearest water, whether it be ahead or behind. In this case, it would be the spring where their camp had been. The brutes would practically gather themselves. All the outfit had to do was free Van and Rosa, recover the horses, and somehow escape with their lives. Gil's silence and the hard line of his jaw set the mood, and the outfit rode on.

Despite their bound hands and cramped positions, Van and Rosa slept. When they awoke, it was to the sound of voices and the arrival of many horses. Even in the gloom of the tepee, they could tell it was still daylight, though they had no idea how late in the day it might be.

"They've brought in some of our horses," said Van.

Rosa said nothing. Once the entire band was together, she suspected they'd begin devising plans for their captives. They didn't have long to wait. The tepee flap was drawn back and one of the men entered. Rosa had seen the face of only the one who had abducted her, and even now she wasn't sure this was the same man. Not that it mattered. He dragged her roughly to her feet.

"Esposa," he said. *"Esposa."*

Rosa ground her teeth in despair. Didn't an Indian *ever* look at a woman with anything else on his mind? He shoved her ahead of him, out of the tepee.

"Van," she shouted, "if there is a chance to escape, go!"

Van swallowed hard. He had an idea what was about to happen to Rosa, and fought his bonds. The girl had sand, and deserved better than this. But he was bound tight and could only sit there and listen in dread.

"Esposa," said the Apache, shoving Rosa into another tepee. This one, she suspected, was his own. Many other Indians waited in anticipation, as though aware of what Rosa's captor had in mind. At least, Rosa thought, for what it was worth, he wasn't going to ravish her in view of the entire village.

"Desnudo," said the Indian once he had closed the tepee flap. *"Esposa."*

"I am not your wife," shouted Rosa in angry Spanish, "and I do not wish to be naked!"

The Indian laughed. He caught the waistband of her trousers, popped off the buttons, and she stood naked from the waist down. Next came her shirt, but he had to free her bound hands to get her arms out of the sleeves. Rosa's hands and arms were numb, but her feet and legs worked. She drove her right knee into his crotch, and he doubled up with a grunt. Since he was blocking the tepee entrance, Rosa threw herself against the side of the thing. A pole snapped, and she flung herself against the other side. By now her furious captor had recovered and was trying mightily to get his hands on her. But Rosa had become a kicking, screeching, clawing demon. Again she threw herself into the side of the tepee, and a second pole gave way. She dropped to the ground as the burly Indian came after her, and he charged into the wall of the tepee before he could stop himself. Sturdy as the tepee was, it had been weakened, and it began to collapse. The wooden pegs securing the bottom edges to the ground gave way, and Rosa rolled out. For a blessed moment she thought her captor was trapped in the collapsed tepee, but he had managed to grab one of her ankles, and was escaping as she had.

The spectacle had excited the rest of the Indians, and they seemed to have all gathered around in a circle, laughing and shouting. Once the two of them were in the open, Rosa used her free foot and kicked her tormentor in the face. That loosed his grip for a second, and she broke free, only to have him catch her again. She clawed his face, yanked out a handful of his shoulder-length hair, and bit him. When he smashed a huge fist beneath her left ear, everything went black before her eyes. When she again came to her senses, she was facedown. The big Indian sat astraddle her, binding her hands behind her back. Finished, he got up, took her by the ankles and slung her over his shoulder. His comrades were whooping, and she could only conclude that he had been disgraced. She had no idea where she was being taken or what her fate would be. Finally, he leaned forward and she literally fell from his shoulder. She came down flat on her back on the hard ground, and found herself before the tepee from which she had been taken. Her captor, vicious now, drew the flap aside and literally flung her inside.

"Loco gato montés," snarled the Indian as he drew the flap closed.

Despite her ordeal and her many hurts, Rosa

laughed. Van, aware that the girl was stark naked, averted his eyes. There was a long, painful silence. Irritated, Rosa was the first to speak.

"Why will you not look at me? I know you have seen at least one naked woman in your life."

Embarrassed, Van was thankful for the poor light in the tepee. Finally he found his voice.

"What did he . . . do to you?"

"Broke some of my bones, I think. He wanted me for a wife, but I believe I changed his mind. What will they do with me now?"

"You'll get a dose of whatever they have planned for me," said Van. "Do you know what time of day it is?"

"Near sundown," she said. "Why?"

"Once they've had supper, they'll let us entertain them, I reckon. You might want to reconsider that big war whoop's proposal and become a wife."

"I'd sooner be dead," Rosa snapped.

"That's a damn good possibility," said Van. "Pray for a miracle."

"Gil and the rest of the outfit will do something to help us."

"I don't know what they can do," said Van, "until dark. That'll be too late for us."

A shallow arroyo on the west side of the Indian camp ran within a hundred yards of the nearest tepees. There were places where the arroyo was barely deep enough to hide a man on his hands and knees, and it was from here that Mariposa, Estanzio, and Gil observed activities in the Apache camp. While they were aware of the commotion that had resulted from Rosa's resistance, they couldn't see from their position, and were unaware of her fight. However, they could see the evening meal being prepared, and from the positions some of the Apaches were taking, Gil thought he knew what they had in mind for Van and Rosa.

"Let's go," he said. "We have to get back to the rest

of our outfit. I think I know what they aim to do, and
we'll only get one chance to help Van and Rosa."

They crept away on hands and knees until sagebrush
and greasewood grew high enough along the arroyo to
conceal them on their feet. Reaching the other riders,
Gil tried to tell them what he felt was about to happen.

"I believe they're going to force Van and Rosa to run
the gauntlet. Some of you may not be familiar with it,
and here's how it's done. The Apaches line up in two
rows, facing one another. The captives, stripped naked,
are forced to run between these two rows of Indians.
The Indians are armed with knives, lances, and clubs."

"We purely can't let it happen," said Long John.
"Our folks won't never git t' the end o' that gauntlet
alive."

"That's how I see it," said Gil, "and there's damn
little we can do to help them. We just counted twenty-
one tepees, and that's all we could see from our position, but there's more. I'd say there's at least sixty fighting men in this bunch, maybe more. That means we're
outnumbered at least five to one. While that's a hell of a
risk, it's the only edge we have. There are so many of
them, they'll be overconfident and won't be expecting us
to try anything in daylight. I can think of only one way
Van and Rosa might be saved. This arroyo is shallow,
especially where it's closest to the Apache camp. We
had to take to hands and knees to avoid being seen. A
man hidden in that arroyo with a rifle could likely pick
off an Indian once they've gathered for the gauntlet
run."

"We draws the coyotes away from Van an' Rosa, an'
brings 'em down on us," said Long John.

"I'm afraid that's what it amounts to," said Gil. "We
kill enough of them, and we become more important
than Van and Rosa. Now here's the problem, pards.
Once we've emptied our rifles, we don't dare try to
reload and stand our ground. They'll overrun us by
force of numbers. So that means we grab our hats and
run for the horses. Retreat. Because this arroyo is so

shallow, we'll be forced to go afoot. Once our damage has been done, we'll be more than half a mile from our horses. Now this bunch of Apaches will not only know our position, they'll have horses, and they'll outnumber us. Van is my brother, and Rosa . . . well, I can't risk the lives of all of you when those I'm hopin' to save may die anyway. Now, I aim to be in that ditch with my rifle, to do whatever I can, but I won't fault any man who chooses not to take the risk."

"By God," said Long John, "them's our people. I'll be alongside ye."

"And I," said Bo.

The rest of them stood fast in their loyalty, backing him to a man. For a moment Gil couldn't speak; he couldn't get the words around the big lump in his throat. When he did speak, he offered no thanks, for they would have been insulted if he had.

"One shot for each of us," he said. "Be sure your Colts and your extra cylinder are fully loaded. If they crowd us too close, before we're able to reach the horses, we'll use our Colts. But don't stop to fight. Shoot on the run. Our only chance is to reach our horses and outride the bastards."

"When they take us from here," said Rosa, "we must escape."

"They'll be lookin' for that," said Van. "One wrong move, and they'll run you through with a lance or knife. They'll not let down their guard until we're spread-eagled stark naked and staked down."

"Is that the only . . . Is there nothing else . . . they might do with us?"

"Nothin' you'll like any better," said Van. "We might run the gauntlet."

"The gauntlet?"

"They line up in two rows, facing," said Van, "every Indian armed with a knife or club. We will be made to run between the rows, and they'll beat and cut us as we go. When we're beaten to the ground, if we're still alive,

we'll be staked out for other torture. I don't know how
they feel about women, but they especially enjoy building a fire in a man's crotch."

"*Madre de Dios!*" cried Rosa. "How can men be so
heartless and cruel?"

"I reckon the Spanish made a bad impression on
them," said Van, "and this is their idea of revenge."

There was the tantalizing smell of roasting meat, but
no food was brought to the captives, nor were they given
water. They waited. Suddenly the tepee flap was drawn
aside and two Indians entered. Van and Rosa could see
the sun was down. Supper was done, and it was time.
One of the Apaches got Van to his feet, loosed his belt,
and ripped his trousers open. His shirt got similar treat-
ment, and when the Indian yanked down his drawers, he
stood there naked as Rosa. Van's bound hands were
freed, so the shirt could be ripped off. Van fell when the
Indian tried to force him through the tepee's open flap.
The trousers and drawers wouldn't come off over his
boots, so the Apache ripped off the boots and flung
away the ruined trousers. Van was again forced to his
feet, while the second Indian dragged Rosa to a standing position.

Van was taken out first, and then Rosa. When her
bound hands were freed, there was blessed relief for her
aching arms and shoulders. Once the captives were
marched out beyond where the cook fire had been, they
could see what awaited them. There were twenty or
more Apaches in each line, some with knives, some with
lances, and some with clubs. Some of the women were
pointing to the naked Van, and while he didn't know the
language, he could understand their laughter. At the
very head of one of the lines that was the gauntlet was
an Apache who had a wolfish grin on his ugly face, and
Rosa thought he was the one she had humiliated. He
looked ready, willing, and eager to extract his revenge.

"*Silencioso!*" bawled an Apache who had the look of
a chief. The chatter of the women, the shouting of the
braves, and the barking of the dogs ceased.

Van and Rosa were shoved into position, but the distant bark of a rifle broke the silence. The chief—if that's who he was—had a look of surprise on his face, and a hole in his chest that spurted blood. He stumbled backward, and before he hit the ground, Van was running. But not between the rows of armed men. Rosa was right behind him, and not a knife, lance, or club touched either of them. Other shots had followed the first, and there was total chaos. Men shouted, women cried, dogs barked and howled, while more men fell victims of the unseen riflemen. Van ran toward the nearest cover, a line of sage and greasewood to the southwest. Before he knew it, he had fallen headlong into a shallow arroyo, and Rosa was right on top of him.

"Damn," Van grunted. He shoved Rosa's foot out of his face and spat out a mouthful of dirt.

"Por Dios," Rosa panted, "never have I run naked through the woods and briars before."

"Neither have I," Van said, "and given a choice, I won't do it again."

Rosa laughed. For a while they didn't move, listening. While the dogs were still barking, they heard nothing else.

"We'll stay with this arroyo," said Van, "and we'd best keep to the south. Gil and the boys gave us a chance, but now they've got the whole damn bunch on their trail. My God, there must be sixty or seventy Apaches in this band."

By the time the arroyo played out, it was dark enough for Van and Rosa to feel safe. Their bodies a mass of cuts and bruises, they stumbled on. While they were weak with hunger, their real need was water.

"For so large a camp," Van panted, "there has to be water. Unless it's just a spring with limited runoff. We must have water."

When the last rifle was fired, Gil and his riders hunched as low as they could and ran for their lives. Pursuit was swift. Almost within seconds, they could hear the pound of horses' hooves. One quick look confirmed Gil's fears. While the Apaches knew from whence had come the lead, they also knew Gil and his riders were afoot. While some of the Indians charged the arroyo, others angled off, getting ahead of the Texans. They were going for the horses, and if they reached them first, Gil and his men were done. Already Indians raced their horses along the arroyo, seeking a break in sagebrush and greasewood. Arrows whipped through the brush, thunking into the dirt walls of the arroyo. Gil drew his Colt, shot an Apache off his horse, and it seemed two more took his place. Ahead of Gil, Long John stumbled and went down, an arrow through his thigh. Gil helped the fallen Cajun to his feet, while Bo covered them, his Colt roaring. Suddenly, in the very teeth of the attack, Mariposa and Estanzio were on the lip of the arroyo, and Gil thought he knew what they had in mind. It was a bold move, and it was also crazy and impossible. But it was their only hope of coming out of this alive. But for a miracle, the end was only seconds away . . .

The closest thing Van and Rosa found to water was damp sand, probably the tag end of the runoff from a spring near the Indian village. Van began to dig with his hands, and when he had dug almost a foot, water began to seep into the hole. The water was muddy, but it was cold and wet. Again and again they drank. With a sudden rustling of leaves, Van and Rosa froze. Two malevolent eyes looked at them out of the gloom, and a dog growled.

"Get away from us, you bastard!" Van hissed. "Scat!"

But the dog began barking, and within seconds every other dog within hearing had joined the clamor.

13

*B*owie in his hand, Estanzio leaped on a galloping horse behind its Apache rider. His left arm around the man's throat, Estanzio drove the big Bowie into the Apache's belly. The horse didn't even break stride as its new rider flung the dying Apache to the ground. Right on the heels of Estanzio's move, Mariposa had performed a similar feat. Mounted, Colts in their hands, the two now galloped toward the thicket where their outfit's horses were waiting. This brazen move by Mariposa and Estanzio had so angered the Apaches, they seemed to forget the besieged Texans in the arroyo. Gil had the wounded Long John on his feet, and with Bo covering from behind, they went on toward the horses. The rest of the riders had continued their mad run down the arroyo, and with the diversion created by Mariposa and Estanzio, the Apaches found that taking the Texans' picketed horses was no longer a sure thing. In the best Indian fashion, Mariposa and Estanzio clung with one leg to the backs of the Indian ponies and fired their Colts under the necks of the galloping horses. A dozen Indian ponies raced away riderless. It was now almost dark, and except for Gil, Long John, and Bo, the outfit had reached the upper end of the arroyo, near where their horses were tied. Their fire, added to that of the hard-riding Mariposa and Estanzio, was deadly. With half their attacking force dead or wounded, the

Apaches retreated. A day that had held so much promise for them had gone sour, and there had been much bad medicine.

"By God," said Long John, through gritted teeth, "she was some fight. I wouldn't of missed it fer nothin'. Did Van an' Rosa git loose?"

"They lit out for the brush," said Gil, "and I don't think they were pursued. The way we cut them down, they wanted us bad, so they dropped everything else and came after us. Now we have to get away from here, remove that arrow from your leg, and then stampede every horse in this Apache camp."

"The arrer jus' tore the meat," said Long John. "It ain't hit the bone."

"No, but there'll be infection," said Gil, "if we don't attend to it."

Without further difficulty they reached their horses, where the other riders waited. Mariposa and Estanzio still had the captured Indian ponies.

"Bring them along," said Gil. "It'll be two less for them to use. When we come for our horses they took, we'll stampede the rest of theirs."

They rode out, bound for the spring where they'd camped the night before. For the night, at least, Van and Rosa were on their own, and Long John's wound needed attention.

"Don't move," Van whispered, his hand on Rosa's arm. "Don't breathe."

They had backed away from the muddy water Van had brought to the surface, and one of the dogs from the Indian camp had roused all the others. Worse, he had attracted the attention of some of the Apaches. Van and Rosa could hear their voices as they came to investigate. But Van still had hope. There was a faint but distinct odor of skunk, for the animal had gone to the water they had left. Van wasn't sure if the curious dog had first discovered them or the skunk, but that no longer mattered. The skunk, if it tarried a little longer, could save their lives. As the Apache voices came closer, the dog's barking grew more frenzied. The foolish dog waited until its human companions were near, and then, encouraged, it went after the skunk. Even from where Van and Rosa hid, the stink was all but unbearable. But the unfortunate dog and the pair of Apaches seemed to have gotten full benefit of the skunk's temper. The dog whimpered and cried, and the Apaches coughed and wheezed. There was a final shriek from the offending dog, as one of the Apaches silenced him forever. Van and Rosa waited until the skunk-smitten Apaches had departed and until the camp dogs were quiet.

"Now," said Van, "let's get away from here."

But it would be a while before moonrise, and they couldn't see where they were going. Finally they came upon a windblown pine, and the upended root mass had left a hole as big as a buffalo wallow. It was waist deep and full of dried leaves. A light wind had risen, and Rosa's teeth chattered.

"God knows what may be in among those leaves," said Van, "but we can't see standin' here jaybird naked, with our teeth chattering, while we wait for the moon to rise."

Van fumbled around in the dark for a stick, a limb, something with which to probe the mass of dry leaves. He eventually found a stone by smashing his big toe into it. When he dropped the stone into the hole, there was no evidence of any animal or reptile that might object to their company. The naked pair sank gratefully into the dry leaves and out of the chilling wind.

"*Por Dios,*" sighed Rosa, "I have never been so tired, so sore, or so hungry. How far are we from the spring where our camp was?"

"God knows," said Van. "That big bastard that grabbed me almost bashed my brains out. I don't know how far we had ridden when I finally came to my senses. I'm afraid we're far enough away that we won't make it tonight, and that forces us to go the rest of the way in daylight. From all the shooting, I reckon Gil and the outfit got out alive, and I look for them to come back after the horses sometime tonight."

"All they can do is stampede the horses," said Rosa, "and that means they must round them up in the daylight. Could we not just stay here and wait for them to find us?"

"Rosa, these damn Apaches will still be here, and they may be hunting horses too. Knowin' Gil, he'll stampede every horse in camp, leavin' these war whoops afoot. They may be out here beatin' the bushes too, and what do you reckon they'll do to us if they find us?"

"I am sorry," she said. "I am so tired, I am not thinking."

"I know how you feel," he said, more sympathetic. "I just believe Gil will expect us to try and make it back to the spring, to our old camp. He won't expect us this near the Indian camp, and he can't risk coming to look for us."

"Van, what do you think of me? Be honest with me, and do not spare my feelings."

"Now that I've seen you stripped to the bare hide," he said, "I think you're a hell of a lot older than Gil believes you are."

"Had you felt that way before . . . today?"

"I've suspected it for at least a year," he said, "and I was sure of it . . ."

"Today," she finished.

He said no more. Irritated, Rosa again took up the conversation.

"Damn it, Van, why will you not talk to me? Just because you have seen me without my clothes, does that make me less a person? Are you going to pretend I do not exist?"

"Rosa, I'm a married man with a child. How am I supposed to feel, the two of us together possum naked? Besides, I'm not sure how Gil's goin' to take this."

"He will be satisfied that we are alive," said Rosa. "Do you fear he is going to think you took advantage of me while we were half frozen, tired, and hungry, with the Apaches after us?"

"No," he said wearily, "it's not that. I . . . damn it, Rosa, I don't know *what* I'm afraid of, *what* I think. I was sittin' there in that tepee, hogtied, not knowin' if I'd live or die. I should have been praying, but when that Indian brought you in . . . like that . . . stark naked, I . . ."

"You forgot the wife and child," said Rosa. "You have been on the trail many weeks, and you wanted me. As a woman. Your conscience hurts you."

"My God, yes," he said, his voice breaking. "I wouldn't have, couldn't have, but God help me, I wanted you. What would Dorinda say if . . . she knew?"

"I think she would say she is proud of her husband," said Rosa. "It is no sin to be tempted. The sin comes with the yielding. You are a bueno hombre, Van, and I could be tempted of you as you are tempted of me, but I think your feelings for Dorinda are my feelings for Gil."

"Thank you," said Van. "I needed to hear you say that, and I don't regret my feelings for you. I don't understand Gil, but if he ever lets you down or hurts you, I'll personally kill him."

"Thank you," said Rosa. "I know he wants me, but there are times when he is so distant I cannot reach him. He is searching for something only he can see. Perhaps it is something he wants more than me. I think I shall know by the time we reach the end of this California Trail. . . ."

Gil and the outfit returned to the spring that had been their camp when the Apaches had struck. The moon had risen, and they found that during the day, most if not all the longhorns had returned to water. So had the horses the Apaches hadn't been able to gather.

"We must have hot water," Gil said, "to cleanse Long

John's wound, and that means a fire. None of us have eaten since last night, so let's eat while we can. We have a long night ahead of us, and maybe a fight in the morning."

"Could the Apaches strike again tonight?" Bo asked.

"Maybe," said Gil, "but I don't think so. We hurt them, and except for the arrow in Long John's leg, they didn't make much of a showing. They've had a bad day. No matter how hard they hit us, those of us still able to ride would go after them, but Indians don't think that way. When things just go to hell for them, like today, they'll back off. In fact, they're liable to pack up at first light and move the camp. That's why we have to go after them tonight, and recover the rest of our horses."

"Ye'd best git started drivin' this Apache toothpick outta my leg," said Long John. "Time the moon sets, we ought t' be back at that Injun camp."

"You're goin' to be right here," Gil said, "and Bo will be with you. By morning, you'll have some fever. I want you to start sweatin' out that infection, so when we recover the horses, we can get on with this drive. I reckon it's time to break out that little keg of whiskey we brought along for this occasion."

It was a sensible solution, and Long John didn't object. A man could die from a minor wound if he didn't whip the infection. While the wound would be painful, when the danger of infection was past, Long John could ride. Once the Cajun had downed enough of the whiskey to make the procedure bearable, Gil made preparations to remove the arrow.

"This won't be a pleasant thing to watch," Gil said, "but those of you who don't know how it's done, ought to know. I think this Indian problem on the frontier may outlive all of us, and every man should know how to treat arrow wounds."

The procedure was as simple as it was painful. Gil snapped off the feathered shaft of the arrow, leaving just enough of its length to drive it on through the flesh. With the butt of his Colt, by the light of the fire, he drove the shaft far enough for the barbed tip to emerge. Gripping the tip, he drew the rest of the broken shaft through the wound. Long John, in a stupor from the whiskey, still grunted with the pain. Once the arrow had been removed, Gil used plenty of hot water—almost too hot—to cleanse the wound. He then poured a generous amount of the whiskey into the wound. An old shirt became a bandage. Gil bound thick pads over the entrance and exit wounds, soaking each pad with the whiskey.

"Now," said Gil, "let's get some grub ready and eat. I want us at that Apache camp by moonset."

Out of the chill wind, despite her cuts and bruises, Rosa slept. It was an escape from the hunger that gnawed at her empty belly. When she woke, it was to a mournful sound that seemed borne on the wind.

"*Por Dios,*" she whispered, "it sounds like the wind is crying."

"I've never heard it before," Van said, "but I've heard of it. It's the Apache death song. Gil and the outfit must have done some real damage. That was a smart move, cutting down on them just as they were about to force us to run the gauntlet."

"I knew that somehow Gil would help us," said Rosa. "In many ways, I do not understand your brother, but he is a fighting man who is quick to do what must be done."

"I know," said Van. "That's how he ended up with you, in the wilds of Mexico, with the Mexican army all around us."

"You say it as though I were a *puta,* as though I forced myself on him. It was not that way. The *soldados* had murdered my *madre* and *padre,* and I was afraid. Gil's hands and face had been browned, like that of a Mejicano, and I feared he was one of the *soldados.* I tried to kill him with a hay fork. He tied my hands and forced me to look at his blue eyes and the white skin above the tops of his boots. He has told you none of this?"*

"He told us nothing, except that the Mex soldiers had killed your mama and daddy. I'm sorry for what I said . . . the way I said it. I know you were alone and afraid, and there was nowhere for you to go except to our trail drive. Gil only did what any man of us would have done, given the chance."

"The moon is rising," Rosa said. "I know we must go, but I wish we did not have to. I am warm here, and the wind is so cold."

"We'll have to take advantage of the moonlight," said Van, "and get as far from these Apaches as we can. I just wish I knew where we are in relation to that spring where we camped last night."

"We could just go north," said Rosa.

"We could, but we don't know if we're east or west of our old camp. Maybe we ought to circle the Apache camp to the west, and then travel north. We might even strike the trail the Apaches left, returning after their attack."

"When the longhorns and the horse remuda stampeded, they would have left a trail," said Rosa. "Perhaps we could find the path of the stampede, and it would tell us the direction we should go."

"The longhorns wouldn't run this far," said Van. "Once they get thirsty, they'll head for the nearest water they remember. If we're goin' to backtrack horses, I aim to look for the trail of the Apaches after their attack on us."

"Suppose they scattered, and all returned by different ways?"

"I'm sure they separated right after the attack," said Van, "but if you can remember, when we reached their camp, all of them had come together. I don't need a trail all the way back to our spring. Just enough to establish a direction, so we don't pass up our camp by bein' too far east or west."

Once the moon was high enough to afford them some light, Van and Rosa left their comfortable sanctuary, again braving the chill night wind.

"We'll go north three or four miles," said Van, "and then west about the same distance. From there, we'll head north. We're lucky we're downwind from the Apache camp, and we want to stay well away from them. All we need is for another of their dogs to discover us."

"There must be a hundred dogs. Why do they keep so many?"

"For hard times," Van said. "When the hunting is poor and meat becomes scarce, they'll drop a dog or two in the cook pot."

"Por Dios!" said Rosa. "I would starve first."

Van and Rosa, east of the Apaches, trudged north until there was no sound from the Indian camp. Even the multitude of dogs had become silent.

"Here is where we turn to the west," said Van, "and once we're far enough beyond the camp, we'll turn back to the north. By then it'll be daylight, and maybe we can start lookin' for a trail that'll lead us back to our old camp."

"Perhaps we will meet Gil and our riders when they come to take back our horses," said Rosa.

"Not likely," Van said. "Gil will want this to be a surprise attack, so I look for him to hit the Apaches from the south. That means our outfit will ride far to the east or west. Too far for them to find us."

"An attack from the south would stampede the horses to the north," Rosa said.

Van chuckled. "Now you're thinkin' like a Texan. Hit them directly from the north, and our horse remuda would end up in Mexico. If I know Gil, he'll stampede every damn horse in the camp. I think that bunch of Apaches will be glad to see us go. If there's any with revenge on their minds, they won't get far without horses."

* * *

"Bo," said Gil, "I don't look for you and Long John to have any trouble while we're gone. We're going to deal those Apaches enough misery that they'll leave us be. I aim to hit them from the south and stampede all the horses this way, so we shouldn't be away too long. If you hear something, don't be too quick to shoot. I look for Van and Rosa to find their way here."

Long John was still out of it, sleeping off the whiskey he'd taken prior to having the arrow removed. Bo had found a place away from the spring, where it was unlikely he and Long John would be discovered. From there, Bo could see the remainder of the horse remuda. When the outfit was mounted and ready to ride, Gil had some final words.

"Bo, if there is trouble—any kind of trouble—stay where you are. If Long John comes around and is in pain, or if he has fever, give him another slug of the whiskey. There's nothing more we can do for him."

Gil led out, the outfit following. The wind was from the west, and they rode ten miles eastward before turning south. That would keep them downwind from the Apaches until they were far enough south to double back for their attack. They rode in silence. Gil's thoughts were of Van and Rosa. The Apache camp was a good thirty miles south of the spring where Bo and Long John waited, and it was to there that Gil expected Van and Rosa to return. But even if they had escaped uninjured, they couldn't cover thirty miles from moonrise to moonset, so they would have to continue their journey in daylight. If the attack on the Apaches came off as planned, the Indians would have no horses, but Van and Rosa would have no way of knowing that. He concluded that he had to depend heavily on Van's savvy and intuition. His brother had too much Austin in him to hole up and depend on somebody to come looking for him, and from a purely practical standpoint, he should know that recovery of the horse remuda couldn't wait. At dawn the Apaches might pull up stakes and move on, taking the horses with them. Gil hoped that after the attack, when they returned to the spring, Van and Rosa would be there. What bothered him most was that he couldn't be sure they were still alive. Perhaps they had been recaptured. If they had, and were yet alive after tonight's attack, their deaths would be swift and sure. Gil rode on, uncertain, but knowing what he must do.

"I reckon we'd better be lookin' for a place to hole up until daylight," Van said. "If we don't, once the moon's down, we'll have a long, uncomfortable night ahead of us."

"My hands have no feeling in them," Rosa said, "and my feet are so dead, they could be full of cactus thorns and I would never know. I fear that when I get warm, the pain will be terrible."

"Come mornin'," said Van, "you'll be wishing you had some of this cool night air. This is still early summer, and the sun will be hot. You ever had all-over sunburn?"

"Once," said Rosa, "and *por Dios,* I could not sit, lie down, or bear having clothes touch my body. But then I was very young, and *madre* covered me with bacon grease."

"You've filled out some since then," said Van, "and we don't have that much bacon. Besides, I'm almost certain Gil wouldn't like it, you wearin' nothing but bacon grease. We need to get as far as we can tonight, before the sun has a chance to work on us."

Wearily they went on, until they came to what seemed the runoff from a spring.

"Let's follow it," said Van. "The spring's likely at the foot of a ridge, or the water may be out of a rock crevice higher up. We need somethin' to keep the wind off us, even if it's a bunch of boulders or the lee side of a ridge."

It was a small spring on the side of a hill, and above it they found a ledge of rock that faced the east. While there wasn't much room, it kept the west wind from their half-frozen bodies. Their crevice was too shallow to have gathered any windblown leaves, and they had to settle for the bare ground.

"At least we are out of the wind," said Rosa, "and that is enough."

14

Though they had ridden far to the east of the Apache camp, Gil had no trouble knowing when they were even with it. The wind was still from the west, and it brought the distant yipping of a camp dog. Gil led out, and they rode on, reining up when he judged they were half a dozen miles south of the camp.

"Now we ride west a ways," he said, "but before we hit the camp, we need to know where the horses are. We also need to eliminate their sentries. This is a tricky piece of work for Mariposa, Estanzio, and their Bowies. Ready, hombres?"

"We ready," said Mariposa. "Kill all?"

"All that's in the way of us gettin' to the horses," said Gil, "and that'll likely just be the sentries. When you've cleared the way, slip back and join us, and then we'll hit them all together."

The moon had set. Mariposa and Estanzio slipped away like shadows. Despite anything Gil had said, the intrepid pair still regarded the loss of most of the horse remuda as their personal disgrace. They were eager to redeem themselves, at least in their own eyes. But the camp was full of dogs, and within a matter of minutes one of them yipped a question. His answer came with a fifteen-inch blade, and his first yip became his last. Mariposa and Estanzio finished what they had been sent to do and made their report.

"Apach' watch horse," said Estanzio, "them die."

"Where are the horses?" Gil asked. "This side of the camp, or the far side?"

"Tepee," said Mariposa, "then horse. No picket. Them loose."

"Bueno," said Gil.

The Apaches on watch had been removed, the horses were being held north of the tepees, and the incredible Indian duo had quietly and swiftly freed all the horses!

"We'll fan out in a wide enough line," said Gil, "that way we'll have a chance to keep the horses bunched. We don't want them breaking east or west if we can help it. Once they're on the run, keep 'em moving. We'll strike just minutes away from first light, and I want every horse to pile out of there like it's Judgment Day and the Hell fires have been lit. Use your Colts to make the horses run, but don't waste any lead on the Apaches unless they try to counter our attack. Once we leave this bunch afoot, taking their horses with us, that ought to be enough bad medicine to rid us of them."

When Gil gave the order to ride, they moved out in an east-to-west line, a dozen yards apart. The camp dogs began the expected clamor, but the riders were already among the tepees before the Apaches could get to their weapons. At a fast gallop, Gil and the riders thundered toward the horse herd.

"Hiiieeeyah!" Gil shouted. "Hiiieeeyah!"

Some of the riders were firing their Colts, and such a spectacle, roaring out of the gray of dawn, was more than enough for the horse herd. They all broke into a gallop and headed north, with Gil and the riders in pursuit.

"Malo," said one of the Apaches. *"Malo medicina."*

Some of his companions grunted, and one of them kicked a barking dog.

Van and Rosa set out in the first light of dawn. The wind had died, and a golden glow to the east promised an end to the coolness of the night. Van suddenly stopped, listening. There was the faint but unmistakable sound of gunfire to the south.

"Gil and the boys are attacking the Apaches," said Rosa.

"Yes," said Van, "and they'll be driving the horses north. If I'm figurin' right, and we're heading anywhere close to our old camp at the spring, there's a small chance that the outfit and the horse herd might catch up to us. But only if we're in the right place, and in time."

"Perhaps we should wait for them," said Rosa.

"We can't risk that," Van said. "We may be too far east, and they may not be coming due north. If our old camp lies farther west, then they'll be riding northwest. They'll pass us by without knowing that we're here. I reckon we'd better keep moving, and if they don't find us, we'll still be a little closer to our old camp. I think we ought to just plan on walking the rest of the way. We get to dependin' on the outfit finding us, and we'll start to slack off, not doing anything for ourselves. By tonight we're goin' to be hurtin' for grub."

"*Por Dios,*" Rosa sighed, "do not speak of food. A bellyful of water does nothing to satisfy one's hunger."

By the time the sun was an hour high, Van and Rosa were sweating, and every cut and scratch on their bodies came alive.

"I wish for a creek or a river," said Rosa. "Water deep enough that I might get into it up to my neck, to free myself of the dirt and sweat."

"I know how you feel," Van said. "The chill of the night kind of numbs us to our hurts, and the sun thaws them all out again. I didn't realize I was so skint up and raw. There's a cut across my backside that feels like I've been raked with a grizzly's claws."

"It looks that way too," said Rosa. "You have been bleeding. You need some of the sulfur salve from our supplies."

Suddenly, just ahead of them, there was a rustling of leaves. Something or somebody was coming. The fugitives froze, relaxing only when they found themselves face-to-face with a horse.

"Indian pony," said Van. "With all this dirt, blood, and sweat, maybe I smell enough like an Apache to catch him."

Gil and the riders kept the horses moving, flanking the herd, turning them to the northwest. By Gil's estimate, they had lost only three or four of the Indian ponies. Those had broken away to the east, and they were so few they weren't important enough to be pursued. Most of the Indian mounts were still part of the herd the Texans had bunched and were driving toward the distant spring where Bo and Long John waited.

"Better we keep Injun horses," said Juan Padillo as he rode next to Gil.

"I think so," Gil said. "At least until we reach Tucson. With Long John hurt, we can't just pick up and go. I look for us to be there at the spring another day or two, and I'll feel better if those Apaches are thirty miles away and without horses."

What Gil didn't say was that he couldn't move on without Van and Rosa. If they hadn't returned to the spring by the following morning, something was wrong, and he would have to search for them or their bodies. Apaches or not.

Van took a cautious step forward, and the horse back-stepped. He was silently cursing himself for not having spent more time at the horse ranch, observing the Indian trainers and learning their "horse talk." Coming from Solano, Mariposa, and Estanzio, it sounded like meaningless gibberish, but it had a calming effect on horses. Van took another step, and again the horse back-stepped. Now his ears were laid back, and that wasn't a good sign. One more wrong move on his part, Van decided, and he was going to lose this horse. He couldn't remember the strange words of the Indian trainers because the words seemed to have no meaning, except to the horses. Though he didn't know the actual words, he still might imitate the sounds. He had nothing to lose except this skittish Indian pony, and he was about to lose it anyway.

"Hoh," said Van. "Hoh, hoh."

Van didn't move. He dared not, until he saw some change in the horse's disposition. Van tried again.

"Hoh, amigo. Hoh."

Van had made no threatening moves, and the voice was soft, soothing. Slowly the flattened ears rose, and Van spoke to the horse again. This time when he took a step toward the horse, it stood its ground. Van continued to talk softly until he was within reach of the animal. It trembled at his first touch, but with his stroking and continued "horse talk," he was able to win its trust. Rosa moved next to Van, letting the horse get used to her.

"No saddle, no bridle, not even a rope," said Van. "Just a horse."

"I always rode a mule without a saddle," said Rosa.

"But not with your backside naked, and raked raw from briars and thorns."

"I am so hungry, so weak, and so tired," said Rosa, "I am not sure I can mount, since there is no stirrup. But if you will help me up, I promise I will stay there."

"Here," said Van, linking the fingers of his right hand with those of his left. "Now you have a stirrup. But I can't do this and hold the horse. Put your arms around his neck while I help you up."

Weak from hunger and exhausted from the unaccustomed walking, Van had trouble mounting the horse behind Rosa. He eventually managed it by first hoisting himself to the trunk of a fallen tree, and from there mounting the horse.

"We must allow him to take his time," said Rosa, "since he is carrying both of us."

"We'll take it easy," said Van, "as much for our sake as his. I feel like I been throwed and stomped. I can understand ridin' bareback when you have to, but not with a bare bottom that's cut, bleedin', and sore."

By the time the sun was two hours high, Long John had some fever. Bo poured a pewter cup half full of the whiskey, and a little at a time the half-conscious Cajun downed it. Bo wondered if the attack had been successful. He had strained his ears, listening for gunfire, but he had heard nothing. The distance had been too great. From his and Long John's position, he could not see the spring, but he could see what was left of the horse remuda. Beyond a doubt, they had to recover the horses the Apaches had taken. The morning drew on, and Bo dozed. Suddenly he was wide-awake, his hand on the butt of his Colt. A horse had nickered. Of course, it might have been one of theirs, but he didn't think so. Their horses had ceased cropping grass and had their heads up, looking back toward the spring. Gil had specifically warned Bo to avoid trouble and remain with Long John, but the Argentine cowboy crept toward the spring. Before he could see anything, he heard a voice. A very familiar voice.

"I reckon nobody's here," said Van, "and it's just as well. We'll have time to clean ourselves up and get into some kind of clothes."

"Van," cried the Argentine, "it's Bo. Long John was hurt, and I have remained with him. Have either of you been wounded?"

"Not by the Apaches," said Van, "but we've been scratched and clawed, and we need to wash off the blood, sweat, and dirt. The Apaches took our clothes. When we're decent, we'll join you. We're goin' to take one of the iron pots to heat some water, and go down near the end of the runoff. I'm goin' to take some matches and a tin of sulfur salve from our supplies."

"I have no extra clothes," said Rosa. "I will have to use a blanket."

"You can't go from here to California in only a blanket," said Van.

"Rosa," said Bo, "I have extra clothes in my roll. I am closer to your size than any man in the outfit. Take a pair of trousers and a shirt."

"Thank you, Bo," said Rosa. "There are stores in Tucson, and I can buy something there."

Suddenly she remembered the gold coins. She found her own saddlebags, and to her relief the little treasure was still there, knotted in a bandanna. She followed Van along the runoff, taking with her a pair of Bo's trousers and a shirt. She was glad Bo and Long John were above the spring, leaving them free access to the runoff, where they couldn't easily be seen. Van got a fire going, and they waited impatiently for the water to heat. Once it was a little warm, they scooped out handfuls and began washing away the blood, dirt, and sweat. They weren't more than half finished when Gil and the riders returned, driving the recovered horses and the captured Indian mounts. Uneasy, Rosa looked at Van, and he tried to reassure her.

"Bo will tell them we're tryin' to clean ourselves up. Not a man in the outfit would come stompin' down here, knowin' what we've been through."

But Rosa had her doubts, and it took Gil just a few minutes to confirm them.

"What'n hell's goin' on here?" Gil demanded.

"What'n hell does it *look* like?" Van responded. "We've been out in the briars and brush all night, and we're dirty, sweaty, and bloody. Since you can't seem to figure it out, we're tryin' to make ourselves look and feel human again."

"And I reckon you have to do it together," said Gil.

Van's face was livid with anger, but before he could speak, Rosa took up the conversation.

"Of course we have to do it together," she said calmly. "There are cuts that need salve that we cannot reach. Turn around, Van."

Speechless, he did. Rosa grabbed the tin of sulfur salve and started rubbing it into the vicious cut that angled across Van's backside and was again oozing blood. Gil went white all the way to his shirt collar, and without another word turned and stalked back the way he had come.

Van laughed. "Rosa, I could kiss you! He's so damn jealous, so poison-mad, he could bite a rattler and it wouldn't stand a chance. He'll give us hell until this wears off. If it ever does."

"We have done no wrong," said Rosa, "and I will not be punished for something I have not done. Before this trail drive is over, Gil Austin is going to learn *one* thing, if he learns nothing else. I am not seeking a man to replace my dead father, to spank me when he believes I have been naughty. Gil has no claim on me. When it is time to decide whether or not he *ever* does, the decision may not belong to him. Perhaps it will be mine."

"Have you told him that?"

"No," said Rosa, "but I will, and knowing him, I will do it before the sunrise tomorrow."

The outfit was into their third day with virtually no sleep, so Gil made no demands on them for the rest of the day. After some jerked beef to satisfy their hunger, Van and Rosa slept for a while. Long John was awake, sweating and hung over. Mariposa and Estanzio spent the afternoon making moccasins for Van and Rosa from a deer hide. Two hours before sundown, Van and Rosa were up and about.

"If you will start the fire," said Rosa, "I will begin the supper."

"I ain't et since ye left," Long John joked. "Cain't nobody else in the outfit cook wuth a damn."

Van got the fire going, and they finished supper well before dark. Gil had said little, speaking only when he had to. When it came time to assign the watches for the night, he would have to. Whatever mood Gil was in, he never ceased to be cautious, nor did he underestimate an enemy. Even with the Apaches thirty miles away and afoot, the outfit would stand watch as usual. Gil asked for first-watch volunteers, and those who were left were considered the second watch. Van usually took the first watch, and he did tonight. Rosa said nothing, and Gil's eyes paused briefly on her. Was he expecting her to take the first watch, to avoid him? Now he knew she had no intention of avoiding him; and they both knew a storm was building, and that before the morning lightning would strike.

They were well into the second watch before Gil said anything, and his first overture was milder than Rosa had expected. "You didn't have to stand watch tonight," he said. "We could have managed without you."

"It was I who insisted on being part of this drive," said Rosa, "and I will do my share."

"Today," said Gil, "I . . . I . . ."

"Today you were jealous," said Rosa, "and you made an *asno* of yourself."

"Well, what the hell did you expect?"

"No more than I got," said Rosa shortly.

"But you told me nothing about—"

"Nor will I," said Rosa, "because you are expecting me to prove myself, to confirm my innocence. I have but one thing to say to you. Your brother has grown up in ways that you have not. Dorinda is a fortunate woman."

"Thanks," said Gil, with all the sarcasm he could muster. "Did you make those decisions before or after you looked at his naked carcass?"

"Only a man judges other men by what his eyes can see," said Rosa. "A woman sees with her heart first, and then with her eyes. Van is a man on the inside, as well as the outside."

"I reckon that means I ain't, then."

"I reckon it does," said Rosa. "After you returned with the horses and came stomping after Van and me, did you ask how we were, or if we had been hurt? No, you spoke down to us, like we were a sinful Adam and Eve, and you the Almighty. You are not the man I knew on Bandera Range, who looked at me with compassion

and read his Bible. You have come to treat me as one of
your possessions, like your horses, your cows, and your
land."

"Are you workin' your way around to tellin' me I
should have said to hell with the horse remuda and
come lookin' for you?"

"No," said Rosa, "I understood the need for the
horses, and I did not fault you for going after them. I
fault you for treating Van as though he took your toy
when you weren't looking, and for you looking at me as
though I already had my ears cropped and your brand
burnt on my backside."

"Are you done preaching?"

"No," said Rosa.

"Well, that's just too damn bad," Gil shouted, "because I aim to have my say. I know the pair of you didn't
aim to get captured and stripped by the Apaches just so
you could spend the night jaybird naked. But the two of
you seemed mighty familiar with one another when I
found you below the spring, and it's askin' an almighty
lot of a man to believe that nothin' serious went on
durin' the night. All I'm askin' is that you tell me nothin'
did."

"I don't intend to tell you any such thing," said Rosa
bitterly. "You may think what you wish, and I will not
speak to you again tonight."

That's how they left it, each knowing it was far from
finished.

Come first light, the first thing Gil did was talk to
Long John, and the Cajun vowed he could and would
ride. Gil took him at his word, and his wound was bound
securely. Besides recovering their own horses, the outfit
had acquired about fifty Indian horses. Gil seemed in a
surly mood, so Rosa asked Ramon about the Indian
mounts.

"We take them to Tucson, I think," said Ramon.

"I wish Gil would just turn them loose," Rosa said.

"The Apaches have had most of yesterday and all night last night, and they know the direction we are going. Even afoot, they could be somewhere ahead of us."

"Gil think of that," Ramon said. "Mariposa and Estanzio scout ahead for water. They watch for Injuns too."

Rosa, Long John, and Bo rode drag. Juan Padillo had joined Gil and Ramon to help handle the increase in the horse remuda. The horses were kept at a faster than usual gait, and the longhorns had to be pushed to keep up. When the herd was moving, and there seemed to be no bunch quitters, Van rode from the flank back to drag, where he could talk to Rosa.

"We all heard him pawin' the ground last night," said Van. "If the wind had been right, I expect the Apaches could have heard him too. He thinkin' we got ourselves captured and stripped so we could spend the night naked in the woods?"

"He knows it was not something we planned," said Rosa, "but he is not sure we did not yield to temptation after our escape. He only wants me to assure him that what he fears might have happened did not."

"So you didn't tell him what he wanted to hear."

"No, and I will not. He is a selfish *asno* who is never wrong, who must have everything his way. He is too stubborn to admit he is at fault, even when he knows better. I am tempted to confirm the lie he is trying to force me to deny, to tell him we spent the night doing that of which he accuses us. But then there would be trouble between you and him, and I cannot become the cause of that."

"Leave him be," said Van, "and when he can think of some way to back off without seemin' to, he'll leave us alone. It's still a long ways to the goldfields."

"If there is no change in him, Van, if he still does not trust me out of his sight, I will not be returning to Bandera Range. I will remain there in California, and if there is nothing else for me, I will take in washing."

Gil picked that particular time to ride back to the drag, supposedly to talk to Long John, but his eyes were on Van and Rosa. Without a word to either of them, he turned his horse and rode back to join Juan Padillo and Ramon.

15

May 13, 1850. Four days east of Tucson, Arizona
Territory

$\mathcal{M}$ariposa and Estanzio had ridden about fifteen
miles when they found the second spring. It
was larger than the one the trail drive had just left.
While there was no Indian sign near the spring, the duo
had not forgotten the surprise attack by the Apaches at
the last camp. In a widening circle, they rode south,
then west, and returned to the spring from the north.
When they were satisfied the area was safe, they rode
back to meet the drive.

"Fifteen-mile drive," said Juan Padillo. "I think we
make it."

"We'll have to," said Gil, "because we have another
one tomorrow. That's how far we are from this next
spring to the San Pedro River. From there, we'll be forty
miles from Tucson, Cienega Creek bein' the only sure
water in between. That means two twenty-mile days,
back to back."

"Make horse, cow run," said Mariposa.

"Better that than dry camp," said Ramon.

Nobody argued with that. Twelve miles was considered a good day's drive. Fifteen was possible, but anything beyond that was so rare as to be unheard of. Yet

Gil and his outfit had done the impossible a time or two, and not a man doubted they could do it again. It meant driving the longhorns at a faster than normal pace, and constant vigilance on the part of every rider to avoid straggling and bunch quitting. It was hard on the horses, hard on the riders, and hard on the longhorns, but when the alternative was a dry camp, it was worth any sacrifice. The weather had been mostly dry and hot, but that was about to change. By afternoon the western sky had become a smoky gray, darkening as the day wore on. Two hours before the sun would say good night to the prairie, it hid its face behind rising thunderheads and painted the western sky with shades of pale rose to vivid crimson.

There was no wind, and even with the sun behind a cloud bank, it seemed oppressively hot. When they had a chance, the riders fanned themselves with their hats. Sweat dripped off their chins and noses, burned their eyes, and dust became instant mud as it touched bare skin and sweat-soaked shirts. The longhorns had been run hard, and as they grew tired and thirsty, they became cantankerous. There wasn't a moment's respite for any rider, as they fought to keep the herd bunched and moving.

"Don't let 'em slack off," Gil shouted. "Don't let the brutes see daylight between themselves and the backside of the steer ahead!"

It was good advice. The ranks must be closed and kept closed, so that no matter where a steer looked, he saw only the rumps and horns of his companions. Thirst, a memory of yesterday's water, and "daylight" within the ranks made any steer a potential bunch quitter. And there were always some followers. To a lesser degree it was a stampede, one steer bolting and others attempting to follow. Gil rode ahead and caught up with the horses. Since the herd had been greatly increased, Juan Padillo had joined Mariposa and Estanzio, but the horses hadn't yet become unruly. Estanzio pointed toward the red glow of the westering sun.

"Mebbe hail," he said.

Gil wasn't sure whether the Indian had predicted "hail" or "hell," and with the run of dry weather they'd been having, he wouldn't be surprised at a devastating combination of the two. If they could reach water in time, at least the herd wouldn't stampede at the first hint of rain. While there was some open plain, there was some sheltering forest, with stands of aspen, oak, maple, fir, and pine. If they did not reach water, and the storm came roaring out of the west, it might send an already thirsty herd running hell-for-leather back the way it had come. Less than an hour had passed when Mariposa rode back to confirm Estanzio's prediction.

"Storm come," said Mariposa. "Stones of water. Bring cow pronto. We wait."

Gil galloped his horse along the flank and back to drag, warning the riders. With doubled lariats they swatted dusty flanks, and the longhorns bawled their weariness and frustration. Estanzio, Mariposa, and Juan Padillo had already secured the horse herd in a stand of oaks. Gil and Ramon led the longhorns for another quarter of a mile, taking shelter in a covering of oak and aspen. Gil wished the horses had been taken west of the longhorns, so if the steers stampeded, they might not take the horses with them, but it was too late for hindsight. Some of the longhorns stubbornly refused to be confined beneath the sheltering oaks and broke loose. They lit out west and ran headlong into a barrage of hailstones, some of them as large as eggs. The steers changed their minds and bolted back to the shelter of the trees. The hailstorm hit hard, littering the ground with leaves and small limbs. Some of the horses, some of the longhorns, and most of the riders were struck by the hailstones. Horses nickered and steers bawled, but they were confused. There was no thunder and no lightning, and there seemed no escape from the onslaught. While the longhorns milled and bawled, there was no spark to ignite a stampede. The hail gradually diminished, giving way to the rain. It became a steady down-

pour, and while there eventually was thunder, it was
subdued. Finally the rain fell faster than the thirsty
earth could swallow it, and there was water for the
horses and longhorns.

"No matter if we reach spring now," said Vicente.

"It does matter," said Gil. "We have to make twenty
miles tomorrow, and twenty more the day after, so that
means we finish our fifteen today. Let's move 'em out!"

The rain remained steady, cooling the land, and Rosa
shivered in her sodden clothes. The wind had risen, and
with the rain, there was an almost uncomfortable chill.
When they finally reached the spring, there was a pleasant surprise. While water pooled at the foot of a ridge, it
came from higher up, tumbling down over rocks. There
was a substantial runoff for the watering of the stock,
and it ran deep, supplemented by the rain. Along the
base of the ridge down which the water cascaded was a
rock overhang a dozen feet high and forty feet long.
With the wind and the rain out of the west, there would
be a dry place to cook, eat, and spread blankets.

"Come on, Bo," said Van, "and let's find some pine
knots and some dead fir and get a fire going. I got a wild
hankering for some hot coffee."

Ramon, Gil, Juan Padillo, Long John, Vicente
Gomez, and Juan Alamonte began unloading the
packhorses. Rosa got the iron spider ready, and filled
the two-gallon coffeepot with water. She filled a soft
leather bag with coffee beans, crushing them with a
stone. Van and Bo returned with some fir and some oak
and the resinous heart of a long dead pine, with the
knots still attached. They soon had a fire going, and the
savory aroma of coffee lifted their spirits.

"I ain't got nothin' agin beans an' bacon," Long John
said, "but oncet we git t' this Cienega Creek, mebbe me
an' Bo can git us a mess o' fish."

The rain let up just before midnight. Gil, Rosa, Pedro
Fagano, Juan Padillo, Vicente Gomez, and Manuel
Armijo had the second watch. Rosa had taken to riding
the Indian pony on which she and Van had returned to

camp, following their escape from the Apaches. The horse had scars on its face, evidence that it had seen little kindness in its life. Rosa had made friends with the animal partly out of sympathy and partly because her affection for it seemed to irk Gil. Estanzio had patiently trimmed the horse's hooves and had shod it for her. Gil didn't waste any time or pass up any opportunity to rag her about the horse. This night on watch, even after a hard day on the trail, was no exception.

"Don't we have enough decent horses without you ridin' that scrubby, ugly Apache nag?"

"He is no scrubbier or uglier than the rest of them," said Rosa shortly. "Since you find them so undesirable, why do we take them with us? Once we were far from the Apache camp, you should have set them free."

"Ugly and scrubby or not," Gil said, "I reckon they'll bring a few dollars in Tucson, and I don't need any advice on how to handle Apaches."

"Or on anything else," said Rosa.

"You never back off, do you?"

"Without cause, you spoke unkindly of my horse. He is an honest horse, and he trusts me, which is more than can be said for you."

"All right, damn it," he growled, "maybe I *was* a mite hasty, when I . . . when I thought you and Van—"

"Is that your Tejano *asno* way of admitting you were wrong?" she broke in.

"Hell, no," he snapped, losing his temper. "I don't know that I *was* wrong, but I'm willin' to put that behind us and just forget it. But you can't seem to; you're hell-bent on keepin' it a burr under your tail forever."

"Madre de Dios." Rosa laughed. "You will forget, but you will not forgive. I do not believe you will do either. When I am old and dying, you will come to me and ask, 'Rosa, what *did* you and Van do while you were naked in the woods?' "

"I try to make amends," he snarled, "and you laugh at me. By God, I won't get down on my knees."

"I laugh so that I do not cry," said Rosa, "and I

couldn't believe you if you *were* on your knees. As I have told you, a woman sees first with her heart, and what I see, I do not like."

"Well, just put the rest of the cards on the table," he said, "and tell me what it is you see that you don't like."

"I see a man who is not satisfied with his life," said Rosa. "Your brother has a wife and child. All you have —or had—was me, and your uncle Stephen's law books. You found no comfort in the books, and you have used my young years as an excuse for turning from me. You wanted me, but only as you might want any woman to satisfy your needs. That is why you left me in Texas. Foolishly, perhaps, I followed, and again you want me, but not in the way that I wish you to. While you need a market for cattle, that is not the real reason for this trail drive. What you seek is within yourself, and if you could not find it in Texas, neither will you find it at the end of this California Trail."

"You're dead right about one thing," he said grudgingly. "I wanted you, and I still do, but not in the way that you wish. You've tempted me, and when you left Bandera Range and joined the drive, you spoiled all my good intentions. I needed to be away from you for a while, to know if I felt more for you than just a need for what you were tempting me with."

"That's why you have been so ugly and cruel to Van and me," said Rosa. "Had you been in Van's place after the two of us had been stripped by the Apaches, our night in the woods would have been different. You would have done the very thing you have accused Van of doing, wouldn't you?"

He was silent for so long, she thought he wasn't going to answer, and when he finally spoke, she barely heard him.

"Like Uncle Stephen used to say, a thief thinks we are all thieves, that everybody steals. Go ahead and laugh. I reckon I got it coming."

"There is nothing to laugh about," said Rosa. "No more will I tempt you, and no longer will you be forced to ponder your feelings for me. When we have reached the end of this California Trail, if you do not want me, than I will not return to Texas with you. I will know your feelings in my heart, and when it is time for a decision, it will not be yours, but my own."

Gil had the herd on the trail when it was barely first light. While there would be no difficulty in finding Cienega Creek, it must be scouted for Indian sign. There were now so many horses, Gil left Mariposa and Estanzio with the horse herd and attended to the scouting himself. He left Ramon in charge of the cattle, with specific instructions.

"Push them hard, Ramon, just like we did yesterday. We have to make a twenty-mile drive today, and we must make it all the way."

Gil rode out, and while his eyes searched the country ahead, his mind was on Rosa and the line she'd drawn last night. He felt better, in a way, having cleared his conscience of the foolish things he'd said and done, but he was uneasy. The girl understood him better than he understood himself. Back at the Bandera ranch, he believed he could have proven himself by taking her to bed. But the days and weeks on the trail had changed her, matured her, and her stern, unbending attitude last night had reminded him of Granny Austin. In his mind's eye he could see her yet, pausing in her Scripture reading to look at him sternly over the tops of her spectacles. While she could not have known his every thought, she had convinced him that she did. He was thirty-eight years old, he thought ruefully, and still having to answer to Granny Austin. As she had bent the twig, so had the tree grown. While he didn't even want to think of returning to Texas without Rosa, she would make the decision, and there seemed no way he could influence her. He made up his mind not to speak unkindly to her, or to force his thoughts or opinions on her. While that might not help his cause, it was a start.

Van, Rosa, Bo, and Long John rode drag. After last

night's rain, it was still too early in the day for dust to be
a problem, and the herd was still fresh enough that the
longhorns were trailing well. Van rode his horse next to
Rosa's, and she smiled at him.

"Not a bad horse for an Injun mount, is he?"

"He is a fine horse," said Rosa. "Even if we hadn't
needed him so badly, I am glad we found him. One who
has been mistreated, when you have won his trust, he
will die for you."

"Your talks with Gil have done some good. He was
almost friendly this morning."

"I have told him I may not be returning to Texas with
him, and that if I do, the decision will be mine alone. I
have begun to believe that my coming on this trail drive
was a mistake, but it is too late to change that."

"For Gil's sake," Van said, "I hope he measures up,
and that you'll be goin' back with us. I don't know how
old you are in years, but you're the kind of woman the
frontier needs. If I didn't already have a wife, old Gil
wouldn't stand a chance. I'd grab you for myself."

"Thank you," said Rosa, touched by his sincerity.

Gil kept his horse at a slow gallop, and in a little more
than two hours reached Cienega Creek. He found, while
the map called it a creek, it was more a river. The previous night's rain had swelled the stream until it ran bank
full. Gil rode upstream two or three miles. From there
he rode west, in a half circle. When he again reached
the fast flowing creek half a dozen miles south, he followed it north to the place where he had first approached it. While he saw no Indian sign, it told him
nothing prior to last night's heavy rain. Before the trail
drive approached the creek, it must again be scouted for
recent Indian sign. For now, it would do. When he had
rested his horse and allowed it to drink, he mounted
and rode back to meet the oncoming trail herd. By the
time the sun was two hours high, there wasn't a hint of
last night's rain. The "wet weather" streams and water

holes were only mud, and another day's sun would see them dried stone-hard, spiderwebbed with cracks.

Much to his satisfaction, Gil found that Mariposa, Estanzio, and Juan Padillo had the horses moving at the kind of gait it would take to reach Cienega Creek in a one-day drive. Gil regarded his outfit as superior to most, because his men had originally been riders for the famous Mendoza horse ranch, in Durango, Mexico. They understood and respected horses, but they also knew the limits of an animal's endurance. It was better to drive them hard all day than to have them suffer a night in dry camp. The same held true for the longhorns, but unlike horses, they knew no loyalty that inspired them to greater effort. They trailed best at a steady, comfortable walk, and when forced to exceed that, they became rebellious and mean. That was the state in which Gil found them on this day when their choice was a killing twenty-mile drive, or dry camp. While the flank riders were having their problems with bunch quitters, it would be far worse at the drag, and that was where Gil headed. With the greatly increased horse herd, Juan Padillo was working with Mariposa and Estanzio. Ramon rode the point, and Gil had shifted everybody he could spare to the drag. There was Long John, Bo, Rosa, Pedro Fagano, and Juan Alamonte. On a normal day that would have been enough, but one look at the cantankerous herd told Gil this was anything but a normal day. Rosa headed a big brindle just in time to ride madly after another that had just broken away. The rest of the riders were equally busy. Long John's horse had a bloody gash along its left flank, having been raked by a horn.

"Swap horses, Long John," Gil said, "and smear that gash with sulfur salve before the blowflies get to it."

Long John nodded and rode away. While he understood what had to be done, he wasn't neglectful. The herd had been so unruly, he couldn't be spared. Gil quickly got a taste of the kind of day they had in store. The same old stubborn brindle that Rosa had just sent bawling back to the herd again decided to back-trail. Gil tried to head him, failed, and finally was forced to rope the brute. He came up fighting, and his mad rush for Gil was cut short when Rosa caught him by the hind legs with a second loop and sent him crashing down in a bawling heap. With both cow horses holding him help-less, Gil bound his front and hind legs with piggin string.

"Three times he has run away," said Rosa.

"We'll leave him lay here awhile and fight the raw-hide," Gil said. "If he still won't trail with the rest of the herd, I'll shoot the bastard. One ornery steer can be more trouble than he's worth, and he sets a bad example for the others."

An hour down the trail, Gil rode back and cut the brindle loose. Meekly the steer trotted ahead of him until they caught up with the tag end of the drive.

"I reckon he's yer pet," said Long John with a grin.

"Yeah," said Gil. "He runs one more time today, and we'll have fresh steak for supper."

"We ain't took enough vinegar out'n 'em," said Long John. "Why don't we bust ther' backsides an' make 'em lope faster?"

"They'd just get more ornery than they are already," Gil said. "Let's see if we can't keep 'em bunched so tight they can't break loose and run. If we keep 'em moving, we'll make our twenty miles. It's the bunch quitting that's costing us. Let's close the ranks and keep 'em closed. I want them bunched so tight, none of the brutes can see anything but the ugly backside of another longhorn."

They swatted the drag steers unmercifully, until they got the idea and closed ranks. The drag animals could set the pace for the herd, as those behind, with their sharp horns provided a powerful—and painful—incen-tive for their companions ahead. By the time the sun was noon high, Gil judged they had covered ten miles. Their hard driving would get them to Cienega Creek before dark. Gil rode ahead and caught up to the horse herd.

"Estanzio," he said, "I'll take your place here. I want you to ride on to the creek and look for Indian sign. I found none this morning, but I don't want any surprises. Ride on beyond the creek a ways, and then get back to us pronto."

Estanzio rode out, and Gil felt better. While he trusted his own eyes, ears, and judgment, nobody was better at Indian sign than another Indian. The relentless sun bore down, kindling a thirst in man and beast. The longhorns, weariness and thirst added to their already cantankerous mood, made it hard on the riders. When the troublesome brindle steer again lit out down the back trail, Rosa lost her temper and her patience. She kicked her faithful Indian pony into a gallop until he was neck and neck with the big brindle steer. Rosa doubled her lariat, then doubled it again, making it a veritable club. Swinging it as hard as she could, she brought it down on the brindle's tender muzzle. Bellowing in pain and rage, he hooked at her, but her shrewd Indian pony was ahead of him. No sooner had the horse drawn away, when he darted back in, and again Rosa laid a mighty blow across the brindle's nose. Then she urged the valiant horse on until she was ahead of the stubborn steer. She was prepared to slug him again, and he apparently realized it. Wheeling, he ran to catch up to the herd. Rosa laughed and tickled the ears of her horse.

"No see Injun sign," said Estanzio when he returned.

By late afternoon there was only one lingering benefit from the last night's rain. There was no dust, and that was something for which the drag riders were thankful. Two hours away from sundown, Gil rode ahead and caught up to the horse herd. He had an idea, and he needed to talk to Estanzio, Mariposa, and Juan Padillo.

"Take the horses on to the creek," he told the trio. "With their stride, they can get there an hour ahead of the longhorns. Water them and get them on some good graze for the night. Move them well out of the way. If we get rushed for time, we may have to run the longhorns the last couple of miles."

It was the only way he could compensate for the un-predictability of the ornery longhorns. Not only would the horses be watered and safely out of the way, the Indian riders would select the graze with an eye for de-fense. Gil rode back to the herd, pausing to speak to Ramon.

"I've sent the horses on ahead. We'll keep the long-horns moving, but they can run the last two or three miles, if that's what it takes to get them to water before dark."

"Bueno," said Ramon. "You start them running, I get out of their way."

It was a controlled stampede that Gil had found ef-fective, depending on the time and place. Terrain was a big factor. A stampede, however brief, was the last thing a trail boss needed if there were deep canyons or drop-offs. But there were no such dangers these last few miles to Cienega Creek. If need be, some riders could be sent ahead to slow the herd as they neared the water, but Gil had no fear of the thirsty longhorns running beyond the creek. He had only to be sure the horses had been watered and were out of the way.

"Ye reckon we gon' make it?" Long John asked when Gil rode back to the drag.

"One way or the other," Gil replied. "I've sent the horses on ahead. Once they're watered and the creek's clear, we can stampede the longhorns the rest of the way. That's the only thing predictable about a longhorn. If he's thirsty, he won't run beyond the nearest water."

When it came to running the rest of the way to Cienega Creek, the herd made its own decision, aided by a cooling west wind. Just minutes after the sun had slipped beyond the western horizon, a playful breeze had sprung up, bringing with it the tantalizing smell of water. The lead steers lifted their heads, forgot all about how tired they were, and lit out in a dead run. The rest of the herd followed, and for the first time that long, hard day, the riders relaxed. The herd would run no farther than the creek.

"How 'bout this Cienega Creek?" Long John inquired. "Is she deep?"

"Deep," said Gil. "More like a river."

"Sincet the herd has took care o' itself fer the night," said Long John, "they's enough time 'fore dark fer me an' Bo t' try fer some fish."

"Go ahead," said Gil, "but you'll have a long ride upstream. Once those longhorns hit the creek, there won't be a fish for miles."

So Bo and Long John rode away, taking Van, Pedro Fagano, and Vicente Gomez with them.

"If there be any fish, we have plenty," said Ramon.

"I hope the others are as thoughtful as Bo and Long John," Rosa said. "When they catch fish, they clean them. The cook does not clean the fish."

The longhorns were strung out along the creek, while the horses grazed well away from it. Juan Padillo had already begun unloading the packhorses, but he was receiving no help from Mariposa or Estanzio. It was not the nature of an Indian, whatever his origin, to so demean himself.

"I'll round up some wood for a fire," Gil said. "Ramon, take a couple of riders and haze the longhorns back into a herd. Now that they've watered, there's no reason for them to graze for two miles along the creek. Our watch won't be worth a damn with them stretched halfway to Mexico."

Gil built the fire, Rosa put the three-legged iron spider in place and soon had the coffee ready. When the fishermen returned, every man with a big string of trout, Rosa threw up her hands in despair.

"Now, now," soothed Long John, "we gon' clean 'em fer ye. We jus' brung 'em back like this so's we could git here 'fore dark."

16

*D*espite the long, hard day, the outfit was elated. Even if it had been necessary for the longhorns to run the last two or three miles, they had reached Cienega Creek in a single day's drive. Rosa put a big iron skillet on the fire, rolled the trout in cornmeal, and fried them in bacon grease. It was a good camp and an excellent meal. To Gil's surprise—and probably that of everybody else—Rosa volunteered for the first watch. No more would she tempt Gil, nor would she make it convenient for any more late night arguments. Instead she spent her first watch in conversation with Bo, Long John, and Van.

"Oncet we git back t' Texas," said Long John, "I'm takin' some time an' goin' t' see my mama, back in the bayou country. Bo, he aims t' go wi' me, an' git a bait o' Cajun cookin'."

There was a depth to Bo that few of them had suspected, and before the night was over, they would regard the little cowboy with respect and awe.

"There is a legend," said Bo, "that each of us is born under a star. It influences us, directs our footsteps, and is our link with God. It shines upon us all the days of our lives, and to follow it is our destiny. When our star grows dim, we may yet be young in years, but when it dies, so do we."

"Ye soun' like my mama," said Long John. "She

reads tea leaves, coffee grounds, playin' cards, the stars, the moon, an' God knows what all else."

"*Madre de Dios,* Bo," said Rosa, "you speak like the *profeta.* If your star does not permit it, you cannot go with Long John to visit his *madre?*"

"Should my star grow dim and flame out," said Bo, "I will not be returning to Texas."

"Ye need fer my mama t' git a holt o' this damn star," said Long John, "an' figger out what it aims t' do. How'n hell can a man go anywher', er do anything, with this know-it-all star a-tellin' him he may be dead nex' week?"

Bo laughed. "Long John, how can any of us know if we'll be alive or dead next week? For that matter, even tomorrow? Our star is our friend, not limiting our days, but marking them. To worship the creation instead of the Creator is paganistic. The star is not my God, but a manifestation of Him. When your star dims, it is His way of preparing you for that which is to come."

"*Por Dios,*" said Rosa, "I have read Gil's Bible, and I think you have been reading it also. You seem to have a better understanding of it than I. Does it tell you that your star is growing dim?"

"Tonight," said Bo, "my star is at peace, as am I. But in times of great danger, the star becomes restive. I tell you none of this to frighten or sadden you, but so that you may know I enjoy each day as it is given to me. I cannot plan for next week, next month, or next year. I suppose that what I wish to say is that when my star flames out, you should have no regrets, for I will be ready. You are my friends, and I am glad that my life touches yours, however briefly, and for as long as my star permits."

Van and some of the other riders had been witness to the strange conversation. None of them had ever heard anything so profound, and in the light of what was to come, they would understand it for the premonition it had been. Darkness hid the tears in Rosa's eyes, and Long John was strangely silent. . . .

* * *

Cienega Creek had been a memorable camp, and every rider felt some reluctance in leaving it. But Gil had the longhorns on the trail at first light, driving them hard to stay within sight of the fast-moving horse remuda. This day demanded yet another twenty-mile drive, which should take them to Tucson. The visitors from the town had told Gil the herd must be driven to the south of Tucson, then west four or five miles, to Saguaro Springs. That posed a question Gil should have asked the visitors, a question that now bothered him. Had their estimate of the twenty miles from Cienega Creek to Tucson included the extra miles beyond the town, to Saguaro Springs? He suspected it had not, and once they were near enough, he must ride ahead and learn for sure just how far they must go to reach water. The longhorns had already begun to lag.

"Good water an' good graze, an' they's still cranky as hell," said Long John in disgust.

"They don't like bein' pushed this hard," Gil said. "We run them ragged yesterday, for sure, but they were rewarded with a night of good graze and plenty of water. It's a damn shame longhorns learn nothing from experience. They'll be just as mean and ornery today as they were yesterday, and they'll give us hell for our good intentions."

The longhorns had become such a trial that Bo had been forced to use a lariat, saving the unique bola for deer hunting and special occasions. The lariat could be doubled and used as a whip, a necessity in the daily battle with bunch-quitting longhorns. Rosa rode and worked as hard as any cowboy, while the nondescript Indian pony she had adopted became one of the best cow horses in the outfit.

Gil rode out when the sun was noon high, bound for Tucson. After he knew where the water was, he aimed to call on the man who bought and sold livestock. They had no need for the many horses they had taken from the Apaches. Even if there was little, or no market for beef, the horses might bring enough to supply their needs from Tucson to the goldfields. Unsure as to how far he was from his destination, Gil topped a ridge and his horse nickered. Hand on the butt of his Colt, he reined up and waited, but there was no answering nicker. Cautiously he rode down the slope, and as he emerged from a forest of fir, he couldn't believe his eyes. At the north end of the valley below was a cluster of greenery, like an oasis. His thirsty horse had scented water! Warily, he rode on. At best it could only be a spring, but why had their visitors from Tucson not mentioned it? Slowly an answer—or what might be an answer—came to him. Had they passed to the north of Tucson—and at one time, they might have—this little patch of green with its spring would have been well to the south of them. Now he suspected they had drifted off their original course and were actually somewhere to the south of Tucson. But what did it matter, if they were miles closer to water?

Gil scouted the spring, finding it more than adequate, with a good runoff. Using the sun as a guide, he estimated the trail drive could easily reach the water before dark. Tomorrow would be soon enough to correct their course and ride ahead to Tucson. He turned back to meet the herd with the good news. Not only was there water, but it was near enough that they need not kill themselves getting to it, as they had been forced to do yesterday.

"Bueno." Ramon grinned. "Is better than having cows stampede through the town."

While the horse herd had been behaving well, the longhorns had not. But once they were allowed to assume their accustomed gait, they settled down. The drag riders removed dusty bandannas from their sweaty faces and fanned themselves with their hats.

"I ain't complainin'," said Van, "but why didn't those hombres from Tucson tell us about this spring?"

"The way we were headed at that time," said Gil, "I don't think it would have mattered. I expect we're somewhere to the south of Tucson now. But we should be able to change direction and still reach Tucson within a day's drive. The important thing is, we have water for tonight."

"So we takes this hellacious long day," said Long John, "an' makes two out'n it."

"Looks that way," Gil said, "but it'll be easier on the horses, the longhorns, and us. We need that extra day, and the only reason we weren't takin' it was because we thought the next water was beyond Tucson."

"We have not drifted far enough south, then," said Bo, "for tomorrow's drive to become a hardship."

"I doubt it," said Gil. "I'll ride out at first light, find out just how far we are to the south of Tucson, and get us back on course. Right now, I couldn't be more satisfied. Some of a man's mistakes turn out for the best, thank God."

He was looking at Rosa, but she seemed not to have heard. Gil rode on ahead, and catching up to the horse herd, decided to use the procedure that had worked so well at Cienega Creek. He gave the same orders to Estanzio, Mariposa, and Juan Padillo as he had the day before.

"Give it another hour, and then take the horses on to the spring. It has a pretty good runoff, but the steers will hog it all. Water the horses and move them down the valley to graze. Once you've done that, split up and ride beyond the spring a ways. I didn't see any Indian sign near the spring, but I didn't take the time to ride any farther."

Sundown was just minutes away when the longhorns reached the ridge from which Gil had first sighted the spring. While there was no betraying breeze, the water was close enough. Just as it had excited Gil's horse, it had a similar effect on the longhorns. Bawling their eagerness, the leaders tore off down the slope, the rest of the herd close behind.

"I believe in givin' credit where credit's due," said

Van, "and sending the horses to water ahead of the longhorns is a plumb good idea."

"That it is," Long John agreed. "Them longhorn bastards would of gored half the hoss herd by now."

Gil grinned at the unexpected praise and said nothing. When they got to the spring, Juan Padillo had unloaded the packhorses and had filled the coffeepot before the longhorns had invaded the spring. Van and Long John soon found enough wood for the supper fire.

"Ramon," said Gil, "take a couple of riders, and as the longhorns drink, drive them off a ways. If they're still thirsty, let them drink from the runoff. I purely can't stomach drinkin' from a spring when there's a cow standin' belly deep in it."

"I did not think a Tejano drank from a spring unless a cow *was* standing in it," said Rosa.

The riders laughed, Long John howled, and there were rare grins from the usually impassive Mariposa and Estanzio.

May 17, 1850. South of Tucson, Arizona Territory

"Let's move 'em out!" shouted Gil.

So sure was he of their having drifted off course, he headed the drive to the northwest, and then rode out ahead of it. He would find the town, locate the water, and again change the course of the trail drive, should it be necessary. Yesterday they had traveled a good twelve miles. Added to today's drive would be the miles they had drifted to the south, but he didn't believe it would increase the distance enough to hurt them. Gil had ridden about ten miles when he heard the faint but distinct barking of a dog. He reined up, listening. He reasoned there wouldn't be an Indian camp so near the white man's town, so it had to be the cabin—or at least the camp—of a settler or rancher. He rode due north, and was rewarded when the yipping of the dog grew louder. Finally there was another sound that assured him he was, indeed, nearing civilization. It was the crowing of a rooster, and Gil grinned in appreciation as the fowl crowed again. He couldn't recall having heard a rooster crow since leaving Missouri, in '33. They'd had occasional eggs and fried chicken at the Bandera ranch only because Dorinda, Van's wife, had come from a farm. Since the Jabez farm was but a few miles south of San Antonio, Van was always swapping beef for eggs, poultry, pork, and vegetables. Pangs of guilt reminded Gil that Rosa had wanted chickens of her own and he had refused. He vowed, once they returned to Texas, that she would have the fowls, and a big red rooster to go with them. That was, *if* she returned to Texas with him. When he rode into a clearing, he found himself approaching a barn, and it was substantial, built from logs. In an adjoining corral there were four mules, sleek and well-fed.* This must be, as Long John had once suggested, mining country, requiring "mule work."

Gil rode past the barn, and by the time he could see the log house beyond a stand of oaks, the dog had discovered him. Gil rode on, reached the yard and reined up. The house was as substantial as the barn, the morning sun reflecting off a glass windowpane. Smoke curled lazily from a stone chimney, and there was a long porch that covered three-quarters of the front of the log house.

"Hello the house!" Gil shouted.

There was no immediate response. Finally the front door eased open a little, and it was a foregone conclusion that whoever stood behind it had a gun. This was still very much the frontier. Gil needed more than a simple hello. He tried again.

"I'm Gil Austin, trail boss for a cattle drive. We're

---

* William Becknell opened a trade route from Missouri to Santa Fe in 1821. The first "Missouri" mules were brought into the southwest over what was to become the famous Santa Fe Trail. Half a century after Becknell's initial journey, the Santa Fe Railroad followed the same route as had the trail.

aimin' to spend a day or two at Tucson, but we're a mite unsure of our direction. We met Vento Henneagar on the trail, if that means anything."

The door eased open enough for a skinny, bearded old fellow to emerge. He limped, seemed old enough to have come with the territory, and held onto what looked like a Hawken long gun.

"Lot o' folks knows Vento," he grunted. "Don't mean diddly."

Gil laughed. "I reckon, but my Texas outfit gunned down a pair of Mex sidewinders that had ambushed Tucson's sheriff and his deputy. Vento seemed to take that as a favor, and told us to come on. Said his brother buys and sells livestock, and we hope to sell some cows, and maybe some horses."

"Wal, now," said the old-timer, more jovial, "thet's better. Vento's my oldest boy, an' he owns the mercantile. Gid's the youngest, an' he's got the livery. Owns the livestock barn too. Me, I'm Jeremiah, too damn old an' stove up fer anything 'cept keepin' the varmints off the place. But by the Eternal, I can still shoot."

"You got the best there is," said Gil. "A Hawken."

"Damn right," said Jeremiah, pleased. "Git down an' rest yer saddle."

"Like to," said Gil, "and likely I'll see you again before we move on, but I need to know where I am in regards to Tucson. I'll need to get back to the trail drive and aim them toward the nearest water. Vento said that's Saguaro Springs, a ways west of town."

"Reckon he's right, if they's that many critters in yer herd. Ridin' west from here, it ain't more'n three miles t' town. Yer maybe six miles from the springs now."

"Thanks," said Gil. "I won't have to check out the water, but since I'm this close, I'll ride in and say howdy to Gid and Vento. Keep that big Hawken loaded and handy."

"Keeno," said Jeremiah Henneagar, standing a bit straighter. "Ride careful, Texas."

Established by the Spanish, Tucson was almost three

centuries old, and it was considerably more than just a village. There were no mud huts, leantos, or temporary shelter. The very least of the structures was log, and a few were of seasoned, dressed lumber, freighted in from God knew where. A much more common building material was adobe brick. Many a roof was of pine or cedar shake, some of them greened over with moss, attesting to their many years of service. Vento Henneagar's store was a low, lumber-constructed, flat-roofed building. It had the name across the false front in neat, black letters: V. HENNEAGAR'S MERCANTILE. If Vento ever had a son, Gil thought with amusement, they'd have to enlarge the building to get the boy's name on the front. Vento Henneagar was alone in the store, since it wasn't too far from the noon hour. He seemed shorter and heavier than Gil remembered, probably because he wore shoes instead of boots, and no hat.

"Well," he said, affably enough, "I see you made it. Any trouble?"

"Nothin' we couldn't handle." Gil grinned. "We strayed a mite too far south, and spent the night at a spring we didn't know was there."

"I thought of that, after we left you," said Henneagar, embarrassed. "It wasn't that much out of your way, and would have made a good stop between Cienega Creek and here. But you know that now."

"No harm done," said Gil, and changed the subject. "I rode in to say howdy to you and your brother Gid. I stopped by your house, and your daddy was about to bore me with his long gun until I convinced him who I was."

"Jeremiah and his Hawken." Henneagar laughed. "That's why we almost never have Indian trouble around here. You don't believe it, just ask him."

Gil mounted and rode on down the dusty street toward the livery and the distant livestock barn. He continued to marvel at the town. Even the saloons looked to have been there a hundred years. One of them had a giant four-armed saguaro growing out front that was taller than the flat-roofed building. The place was appropriately named the Cactus Saloon. Another, blatantly catering to miners, called itself the Pick and Shovel. Quickly, a man turned from the doorway back into the dim interior of the saloon. For a moment he seemed familiar, like someone Gil should know. As he rode past, a few people watched him curiously from open doors. He dismounted before the livery, half-hitching his reins to the rail. The sign across the front simply said LIVERY, not mentioning the owner's name. A lesser sign above the door said *Blacksmith. Horses and mules shod.* Gil stepped into a small but neat office, and found it empty. He was about to depart the way he had come in when a second door opened and he found himself facing the younger Henneagar. Gid's features and build were similar to Vento's, and Gil saw little difference between the two, except the years. And the sheriff's star on Gid's vest. Gil spoke.

"I'm Gil Austin, trail boss for a Texas trail drive. I met Vento a few days ago. My outfit gunned down a pair of killers who had ambushed your sheriff and his deputy. I see you won the star."

"Won, hell," said the younger Henneagar, "we cut the cards and I lost."

He didn't smile when he said it, and Gil changed the subject.

"The herd's on the way, and should be at Saguaro Springs by sundown. We aim to be here maybe a couple of days. Vento says you buy and sell livestock. We need to sell some horses, and maybe some beef. Interested?"

"I'd be more interested in some good mules," said Henneagar. "Beef, if the price is right. Horses, they'd have to be mighty cheap."

"Big Texas steers," said Gil, "two-year-olds or better, ought to average twelve hundred pounds. I figure thirty dollars a head. Forty-five horses, Apache broke. Make me an offer."

"Seventy-five steers at twenty-five dollars a head. The horses I'd have to see."

"You have a deal on the steers," said Gil. "Why don't you ride out in the morning and look at the horses?"

"I'll do that," said Henneagar.

Gil took that for dismissal and turned toward the door.

"Austin?"

Gil turned back to face the livestock buyer turned sheriff.

"You and your riders are welcome for as long as you care to stay," said Henneagar, "but I want no trouble."

"None of my riders will start any trouble, Henneagar," said Gil.

Gil closed the door behind him and stepped out on the boardwalk. He wondered what had prompted the warning, but it didn't matter. His promise had carried a warning of his own. While he and his riders wouldn't start any trouble, neither would they run from it. A Texan was a breed unto himself, and while he might not have started the trouble, he would be there until the finish of it.

Gil was elated to learn that his change in direction had been exactly right. When he left Tucson, he rode southeast, and within four or five miles he met the horse herd. He couldn't see the longhorns, but he saw their dust; his riders were pushing them hard. Juan Padillo rode ahead of the horse herd to meet him. Juan grinned, anticipating the welcome news he saw in Gil's expression.

"We're maybe four miles from town," Gil said, "and the water's three miles beyond. We'll sell some steers for sure, and some horses maybe. Get the word to Mariposa and Estanzio. There'll be more supplies, ammunition, clothes, horseshoes, and maybe eggs for breakfast."

"Bueno," said Juan. He swatted his dusty hat against his thigh and rode ahead to meet the oncoming horse herd. Gil waved his own hat to Mariposa and Estanzio as he rode past the now visible lead steers. The herd was moving fast enough to keep the horse remuda in sight, and for just a moment Gil paused to speak to Ramon. The flank riders would get the word from Ramon, and Gil rode on to the drag. Van, Long John, Rosa, Pedro Fagano, and Vicente Gomez were riding drag. They whooped their excitement as Gil rode in among them, speaking loud enough for all to hear.

"Only seventy-five cows," said Rosa, "and it is almost two thousand dollars."

"It's been so long," said Van, "I didn't know Texas steers could still be swapped for honest-to-God money. We've swapped beef for vegetables, ham, and frying chicken until I can't imagine gettin' anything else."

Gil laughed. "Get used to it. I only asked thirty, and settled for twenty-five. We'll get three times that in the goldfields."

Gid Henneagar watched Gil ride away, and he shifted his pistol belt, the unaccustomed weight of the Colt bothering him. He was no gunman, and while he had accepted Gil's promise at face value, he'd be uneasy with this Texas outfit in town. He had known Texans before, and they were all men with the bark on, willing to fight at the drop of a hat. If you didn't have a hat, they'd loan you one, and then drop it for you. While they might not start trouble, they'd sure as hell finish any that came their way. Tucson's reluctant sheriff already had one potential troublemaker in town. A saddle tramp had ridden in a few days ago, had begun haunting the saloons and taking more than his share of winnings from the poker tables. He wore a tied-down Colt and had the look of a killer. He apparently had no intention of leaving, and the town had begun to look questioningly at its new sheriff. What could he do? There were no laws against gambling, and for that matter, none against "slick dealing," unless the victim had a fast gun to back up his charge. While there had been a few complaints, none of the miners felt froggy enough to jump the visiting hardcase. Just maybe, thought Sheriff Henneagar, he might welcome this Texas outfit after all. Once they sold some steers and had some money, they would visit the saloons. He could imagine, with some satisfaction, these Texas cowboys buying into a poker game and having this slick-dealing Morgan Pinder clean them out. Sheriff Henneagar grinned to himself.

Morgan Pinder, standing in the doorway of the Pick and Shovel saloon, had immediately recognized Gil Austin as he rode toward Henneagar's livery. Pinder had hastily retreated into the dim interior of the saloon, hoping that the Texas trail boss hadn't recognized him. Hate flamed anew in Pinder. He had been tortured and humiliated by the Texan, and, afraid for his very life, forced out of the Clanton gang. Now he would have his revenge. He had no doubt the Texans would be in town for a day or two, and he vowed a pair of them would die. One was the high-handed trail boss, and the other was that Indian bastard who'd used a Bowie on him.

Once the trail drive was near Tucson, Gil sent the horse remuda ahead, so they would reach the springs well ahead of the longhorns. There they would again be watered and driven to graze before the longhorns arrived. It was one of those rare good days when the big Texas steers were not thirst-crazed and were driven in an orderly fashion to the water.

"Any of us goin' to town tonight?" Van asked.

"No reason for us to," Gil said. "We're broke. Gid Henneagar's goin' to ride out in the morning to look at the horses and deal with us for the longhorns. Tomorrow afternoon, and maybe tomorrow night, we'll all have a chance to go in and buy what we need."

17

∗⁓✦⁓∗

Nothing disturbed the silence of that first night near Tucson. Even though they would be here several days, habit had them all up and about before first light.

"Estanzio," Gil said, "you and Mariposa decide how many horses ought to be reshod. Any shoe that may wear thin before we reach the goldfields, let's replace it now. We'll take some extras with us to replace thrown shoes, but let's head off as many as we can, by replacing them here. First thing we'll do, once we collect for the steers, is replenish horseshoes and nails."

"Bueno," said Mariposa. "No shoe Apach' hoss?"

"No," said Gil. "We have entirely too many horses, and with Mendoza breeding stock, I can't see wasting time with anything less. Once you know how many must be reshod, the rest of us will help you."

Neither Mariposa or Estanzio said anything. With the help of Solano, they had prepared the horse remuda for the trail. Gil had a suspicion the pair wanted to replace all the spent shoes themselves. It would be hot, dirty work, and they'd get no argument from the rest of the outfit. But Gil always felt guilty when the Indian duo undertook such a task, although he knew the pride they took in the horses.

When Gid Henneagar arrived, he wasn't alone. Vento was with him.

"I'd like to look at those steers," said Vento. "Might take twenty-five myself and make it an even hundred, if you'll part with that many."

"No problem," said Gil. "Got forty-five Apache horses too. All broke to ride, far as we know."

"Didn't know the Apaches was hoss traders," Vento said.

"We didn't trade for these." Gil grinned. "More like a gift. Apaches stampeded our horse herd one night and took half our remuda. When we took our horses back, we took theirs. Partly for our trouble, but mostly to keep them off our trail. Texans don't usually hold with horse thieving, but we occasionally make exceptions."

Vento laughed, appreciating the boldness of the act. Gid, who didn't seem like the laughing kind, managed a grin. He left them, going to take a closer look at the horses.

"Be worth more," said Vento, "if they was mules."

"That's what Gid already told me," Gil said.

"Mus' be lots o' minin' here," said Long John. "That's mule work."

"Yes," said Vento, "and a good mule's worth fifty dollars. Most of ours are trailed in from Santa Fe."

When Gid Henneagar returned, he didn't look too enthusiastic about the Apache horses.

"Five dollars a head," he said. "At that, they may die of old age in my corral."

"You got a deal," Gil said. "We'll drive them in, along with the steers."

"The traders will be in from Santa Fe in July," said Vento. "Maybe you can trade them for some mules."

"Maybe," said Gid. Clearly that's what he had in mind, and he cast a warning look at Vento, who laughed.

Gil appeared not to notice, and the pair rode back toward town.

"He's a horse trader," said Van, "and he'll double or triple his money. We might do the same, if we took that bunch of ponies on to the goldfields."

"Maybe," said Gil, "but they're more trouble than they're worth. We're selling beef, because that's what's needed. Be our luck for every jaybird in California to already have a horse."

"For twenty-five more cows and the horses," said Rosa, "it will become a fortune. It is almost three thousand dollars."

"I'll divvy the money from the sale of the horses among all of you," Gil said. "That'll be about nineteen dollars for each rider, and since we're selling a hundred steers, I'll add enough to that so each of you will have seventy-five dollars. That ought to make a visit to town worthwhile. But we don't all go at the same time. Those of you who drive the steers and the horses to Henneagar's corral can do your town visitin' while you're there. Soon as I make a deal for horseshoes and nails, I'll be ridin' back to camp. There's a pile of work to be done."

While the riders cut out a hundred head of steers and rounded up the Apache horses, Gil caught up a pair of packhorses. He had decided Rosa would go to town first, because he didn't want her there after dark. With her, he was sending Van, Long John, Ramon, Juan Padillo, Bo, and Vicente Gomez. He wanted the majority of the outfit back with the herd before dark. Town held no interest for Mariposa and Estanzio. They would remain in camp to see that the horses were properly reshod. Fortunately there was more than enough horseshoes and nails to keep them busy until Gil could return with what he intended to buy.

"Come on in the office," said Gid Henneagar once the horses and the steers were safely in his corrals.

Gil and the riders had gotten plenty of attention driving the horses and longhorns through town. This was the frontier, all right, Gil thought. Ten o'clock in the morning, and all the saloons were open.

"Vento arranged for me to pay for his steers along with mine," said Gid. "You'll have to take gold. We got no confidence in anybody's paper out here."

Gil laughed. "My kind of town. Now I'll do some business with you. We have forty horses that need to be reshod. I'll need shoes and nails."

While Henneagar went about supplying Gil's needs, Gil went out to the corrals and gave each of the riders their promised seventy-five dollars.

"Now," said Rosa, "I can buy some new clothes for Bo, to replace those I have ruined."

"Me," said Long John, "I'm gonna buy me 'nother Colt. Man cain't have too many Colts."

"New boots for me," Van said. "Moccasins are better than barefooted, but I purely feel like a digger Injun without my boots."

"Remember," said Gil, "the rest of the outfit will want to spend some time in town. Give it three or four hours and then give the others a chance. Go easy in the saloons."

Gil took his two packhorses and rode to Vento's store. He could go back to the livery on his way out of town. On pages torn from a tally book, he had listed what they needed to replenish their supplies. For the first time in years he was not buying on credit, or limited only to items for which there was a dire need. He knew of only two things Mariposa and Estanzio would want from the white man's store: tobacco and rock candy.

Gil had just passed the Pick and Shovel saloon, when there was a shot, and the slug snatched the hat off his head. He piled out of the saddle, Colt in his hand, running toward the saloon. The shot had drawn one man to the door, but when he saw Gil coming, he ducked back inside. Thinking it unlikely the shot had come from within the saloon, Gil headed for the rear of the building. He smelled burnt powder and found boot prints, but that was all. He kicked open the back door of the saloon and stepped inside.

"What'n hell's goin' on?" shouted one of the three men at the bar.

Gil said nothing, walking the length of the room. From the front door, he could see Van and Long John coming on the run. From the opposite direction came Sheriff Gid Henneagar, and several men had just left the barbershop. Gil waited. He didn't intend to tell it but once. Henneagar was first in the door, the others on his heels.

"Did you fire that shot?" the sheriff demanded.

"No," Gil replied. "Somebody shot at me from behind the saloon. He got away before I could get back there. I'm thinkin' he might have ducked in here through the back door."

The three patrons at the bar began to look uncomfortable. Henneagar turned to the barkeep.

"Harvey, has anybody been in or out through that back door in the past few minutes?"

"Nobody went out," said Harvey, "and nobody come in, 'cept the gent right next to you. Kicked the door open and come in with a pistol in his hand."

"He's right," said one of the men at the bar. "Wasn't nobody in here but us, an' we ain't went out."

This was getting them nowhere. Gil pushed through the swinging doors, Van and Long John following.

"Mebbe we oughta mosey along wi' ye," said Long John.

"No," said Gil. "Take care of your business here, and don't stay longer than you have to. We don't know if somebody just has it in for me, or if I just happened to be the best target. He might take a shot at any one of you."

Gil got his ventilated hat, loosed the reins of the horses, and swung into the saddle. Leading the packhorses, he rode on to Vento's store. Rosa stood on the long porch, her eyes full of questions. Gil dismounted and half-hitched the reins of his horse and the lead ropes of the packhorses to the rail. Then he turned to Rosa.

"Somebody took a shot at me," he said. "I'll be in the store awhile, and then I'll have to go back by the livery. When I leave, I want you ready to ride out with me."

Her eyes on the hole in the crown of his hat, she

didn't argue. Instead she returned to the store, and Gil followed. When they were finished, Gil secured their purchases on one of the packhorses and they rode on to Gid Henneagar's livery. Henneagar had stashed the horseshoes and nails in four open-topped wooden kegs.

"Any idea who might have been shooting at you?" the sheriff inquired.

"No," Gil said. "There's some, I reckon, that'd like to cash in my chips, but I don't know of any this far west. Anyway, we won't be in town that long. Another day at most."

Gil and Rosa rode out, Gid Henneagar thoughtfully watching them go. It was just as well he didn't know that Gil only wanted to get Rosa out of town.

Gil had decided that once Van, Long John, and the other riders returned to camp, he would allow the rest of the outfit to ride in, and he would go with them. If somebody wanted him dead, the bastard wouldn't stop in Tucson, and Gil Austin purely didn't aim to dodge a bushwhacker all the way to California. With himself as bait, he would end it here. Now that he knew he was in danger, he had an edge. He would do some sniping on his own, and the hunter would become the hunted.

Morgan Pinder hid out in the brush, cursing himself for having missed a perfect opportunity. Now he had to stay out of town and out of sight until dark, lest he be recognized. All this Texas outfit had seen him clearly as the Indian had tortured him. If any one of them saw him now, they'd know he had tried to kill their trail boss, and he'd be hunted down like a coyote. Sweat dripping off his chin and burning his eyes, he hunched in the meager shade of some greasewood, longing for the cool gloom of the saloon. The time dragged. Impatient, he considered sneaking to the springs where the herd was, and trying for a shot at the hated Indian. Then he recalled how Estanzio had moved like a shadow, taking him captive in total darkness. What chance did he have in broad daylight? Morgan Pinder shuddered, sleeved the sweat from his face and waited for the night.

Within two hours after Gil and Rosa had returned to the herd, the rest of the riders who had gone to town rode in. Those yet to visit Tucson had been given the money Gil had promised them, but only Juan Alamonte, Manuel Armijo, Domingo Chavez, and Pedro Fagano would be going. While Mariposa and Estanzio had accepted the gold, they had declined a trip to town. As soon as the first riders returned, and before the last four rode out, Gil spoke to them all.

"As those of you who were in town know, and as the rest of you are about to find out, somebody tried to ambush me this morning. Those of you who have yet to ride into town, I'm asking you to tend to your business and return as soon as you can. Maybe this bushwhacker tried for me because I was alone and the best target, but I don't know that he won't cut down on some of you if he gets the chance. I believe, or at least I hope, he's just gunning for me. If he is, I aim to give him a chance he can't pass up. I'm riding back to town for as much of the night as it takes to end this thing. While he's hunting me, I'll be hunting him."

"That's a damn fool scheme," said Van. "Take some of us along to watch your back."

"No," said Gil, "it has to look like a sure thing, and it won't with some of you following me. Van, you're in charge, whatever happens."

While Gil was saddling his horse, Rosa went to him with a final plea.

"I fear for you," she said, "and I wish you would not do this thing."

"It has to end here, Rosa. Would you like it any better if I ran away from this, only to be shot in the back somewhere along the trail? Besides, if he fills me full of lead, it might solve your problems where I'm concerned."

He had said it as a joke, but she ignored his grin.

"I do not wish to have my problem with you solved in that way."

"Then you *do* care," he said, serious now. "A little, anyhow."

"I will always care, and you know it. Even if I must leave you, I would not wish you hurt or dead. I do not want you tempting this bushwhacker. It does not matter to you that I care this much?"

"It matters," Gil replied, "but there are things a man has to do if he aims to go on callin' himself a man. A woman's got no right to set limits, and if that's your test for my carin', then I reckon I've failed it."

He mounted and rode away without looking back. Reaching town, he found the horses of his four riders tied outside Vento Henneagar's store. He wanted them out of town, reducing this conflict to the simplest possible terms: himself against the unknown gunman. Since it was Saturday, the stores would be open late, and the saloons maybe all night.

A good two hours before sundown, Gil stopped in a little café and had supper. There was roast pork, potatoes, onions, and apple pie. Twenty-five cents seemed a little high, but it was a good meal, and Gil enjoyed it. He hoped he could rid himself of this bushwhacker in time for them to have one quiet day in town before they moved on. He would have enjoyed treating Rosa to a town-cooked meal. Now he doubted she would go with him. He figured he was on the bad side of her again, which would diminish the pleasure of the first cash money they'd had in a coon's age. With time on his hands, he lingered in the café. When he stepped out the door, he saw the hitch rail at Vento's was free of horses. His riders had gone elsewhere. Except for the saloons and the cafés, there were few other places a man could go. He thought, after his warning, they had already ridden back to the herd. Gil went into the store and found Vento Henneagar alone.

"Vento, I need to know about the country between

here and Fort Yuma. I need to know where the water is. Want me to bring you some supper from the café?"

"Thanks," said Vento, "but I have a late dinner on Saturday, and delay supper until I close. Gid's got his bowels in an uproar 'cause somebody took a shot at you this morning."

"Somebody did," Gil replied, "but I aim to ride out alive, for my sake as well as Gid's. That star he's wearin' is gettin' mighty heavy."

"I know," Vento sighed. "Makin' him sheriff was a mistake, but nobody wanted the job. You know Jeremiah, our daddy. He shamed Gid into takin' the star. Jeremiah's an old stove-up mountain man, and he's never been satisfied with Gid and me living in town, running a business. Gid's been touchy as a bronc with a burr under his tail ever since he pinned on that sheriff's star. There's some hardcase that's been here a few days, hanging around the saloons, living off his poker winnings. Slick dealer, I hear. Gid looks for trouble, and he's no gunman. But this Morgan Pinder is. Wears his Colt low, like a real gun-throwin' killer."

"Sounds like a bad one," said Gil, with no change in his expression. "I reckon I'll mosey on; there's somethin' I have to take care of."

"What about the country between here and Fort Yuma?"

"It'll wait," said Gil. "I'll get with you before we leave."

Warily Gil left the store. Now he recalled the man who had seemed so familiar yesterday, the man who had ducked hurriedly into the saloon. Gil had no doubt it was the same man who had shot at him this morning, and it left him facing a dilemma. Should he confide in the nervous Gid Henneagar, or just do what had to be done? The sheriff obviously had his pride, since he hadn't mentioned the troublesome Morgan Pinder to him. Now, confronted with the virtual certainty that Pinder had fired at him, what would Sheriff Gid Henneagar do? Gil had no trouble answering that question.

The nervous sheriff would get himself shot dead. Gid was just stuffy enough, prideful enough, to allow his vanity to override his common sense, and Gil decided what the younger Henneagar didn't know might save his life. Though it wasn't even dark, the saloons were tuning up for the night. Gil shouldered his way through the bat wings of the Pick and Shovel.

"I'm lookin' for Morgan Pinder," said Gil to everybody in general and nobody in particular.

The room became suddenly quiet. Finally a brawny, red-faced man kicked his chair back from the table and stood up.

"What might you be wantin' that bastard for? You a friend of his'n?"

"I'm a Texan," Gil responded quietly, "and where I come from, we don't bother answerin' a man's questions that are none of his business."

"Siddown, Charlie," growled the barkeep, sensing trouble. He turned to Gil and spoke. "We ain't seen Pinder today, and if we never see him again, it'll be too soon."

Gil visited the other four saloons, receiving the same answers, the same negative response. Following his unsuccessful ambush, Pinder was laying low. He was the kind who wouldn't try again until he had an edge. He would wait for darkness. Since Gil had nothing to do except wander about town, it was inevitable that he would encounter the sheriff.

"You've made all the saloons," said Henneagar, "and you're not a drinking man. It's like you're lookin' for somebody."

"No law against walkin' in a saloon and out again," Gil replied.

"None that I know of," said Henneagar, moving on down the boardwalk.

Gil watched him go. The sheriff knew he was looking for Morgan Pinder. Add that to Pinder having disappeared for the day, and the nervous sheriff also knew *why* he was looking for Pinder. Gil only hoped Henneagar had the good sense to stay out of it, now that his riders were out of town and he was free to hunt Pinder without interference. But now, when it was shoot or be shot, how could he be sure this dedicated but inept sheriff wouldn't be caught in the cross fire?

Gil had thought Gid Henneagar was bound for Vento's store, but somebody from the barbershop called to the sheriff, and he went there. Hurriedly, Gil crossed the street to Vento Henneagar's store. He needed help, and Vento was the only man he could turn to. The older Henneagar was alone in the store, and Gil didn't waste any time.

"Vento, Gid may walk in before I finish, so I'll lay the important part on you first. I know who tried to bushwhack me, and I aim to settle with him. I've managed to keep my outfit in camp, but now it looks like I might have Gid in my way. Is there any way you can get him off the street for a while?"

"Since he took the star," said Vento, "he's got night help at the livery. But he'll fill in for me in a pinch. If I was sick, I could keep him here until maybe ten or eleven."

"How are you feeling?"

"Great," said Vento, "but I could be feelin' poorly by the time Gid gets here."

"For his sake and mine," said Gil, "keep him here as long as you can."

Without awaiting Vento's response, Gil left the store, just as the new sheriff left the barbershop.

When Gil had ridden away, Van sat down beside the dejected Rosa.

"He said that if his going was a test of his feelings for me, that he has failed," said Rosa. "Why must a man get himself killed to prove he is a man? I have demanded no proof."

"He's demanding it of himself," said Van. "It's something he has to do."

"You said it is a fool scheme."

"It is," Van replied, "but there is no better way. He'll have to settle it here or risk being shot in the back when he's least expecting it. I'd have gone with him if it had been possible, but if half the outfit was there watching his back, the killer would just ride away and wait for a better chance."

"Will he . . . can he . . . win against one so devious and cowardly?"

"I think so," said Van, "and more important, so does he. It isn't that he wouldn't have liked for some of us to side him. He has to make the odds look good enough for the bushwhacker to come after him."

"If he is right, then I will have to admit that I was wrong. But *was* I wrong, not wishing to see him shot dead?"

"No," Van said, "you were not wrong in that. You were wrong only in trying to stop him from doing what he had to do. Gil can be mule stubborn, but I think he knows why you didn't want him to go. I'd leave it alone. When he rides in with no bullet holes and no blood leakin' out, that ought to satisfy his ego."

Once it was dark, Gil rode from one end of the town to the other and back again. When he passed a saloon or store where lamplight bled through a window or open door, he kept to the far side of the street. But nothing happened. The bait must become more attractive, and the odds must be bettered in favor of the bushwhacker. Gil rode almost to Gid Henneagar's livery, dismounting before the last saloon on the street. It was called the Silver Dollar, and it suited his purpose in several ways. Since it was at the very end of the street, who could doubt that he would ride back the way he had come? Next to the saloon, along the way he would ride, there were no less than three dark, vacant buildings. Once he left the saloon, there was all the cover a bushwhacker could ask. Gil slipknotted his reins to the hitching rail and shoved in through the saloon's swinging doors. While he wasn't a drinking man, he could stand an occa-

sional beer, and he ordered one. He needed some excuse to remain in the saloon awhile. He feigned interest
in a poker game for a few minutes, and then stood
through another beer at the bar. Judging he had been
there half an hour, he pushed back through the swinging
doors.

It was still too early for the moon, and in the dim
starlight the three vacant buildings stood dark and silent. Earlier Gil had decided that the space between the
first and second, or between the second and third,
would provide excellent cover for his bushwhacker. That
meant as he rode even with the killer, Pinder would
have only a few seconds to shoot before he passed into
the protective shadow of the next building. Pinder
would have to wait behind the Silver Dollar so the bushwhacker would know when he left the saloon. The hitching rail extended along the boardwalk toward the first of
the three vacant buildings, and Gil had purposely tied
his horse a little away from the front of the saloon. If
Pinder were hiding behind the saloon, he must be able
to see Gil mount. Pinder might shoot from there, but
Gil doubted it, because the saloon's back door was
open. Gil counted on Pinder taking the safest position,
with less risk to himself, and that had to be between two
of the vacant buildings.

Loosing his reins from the hitch rail, Gil took his time
mounting, as though he might have had one drink too
many. Once he had passed into the shadow of the first
darkened building, he stepped out of the saddle, the
reins in his left hand. In his right he held his Colt. The
horse kept walking, Gil between it and the dark, vacant
buildings. Just as they came even with the darkened gap
between the first two structures, from the narrow tunnel
of darkness came the roar of a Colt. The lead went high,
perfect to knock a man out of his saddle. But there was
no rider in the saddle. Gil crouched on the ground and
fired three times. Once at the muzzle flame, again to the
right, and a third time to the left of it. There was a

cough, a groan, and then silence. But the silence was short-lived. The Silver Dollar emptied in a hurry.

"Who's shootin'?" somebody bawled.

"The shooting's over," Gil answered. "Somebody took a shot at me, and I shot back. One of you ride down to Henneagar's store and get the sheriff. Tell him to bring a lantern."

Gid Henneagar came at a mad gallop, the lighted lantern swinging wildly. In his eagerness to dismount, he almost fell off the horse.

"Sheriff," said Gil, "I just shot the bushwhacker who shot at me earlier today. His name is Morgan Pinder. He's a killer and a thief, part of an outlaw gang that jumped us in New Mexico Territory. I'll be around for the hearing or inquest, or whatever the law requires."

"Inquest, hell," growled a voice. "Drag the slick-dealin' son off in the brush fer the coyotes an' buzzards."

Gid Henneagar, accompanied by a pair of the saloon patrons, had gone in between the buildings and confirmed the identity of the dead man. Morgan Pinder had played out his last hand.

"My God," said one of the men who had seen the body, "three shots, three hits. That's some shootin' in the dark. Mister, you must be thunder and forked lightnin' in daylight."

"Sheriff," said Gil, "unless you have some objection, I'm ridin' back to my outfit. I'll see you again before we move out."

"Ride on," said Henneagar. "Self-defense if I ever saw it. Anybody disagree with that?"

"Hell, no," said a voice. "We oughta pass the hat an' raise a reward."

There were shouts of agreement, but Gil heard no more. He mounted and rode out, feeling no elation. A burden had been lifted, but there was only relief. It was still early, but Gil sang out so the riders on watch knew who he was. Feeling safe with the nearness of town, Rosa still had a small fire going, and the coffee was hot.

"Morgan Pinder," said Gil as the riders gathered around. He told them nothing more, nor did he need to. He was alive, and that told them the rest. Rosa poured coffee from the big pot into a pewter cup, bringing it to him.

"I am glad you are unharmed," she said.

Strong on her mind were the hard words they'd had. She turned away.

"Rosa."

She turned to him, expecting retribution. If he spoke unkindly, hadn't he earned the right? But he surprised her, and perhaps himself.

"Rosa, it'll be safe enough in town now. Would you like to ride in for Sunday dinner tomorrow? We'll eat at a café."

"I would like that," she said. "I have never eaten in a café before."

Gil sipped his coffee, more at peace with himself than he'd been for weeks. For the first time in years he had gold—more than two thousand dollars—from the sale of Texas steers. He estimated they were at least halfway in their conquest of this California Trail. Surely, he thought, the frontier could not imperil and punish them any more than it already had. But on the trail ahead, it could and would. At Fort Yuma . . .

18

Gil's second day in Tucson was as tranquil as the first had been hectic. He found himself an unwilling celebrity for having rid the town of the arrogant, troublesome Morgan Pinder. He first became aware of his notoriety when he took Rosa to Sunday dinner at the café and they wouldn't take his money. Later, when Bo, Van, Long John, and several other riders came in, they also were not allowed to pay.

"Damn it," said Gil, to the amusement of his outfit, "this is embarrassing. I shot Pinder because he was trying to kill me, not to get myself set up as a gunfighter."

"Ye should of jus' bored him oncet." Long John chuckled. "Takes a real heller with a pistol t' shoot three times an' git three hits, even in daylight. Ye done it in the dark, an' t' be honest, I couldn't of done better myself. Like it er not, ye got the name of a real pistolero."

"We can take the herd on to California," Van jibed, "if you wanta stay here and run for sheriff."

Rosa laughed and Gil grinned, trying to ignore them. But it wasn't easy, ignoring a whole town. Vento Henneagar closed his store on Sunday, and Gil rode out to the house. He still needed to know something about the country west of Tucson. The dog announced his arrival, and was called off by Jeremiah Henneagar.

"Git down an' come in," the old man bawled. "Pleasure t' meet an honest-t'-God fightin' man."

Vento rescued Gil from the old mountain man, who wanted to talk about the very thing Gil wished to avoid.

"Jeremiah," Vento said, "I promised Austin some information on the trail between here and Fort Yuma. We have some talkin' to do."

"Wal, I got some talk of my own," said old Jeremiah. "Some gun talk, somethin' we never hear much of in these parts."

It was an obvious slap at the "town living" of his sons. Vento overlooked it, and Gil followed him into the house. Jeremiah stomped along behind, mumbling under his breath. Vento took a seat at the big kitchen table, and Gil sat down across from him. Leaning back, Henneagar opened a sideboard drawer and took out a pencil and tablet.

"Right smart for a man to remember," said Vento, "so I wrote it all down for you." He placed the tablet on the table. "This will get you to Fort Yuma, which I'm figurin' at two hundred fifteen miles."

"Some mighty hard days," Gil said, "if your miles between water are even close, and I'm not doubting you."

"You could maybe lessen the total miles," said Vento, "but you'd have to gamble on the water. You're better off to go a little out of your way, like you did when you stumbled on that spring to the south of here. You'll drop down near the Mexican border a time or two, but that's to get you to sure water. First you can count on, once you leave here, is at Queens Well. I'd figure it a good twenty miles. Could be less, but not much. Second day, you'll need to reach Santa Rosa Valley, and that's eighteen miles. Third day, figure another eighteen miles to Quijotda valley. Day four you'll be lookin' for dripping springs in the Ajo Mountains, and that's a good twenty miles. The next day is maybe twenty-two miles, and that gets you to Papago Wells."

"Five days to Papago wells," Gil said, "and then we turn due north."

"You do," said Vento, "and there's a good reason. After twenty miles, you'll reach San Cristobal Wash. It carries a runoff from the Gila River, in the Mohawk Mountains. You follow San Cristobal north forty miles. Now I know this is roundabout, out of your way, but it's sure water. Once you reach the Gila River, follow it west sixty miles to its confluence with the Colorado. That will take you to within sight of Fort Yuma."

May 20, 1850. Tucson, Arizona Territory

"Move 'em out!" Gil shouted.

The horse remuda, down to its original size, took the lead. The longhorns moved into position behind the horses, and the trail drive was again headed west. Some of the folks from Tucson, including Vento and Gid Henneagar, had ridden out to see the Texans off. Before the tag end of the herd disappeared over a ridge, Rosa waved her hat one last time.

"Them is good folks," said Long John.

"It saddens me to leave here," Rosa said, "when I do not know what might lie ahead of us."

"All the more reason to press on," said Bo. "If we could see what lies ahead, the little bad would frighten us away from the good. We would become slaves to our fears, huddling together and dying of stagnation."

"He talks like a politician I knowed oncet, back in the bayous," teased Long John. "Feller talked like ever'thing was jus' purely goin' t' hell if'n he dint git elected."

"I reckon you voted for him," said Van.

"No," said Long John, "but ever'body else did. The bastard got elected, and *that's* when ever'thing went t' hell."

The conversation ended when Gil rode back to the drag.

"We're twenty miles from water," he told them. "It's swing some lariats, bust some behinds, or face a night in dry camp. Get with it!"

By noon the pleasures of Tucson and the restful camp

were forgotten. The smaller horse remuda moved at a gait the longhorns found difficult to maintain. As usual, there were many who decided to forsake the drive and return to the good graze and water at Cactus Springs. While the riders fought to keep the steers bunched and the ranks closed, there were always some that managed to break away. There was no wind, and the heat from a vengeful sun seemed all the more intense. Every rider wore a bandanna over nose and mouth, but it spared them little, and their eyes not at all. Sweat blinded their eyes, soaked their hair, dripped off their chins. Dust became so thick they could scarcely tell if the steers were bunched or not, beyond the first few at the tag end.

"I reckon we're halfway there," Gil shouted when he next rode back to the drag. "Keep 'em moving, and keep 'em bunched."

It was becoming more and more difficult to do either. As the day wore on, the hard traveling took its toll. As the steers began to tire, they became more ornery, and the hard drive rapidly increased their thirst. Gil was thankful for Vento Henneagar's directions, giving him some idea where the water was. But as the day seemed to grow hotter, he became increasingly uneasy. He must know for a certainty how far away that water was!

"Ramon, I'm riding ahead to check out the water at Queens Well. Keep the longhorns in sight of the horses, and keep 'em moving."

Gil paused long enough to tell Mariposa and Estanzio where he was going. They well understood the urgency, and he didn't have to tell them to keep the horses at a fast gait. To Gil's relief, he found Vento's mileage accurate. The drive was within half a dozen miles of the water. It was in a valley amid a forest of Joshua trees, and Gil was struck by the unusual water source. While it was actually a big spring, it *did* look like a well. Fed from underground, it was a dozen feet across, and seemed bottomless. Any man, horse, or cow falling in there had better be prepared to swim. There was excellent runoff, with a profusion of Joshuas and other greenery, and it wouldn't be difficult to keep the long-horns away from the spring itself. Gil found no remains of old fires, and the only tracks those of coyotes, wolves, and wild turkeys. He watered his horse, satisfied his own thirst, and rode back to meet the herd. He hardly needed to tell Estanzio and Mariposa to take the horses on to water. It was what they had come to expect, and they soon had the horses at a gait that would put them at the water well ahead of the longhorns. Gil rode on to meet Ramon.

"Keep them moving like they are, Ramon. We're maybe two hours from the water, and I've sent the horses on ahead."

Gil rode to the drag with the same cheering words, finding the riders sorely in need of encouragement.

"Five more hard days," Gil said, "with a drive about like today's, but when we reach San Cristobal Wash, we'll be about a hundred miles out of Yuma. We'll be following the wash north, and since it carries a spill-off, we'll be sure of water all the way to the Gila River. Then we follow the Gila west until it joins the Colorado, near Fort Yuma."

"All we got to do," said Van, "is live through five more days like today, and we can ride easy the rest of the way to Yuma."

Gil laughed. "That's it."

"Please," said Rosa wearily, "explain that to the cows. They do not believe there is water anywhere else in the world, except back at the Cactus Springs."

Sweat-soaked, dirty, and exhausted as they were, they laughed. But they pressed on, and before sundown the longhorns were strung out along the runoff from Queens Well.

"By damn," said Long John as they sat around the supper fire, "we must of done somethin' right. Ain't this the fust twenty-mile day we done, that them critters didn't stampede the last two er three mile?"

"I think you're right," said Gil, "but it wasn't so much

our doing. We had no wind bringing the smell of water to the herd. But we can take credit for getting them here before sundown. Usually that's when the night wind rises and they discover there's water ahead. The secret is to start early and just drive the hell out of them, getting as far as we can, as quick as we can. Like we did today."

The night was peaceful, and again Rosa took the first watch, avoiding any time alone with Gil. The outfit was up, had breakfast done, and were on the trail at the first gray of dawn. Gil was determined that their second day out of Tucson would be as successful as the first. Everything seemed to be a repeat of the previous day's hard drive. The sun rose hot as ever, there was no wind, and the longhorns rebelled when they were again forced to keep up with the fast-moving horse remuda. Bunch quitters broke away, were chased back, and at first opportunity broke away again. At noon Gil had the riders change horses. One at a time they rode ahead to the remuda for a fresh mount. But there was no relief for the riders. Again Gil rode ahead, seeking the Santa Rosa Valley and the water Vento Henneagar had said was there. He found they had again drifted too far south. He rode north several miles and then doubled back to the spring. It was adequate, but with a lesser runoff than Queens Well. Gil scouted the area before returning to the herd. As usual, when he reached the horse remuda he sent Mariposa and Estanzio ahead with the horses, having them adjust their direction to the north. Then he rode on to meet Ramon.

"Little more to the north," said Gil. "I missed the water at first and had to ride back. Today's drive is about eighteen miles, so we ought to do at least as well as yesterday."

Gil found the drag riders in about the same state of exhaustion as the day before. The good news that the water was a little closer than yesterday cheered them only slightly. They were as dirty and sweat-soaked as ever, and if anything, the ever-present dust was even

worse. Gil pitched in to help, and the very first bunch
quitter he tried to head turned on him. Only his fast-
moving, quick-thinking horse saved him from a horn in
the belly. What happened next was bizarre, something
none of them had ever seen or heard of before. While
the steer's horn missed Gil's belly, so near was the miss,
it caught under his pistol belt and he was plucked from
the saddle. The unruly steer, as though he had planned
just such a maneuver, lowered his head and slammed
Gil to the ground on his back. The angry brute then set
about to finish what he had started. But two loops
snaked out as Long John and Van roped the lethal
horns. Frustrated, the steer kicked the air, allowing
Rosa to ride in and catch his hind legs with an underhand throw. With her lariat dallied around the horn, her
horse took up the slack, and the stubborn steer was
thrown to the ground in a cloud of dust. Gil was up in
an instant, piggin string in his hand and a second one
clenched in his teeth. Seizing the big steer's flailing front
legs, he tied them, and then went for the hind legs. Then
he loosed all three lariats, allowing Rosa, Van, and Long
John to go after other bunch quitters. To his disgust, he
saw that others within the herd had taken advantage of
the absence of the riders who had come to his aid. A
dozen or more longhorns were raising a cloud of dust
down the back trail. Feeling like every bone in his body
had been broken at least once, Gil swung into his saddle
and kicked his horse into a gallop. Sensing trouble, several flank riders had dropped back, trying to bunch the
herd. Gil threw in with them, allowing Van, Long John,
and Rosa to gather the bunch quitters along the back
trail. When the herd was finally gathered, bunched, and
moving, every rider was drenched with sweat, caked
with dust that had become instant mud, and totally exhausted. When Gil managed a feeble grin, it felt like his
face was going to crack like a looking glass.

"Them brutes knows it's you that's makin' it hard on
'em," said Long John. "Ye'd best stay up front, so's they

cain't git at ye. Never seen one o' the bastards grab a
rider thata way."

"Freak accident," said Gil wearily. "All he had in
mind was a horn in the gut. Worst of it was, he took four
of us away from the herd and allowed others to break
loose. Damn him, I ought to shoot him between the
eyes."

"Then you would have to shoot them all," said Rosa.
"Given the chance, would not any one of them gore you
and your horse?"

"Yeah," said Gil sheepishly, "I reckon they would.
Let's burn their behinds and force 'em to use up all that
cussedness gettin' to water."

Again their determination paid off, as they reached
the spring without further difficulty. Gil estimated they
were forty miles west of Tucson and 175 miles from Fort
Yuma.

May 22, 1850. Santa Rosa Valley, Arizona Territory

"Eighteen to twenty miles today," Gil said as they
saddled their horses. "Place called Quijotda Valley. Another spring, I reckon."

So began another wretched day of blistering sun,
dust, sweat, and ornery bunch quitters that wanted to go
anywhere except California. When the sun was noon
high, Gil rode out, anxious to find the water and to
estimate their chances of reaching it before sundown. It
was a spring, as he had expected, and as good as the one
of the day before. Judging by the time it had taken him
to reach it, the herd had been better than halfway when
he had left them. For the third time in as many days,
they were about to reach water without a stampede.
While the hard drives were hell on the riders, they were
worth the effort, and Gil was elated. They should reach
Fort Yuma no later than June first! Soon as Gil met the
horse remuda, he sent Mariposa and Estanzio ahead
with the horses. That was another innovation of his that

had proven itself. Jubilant, he rode on to the drag with the good news. Water was near!

"I believe ye," shouted Long John. "Now if ye kin jus' git it through the head bones o' these stupid, cantankerous, horned sons o' the devil . . ."

Gil laughed and threw himself into the task that had so infuriated Long John: keeping the longhorns moving west, returning one bunch quitter to the herd just in time to tear out after the next one.

In contrast to the long, hard, hot days, the nights were cool and peaceful. And there were no dry camps. Nobody complained. On a trail drive, it never got any better, and most of the time it was infinitely worse.

May 23, 1850. Approaching the Ajo Mountains

"This will be another hard day," Gil told them at breakfast as they were preparing to move out of the Quijotda Valley. "We'll have to cross the Ajo Mountains to reach dripping springs, so we'll be travelin' uphill some of the way. That means the steers and horses will tire quickly. We'll have to fight twice as hard to cover the same ground."

Gil had the herd moving at first light, and he immediately rode out to scout the mountainous terrain ahead. It would be the most difficult part of the day's drive, and he wanted it behind them before man and beast became exhausted. While there would be little danger in the ascent, the drive down the opposite slope could be hazardous if there were sudden drop-offs or shale outcroppings. This was Gil's concern, but when they reached the foothills, he felt better. While the land became more mountainous, the rise was gradual, but he still had to see the other side. At the higher elevation there were stately ponderosa pines and thick forests of fir. Reaching the crest, Gil reined up, his eyes searching the valley below. He marked the position of the spring by the profusion of greenery that surrounded it and the runoff.

Beyond the spring and as far as Gil could see, there was a literal forest of cactus, treetop tall. Magnificent, they dwarfed anything he'd ever seen.* Suddenly his eyes were drawn back to the spring. Briefly something had caught his attention, and then he'd lost it. Just as he was about to blame it on his overactive imagination, he saw it again. A wisp of smoke, barely visible against the blue of the sky, quickly dissipated. Somebody was or had been at the spring! Warily he rode on, avoiding bare spots, staying well within a sheltering growth of fir and pine.

Gil reined up at the foot of the slope, not daring to ride closer. If there were men at the spring—white or Indian—they would be mounted, and the nickering of a horse could betray him. Gil half-hitched his reins to some greasewood and began his cautious advance toward the spring on foot. Such was the undergrowth, he could see only a few feet ahead. He avoided approaching the spring directly, and when he reached the runoff, he found it a substantial stream, shaded by pinion, willow, and oak. Staying within the shadow of the trees, Gil followed the runoff until he was within sight of the spring. While it was shaded by trees, it flowed out of rock and there was little underbrush. Stone outcroppings provided a natural clearing, and within it was the remains of a fire that had been left to burn itself out. Only an ember remained, and the smoke was becoming less and less. Leaving an unattended fire was wanton carelessness, certainly not the act of a frontiersman or Indian.

Gil drew his Colt and moved closer. Birds chattered in the trees, and a pair of jays dipped down to the spring. Whoever had been there was gone. Holstering his Colt, Gil went on to the spring. The jays escaped to the safety of an overhead limb and, in a language of their own, swore at him for his intrusion. Gil didn't

* Now Organ Pipe Cactus National Monument, in southwestern Arizona

pause at the spring, but continued beyond it, until he found where the horses had been picketed. It took him only a few minutes to find where the riders had approached the spring from the south, and he accounted for fourteen horses. Where the men had dismounted there were some boot prints, and Gil found several where the heel had gone deep. There was a distinct imprint of big roweled spurs. Cartwheel spurs, the kind favored by Mexican riders.

In a widening circle Gil moved away from the spring until he found where the riders had departed. Westward. He had no time to trail them. It was a task better suited to Mariposa or Estanzio, once they had brought the horses to the spring ahead of the longhorns. Gil rode back, and when he met the horse herd, he spent a few minutes with the Indian riders. From there he went on to meet Ramon and the herd.

"Mostly good news, Ramon. Looks like we'll end another day without a stampede. Mariposa and Estanzio are takin' the horses ahead, as usual. One of them will be ridin' west, trailing some hombres who left the spring sometime this morning. May not mean anything to us, but we can't risk it."

Reaching the drag, Gil found that most of the other riders shared his caution. Things had been going entirely too well.

"Mex outlaws," Van declared, "and up to no good. You can bet your last pair of good socks they're not here among the cactus and rattlesnakes just to visit their kin."

"Ye purely got the straight o' it, son," said Long John. "I reckon we gon' be payin' fer them peaceful nights we had."

"They have left their fire and ridden away," said Rosa. "Perhaps they do not know of us."

"Perhaps they do," said Bo, "and they are waiting until we reach Papago Wells. Is it not very close to Mexico?"

"Within hollerin' distance," Gil said, "and your

thinkin' is running neck and neck with mine. If this bunch figures we're trailwise enough that they can't hide from us, leavin' the fire and a plain trail makes sense. Obviously they have no interest in us, and it purely fans the fires of my suspicions. If they know we're headed for dripping springs, they'll also know our next sure water will be at Papago Wells. If they're up to devilment that involves us, it'll happen at Papago Wells. Once we leave there, we move north, following San Cristobal Wash to the Gila River."

"So we'll sleep with one eye open at Papago Wells," said Van.

"Don't plan on sleeping at all," Gil replied.

They topped the Ajo mountain range an hour before sundown, and the longhorns were allowed to take their time on the descent. The riders reined up, awed by the mystic beauty of what seemed literally thousands of organ pipe cactus.

"Madre de Dios!" Rosa cried. "I could stand here on this mountain and enjoy them forever. Perhaps instead of returning to Texas, I will live here."

Bo laughed. "One could do worse."

Gil started to say something, saw Rosa looking at him, and kept silent. They followed the longhorns down the slope, falling behind as the brutes became aware of the water ahead. Following Gil's orders, Ramon had taken the herd over the slope at a point that would lead them not directly to the spring, but to the runoff.

"You aim to keep some distance between the horses and the longhorns tonight, I reckon," Van said.

"Tonight, and especially tomorrow night," said Gil. "If those Mex outlaws have any ideas about stampedin' our stock, they'll have to choose horses or cows. I don't aim for them to get both."

Estanzio waited at the spring with the packhorses. Mariposa had not returned from trailing the mysterious riders. Gil, Van, Long John, Ramon, Bo, and Juan Armijo began unloading the packhorses. Rosa quickly got the supper started. The fire had to be doused before dark. Mariposa returned, and his report was brief.

"No could trail more," said the Indian. "Sun go, them no stop."

"We'll pick up the trail tomorrow," said Gil. "I just wanted to be sure they didn't double back and hit us tonight."

"Still might," said Long John. "They could of doubled back after the Injun quit the trail."

Mariposa cast Long John a black look. He might or might not have understood the words, but he had caught the doubt in the Cajun's voice.

"Even you couldn't follow their trail in the dark," said Gil. "We'll be on watch tonight, and we'll scout ahead tomorrow. We don't dare drive on to Papago Wells without scouting it first, and if they aim to hit us, I still think that's where it'll happen. We won't be more than four or five miles from the Mexican border, and if they manage to run our stock into Mexico, they'll steal us blind."

"Ye kin count on 'em comin' fer the hosses," Long John said. "Tomorrer night, if'n we all stakes out the hoss herd, we kin blast 'em outta their saddles."

"No," said Gil, "that's a gamble. We'll do what we've been doing. We'll leave Estanzio and Mariposa with the horses, and the rest of us will be with the longhorns. We'll move the horses to the north of our camp, and the longhorns to the south. You could be right, Long John, and if they *do* come after the horses, they'll have to run them past us if they aim to cross the border. But they'll have a fight on their hands, because we'll have enough distance between horses and longhorns so's we can head the horses before they get to the steers and stampede them."

Van laughed. "Not bad, big brother. On the other hand, if they decide on the longhorns, they'll be up against a dozen of us, and we'll be expectin' a stampede to the south."

"Dead right," said Gil. "We don't know if they'll try for horses, steers, or both. But we'll be prepared to defend either herd, and in either case, we'll be between them and the border."

"Por Dios," Rosa said, "in Mexico it is the *soldados;* here it is the *Indios* and *banditos.* Is there no place in the world where one's life, cows, and horses are safe?"

"I have seen some of the world," said Bo, "and no man's possessions are any safer than his willingness to defend them. Nor is his life. Governments, laws, and politics are tools men employ to steal what others have earned."

"The Good Book says the world is goin' t' hell." Long John chuckled. "An' Bo says it's done gone."

"Quoting the Good Book," said Bo, "men love darkness because their deeds are evil. Words of the ancients tell us Diogenes went looking for an honest man, carrying a lamp to light his way. His search was in vain. I suspect he said to hell with it, after someone stole his lamp."

It was a humorous remark that none of them fully understood except Gil. He remembered it as a nugget he had laboriously dug from one of Stephen Austin's books. He looked at the little cowboy with new respect and some envy, and was troubled by his own thoughts. How many months and years had he known Bo, without *really* knowing him? He felt a sense of loss, and silently vowed to spend some time with the Argentine. But with each passing day, time was running out. . . .

19

～✦～

Despite Long John's misgivings, there was no trouble at the dripping springs. Vento Henneagar's directions said the distance to Papago Wells was twenty-two miles, and it would be their longest drive since leaving Tucson. Gil had the herds on the trail at first light. The riders were grimly determined, each resigned to a hard day with little or no sleep at the conclusion of it. Strong on their minds was the possibility of an outlaw attack at Papago Wells. But Gil intended to take every precaution, and once the trail drive was moving, he rode west. He took the trail that Mariposa had followed until darkness had overtaken him. While the Indian hadn't had time to trail the bunch as far as Papago Wells, Gil faced no such limitation. After leaving the spring, he fully expected the band to continue west, but how far? If his suspicions were justified, once they were well beyond Papago Wells, the riders would double back, either north or south. Soon afterward they would swing back to the east until they were close enough to Papago Wells to lay in wait. He believed they would ride north, attacking from that direction with intentions of stampeding the horses and the longhorns across the border. It made sense, and if such an attack came, Gil hoped it was from the north. That meant they would have to hit the horse herd first, with Mariposa and Estanzio waiting for them. Even if they successfully stampeded the horses, Gil and the rest of the outfit would be riding in from the south. Not only could he and his riders head the horses before they reached the longhorns, they could, and would, empty some outlaw saddles.

Unsure as to how far he might have to ride, Gil had kept his horse at a slow gallop, a mile-eating gait that was easiest on the animal. When he had been in the saddle about two hours and was nearing Papago Wells, he slowed the horse to a walk. While he didn't expect to find the riders at the spring, he dared not risk riding too close. He would have to picket his horse and approach on foot. Once he had left his horse, he paused every few yards, looking and listening. Around him he could hear the twitter of birds, and that was a good sign. The spring, when he sighted it, was surrounded by the usual greenery. Surprisingly, much of the small valley's growth was devoted to yucca, greasewood, and buffalo grass. Given a choice, horses and cows usually bedded down near water. Tonight they would have no choice, for the spring wasn't large, and the runoff was correspondingly small. The horses, when they had been watered, would be driven considerably north of the spring, while the longhorns would graze to the south.

Near the spring, Gil found the ashes of last night's fire and other evidence the band of riders had spent the night here. He quickly found where they had ridden away, leaving a clear trail heading west. Sweating in the mid-morning sun, Gil trudged back to his horse and again took up the trail. Five miles west of Papago Wells he had his suspicions vindicated and verified. The trail took an abrupt turn to the north.

The bunch wouldn't work their way too near the spring, lest they be discovered, so Gil doubted he had been seen. Still, he would take no chances. He rode south several miles before he turned back to meet the herd, bypassing the spring. His relief was tempered by his anxiety. While they had an edge, knowing what to expect, there was always a chance that some of his riders would die in the attack. Could he keep Rosa out of it, even with a direct order? As if that weren't enough of a dilemma, he found himself facing yet another. Should he send Mariposa and Estanzio ahead with the horses, knowing more than a dozen bandits lay in wait somewhere north of Papago Wells? They might simply gun down the Indian riders and take the horse herd. Once across the border, they could lose themselves in the wilds of Mexico, or set up a deadly ambush. By the time Gil had reached the oncoming horse herd, he had made up his mind what he must do. Quickly he explained the situation to Mariposa and Estanzio.

"There's fourteen of them," said Gil, "and I won't risk having the two of you ride in there with the horses an hour or two ahead of the rest of us. Once the longhorns get close to water, we can't hold them; you know that. This time, with those outlaws layin' for us, we'll have to take the longhorns to water first. That'll mean holdin' the horses back, not allowin' them to break for water when the longhorns run. Can you hold the horses back until the steers have watered and been put out to graze?"

"Hoss herd wait," said Estanzio. "Let cow go."

Gil had considered leaving at least one other rider with the horses, but thought better of it. This pair of Indian riders had more than their share of pride. He rode on, taking the word to Ramon and the rest of the riders, knowing they weren't going to like what lay ahead.

"From here on to the water, Ramon, we'll have to run 'em harder than we ever have. It'll take longer to water the steers, and we'll have to get them out of the way while there's still enough daylight to water the horses."

"It be some hell of a day," said Ramon doubtfully. "Already we run them hard, and they do not like it. Now we must drive them still harder."

"That's it," said Gil, unrelenting. "They're already givin' us hell, I know, but it's gonna get worse. Once we're past Papago Wells, we can ease up."

"That is how it must be, then," said Ramon. "Cows give us hell, we give it back."

Not unexpectedly, Gil found the rest of the outfit less agreeable to his plan, especially the drag riders.

"Wal, hell," growled Long John, "if'n this bunch o' Mex bastards is wantin' t' fight, how come we got to faunch aroun' an' wait fer 'em t' jump us? Why cain't we jus' leave the herd, shoot 'em dead, an' git it over?"

"Because," said Gil, his patience wearing thin, "they'd shoot some of *us* dead. Let them think they have an edge, that they're takin' us by surprise. One on one, in daylight, some of us will die. I don't want that; do you?"

Long John couldn't answer that, and didn't try. Bo took up the slack, easing the burden off the lanky Cajun.

"Long John wishes this to be finished," said Bo, "and so do we all, but our impatience could be the death of some of us. A good general chooses his own ground, and fights on his terms. Let us first get the horses and steers to water, and then give these bandits our undivided attention when they come for us."

Gil could only admire the little rider's diplomacy. His words had been conciliatory, while Gil had been tempted to respond by flaying Long John with the Austin temper.

"Wal," Long John sighed, "if'n we got it t' do, ain't no use talkin'. I say we doubles our ropes an' busts some longhorn behinds."

Even Gil laughed at that, and they set about doing the impossible. Some of the herd, already driven hard, responded by hooking at their companions, or trying to break away. Gil shouted until he was hoarse and swung his lariat until his arm and shoulders were numb from exertion, and finally their efforts began to take effect. The longhorns eventually discovered it was easier to remain with the herd than to bear the punishment bestowed upon bunch quitters.

Mariposa and Estanzio had driven the horse herd out

of the path of the longhorns, bringing the horses back
into line once the steers were well past. The hardest day
the outfit had endured since leaving Bandera Range
couldn't equal this one. The longhorns lagged constantly, and any gap within the ranks inspired a new
wave of bunch quitting. Clouds of dust painted the blue
of the sky a murky yellow, and bandannas offered scant
protection for a rider's nose and mouth. Hats had been
secured with piggin string, lest the fury of movement
tear them loose and send them flying. Every weary mile
became a hard won victory, and the riders had but one
consolation: the longhorns had begun to tire, becoming
victims of their own cussedness. Only a time or two was
Gil able to look down the back trail, and he saw nothing
of the oncoming horse herd. He was thankful for the
wisdom of his Indian riders. They well knew that once
the longhorns reached the water, getting them to drink
and move on might become the worst part of an already
wretched day. Exhausted as the steers had become, the
leaders were still capable of a shambling run once they
smelled water. With a groan, Rosa spoke for them all.

"I do not know which I hate the most—Tejano cows
or Mejicano outlaws."

"One's 'bout as lovable as t'other," said Long John.

"Keep that mad on a slow fire," Gil said, "and save it
for the outlaws. Let's go finish what we started, and get
those troublesome brutes out on that buffalo grass to
the south. Let the water clear up a mite before the
horses get here. Then we'll get our supper and lay our
plans for tonight."

Their task was far from finished. The longhorns
reaching the water first were in no hurry to leave, and
had to be driven away so their thirsty companions could
drink. Some of the stubborn brutes were still muddying
the water when the horse remuda arrived. Estanzio and
Mariposa joined the rest of the outfit in driving the
longhorns almost a mile south, where there was abun-
dant buffalo grass. When the horse remuda had been
watered, Mariposa and Estanzio drove the animals

north, leaving them to graze. Despite the long drive, supper was over and the fire doused before dark.

"Them boneheaded bastards is comin' fer more water," said Long John.

Though the longhorns had been watered and taken to graze, some of them had begun wandering back toward the spring.

"Those of you on the first watch can drive them back," Gil said. "It'll be dark in a few minutes, so we might as well get started."

Long John, Van, Bo, Manuel Armijo, Pedro Fagano, and Vicente Gomez took the first watch. Gil was surprised and relieved, knowing that Rosa would be near him. When danger threatened, she turned to him, and he found that gratifying. Immediately after supper Mariposa and Estanzio had ridden north to take their position with the horses.

"If they're comin'," Gil said, "I don't look for 'em until after midnight, but I want every one of us ready to hit the saddle and ride. That means we saddle and picket our horses, and even if your watch is done, take off nothin' but your hat. I look for them to ride in from the north, and that means they will hit the horses first. Mariposa and Estanzio will cut down as many as they can, but they've been told not to pursue, even if these owlhoots manage to stampede the horses. That throws it all on us, but I can't gamble on our riders shooting some of us, or us shooting one of them. That means any rider comin' at you in the dark is one of the outlaws. Make every shot count. If you shoot first, the return fire will be at your muzzle flash, so don't fire until you can empty a saddle. Remember, our first priority is to gun down as many of these rustlers as we can, and our second is to head the horses before they reach the longhorns. If we burn enough powder, put enough lead into these outlaws, we ought to raise enough hell to turn the horses."

There was nothing more to be said. The first watch mounted and rode out, pushing the strayed longhorns back toward the grazing herd. Gil and the rest of the riders saddled and picketed their horses. After that they could only wait—for their nighthawking to begin at midnight, or for the attack they believed was coming. Tension ran high, and as Gil had predicted, nobody would sleep. Outwardly they were calm, but as the night wore on, the second-watch nighthawks became increasingly aware that the attack, if it came, would take place in the small hours of the morning. Gil's own nerves were on edge, and he reflected that going into battle never got any easier, whoever the enemy and whatever the cause. While a man was born with seeds of death within him, its being inevitable never enhanced its reality. These riders were more than just an outfit; they were his friends, and this night he might be leading some of them to their deaths. But had he any choice? This was the frontier, where violence was the rule and seldom the exception, where the greatest honor a man might possess was having it said "he rode for the brand." Even if it became his epitaph. Midnight came, and before Gil and his riders began the second watch, he had some last words of caution for them.

"Stay within sight of one another, but don't bunch together. We can't be sure they won't come gunning for us, so don't make it easy for them."

Gil tried to think of some way to keep Rosa out of the fray, but gave it up. Since the day she had caught up to the trail drive, she had resented his attempts to make it "easy" for her. The stubborn girl was determined to prove herself a worthy rider, if it killed her, and Gil feared it might.

"Perhaps they will wait until just before the dawn," said Ramon, riding close. "They will know we are watching, and they will wait until we are all weary from the long night."

"No," Gil said, "I don't think they'll wait until just before the dawn, because there is no moon. They'll know we're watching, but I'm counting on them *not* knowing we're waiting especially for them. No trail boss with the brains God gave a *paisano* would bed down a herd out here without nighthawks, but normally some of the outfit would be sleeping. Our edge, if we have one, is that every rider can be in the saddle at the first sign of attack."

Time dragged, and the long, hard drive to Papago Wells began to take its toll. A dozen times Gil was jolted awake, aware that he had dozed in the saddle. The harder he strove to remain awake, to be alert, the more surely his weary body betrayed him. But nothing brought a frontiersman to full awareness as quickly as gunfire, and such was the case with Gil Austin and his companions.

Just as Gil had expected, the night riders came in from the north, shouting and shooting. Gil and the rest of the nighthawks kicked their mounts into a gallop, and by the time they reached the spring, the rest of the outfit was in the saddle. Amid the shouting, there was a scream of terror; a Bowie in the hand of one of the Indian riders had found a victim. The outlaws had been successful in stampeding at least some of the horses, but when Gil and his riders began throwing lead at the oncoming rustlers, a strange thing happened. The horse herd, with mounted, gun-wielding riders behind and in front of them, split. The horses ran east and west, leaving the surprised outlaws in a confrontation with not just the nighthawks, but the entire Texas outfit! It was more than they had bargained for, and they split their ranks, breaking east and west. While starlight made for poor shooting, Gil had seen several empty saddles.

"Hold it," Gil shouted. "Don't ride after them."

If the outlaws didn't scatter, which was likely, they could take cover and ambush the pursuing cowboys. The stampede had been aborted and the outlaws had lost some men. In the darkness Gil and his riders could do no more.

"Gather 'round, Tejanos," Gil said.

One by one they reined up their horses near his. Estanzio and Mariposa approached on foot.

"Bueno," said Gil. "We gunned down some of them, but none of us were hit. I can't ask for more than that."

"Some of the horses have run away," said Rosa.

"But not across the border," said Gil. "We headed them, and we'll round 'em up at first light. Even so, the whole herd didn't run."

"No get 'em all," said Estanzio. "Two Mejicano *busardos* die."

"Bueno," said Gil. "We shot some of them out of the saddle too. We hurt them enough that I don't look for them to bother us again. Besides, we're not that far from first light. Those of us on the second watch had better be gettin' back to the herd. Mariposa, you and Estanzio stay with the rest of the horses. Come daylight, we'll go after the scattered ones. All of you from the first watch are welcome to the little sleep you can get before time to roll out."

"No sleep for so long," said Juan Padillo, "I forget how."

"Ye kin go wi' me, then," Long John said. "I aim t' scout aroun' an' see how many o' them bastards we kilt, besides them two the Injuns got."

"Count me in," said Van. "A little sleep's worse than none."

Most of the riders from the first watch agreed, and while Gil and his nighthawks rode back to the longhorn herd, the others searched for the dead.

"If there be two more Mariposa and Estanzio with the horses," said Pedro Fagano, "that be enough. The others of us could protect only the cows."

"They's somethin' purely devilish 'bout them Injuns," said Long John suspiciously. "They's somethin' onnatural 'bout the way they comes out'n the dark at a man, an' him never knowin' what's took 'im."

Van laughed. "Count your blessings, Long John. They're on our side."

"Makes no never mind," said Long John stubbornly. "I ain't trustin' nothin' er nobody I cain't understand."

They found two of the outlaws, one dead and the second close to it.

"We ought t' git a rope," Long John said, "an' finish what the lead started."

"He won't last that long," Van said, kneeling beside the wounded outlaw. "You're done for, mister. You got anything to say, any last words?"

"Only this, gringo," gasped the hard-hit man. "You have killed me, but my *hermano,* Perra Guiterro, lives. He . . . will make . . . you . . . pay."

It was a dire prediction from a dying man, and it had a sobering effect on the riders. Before any of them could speak, the outlaw was dead.

"He was very young," said Juan Padillo.

"Young coyotes grows inter older coyotes," Long John said. "This'n won't be raisin' no hell in his later years."

"Perhaps we should remember the name," said Manuel Armijo. "This Perra Guiterro must be the leader of the outlaws."

"We'll remember to tell Gil," said Van, "but I can't see them coming after us again. We've cost them four men, and they have nothing for their efforts."

"To the Mejicano," said Vicente, "blood ties are strong. Perra Guiterro may be the leader of this band of outlaws."

"He'll bleed jus' like these other coyotes," said Long John. "What kin the rest of 'em do t' hurt us?"

When the answer came, Long John wasn't going to like it. . . .

By dawn the scattered horses had returned, for this was the nearest water, and they were thirsty. When it was light enough to see, Gil sent Mariposa and Estanzio to follow the separate trails of the outlaws. At some point they would come together, and when they did, Gil wanted to know where the band of rustlers went from there. The Indian duo soon returned, and their report wasn't surprising.

"Them meet," Mariposa said, pointing south. "Ride on, same way."

"Back to Mexico," said Van. "They don't aim to follow us, then."

"They won't have to," Gil said. "They can dip into Mexico, ride east until they reach the Rio Colorado, and then ride north to Yuma. For them it's maybe a seventy-mile ride. It'll be a hundred twenty miles for us, because we have to have water every twenty miles."

"Madre de Dios," said Rosa, "they would ride that far, seeking vengeance for those who have died?"

"There's no accounting for what a man will do, where his kin are concerned," Gil said. "This is a violent land. An hombre with enough of a mad on might ride a thousand miles. I'd say until we're out of Arizona Territory, well away from Mexico and into California, those outlaws could be a threat."

From Papago Springs the drive turned north, seeking San Cristobal Wash. So far, Vento Henneagar's directions had proved accurate. Once they reached the wash, with its spill-off from the Gila River, they would have sure water all the way to Fort Yuma.

"Vento says we're twenty miles east of San Cristobal Wash," Gil told them, "but I want to push the herd just as hard as ever. I aim to ride out and scout the area ahead."

By the time the sun was noon high, Gil judged they had done well, with at least half the day's drive behind them. But as the day wore on and the longhorns grew tired and thirsty, the riders would have the usual fight on their hands. From what Vento had told him, Gil suspected that once they'd reached San Cristobal Wash, they might have to follow it awhile before the water became substantial enough for the herd to drink. Once the stream spilled off from the Gila, it flowed south some forty miles. The farther it went, the less it became, until it petered out entirely. When the Gila ran bank full, the farther and deeper ran the spill-off. Though their proposed drive to San Cristobal was twenty miles, the farthest end of the wash might be dry. But since Gil couldn't be sure, he hadn't mentioned it to the outfit. That was one of the things he needed to know, lest their twenty-mile drive take them to a dry wash. If the south end *was* dry, he had two options, either of which meant a longer, harder drive. He could keep the drive moving northwest, and follow the wash until there was water, or he could change direction, reaching the wash farther to the north. The better of the two, he decided, was to change direction, reaching the wash where there would be water, somewhere to the north. But he could make no decision until he knew at what point along the San Cristobal Wash there *was* water. He kicked his horse into a fast gallop, and when he eventually reached the tag end of the wash, he found that his caution had been justified. There had *been* water here, even high water at times, but there was none now. The sand wasn't even damp. This was a thing Vento Henneagar couldn't have foreseen, although he had suggested that it might be the case. With a sigh, Gil turned his horse due north. He would have to follow this dry wash. He knew of no other water near enough to save them, unless they returned to Papago Wells, and that was unthinkable. Reining up, he rested his horse, considering the worst of all possibilities. This damn wash, he reflected, *could* be bone dry all the way to the Gila River. Gil looked at the westering sun, estimating the time, and a tiny movement caught his eye. Bees! He watched until he spotted two more of the little creatures winging their way south. There was water ahead!

At first there was only a shallow, stagnant pool where the dry earth had begun to swallow the stream. He rode almost two miles before the water became deep enough to suit their need, and it would be even farther before there was a flowing stream. Standing water, while better than nothing, was a poor prospect; the first few steers would muddy it beyond redemption. Gil judged he had ridden north four miles since reaching the dry wash.

There was but one choice. From where he was, he must ride as straight a line as he could, back to the herd. They dare not drive to the dry end of the wash and follow it five or six miles to water. After resting his horse, Gil allowed the animal to drink. He then rode out in a fast gallop, angling to the southeast, hoping the drive hadn't moved far enough westward that he would miss it.

Meanwhile, with the cantankerous longhorns on their worst behavior, the riders had their suspicions. Especially Long John.

"Ye calls it a river, a creek, er even a branch," Long John growled, "but not a wash. Back in the bayous, a wash an' a gully's the same, an' the only time they's water in either of 'em is right after a rain. Nex' day, they's so dry, ye could unroll yer blankets an' sleep there."

"I've been thinking that same thing myself," said Van, "and I don't doubt Gil has. Remember, he told us to push the herd just as hard as ever, while the instructions he got from Vento Henneagar says it's a twenty-mile drive. My big brother's smarter than he looks, thank God."

Bo laughed, and the conversation ended as more bunch quitters decided the back trail looked better than the trail ahead.

When Gil came within sight of the horse herd, he estimated he'd ridden at least ten miles. It was two hours past noon, and that would be two hours they had lost. He quickly explained the new direction to his Indian riders, and the need for it.

"Take the horses on to water," said Gil, "and make way for the longhorns. They'll likely hit the water on the run."

Ramon only nodded after Gil had explained the situation to him. There was nothing to say. They had to make up a difference of two hours, and it was going to be hell with the lid off. While there was some mild bitching from the rest of the riders, they accepted the grim news more with resignation than anger. Gil tried to soften the blow.

"Just be thankful," he said, "that I got back to you in time to change direction. If we'd driven on to the wash and then had to turn north, we'd be fifteen miles away instead of ten. They way we're headed, there are no bluffs or deep canyons. The horses will be watered and out of the way, so the steers can break loose and run the last two or three miles without harm."

Wearily they pressed on, fighting the unruly herd, and it was a relief when the longhorns smelled the water. In a bawling, thundering fury, they ran.

20

May 27, 1850. On the Gila River, sixty miles east of Fort Yuma

San Cristabal Wash offered adequate water for the two days it took the Texas outfit to reach the Gila River. For the first time since leaving their Bandera range, they were able to follow a stream. No longer did the specter of a dry camp hang over their heads. It was an unaccustomed luxury, pausing where darkness found them, without the lack of water creating a crisis. The Gila proved to be a clear, fast-running stream with an abundance of fish. The dawn of their first day on the Gila saw Bo and Long John ride in with a deer.

"Por Dios," said Rosa, "with a river so close, it is like another world. There are no thirsty cows running away, there are fish, deer, and a chance to rest."

"From here on to Fort Yuma," said Gil, "and once we reach California, I think we'll travel parallel to the coast. While we can't use water from the sea, there are plenty of freshwater streams flowing into it. Accordin' to our map, there are lakes too. Where water's concerned, I believe the worst part of the drive is behind us. But as we near the goldfields, I expect there'll be other problems, such as thieves and killers."

"Nothin' diff'runt 'bout that," said Long John. "Them wasn't 'zactly a bunch o' pussycats that hit us las' time."

June 1, 1850. Fort Yuma, Arizona Territory

Just after noon of their fifth day on the Gila, they bedded down the longhorns in the triangle where the Gila and Rio Colorado joined. Within sight, on a rise above the west bank of the Colorado, they could see Fort Yuma. Oddly, there was no stockade, and half a dozen men—soldiers—watched them. The sun reflected off brass, and Gil identified one of the bluecoats as an officer.

"First off," said Gil, "some of us need to ride up there and satisfy their curiosity. Who wants to go with me?"

"I wish to go," said Rosa.

Ramon laughed. "Rosa has my old Colt revolver. She wishes to shoot *soldados.*"

"That is not true!" cried Rosa. "I wish to see if there is a store."

"Come on, then," Gil said. "Anybody else?"

"I'll go," said Van, "just to see somethin' besides longhorn rumps."

"I go too," said Pedro Fagano. "I have never seen an American *soldado* fort."

"Wal," said Long John, "I reckon they'll be 'nough o' ye here wi' the herd, so's me an' Bo kin git in some fishin'. This Colorado River is bigger an' deeper. No tellin' *what* we might ketch out'n there."

"Whatever it is," Rosa cautioned, "see that you clean it."

Gil, Rosa, Van, and Pedro mounted and headed for the fort, less than a mile distant. Bo and Long John rode across the Gila and turned their horses down the east bank of the Colorado. Mariposa and Estanzio had already begun an examination of the horse remuda, checking each animal for loose or worn shoes. The rest of the riders, heads on their saddles and hats over their faces, stretched out and dozed in the evening sun.

When Gil and his companions arrived, three soldiers were waiting. Without dismounting, Gil performed his introductions. One of the soldiers, wearing dress blues and captain's bars, responded.

"I'm Captain Tilden Norris, post commander. The gentleman on my right is Lieutenant Maynard, and on my left is First Sergeant Gannon. You are welcome to dismount, and welcome to Fort Yuma, such as it is."

"Thanks, Captain," Gil said. "I'd like to talk to you about the country ahead of us, and my riders want to visit your store, if it's permitted."

"Sergeant Gannon," said Norris, "show these folks the store. The post as well, if they wish to see it. Lieutenant Maynard has been in the field more than I have. You'll accompany us, Lieutenant."

Gil followed Captain Norris and Lieutenant Maynard through the orderly room and into the post commander's office. Norris took a seat behind his desk, nodding Gil and Lieutenant Maynard toward a pair of cane-bottom, ladder-back chairs.

"I envy you, Austin," said Captain Norris. "This thing, this trail drive, is one hell of an adventure. I expect it forces a man to become all he can become, pushing him to the brink."

Gil grinned. "You don't always stop there. I've been over it a few times."

Briefly Gil mentioned their Indian trouble, the fight with the Clanton outlaws, and the latest attack by Mexican rustlers. When Gil spoke of their killing four of the Guiterro gang, Captain Norris whistled long and low. Lieutenant Maynard leaned forward, his hands on his knees.

"Guiterro and his bunch are the most hated men in these parts," said Captain Norris. "They're wanted for murder and horse stealing all over southern California. My God, what the law in San Diego wouldn't give to get its hands on that gang."

"Now there's only ten of them," Gil said. "Why not take some men and track them down?"

"Easier said than done," Norris replied. "Tell him, Lieutenant."

"Guiterro and his bunch are holed up twenty-five miles south of here," Lieutenant Maynard said. "It's a box canyon called Poza de Arvizo, near the Rio Colorado. It's a fortress, in some of the wildest country in Mexico, with plenty of water, grass, and walls of overhanging solid rock. Why, you couldn't root 'em out of there with an army. We can't touch the bastards anyway, thanks to the misguided Yankee liberals in Washington. They're hell-bent on us honorin' Mexico's borders, because after the war, we've forced Mexico to honor ours."

There was a knock on the door, and Lieutenant Maynard opened it to find Sergeant Gannon there. Behind him stood Van, Rosa, and Pedro.

"Gunfire to the south, sir," said Gannon.

"Sorry, Captain," said Gil as he leaped to his feet. "My men are out there."

Gannon stepped aside as Gil and his companions ran for their horses.

"Sergeant Gannon," said Captain Norris, "this may be the Guiterro gang. Saddle horses for the lieutenant and me. Then mount and lead the second platoon after us at a fast gallop."

Gil, Van, Rosa, and Pedro kicked their horses into a run. To the south, far down the Colorado, they could see two tiny, fast-moving horsemen. Behind them, gaining, came a band of other riders, firing as they rode.

"Madre de Dios!" Rosa cried. "It is the outlaws! They are after Bo and Long John!"

"Reckon it's time we was ridin' back," said Long John, checking the time by the sun.

"Past time," said Bo. "I think we have enough fish for everybody at the fort too."

But at that point, Bo and Long John forgot all about

fishing. Around a bend in the Colorado, from the south, came ten riders! Already they were firing their pistols, although they weren't quite in range. Bo and Long John ran for their horses, leaped into their saddles and kicked their mounts into a fast gallop. Their only chance lay in reaching their outfit, more than five miles upriver.

With the first distant rattle of gunfire, the riders who had remained with the herd were on their feet, running for their horses.

"No saddles!" Ramon shouted. "There is no time!"

He kicked his horse into a fast gallop, followed by Mariposa, Estanzio, Juan Alamonte, Manual Armijo, Domingo Chavez, Vicente Gomez, and Juan Padillo. They pounded down the east bank of the Colorado until far down the river, headed toward them, they could see Long John and Bo riding for their lives. West of them, thundering down the hill from the fort, came Gil, Van, Rosa, and Pedro, followed by Captain Norris and Lieutenant Maynard. Within minutes Sergeant Gannon and his platoon would be in the saddle. But none of the rescuers were in time, and in horror they watched the tragedy unfold.

Bo was in the lead, Long John a few yards behind. When the Cajun's horse was hit, the animal's cry was almost human. Bo turned at the sound and saw Long John roll out of his saddle. By the time the Cajun was on his feet, the outlaws had drawn closer and lead began kicking up dust. In the face of it all, Bo turned his horse and galloped toward Long John. The Cajun caught Bo's outstretched hand, leaping astride the horse, behind the little cowboy. But the outlaw fire became more intense, and a slug caught Bo in the chest with such force, Long John felt the shock of it. His left arm holding the hard-hit cowboy in the saddle, the Cajun grabbed the reins with his right hand before Bo lost them. Long John wheeled the horse, kicking it into a hard run. A slug burned the animal's flank, another tore Long John's hat away, while a third left a bloody gash above his right ear.

The eight riders who had been with the horses and longhorns now rode at a fast gallop along the east bank of the Colorado, while Gil and his riders, closely followed by the soldiers, galloped along the west bank. Faced with such formidable opposition, the Mexican outlaws reined up, turned their horses and fled south.

"We'll pursue them!" shouted Captain Norris.

Gil and his riders splashed across the Colorado, riding back to their camp. Long John was already there, kneeling beside Bo, whose eyes were closed. Blood welled from a terrible wound in his bare chest. Rosa, blinded by tears, all but fell from the saddle, and the riders who had gathered around made room for her. Kneeling, the girl took one of Bo's hands in both of hers. Gil and Van were right behind her. Bo coughed, and there was bloody froth on his lips. It was the end of the trail, and they all knew it. Suddenly the little rider's eyes opened and, painfully, he spoke his last words.

"Amigos . . . the star grows . . . dim . . ."

His eyes remained open, but they were empty, for the soul had departed and gone to its maker. The silence that followed was ghastly, broken only by Rosa's sobbing. Gil led the girl away. Ramon brought a blanket and gently covered Bo. Mariposa and Estanzio stood looking toward the south, murder in their eyes. But most of the riders had turned their attention to Long John. The Cajun spoke not a word, and the look in his eyes was a mix of unspeakable grief and killing rage. Slowly, wearily, he got to his feet, and when he did finally speak, his words were cold, deadly.

"One o' ye kindly fetch the saddle off'n my dead hoss. I got me some ridin' t' do."

"Long John," said Gil quietly, "Bo was one of us, and his killers will pay, but we'll go after them as an outfit. Throwing your life away won't help Bo. We're just an hour away from sundown, and I want Bo to have a decent burying before we ride after his killers. One of the

officers at the fort knows where those outlaws are holed
up, somewhere south of here. We'll go after them at first
light, and I promise you, they'll die."

Long John stood there looking forlornly across the
Rio Colorado, his lean jaw set hard, clenching and un-
clenching his fists. Far down the river, Gil saw Captain
Norris and his soldiers returning. He had no doubt they
had given up pursuit at the border, and when they rode
in, Norris confirmed it.

"We couldn't follow them into Mexico," he said.

"But we can," Gil replied, "and we will, tomorrow at
first light. Right now we have a buryin' to do, and we'll
need the loan of some digging tools."

"I can do better than that," said Captain Norris. "Decide where you want the grave, and I'll send you a burial
detail. For that matter, why don't you let us bury him
with military honors? I've never seen a more coura-
geous act under enemy fire."

"Thank you, Captain," Gil said. "I believe Bo would
have liked that."

Captain Norris acted quickly. There was a wooden
coffin in the fort's supply room, and while it wasn't
fancy, it was more than most cowboys had when they
played out their string. The burial detail dug the grave
beneath a sheltering oak on a slope above the western
bank of the Rio Colorado, within sight of the fort. As
the last rays of the westering sun turned the river to
liquid gold, the Argentine cowboy they knew only as Bo
was laid to rest. When the coffin had been lowered, six
soldiers fired a volley over the grave. From the Bible
Captain Norris had provided, Gil tried to read the scripture he had chosen, but was unable to speak. Silently he
passed the Bible to Captain Norris, and the officer began to read the Twenty-Third Psalm. When he had finished, he turned to St. John and read a passage from the
Fifteenth Chapter.

"Greater love hath no man than this, that a man lay
down his life for his friends."

Captain Norris lifted his hand to the bugler at the top

of the hill, and the high, lonesome sound of taps filled the twilight. The melancholy refrain rose and fell, rose and fell again, and when it peaked a third time, it seemed to linger, before dying to silence. Gil led the weeping Rosa away, and the others followed, leaving only the burial detail and Long John. Nobody waited to see the grave filled, except the Cajun, and it seemed he wished to etch the macabre scene in his mind. Once the trio of soldiers had filled the grave, they took their shovels and started back to the fort. Only then did Long John approach the grave.

Estanzio and Mariposa had not gone to the burying, but had remained with the horses. Captain Norris rode back to the Texans' camp, and Gil suspected he had something on his mind. When they had dismounted, Rosa turned and looked at the distant slope where they'd buried Bo.

"Madre de Dios," cried Rosa, "it grows dark, and Long John is still there. We must find a way to help him."

"Nothin' we can say or do will ease his grief," Gil said. "He's better off where he is, than ridin' after those Mex killers by his lonesome, and that's what he had in mind. But it's a job for all of us, and we'll ride at first light."

"God knows, I'd like to help you," said Captain Norris, "and perhaps I can, but it's against regulations, and I could be court-martialed. I'd need a vow of silence from you."

"You have it," Gil said.

"You'd need artillery to run that bunch out of that canyon stronghold, but lacking that, there may be another way. We have some canisters of black powder. Lieutenant Maynard and Sergeant Gannon are skilled in its use, and they believe a few well-placed charges can bring those canyon rims down like the Walls of Jericho. With your permission and vow of silence, Maynard and Gannon wish to ride with you. They will not be in uniform, but will become part of your outfit for the duration of this maneuver."

"A flagrant violation of regulations," Gil said.

"Yes," Captain Norris agreed. "The three of us could end up kicked out of the army, building time in a federal *juzgado*—they, for going with you, and yours truly for allowing them to."

"I'd be honored to have them ride with us," Gil said, "and we'll say or do nothing to endanger their career or yours."

Long John Coons stood in the gathering darkness, looking down at the new-made grave. Never in his checkered life had he cared a damn about anyone but himself. The little rider from the Argentine had been the only friend Long John had ever had. Now Bo was gone, and the Cajun didn't know what to do with his grief. He lifted his eyes to the evening star. For a reason he didn't understand, and in a voice that didn't sound like his own, he spoke.

"Bo said they's a range somewher' beyon' the stars, wher' the grass is always green, the skies is always blue, an' the water runs cool an' deep. I know I ain't good 'nough t' go, an' I won't never be, but Bo said it ain't up t' us. If'n we go ther', it's by faith, an' if we got the faith, then it's the Almighty's way o' tellin' us He put His brand on us 'fore we was borned. Bo believed, an' he's on that range t'night. I got nothin' t' offer, 'cept the same faith Bo had. The faith that somewher' beyon' the sky, Bo an' me will meet agin, that we'll saddle up an' ride that golden range."

A strange feeling of peace crept over Long John. It seemed a burden had been lifted, that something cold and hard within him had released its merciless grip. The tears came unbidden, and Long John couldn't have withheld them if he'd tried. For the first time in all his years, Long John bowed his head and wept. . . .

To Gil had fallen the sad task of going through Bo's few belongings, and he had spread a blanket near the fire for that purpose. He was so engaged when Long John finally returned.

"I have saved your supper, Long John," said Rosa.

Silently Long John accepted the tin plate and sat cross-legged on the ground to eat. He was watching Gil, who soon became uncomfortable.

"This is something you should be doing, Long John," Gil said.

"Don't make no diff'rence," Long John said. "I ain't askin' but one thing. I want Bo's Colt."

Gil handed him the weapon, and Long John slipped it under his belt with his own extra Colt. Except for Bo's few clothes, there was nothing in his saddlebags except a worn King James Bible and the strange leather-thonged, iron ball bola.

"I wish to keep the bola," said Rosa.

"Rosa," said Gil, "Long John—"

"I got no use fer it," Long John interrupted.

Finally Gil opened a little leather bag, emptying its contents onto the blanket. It had held the few items they'd taken from Bo's pockets. There was most of the money Gil had given Bo in Tucson, and a few coins. Rosa's eyes were red and her grief still strong, but she knelt beside Gil. Two of the coins were not coins at all, and Rosa took them. Van, Ramon, Juan Padillo, and some of the other riders had gathered around. Rosa handed Gil one of the objects, which looked like a large silver coin, and he held it up to the firelight.

"Looks like a birthdate on this side," Gil said. "It's April fourth, 1810." He turned it over.

"It is the star he spoke of," said Rosa, peering at it.

"There's an inscription beneath it," said Gil, "and it's in Spanish. Read it, Rosa."

Taking the silver disk, she read: *"Destino en Cristo eterno."**

"If'n ye don't mind," said Long John, "I'd mighty like t' have that."

---

* Destiny in Christ eternal

Gil nodded, and Rosa passed the big silver coin to Long John, who let it drop into his shirt pocket. The second coinlike object that had caught Rosa's attention was as large as the first, but it was some kind of medal, its golden face gleaming dully in the firelight. Gil took it from Rosa, and after looking at both sides, whistled.

"My God," Gil said, "this is a medal presented by the Queen of England, in 1832. When Bo was twenty-two, he was knighted by the queen!"

"Bo was special," said Rosa softly, "and we lost him before we really knew him."

At that point Sergeant Gannon and Lieutenant Maynard rode in, wearing range clothes. They would stay the night, prepared to ride with the outfit in the morning. One of the riders had recovered Long John's saddle from the dead horse. The Cajun took a blanket from his roll, spread it out, and began cleaning one of his Colts. Finished with that, he cleaned the second one. Finally he cleaned Bo's, and then fully loaded all three weapons.

"Long John," Gil said, "we'll ride at first light. Sergeant Gannon and Lieutenant Maynard will be riding with us. They know where this outlaw hideout is, and they have a plan that could bury those owlhoots under tons of rock."

"I ain't wantin' 'em buried under tons o' rock," Long John growled. "I want the murderin' coyotes gut shot an' dyin' slow."

"They're goin' to die," said Gil, "but they're forted up in a canyon, and we may have to take them any way we can get them. They're twenty-five miles south of here, and I want us under way before first light."

"Damn shame there's no moon," Van said, "or we could have gone after them tonight."

"Sergeant Gannon and Lieutenant Maynard have enough black powder to blow the canyon walls," said Gil, "and we'll need daylight to set the charges. Besides, I don't want any of us killed trying to sneak in there. This way, there's no risk."

"I'm turnin' in," said Long John. "Count me fer the second watch."

The rest of the outfit watched with interest as the Cajun got his bedroll, spread his blankets, and stretched out with his head on his saddle. Long John and Bo had always taken first watch, but tonight was different. In the small hours of the morning Long John would need a horse, and the surest means of getting one without any fuss and bother was to nighthawk on the second watch.

His hand gripping the butt of Bo's Colt, the Cajun waited for the start of the second watch, and the time when he would ride south. Alone.

Long John's nighthawking companions were Gil, Rosa, Juan Padillo, Pedro Fagano, and Vicente Gomez. There was no talk. They were all painfully aware of Bo's absence, and their lack of communication allowed Long John to keep to himself.

It was Rosa who first missed Long John, and spoke to Gil. "He has gone after the outlaws!" she cried.

Gil spoke to the rest of the nighthawks, and even to Mariposa and Estanzio, but none of them had seen Long John for a while. A long while, Gil suspected. Rosa was probably right. Long John, damn his stubborn Cajun hide, had ridden downriver to face Perra Guiterro and his outlaws alone. Gil quickly awakened the riders from the first watch, along with Sergeant Gannon and Lieutenant Maynard.

"Long John's gone after those outlaws," Gil said. "Van, I want you, Rosa, Ramon, Juan Padillo, Mariposa, and Estanzio to remain here. The rest of you, saddle and let's ride. We may already be too late."

"I wish to go with you," Rosa cried. "I am afraid for Long John."

"So am I," Gil said, "but whatever he aims to do, he'll have done by the time we get there. I want you here; I have enough to concern me."

Before she could respond to that, he led out, followed by eight fighting men, including Sergeant Gannon and Lieutenant Maynard. Since the military duo knew where the outlaw stronghold was, they just followed the Colorado. Gil had set the pace, riding at a fast gallop. When they reined up to rest their weary horses, the first rosy rays of dawn were touching the eastern sky. Suddenly there were three shots, a pause, and then two more.

"It's started," Gil shouted. "Let's ride!"

As they galloped toward the scene of battle, there were more shots. It was the only assurance they had that Long John was still alive, but as they drew closer, the shots became fewer. Finally there was only silence.

"Rein up," shouted Lieutenant Maynard. "The canyon's just ahead, and they can cut us down from cover."

"Long John's in there," Gil said, "so the sentries are dead. Once we're in the canyon, what's it like?"

"There's a cabin at the box end," said Sergeant Gannon, "backed up under a shelving rock. But if we can get into the canyon, we can get within sight of the cabin and still be out of range."

"Let's ride, then," Gil said.

Cautiously he led out, and when he reached the canyon mouth, he found it narrow and forbidding. Dismounting, he took a stone the size of his fist and flung it as far as he could into the canyon. There was no response. Just a few yards beyond the entrance there was a bend, and boulders had fallen or had been pushed from the rim to provide perfect cover. But something had happened. On the canyon floor lay a hat, and it wasn't Long John's. Gil swung into his saddle, and Colt in his hand, rode into the canyon. The rest of the riders followed, and when they rounded the bend, they could see the bodies of two men sprawled on the canyon floor. As they rode on, the canyon widened, and they could see Long John's horse cropping grass. Three-quarters of a mile ahead, part of the shake roof of the outlaw cabin was visible through sheltering oaks. To the left of the cabin, water tumbled down a canyon wall, and horses grazed around a spring which the riders could not yet see. In places, buffalo grass was knee high, while oaks sheltered much of the farthest end of the canyon. Suddenly there was movement ahead, and the riders reined up. A man leaned against one of the oaks, hatless, his head sagging on his chest. He had heard their horses approaching. Slowly, wearily, he lifted his head.

"Lord God," Gil shouted, "it's Long John!"

The lanky Cajun seemed more dead than alive, looking like an apparition from the pits of Hell. His face was a mask of blood from head wounds, the front of his shirt was blood-soaked, and it dripped off the fingers of his dangling left hand. One of his Colts was in the holster, the second under his belt, and Bo's Colt hung from his bloody right hand. Blood still welled from wounds in his thighs, dripping onto his boots. He stared at them listlessly, through hopeless, pain-slitted eyes. Pedro Fagano helped Gil lower Long John to the ground.

"Some of you work your way toward that cabin," said Gil. "We need to know where those owlhoots are, if they're alive or dead."

Even in Long John's condition, he was trying to speak. Gil turned back to him, leaning closer.

"Kilt 'em . . . all," Long John mumbled. "Got 'em . . . fer Bo. Take me t' the hill . . . wher' . . . he is . . . near the Colorado. Him an' me . . . gon' ride . . . ride the range . . . beyon' . . . the stars. . . ."

21

There was nothing they could do for Long John, except try to get him to the fort, where there would be medicine and a doctor. Sergeant Gannon rode back to report on the whereabouts of the outlaws.

"My God," said Gannon in awe, "I never saw the equal of it. He's gunned down the Guiterro gang, to the last man! When he took the two at the canyon mouth, it must've brought the others on the run. Eight of the bastards come at him in a skirmish line, and he shot them to doll rags. The lieutenant's making sure Guiterro's among the dead. How's your man?"

"Maybe done for," Gil said. "I aim to get him back to the fort and try to save him, but we can't take him there slung over the back of a horse. Pedro, take all the blankets we have and cover him. Maybe there's somethin' in that cabin we can string up for a travois."

"I'll help," said Sergeant Gannon. "He's too good a man for us not to do everything we can to save him."

Gil rode on to the cabin, passing Lieutenant Maynard as he examined the bodies of the outlaws. It was as Gannon had said—they were strung out in the high grass, all the way to the cabin. Gil found Juan Alamonte and Vicente Gomez tearing the frame of a bunk away from the wall. Once they freed it, there would be only a pair of strong cedar poles with wide strips of rawhide latticed between them. But it would serve as a travois, a drag, to make Long John as comfortable as possible on the long ride back to the fort.

"Long John be hard hit," said Vicente. "We think mebbe travois get him to fort and *medico*."

"Good thinking," Gil said. "It'll be a miracle if he gets there alive, but you have the right idea. We might as well spare him more suffering and let him die where he is, as to sling him over a horse."

When the trio returned to the hard-hit Long John, bearing their makeshift travois, they found the rest of the riders there. Lieutenant Maynard had apparently satisfied himself that Perra Guiterro was among the dead. He assisted them in making a bed of blankets over the latticed rawhide. Gently as they could, they lifted Long John onto the bed and then wrapped him in blankets to his chin. But the real difficulty lay ahead. Long John's horse didn't appreciate or trust the strange contraption, one end of it slung over his rump and the other end dragging the ground behind him. The horse bore the unfamiliar burden only because Vicente rode on one side of him and Pedro on the other. Their progress seemed painfully slow, and every man chafed at the delay. Gil and his riders had been concerned only with saving Long John, and hadn't taken a second look at the dead outlaws, but Sergeant Gannon and Lieutenant Maynard had. As they rode, the military duo pieced together the fight, marveling all the more at what one man had accomplished in an act of vengeance.

"He had three Colts," said Sergeant Gannon, "all empty except the one he was holdin' when we found him. If he started fully loaded, that means he fired seventeen times."

"Counting the two at the canyon entrance," said Lieutenant Maynard, "he scored fifteen hits. By God, he's a fighting man, by anybody's standards. He's got to pull through so I can shake his hand."

It seemed forever before they came within sight of their destination, and by the time they could see the fort, they could also see a rider tearing along the bank of the Colorado. It was Rosa, in a cloud of dust and at a fast gallop. She said nothing, riding behind the travois on which Long John lay, tears streaking her dusty cheeks. Gil didn't know if the Cajun was alive or dead, and he feared the worst. Long John was carried, crude travois and all, into the post hospital. It seemed well-supplied, and the post doctor, Lieutenant Scott, took charge in a competent manner. Only Mariposa and Estanzio remained with the herd. The rest of the outfit haunted the post hospital, awaiting some word on Long John's condition. After two long hours it came, and Dr. Scott looked grim.

"He's been hit nine times," said Scott, "and five of them are serious enough to finish him. God knows how his lungs were spared, but they were, and this object in his shirt pocket was all that saved him taking a slug through the heart."

They all gathered around to see what the doctor had dropped on the desk. It was the badly bent silver coin with Bo's birthdate, the medal that Long John had dropped in his pocket the night before. The lead had hit the star dead center. In his own way, Bo had ridden with Long John this last time.

"He has a chance," said Dr. Scott. "We'll have to wait and see."

Gil lagged behind until the others had departed. He then confronted the doctor.

"You say he has a chance, Doc, but how much? What are the odds?"

"One in a thousand," said Dr. Scott. "If I'm any judge, this time tomorrow he'll be dead."

June 2, 1850. Fort Yuma, Arizona Territory

Even as Long John lay grieviously wounded, perhaps mortally, Gil had to make some decision regarding the trail drive. Long John, if he lived, would be weeks, perhaps months, recovering. The drive must go on to California, and with that in mind, Gil had Mariposa and Estanzio begin reshoeing the horses that were in need of it. At suppertime he told the outfit of his decision and the reason for it.

"We're moving out at first light tomorrow," he concluded.

"But we cannot," Rosa cried. "Not until we know about Long John . . ."

"I think we'll know by morning," Gil said, recalling Dr. Scott's grim prophecy.

"You are a heartless Tejano *bastardo!*" Rosa cried. "I will not go until I know that Long John will live!"

Gil sighed. Despite Dr. Scott's objections, Rosa took up her vigil beside the narrow cot on which Long John lay. Gil was there shortly after eleven that night, before he began the second watch, and found Rosa nodding off. A lamp guttered low, smoking the globe. If Long John had so much as moved since being placed on the cot, Gil couldn't tell it.

"Rosa," he said softly. Instantly she was awake.

"I only closed my eyes to rest them," she said defensively.

"Rosa, you're not helping him," said Gil. "You're only hurting yourself. You had no sleep last night, and you're dead on your feet. Give it up."

"No," she said. "I have prayed for a sign that he will live. Sometime tonight I will know. Until then I will stay."

When Gil had gone, she took one of Long John's bony hands in hers and began to talk to him as though he were conscious and listening to her.

"Long John, Gil says we must take the cows on to California, and he says you would understand. But how can you understand if you do not know? How am I to leave you, unless I know you will be waiting for us when we return from California? Something—perhaps it is my star—tells me that I must go, or Gil will be lost to me forever. But I cannot leave you, unless you promise me that you wish to live, and that you will try. I know you are hurt and cannot speak, but I have prayed that some-how, before the morning, you will tell me that you un-derstand. I wish you to know that all of us want you to live, to return to Texas with us, and I cannot leave you until I have that promise."

The laudanum had long since worn off, but Long John felt no pain. In fact, he felt nothing. He feared he was dead, that he had not been one of those the Al-mighty had predestined to ride that range beyond the stars. His limbs felt frozen, he couldn't open his eyes, and his tongue clove to the roof of his mouth. Could his brain be alive and his body dead? At first the voice was only a pleasant but meaningless sound. Only the last few words got through the barrier his tortured body had flung up around his brain. He felt a little warmth in the fingers of his right hand, and slowly he was able to relate that to the distant but familiar voice. Hurt as he was, unable to move, he was aware that he had been on the very edge. There had been no reason for him not to cross that eternal line, until the voice had begged him not to. He wanted to get closer to the voice, to respond to it, and he put his very soul into the effort. He concen-trated on the evening star that he had spoken to just the night before, over Bo's grave. He was unable to do it alone, and he silently begged for help. . . .

Rosa had talked to the silent Long John until her throat ached, and while she still held his bony hand in hers, her head had sunk down in total exhaustion. Sud-denly she was wide-awake. Had she imagined it, or had Long John's fingers moved just a little? Slowly, for just a few seconds, the bony fingers pressed her own, and she knew! He had heard her plea, and it was the answer for which she had prayed! She fell on her knees beside the cot and wept. Dr. Scott came in, expecting to find Long John dead. But Rosa was smiling through her tears. The doctor stepped out and closed the door. He spoke of the strange incident to Gil the next morning, before the two of them went to the little room where Long John lay.

Gil had expected to find Rosa in an exhausted stupor, but she greeted them with a smile and a prediction.

"Long John is going to live!" she said. "He will be waiting for us when we return from California. He understands why we must go."

Rosa didn't see Dr. Scott shake his head, but Gil did. He believed, as the doctor obviously did, that when they returned from California, Long John's bones would be resting in a grave next to Bo's. In fact, unknown to Rosa, Gil had already made arrangements with Captain Norris to see that Long John had a decent and proper burial. He had no idea what had given Rosa new hope, but he was thankful for it. There would be time enough for her to weep over Long John's grave when they returned from California.

June 3, 1850. Fort Yuma, Arizona Territory

"Move 'em out," Gil shouted.

Mariposa and Estanzio led out with the horse remuda, while the rest of the outfit, now short two riders, got the longhorns moving. The day's drive was only ten miles. They crossed the Cargo Muchacho Mountains, bedding down the herd in the foothills beyond the western slope. Again they were relying on springs, and this one was a certainty. The next one promised to be much farther.

"Tomorrow," said Gil, "we'll turn more to the northwest. To the south there's Salton Sea, which may be a salt lake. Beyond that is the Anza Borrego Desert. I think we want to avoid both. We'll keep to the northwest, drive through Palm Springs and to the north of Los Angeles. We'll be in the northern foothills of the Sierra Madres for maybe a hundred miles. Then we'll move in near enough to the coast to see the big water."

Southern California was dry, and Gil was often forced to shorten the day's drive to assure them of water. Leaving sure water to gain a few more miles didn't make sense if it resulted in a dry camp. The land seemed to have an abundance of chaparral, a thorny bush common to the west, whose name had been bequeathed during Spanish domination. From a distance, to those unfamiliar with it, the growth was deceiving. Up close it became a dense thicket of dwarf trees, a virtual haven for wild longhorns. Except for the higher elevations, there was virtually no forest, and that clothing the slopes appeared to be coniferous. On the chaparral plains there were tracks of deer, rabbits, and coyotes.

Once the outfit had left Fort Yuma, little had been said about the critically wounded Long John. Gil had left Bo's saddle at the fort, to be claimed when they started back to Texas. Long John's saddle had been left there with the same thought in mind, but Gil hadn't had any intention of leaving the Cajun's weapons, ammunition, or horse. Rosa hadn't seen it that way.

"When Long John is well," the girl had said, "he will need his horse, and has he not earned the right to keep his weapons and ammunition?"

So Gil had been forced to leave Long John outfitted as though he would one day rise from the cot on which he lay more dead than alive. And again there was a rift between Gil and Rosa. Rosa had told Gil of her prayers and of Long John's response that last night at Fort Yuma. Now she realized he didn't share her faith, that he never expected Long John to rise from that cot. Gil was resentful because Rosa had created a scene that had left him seeming callous and uncaring.

June 18, 1850. East of Los Angeles, on the Mojave River

Gil estimated they were 210 miles northwest of Fort Yuma and a hundred miles from the point where they'd parallel the Sierra Madre foothills.

"Seventeen days out of Yuma," Van said. "That's just a little more than twelve miles a day."

"Which is a *good* day on a trail drive," Gil reminded him. "We've had short days, bedding down near water when we still had three hours of daylight left. According to this map Big Foot Wallace got for us, there'll be lakes and rivers aplenty from here on. We'll be able to follow some of these rivers, like we did the Gila. That means we can keep the drive goin' right up to sundown, with the river there beside us."

"Nex' time," said Juan Padillo, "let us bring the map which has a river all the way from Tejano range to Californio goldfields."

They all laughed, and it sounded strange in their own ears. It was the first cheerful note since Bo had died and Long John had been shot. It might be a turning point, Rosa thought. Perhaps things were about to change for the better. The next morning, three hours on the trail, they came up on a northbound wagon with a smashed rear wheel. A middle-aged man and a younger woman, both dressed in city clothes, stood there looking help-lessly at the disabled wagon. The mismatched team—a roan and a bay—waited patiently, to be unhitched or to continue the journey.

Mariposa and Estanzio drove the horse herd wide of the wagon. Far ahead, but within sight of the longhorn herd, the Indian duo held up the horses. If Gil chose to aid these stranded travelers, it might mean halting the trail drive. But Gil rode far enough ahead of the long-horns to take a look at the wagon without stopping the herd. He waved his hat, signaling Ramon to guide the longhorns wide of the wagon but to keep moving. He then rode to the wagon and dismounted. Taking things in the order of their importance, he considered the problem before he spoke to the travelers. The wagon was far from new, and had been rawhided together. Sev-eral of the wheels had spokes missing, while others had split, held precariously in place with wire. The brake shoe, once a thick pad of leather, had worn through to the wood. In mining country, mules were at a premium, so that accounted for the horses. By the time Gil turned his attention to the people involved, they seemed impatient and half angry. To further complicate things, the longhorn herd had passed the wagon, and Rosa had left her drag position. She reined up beside Gil just in time for the stranded strangers to introduce themselves.

"I, sir, am former judge Lionel Donnegan, recently retired from the New York bench, and this is my daughter, Kate."

"Gil Austin, and this is one of my riders, Rosa."

The two females were appraising one another like a pair of hostile hounds. Kate spoke first, a malicious gleam in her eye.

"A female cowpuncher, and a chili pepper at that. There must be a real shortage of men out here."

"There is a shortage of women as well," Rosa responded angrily, "and I cannot see that it is improving."

"Rosa," said Gil, calmly as he could, "catch up to Ramon and have him hold the herd. We may be here awhile."

Rosa paused, and while she didn't speak, her eyes said plenty. Finally she wheeled her horse and galloped off after the herd. Gil turned back to study the strangers, taking the girl first. Her eyes were blue, and she had curves like a cow path down a mountainside. Her too-tight red dress went well with her red hair, and so boldly did she return Gil's look, he hastily focused his attention on her male companion. His graying hair was over his ears, long in the back to the collar. His once white shirt was dingy gray, the cuffs and collar frayed. One end of his black string tie dangled from the pocket of his gray pin-striped trousers, and a matching coat lay across the wagon seat. His florid face was lined, making him look older than he probably was. He had the look of a man who drank too much, too often, and there was a pompous air about him. Had he been a rooster, he'd have hopped up on a wagon wheel, flapped his wings and crowed. Instead the judge strove for some outward show of humility before he spoke.

"I . . . we . . . damn it, Austin, we're stuck here, and we need your help."

"It's customary," Gil said, "for a wagon to carry an extra wheel, a spare axle, and a wagon jack."

"Obviously, our wagon is missing all those things," said the judge.

"There's no help for the wagon," said Gil. "You'll have to leave it."

"No," Kate cried, "I won't leave my trunk!"

"Then you'll just have to stay here with it," said Gil, his patience wearing thin. "You'll ride out astraddle a horse, or you'll stay here, and don't plan on takin' anything with you that won't fit on a packhorse. You can unhitch your team and ride them, trailing with us to the nearest town. We have bridles, but no extra saddles. But we have cinch strap leather, and with blankets for a seat, I can fix you a pair of Injun rigs. It'll be some better than ridin' bareback."

"I am mortified," Kate snapped. "A lady does not ride astraddle."

"Then the lady will just have to walk," Gil responded hotly. "This is the frontier, ma'am. Male or female, you ride astraddle, or you walk. The choice is yours."

He turned away in disgust, failing to see the murderous look the judge bestowed on the uppity girl. Her entire manner suddenly changed, and when she spoke again, she got Gil's attention.

"I'm sorry," she said contritely. "You're right. We're asking you for help and I'm being difficult. Tell us what we should do."

Unknowingly she had reacted in a manner that appealed to Gil's troubled vanity. How many times had Rosa raked him over the coals, refusing to give an inch? Of course, he recalled guiltily, she had been right most of the time. Now here was a woman who backed down, apologized for her sharp tongue, and had accepted him without reservation. He eyed her with new interest, and she smiled. Gil rode to the horse herd, and from one of the packhorses took cinch strap leather and bridles.

From another he took four extra wool blankets. He then caught up a horse upon which the Donnegans could pack their belongings. He said nothing to the riders who circled the restless longhorns, and they said nothing to him, but he knew they didn't approve of his dallying around with these inept strangers. As he rode back to the duo and their disabled wagon, it was just as well he couldn't hear the comments of his outfit.

"Something tells me," Van said, "this trail drive will be movin' mighty slow for as long as that pair's with us. If they can ride, why were they piddlin' along in a wagon anyhow?"

"There is a trunk," said Rosa. "Dresses, perhaps, all of them showing too much of her. She dresses like a *puta.*"

The rest of the riders kept their opinions to themselves, waiting to see how this situation might affect them. For now, they watched in gleeful anticipation as Gil made preparations to mount these tenderfeet. First he unhitched the bay and the roan from the disabled wagon. Using the long cinch leather straps, he fitted each horse with a front and back cinch. He then folded the blankets, two for each horse, into a passable seat. The pad was held in place by tucking each end under the cinches.

"Now," said Gil, "I'll have to get the two of you mounted so I can rig some makeshift stirrups. You'll have to get used to the horses, and they'll have to get used to you. If you're afraid of a horse, he'll know it, and he'll take every advantage."

The makeshift stirrups couldn't be used as stirrups in mounting or dismounting, else the entire rig slide off the horse's back and under his belly. Such "stirrups" were useful only to steady the rider once he had mounted, and both feet had to remain in place. Gil assisted the judge in mounting the bay, and Donnegan, listing like a sinking ship, slid off the other side. Getting him mounted a second time, Gil managed to get the stirrup loops at the right length on the front cinch, and got his feet into them before he slipped again.

"Keep your feet in those loops," Gil warned, "or you'll end up on the ground again. When you're ready to dismount, kick both feet free at the same time and slide off."

With a sigh, Gil turned to Kate. Getting her mounted wasn't difficult, but keeping her there was. While her long dress was almost ground length, it still hiked higher than decency allowed, and she sat there uncertainly. The roan was as nervous as she, and when the horse suddenly back-stepped, she lost one of the stirrup loops. The rig shifted and she slipped down the offside of the horse as the judge had done, but her descent was far more spectacular. Her startled screech terrified the already skittish roan, and he went galloping down the back trail. Gil did a most ungentlemanly thing. He left Kate sitting there, the voluminous dress over her head like a tent, and went after the runaway roan. When he returned with the horse, nobody spoke. Silently, Gil hoisted the girl back into the position she had just vacated.

"The both of you just sit there until I return," he said. "I've held the drive up as long as I can. I'll load the packhorse for you then."

The riders saw him coming, erasing their grins and wiping the tears of mirth from their eyes before he arrived.

"Ramon," Gil said, "ride and tell Mariposa and Estanzio to take the horses on to water. It's maybe five more miles. Then you take the longhorns ahead, but don't push them. I'll be along as soon as I can."

"Gil," said Van, "while I don't like to interfere with you bein' a good Samaritan, this purely ain't a Sunday evening lark for eastern dudes that don't know one end of the horse from the other."

"But you *are* interfering," Gil said angrily. "Would *you* have left those people sittin' there with a busted wagon wheel?"

"You're just muddyin' the water," Van said. "Long as you're bossin' this trail drive, it ought to come first. If you aim to wet-nurse these dudes at the expense of the drive, then maybe you should just *do* that, and let us appoint another trail boss."

"You, maybe?"

"Why not?" Van replied. "I'd devote all my time to it, and we'll go on to the goldfields like we planned."

The situation was getting out of hand, and the riders hesitated to become involved, because they liked both the Austins. Rosa recalled Bo's quiet way of dousing the flames when tempers flared, and she proposed a truce, if only temporary.

"Let us wait until tomorrow, after we have stopped for the night," she said, "before we judge what Gil is trying to do. Then let us decide if these strangers are costing us miles because they cannot keep up with the drive. If they are slowing us, then we cannot afford to lose time because of them. We can then leave these people some food, allowing them to go as slowly as they wish, or Gil can stay with them. Is that not fair to them and to us?"

"Damn right it is," Van said. "One slow day won't hurt us, but I won't have it plague us any farther."

Gil resented Rosa backing him into such a corner, but he was in no position to argue. If he disagreed, there would be trouble, and he would be the cause of it. He sighed.

"All right," he said, "I'll talk to them and explain our situation. Now let's get this herd moving."

When the longhorns were again on the trail, Gil rode back to the cause of the controversy. He had left the Donnegans astride their mounts, and he noted with a small glimmer of hope that they hadn't slid off. Without beating around the bush, he told them of tomorrow's ultimatum.

"I'm trail boss," he concluded, "and my first obligation is to the trail drive. As I've had pointed out to me, helping you folks is one thing, but teaching you to ride is another. We're still half a dozen miles from water, and the herd will be there before sundown. Whatever it takes, I aim to be there too. Now do you aim to ride sittin' up, or do you want me to tie you belly down across your mounts?"

"I'll try it sitting up," said Donnegan.

"So will I," said Kate. "I'm sorry you're losing time because of us."

Gil looked upon her even more favorably. He loaded their belongings on the packhorse, and while their progress was slow, the Donnegans kept their seats and did better than he expected. But the real test would come tomorrow. By dawn their backsides would be in such a state, neither of the Donnegans would ever want to see another horse. He seriously doubted they could keep up with the trail drive, but he didn't want to abandon them. He wanted to see more of the girl with the red hair.

The horses and longhorns reached water before sundown, but Gil and the weary Donnegans didn't arrive until after dark. The judge rode with his arms around the horse's neck, not so much to avoid falling as to take some of the pressure off his hefty backside. Rosa had saved supper for them, but they had to help themselves. Finished eating, Donnegan abandoned all dignity, found a place away from camp, and stretched out on his belly. Rosa took the first watch, not wishing to encounter Gil during the night. Much to her disgust, but not to her surprise, when Gil arose to begin the second watch, the Donnegan woman was with him. Rosa slept little, worried a lot, and imagined the worst. Gil felt self-conscious with Kate Donnegan walking, so he dismounted and walked with her. He hadn't asked her to come along, nor had she asked permission. Gil knew very little about this father-daughter duo, but he suspected he was about to learn more. While propriety didn't allow him to question her, he could listen.

"Daddy retired from the bench in New York," she

began, "and the West excites him. That's why we're here."

"Gold fever can get to a man, I reckon."

"Oh, we're not here for the gold," she said hastily. "Once our holdings in New York have been liquidated, Daddy plans to select a partner and establish a school of law somewhere in the West."

"I've heard there's a crying need for lawyers in mining country," Gil said. "There's always claim jumping and boundary disputes."

"Daddy's school of law will be in a large city," said Kate. "While I don't mind the West, I'm used to town living, and I think San Francisco will suit me. That's where our funds will be sent. We should have stayed aboard ship and continued there, but Daddy wanted a look at Los Angeles."

"My uncle Stephen was a lawyer," Gil said. "I've enjoyed reading some of his books."

"*The* Stephen Austin who founded the Texas colony? Daddy says he was a brilliant man, that Texas ought to build a monument to him. He's the kind of man Daddy has in mind for a partner."

"It's a mite late for that," Gil said. "Uncle Steve's been dead fourteen years, but I'm sure he'd have been flattered."

"It's never too late to build a monument to him. You could call it the Stephen Austin School of Law, and you could become its first graduate."

"Me? I'm just a cowboy, liking to read, but seldom finding the time."

"But you're not all that satisfied, being just a cowboy. It's just the nature of most men, wanting to fly as high as they can. But you must forgive me. Here I am trying to change the course of your life. This is just Daddy's dream, and I've really no right to be talking about it."

No more was said on the subject, but the seed had been planted. . . .

22

June 19, 1850. North of the Mojave River

*T*he outfit was ready to move out at first light. Except for the latest addition to the drive, the Donnegans. Gil finally roused them up, threatening to leave them behind.

"What happened to breakfast?" Judge Donnegan asked, bleary-eyed.

"Breakfast was an hour ago," Gil said, striving to hold his temper. "You were called. Now you'll wait for supper."

"There's no water on our map," Van said, "until we reach the Cuyama River, and that's a good eighty miles. You got any objections if I send Estanzio to scout ahead for water?"

"No," Gil said, "and have him ride out immediately. We'll have to count on unmarked springs and water holes from here to the Cuyama."

Gil and the Donnegans soon fell behind. Van and Rosa were at drag, and she rode her horse alongside his so they could talk.

"I do not know about this judge," Rosa said, "but the *hija* has not been honest. There is a hardness in her eyes I do not like."

"I don't think Gil's lookin' at her eyes," Van said,

"and for that reason, I have my doubts about this 'good Samaritan' business."

"He cannot get that *gitano* pair to water before dark," Rosa said, "and there will be the big fight. He shirks his duty as trail boss, but he will not allow you to replace him."

"There'll be no fight," said Van. "I'll talk to the rest of the outfit so they'll understand. Without Gil gettin' his hackles up, I learned that these Donnegans are goin' to San Francisco. Accordin' to our map, that's about two hundred forty miles."

"Por Dios, they will be with us for three weeks!"

"No matter," Van said. "If you're right, and this pair's ridin' under false colors, they'll give themselves away. As for Gil, there's nothin' like a good, strong dose of somethin' to make a man sick of it. I'm thinkin' he'll have to be cured by the hair of the dog that's bitin' him."

"From this *hija,* this *puta,"* said Rosa, "I fear that Gil may get a dose of something that will not go away."

"Not if you refuse to leave them alone," Van said. "You played right into her hands last night. From here on, take the same watch Gil takes, and stay within sight of him. I don't think Gil will fall to such temptation, but it won't hurt if he has a conscience lookin' over his shoulder."

"He will hate me," Rosa said.

"No he won't. If he's the kind of man you want, and the kind of man I think he is, he'll end up thanking you."

"I will do as you say," said Rosa. "I would have him hate me before I would see this *perra* get her claws into him."

When Estanzio returned, Van estimated they had to travel about twelve miles to water. It should be an easy day, with only chaparral plains as far as they could see. Rosa looked back but was unable to see Gil and the Donnegans. Far behind, Gil's mood shifted from sympathy to disgust and back again. He contemplated, just as

Rosa had, the long miles ahead. Even if Van and the rest of the outfit tolerated this, he thought morosely, he wasn't sure he could. Suppose there was trouble and they had to ride for their lives? He dared not even consider such a possibility, and forced his thoughts off in another direction. Kate's talk of a school of law named for Stephen Austin intrigued him, and even more so the possibility that he might study law. He wondered what it would be like, spending his days in town, riding home in the evening. But if Donnegan established such a school in or near San Francisco, where did he fit in? He had no intention of remaining in California, and even if he did, it made no sense naming the place after Stephen Austin. A memorial to Stephen Austin should be in Texas. Slowly it dawned on him what Kate had been suggesting. Suppose he, Gil Austin, became the partner Judge Donnegan was seeking? Kate had implied that for the right man, Judge Donnegan's plans might be changed. What better place for the Stephen Austin School of Law than San Antonio? It was an exciting possibility, and Gil determined to explore it further. Once the herd was sold, there would be money aplenty, and perhaps Gil Austin *was* destined to become more than just a cowboy. . . .

The Donnegans were game, and despite their discomfort, managed to reach water before dark. Gil was pleasantly surprised when the confrontation he had been expecting didn't materialize. His good humor lasted until he found Rosa on the second watch with him, and he suspected that accounted for the outfit's acceptance of the Donnegans. Rather than try to convince him of the error of his ways, they were going to keep him out of mischief by keeping an eye on him. In defiance, he sought out Kate and took her with him when he began the second watch. It was a poor watch on his part, he thought guiltily, because he didn't circle the herd as the other nighthawks were doing. He held the reins while his horse cropped grass, and talked to Kate. Rosa made her rounds quickly, often riding close enough to hear their words.

"That little tamale follows you around like she's your mother," Kate said angrily. "Does she take a switch to you when you're naughty?"

"Ignore her," said Gil, thankful the darkness hid the flaming red of his embarrassment. "I want to talk to you about this school of law the judge has in mind. I might consider goin' partners with him, if he'd start it in San Antonio. Once the herd is sold, I could put up some gold."

"I don't know," Kate said, as calmly as she could. "This is his dream, and I doubt he'd accept your money. I don't know how he'd feel about Texas. It seems there's so much potential here. Really, I spoke out of turn when I mentioned it to you. You'll have to talk to him, but not until I have spoken to him first. To justify your interest, I'll have to tell him that I spoke of it to you. He becomes angry when I talk too much."

June 24, 1850. Sierra Madre foothills

After five hard days on the trail, the Donnegans had progressed to the extent they could at least keep within sight of the drag riders. Gil felt better. Just when he had begun to wonder if the judge ever intended to approach him about the proposed school of law, Donnegan did.

"Kate sometimes talks too much," said the judge, "but in your case, I believe her confidence is well-founded. We were strangers to you, but you came to our aid, and we've repaid you by becoming a considerable burden. I like a man with compassion, Austin, and as Kate told you, I'm an admirer of your late uncle. I am willing to consider you as a potential partner, and if we can reach an agreement to your satisfaction and mine, we'll establish the school in Texas. The Stephen Austin School of Law. Do you have some questions?"

"One," said Gil. "If you're willing to go all the way

back to Texas, why did you come all the way to California to begin with?"

Donnegan laughed long and hard before he spoke.

"You've seen me ride. Do you blame me for choosing an area that could be reached almost entirely by water?"

"No," Gil grinned, "I reckon I don't."

"Besides that," said Donnegan, "in my years on the bench, I accumulated some powerful enemies, and my first thought was to get as far from them as I could."

Gil said nothing, and the judge continued.

"I have but two stipulations. The first is something I must ask you *not* to do, and the second is a personal favor to which I hope you will agree."

"I'm listening," Gil said.

"I want no money from you. This is my project, and I'd planned to fund it before I ever laid eyes on you. Now for the favor. As I've told you, my assets in New York are being liquidated. If my funds aren't already in San Francisco, they soon will be. Except for travel money for Kate and me, I want you to take these funds —in gold—back to Texas with you."

"That's some kind of responsibility," Gil said. "How *much* gold?"

"Fifty thousand dollars' worth."

Gil whistled long and low.

"You have the men to protect it," said Judge Donnegan. "I do not. Will you do it?"

"You sure it'll be ready when we get to San Francisco?"

"It should be," said Judge Donnegan. "If it's not there when we arrive, it won't be long in coming. Could you not wait a few days, if you have to?"

"Yeah," Gil said, "I reckon I could. Is that all?"

"One more thing. In your own handwriting, I want you to tell me all about yourself. What you say isn't as important as how you say it. I think you have the makings of a lawyer, and I want to see how well you express yourself."

After supper, while it was still light, Gil took a stub of pencil and a ragged tablet from his saddlebag. With the rest of the outfit wondering what he was up to, he sat with his back against a pine and began to write. He wrote two pages, signing his name at the bottom of the second one. The following morning he would give the manuscript to Judge Donnegan. To Gil's extreme satisfaction, on the sixth day after he'd taken in the unfortunate pair, the Donnegans were able to keep up to the drag riders. Gil resumed his duties as trail boss and began studying the map with an eye for San Francisco.

"I figure we're a day's drive from the Cuyama River," he said. "We'll follow it northwest maybe thirty miles, until it turns west to the Pacific. From there we'll continue northwest another thirty miles, to Santa Margarita lake."

They were within half a dozen miles of the point where Gil estimated they would reach the Cuyama River, when Mariposa left the horse herd and rode back to meet the oncoming longhorns. The Indian paused at the point, spoke to Ramon, and then rode on to find Gil. Mariposa wasted no words.

"Fire come," he said, pointing eastward.

The wind was out of the northwest and told him nothing, but Gil could see a faint yellowing of the sky to the east. It didn't look like smoke.

"Take the horse herd," Gil told Mariposa, "and head them just as hard as you can toward the Cuyama River!"

Ramon was pointing toward the east long before Gil reached him.

"We're goin' to have us a stampede, Ramon, so get ready. We have to make the Cuyama River ahead of that prairie fire!"

"We mebbe got time," Ramon said. "That not be smoke. Is dust."

It *was* dust, and by looking close, they could see the cause of it. A moving line of deer and antelope ran for their lives, and in their midst was a lumbering grizzly, seeking only to escape the flames. Finally they could see the coyotes and jackrabbits, and could hear the frightened chatter of the birds. Gil kicked his horse into a gallop and rode to warn the rest of the riders, if they didn't already know. As they had traveled north, the terrain had changed. While there was still an abundance of chaparral, there was other vegetation. The tall dry grass brushed his stirrups. By the time he reached the drag, words were unnecessary. Smoke hung in a gray cloud in the sky to the east.

"We'll have to stampede the herd," Gil shouted, "and try to reach the Cuyama River!"

Van galloped his horse near the tag end of the herd, drew his Colt and began firing. The rest of the drag riders followed, whooping and swinging lariats. This was going to be the supreme test for the Donnegans, and the last word Gil had was for their benefit.

"There's a prairie fire coming! If we don't reach the river, we'll be roasted like grasshoppers. Ride!"

Gil joined the drag riders as they forced the longhorns to run. The only advantage they had was that the fire was still a good distance away, but it was coming against the wind, and the flames would travel faster and burn hotter. Once the fire came close enough, closing in from the east, it would be all but impossible to keep the longhorns headed north. Their reaction to any danger was to flee from it, and if the stampede broke to the west, the steers would be directly in the path of an enemy they couldn't possibly outrun. Gil looked again to the east, and the smoke against the blue of the sky seemed unchanged. The stampede had begun in earnest, with the sharp horns of the brutes behind providing ample incentive for their companions in the ranks ahead. The longhorns must hit the river at a dead run, with enough momentum to take the herd across. Otherwise the brutes would scatter to drink, and there was no time for that.

"Keep the ranks closed," Gil shouted. "Keep 'em tight!"

Two steers were down. One had stepped in a hole and

had a broken foreleg, and the other had been mortally gored. Gil shot them and rode on. The stampede thundered on, making the first hint of smoke all the more ominous. If the flames came close enough for them to smell the smoke against the wind, their race might be in vain. But no! Ahead Gil could see the leafy tops of distant trees. They were at the crest of a slope, and below them was a small valley through which the river would run. The herd tore out, hell-for-leather, toward the distant water, and Gil could tell when the lead steers hit it. That was always a critical time, for the herd seemed to pause, and the riders had to fight to keep the longhorns bunched and moving. The flank riders suddenly had a problem on their hands, as the farthest ranks of the herd became aware of the water ahead. But hard-riding drag riders kept the ranks tight, making it difficult for bunch quitters to break away. Finally the tag end of the herd splashed across the river, and the riders had an unpleasant surprise.

"It's deep enough," Van said, "but mighty narrow. If the wind shifts, the fire could jump the water."

"More like spring branch than river," Juan Padillo observed.

"I smell the smoke," Rosa said. "The fire comes closer."

There was the roar of Colts, as riders shot the steers gored in the river crossing. The Donnegans had fallen behind, but Gil could see them coming. The longhorns crowded the west bank of the river, seeking water. Mariposa and Estanzio had watered the horses and had taken them well beyond the river. Vegetation flourished along the riverbanks, most of it second growth, providing a dry first generation to fuel the oncoming flames.

"This part of the river's too narrow," said Gil, "with too much brush overhanging the banks. The fire's likely to just jump to the other bank and keep going. We'd better set some backfires as far up- and downriver as we can, in the time that we have. I want Van, Ramon, Vicente, and Pedro to come with me. The rest of you cross and begin driving the longhorns away from the river."

Gil led his companions a hundred yards east of the riverbank. They cut the tops from young pines to beat out the flames, and then positioned themselves thirty yards apart, paralleling the distant riverbank. Here there was only grass, and without heavy brush and chaparral to feed the flames, their backfires could be controlled. Carefully they set their fires, and just before the flames reached the heavy brush along the river, the backfire was beaten out. Gil and Vicente worked their way downriver, and after a few hundred yards found that the stream had begun to widen. The soil had become sandier, and the river had made itself a wider channel. The fire approaching from the east was now close enough for them to see the flames, as clumps of chaparral became huge fiery torches.

"Come on, Vicente," Gil shouted, "we've done all we can do."

Van, Pedro, and Ramon had seen the oncoming flames, and moved to join Gil and Vicente at the point from which the five of them had started.

"We took it as far as we could," Van said. "River widens some upstream, and we backfired it that far."

"About the way it is downstream," Gil said. "I reckon we've burned off the stretch where the fire might have crossed. At some distant point up- or downstream, it still might cross, but we'll have to risk that. Now let's get across the river and keep the longhorns from gettin' skittish as the fire comes closer."

"They be tired from running," said Ramon.

"I hope you're right," Gil said. "They ought to be pretty well used up, and with the fire not comin' too close, I think we can hold them."

"I wonder what happened to the grizzly and the rest of the critters that hit the river ahead of the herd?" Van said.

"They crossed and kept running," said Gil. "They

didn't know the fire would stop at the river. There's been no lightning, and I'm wondering who started that fire, and why. I reckon we'd best ride careful."

They watched the flames advance, and as the smoke reached them, a few of the steers bawled uneasily. But they didn't run again, and when the wind died at sundown, the fire burned itself out against the barren stretch that had been backfired.

"Next two days ought to be easy," Gil said. "We follow the Cuyama north maybe thirty miles. Plenty of water all the way."

The Donnegans seemed to be going out of their way to avoid antagonizing the rest of the outfit, but Gil reckoned there would be trouble enough when they learned he aimed to stop in San Francisco. Especially when they discovered the purpose.

Gil had the drive on the trail at first light, traveling north along the Cuyama. With an assurance of water, the longhorns were allowed to trail at a gait to their liking, so there were no bunch quitters. They were about two hours into the day when, somewhere ahead, there came the ominous rattle of gunfire.

"I don't like the sound of that," Gil said. "I reckon we'd better stop the drive until we know what's going on."

Taking Van, Ramon, Vicente, Pedro, and Juan Padillo with him, Gil rode ahead. He found Mariposa and Estanzio were holding the horses, waiting for him.

"Hold them here," Gil told the Indian duo, "until we return."

The firing continued, and from the pattern of it, a group of antagonists were attacking a lone defender. The riders soon found his position ahead of them, behind some rocks at a bend in the river. While they were unable to see him, they could see his horse behind concealing chaparral. Once the besieged man had fired, no less than eight attackers opened up on his position.

"Shuck your rifles," Gil told his men. "Not much fire-power, but maybe enough to cover that poor devil until he can get away."

Gil and his riders dismounted, leaving their horses concealed near the river. On foot they climbed a ridge, making their way north until they overlooked the positions of the attackers. Gil waited until there was a lull in the shooting and shouted a warning.

"You hombres burnin' all the powder, just hold your fire. I have enough rifles up here to even the odds."

"This ain't none of your affair," an angry voice shouted. "Stay out of it."

"I'm makin' it my affair," Gil said. "You behind the rocks, get your horse and ride."

There was movement below, where the attackers were concealed, and Gil sent a slug screaming into the brush. It came close enough to leave its intended target swearing. There was no more movement from the attackers' position. The lone defender had moved with the stealth of an Indian, coming up the ridge leading his horse, seeking his rescuers. He was Mexican, not far out of his teens, if that. He wore moccasins, was dressed entirely in buckskin, his hat broad-brimmed with a pointed crown. His left arm hung useless, the buckskin sleeve bloody.

"Pardner, you need some doctorin'," Gil said.

"Gracias," said the Mexican youth, "but there is no time. Already you will have trouble enough. Adios, amigos. Joaquin Murrietta does not forget."

Once he had topped the ridge, he swung into the saddle and was gone. Gil turned his attention back to the attackers.

"Now you gents can come out into the open, but keep your hands where I can see them."

Slowly they emerged from behind bushes, trees, and rocks.

"I reckon there's some good reason," Gil said, "why eight of you coyotes are gunnin' for one man."

"Damn right there is," said one of the men angrily. "That no account Mex is Joaquin Murrietta, a thief and a killer. We trailed the bastard all the way from Diablo Plains."

"I have no proof of that," said Gil. "Are you the law?"

"Damn right we're the law."

"I don't see a badge," Gil said.

"Don't make no diff'rence."

"It does to me," said Gil. "Now mount up and ride back the way you came."

"Mister," said the self-appointed leader, "far as I'm concerned, your bunch is part of the Murrietta gang. We'll meet again, when you ain't got the drop." They mounted their horses and rode away.

"They want him almighty bad," Gil said. "The yellow coyotes tried to burn him out. They set that fire, and he crossed the river north of us."

"I kind of wish you hadn't run 'em out of here so quick," said Van, "so we could have learned what town they're from. I'd like to avoid it."

"No matter," Gil said. "This was my decision, and if there's trouble on down the trail, it'll be mine. If that bunch feels froggy enough, they can jump me. Let's get back to the herd."

June 25, 1850. Approaching the La Panza Mountains

In the southern foothills of the La Panza Mountains, the Cuyama turned due west on its way to the Pacific.

"From here," Gil said, "we're thirty miles south of Santa Margarita lake, and our map shows no water in between. I'll ride ahead and see if there's a spring. If not, it's dry camp."

Gil rode northwest through the La Panza foothills, and soon found himself surrounded by towering ponderosa pines. There were other trees, totally unfamiliar to him, and Gil reined up. They were so tall—

more than three hundred feet, he guessed—he could barely see the tops of them.*

The forest was cool, the sun having to fight its way through dense foliage. Some stands of trees grew so thick, it was impossible for Gil to ride through them. The Texas steers, with their massive horn spreads, weren't going to find it easy getting through. Their drive through the forest would be slow, but somewhere the length of this mountain range, there had to be water. Gil saw rabbit, deer, and coyote tracks, and though he watched for bees, he was unable to see them in the gloom of the forest. Suddenly his horse snorted and surged ahead. The water tumbled off a rock shelf into a large pool and then babbled away as a respectable run-off. Gil watered his horse and took a long drink himself. The water was cold, the most satisfying he'd had since leaving the Sierra Madre foothills. Bearing the good news, he rode back to meet the drive, estimating the distance at about twelve miles.

"We're about eighteen miles south of Santa Margarita lake," Gil said as they began their second day's drive through the huge forest.

The Donnegans now rode well enough to keep up to the longhorns, and although Gil hadn't spent any more time with Kate, she smiled at him often. Rosa ignored him with a similar consistency, smiling not at all. Their second day in the heavily forested La Panza foothills was more difficult than the first. They constantly lost time guiding the longhorns around heavy stands of timber. One old steer began hooking a huge ponderosa, forcing Ramon and Pedro to rope the brute and drag him away. Gil rode out at noon, mostly to look at the terrain ahead, hoping there were no steep drop-offs or canyons. They'd lost so much time getting through the forest, he was almost sure they'd have to run the herd if

* This area is now Los Padres National Forest; the unfamiliar trees are redwoods.

they reached water before dark. With that in mind, he paused to talk to Estanzio and Mariposa.

"Take the horses on to water," he told them, "and then move them away from the water to graze."

When they finally emerged from the forest, the elevation was sufficient for them to see the blue of the Pacific, twenty miles to the west. It had been a long, tiring day, and the longhorns began to bawl their thirst and frustration.

"Thank God there's no wind," Van said, "or these brutes would be on their way to the ocean by now."

"We'll never reach Santa Margarita lake before dark," said Gil, "unless we run the herd the rest of the way. We'd need a good two hours, and we have only one."

Again they forced the longhorns to run, driving them northwest. Santa Margarita lake was an elongated body of water, stretching westward as far as they could see. Mariposa and Estanzio had watered the horses and had taken them to graze, so there was plenty of room for the thirsty longhorns. After supper, Gil spent some time with the map. They were 120 miles from Coyote lake, just south of San Jose. Gil figured it at sixty miles from San Jose to the eastern shore of San Francisco Bay.

"How far are we from San Francisco?" Kate Donnegan asked.

"Maybe a hundred eighty miles," Gil said.

"We're not going to San Francisco," said Van.

"But we are," Kate said.

"So Gil and the trail drive will be going there as well," Rosa said.

"Gil's a big boy and can speak for himself," said Kate maliciously. "Why don't you ask him?"

Rosa turned to Gil, and while she said nothing, she didn't need to. He hadn't intended to announce the delay in San Francisco in this way, but now he could only admit to the truth of it. As calmly as he could, he explained his reason for going to San Francisco, without mentioning Judge Donnegan's money. He dwelt on the preparation of the joint venture he and the judge would undertake in San Antonio. Nobody said anything. Rosa and Van seemed struck dumb, incapable of speaking, while the rest of the outfit didn't feel justified in interfering. Gil finally broke the silence.

"It's time to get with the herd. Who wants the first watch?"

The riders had their eyes on Van and Rosa, and when neither of them volunteered for first watch, Gil quickly had the first watch covered. Van and Rosa had held out for midnight to dawn, and everybody knew why. Gil was in for it.

Supper was eaten in silence, and Gil pondered the strange events that had him at odds not only with Rosa, but with his brother as well. He believed they were judging the Donnegans unjustly, Rosa because of Kate's interest in Gil, and Van because he favored Rosa over the flamboyant Kate. But damn it, Rosa had dealt him nothing but misery all the way from Texas, and he was tired of it. He told himself Kate Donnegan was a beautiful woman, near his own age, and obviously interested in him. Besides, there was Judge Donnegan's proposal to honor Stephen Austin, and he, Gil Austin, had been asked to participate. Van had a wife, a child, and a life of his own, while Rosa didn't seem to know *what* the hell she wanted. Who were they to insist on living Gil's life for him? He would ride his own trail, and if they didn't like it, then that was just too damn bad.

23

$\mathcal{P}$edro and Vicente joined Gil, Van, and Rosa on the second watch. Pedro and Vicente quickly distanced themselves from their three comrades, lest they become involved in the controversy that was almost sure to follow. Gil just wanted it over and done with, so he made the first move.

"I reckon the two of you are pawin' the ground to get at me, so go on and work off your mad. Let's be done with it."

"I ain't so much mad as just purely disgusted," Van said. "Now if you aimed to haul fancy-dressed lumber from Shreveport and build yourself some kind of mansion, or if you went lookin' to buy a stable of racehorses, I could maybe understand that."

"I haven't told you this," said Gil, "because I didn't want to say it before everybody else, so I'll tell you now. I'm not being asked to put up any money. What I also haven't told you is that we're going to San Francisco so that I can pick up Judge Donnegan's funds. I'll be taking fifty thousand dollars back to Texas for him. Now how in tarnation can you find fault with that?"

"Because it makes no sense," Van said. "You've known this so-called judge less than two weeks, and not only is he asking no money from you, he's trusting you with fifty thousand dollars of his. Somehow, somewhere, he aims to cash in, and when he does, it'll be your chips, not his."

"You don't *know* that!" Gil shouted. "But what if he *does* expect me to put up some money? Once we've sold the herd, some of the money will be mine. Then, by God, if I decide to build a monument to Santa Anna, who's going to stop me?"

"Not me," Van said. "That would make about as much sense as what you've got in mind."

"Come on," Gil said, turning to Rosa. "It's your turn to get your claws into me."

"It is none of my affair," she said. "It is your money and your life."

Her indifference hurt him more than her anger would have. In all his frustration, he turned back to Van.

"Where is it written that a man who starts out as a cow wrassler can't be something more?"

"Cowboying is honest work," Van said, "and it was good enough for you for seventeen years. We come to Bandera Range in 'thirty-three, strugglin' and starvin' until now. Finally, with a decent stake comin', the best you can do is hunker in some dingy office, feedin' off folks' misery in the name of the law."

"This is gettin' us nowhere," Gil snapped. "Are you finished?"

"No," said Van, "but you are. I don't aim to say another word. I'm just goin' to watch this Judge Donnegan get you where he wants you, and then give you a knee where it hurts the most. When he's picked you clean, if you ain't too proud to be a cowboy, I'll pay forty a month and found."

Gil mounted and rode to the far side of the herd, leaving Van and Rosa alone.

"What are we going to do?" Rosa asked.

"Nothing," Van said, "except keep our eyes and ears open. It's a long ride back to Texas, and I'd bet my share of the herd that before we leave San Francisco, this Judge Donnegan makes a believer out of a dumb cowpuncher."

* * *

By first light the herd was again on the trail, following the Salinas River northwest. They would follow the river eighty miles, to Soledad. Van and Rosa were outwardly calm, and the apparent rift within the outfit seemed healed. But Gil knew better, uneasily recalling Van's doubts, and wondering what lay ahead. For the next six days it looked like an easy trail, simply following the Salinas River. There had been virtually no bad weather since they'd reached California, but their second day on the Salinas, that changed. The sun set red behind dirty gray clouds, and a brisk wind from the west had the taste of salt.

"Storm be coming," said Juan Padillo.

"Yeah," said Gil, "and it may be a storm unlike any we've ever seen. I've heard of these storms that spring up out over the ocean, and I reckon we'd better get ready. Tonight it's everybody in the saddle until this storm passes."

The riders tied down their hats with piggin string, loosed their lariats, and after supper they all took to their saddles. The wind grew stronger, plucking at hats and clothing like unseen hands, moaning through the brush and chaparral along the river. Mariposa and Estanzio had moved the horses well away from the longhorns, so if one herd ran, the other didn't have to follow. One old steer faced the rising lonesome wind, bawling long and mournfully. Three others joined in, forming an eerie quartet.

"It's gettin' to them," Van shouted. "They're just waitin' for something to light the fuse."

If the longhorns ran, it would almost certainly be to the east, away from the storm. With that in mind, Gil had positioned his riders five to the north and five to the south of the herd. When the rain came, it hit with such force, the riders were almost swept from their saddles. Like the longhorns, they turned their backs to the fury of the storm. There had been no thunder or lightning, and just when the riders had begun to hope there would be only wind and rain, there came a clap of thunder of such proportions it seemed to shake the very earth. Before the echo faded, the herd was off and running. The riders charged after them, trying to get ahead of the lead steers. Suddenly the sodden ground gave way beneath the front hooves of Gil's horse, and he was barely able to free himself from the saddle before the animal went down. Gil rolled with the fall, praying he wasn't throwing himself into the path of the stampede. He stumbled to his feet, and in the glare of the lightning that followed the thunder, he could see his downed horse struggling to arise. It got up, limping, and Gil caught the trailing reins. He was out of it, and since the herd hadn't slowed, he doubted the other riders had been able to head it. While it was small consolation, the river from which the longhorns had stampeded was the only convenient water. The herd would eventually return to the river, once the sun sucked up the excess water left by the storm.

The thunder had faded to an occasional rumble, and the lightning to an infrequent illumination of the rain-swept world around them. The wind had died, and the rain become only a soft patter. Leading his horse, Gil started back toward the river. He wondered how the Donnegans had weathered the storm. They had remained in camp, on the lee side of some rocks that might have offered some protection.

"Tejanos," Van shouted, "where are you?"

"Here," Gil replied. "My horse fell and I'm afoot."

"Me here," Ramon cried. "Me and Pedro."

"Injun here," said Estanzio from somewhere in the darkness. "Horse no run."

Whatever the circumstances, the Indian riders never raised their voices, especially at night. Nobody else responded, and that might mean they were still in pursuit of the herd. But there was always the terrible possibility that a horse had fallen and one of the riders had been trampled in the stampede. Gil tried not to think of that. The rest of the riders would have to find their way back to camp on their own, and if somebody didn't make it, there was nothing to be done until first light. The sky had begun to clear, and while there was no moon, there was starlight. Slowly, to Gil's relief, the rest of the outfit returned. Rosa was the last to arrive, and Gil wondered if she had purposely done that, just to worry him. If she had, he dared not let her know how well she had succeeded. Once Rosa was sure there would be a storm, she had found a rock overhang and concealed enough dry wood for a fire. They soon had hot coffee, and that helped. To everybody's satisfaction except possibly Gil's, the Donnegans hadn't escaped the fury of the storm, and were properly drenched and bedraggled.

Dawn found many of the longhorns within two or three miles of the point from which they had stampeded. The sky was clear and blue, and the sun was hot.

"We'll bring the closest ones in first," Gil said. "The sun will soon dry up the water from last night's rain, and the wet-weather water holes will be mud. Then the rest of the herd will come back to the river."

The river ran bank full of muddy water. Along the narrow stretch beyond the east bank where the backfires had been set, the water had flooded past the burned-off area. By noon the riders had half the scattered longhorns back along the river.

"We'll be here at least another day," Gil predicted. "Once they get dry they'll come back to the river, but not necessarily to this point. We'll have to ride up- and downstream a ways. If that fails to get the rest of them, I reckon we'll have to run them out of the chaparral one at a time."

By the end of the day following the storm, most of the temporary water holes were only mud, and by sundown Gil and the outfit had gathered all but three hundred of their original herd of longhorns.

"We can't afford to lose that many," Van said.

"I don't aim to," Gil replied. "We'll ride the river again, first thing in the morning. Then, if we're still missing a bunch, we'll spread out to the east and look for them."

At first light more of the steers had returned to the river, but a quick tally left them still missing 150 head.

"I'll take four riders upstream," Gil said, "and Van, you take four downstream. We'll each cover about five miles, and if we're still short, it's into the chaparral."

Their search produced another 110 head, leaving them forty short.

"After bringin' 'em this far," Van said, "I purely don't like losin' any. We've already lost part of a day here; let's use the rest of it out in the chaparral."

Near sundown they returned to the river with nothing to show for their efforts.

"Damn it," Gil said, "that's it. I don't aim to kill another day here."

Just before dark, Mariposa rode downriver, driving twenty-five steers.

"Them come to water," said the Indian. "We round up."

"That leaves only fifteen," Van said. "The others might show up before we leave tomorrow."

"Maybe," Gil said, "but if they do or don't, we're movin' out."

At dawn Gil again had the trail drive moving, following the Salinas River northwest. In the late afternoon, ten miles north of their old camp, they found the fifteen missing longhorns grazing beside the river.

"I don't believe this," Gil said. "We didn't lose a one."

After supper there was some daylight left, and Rosa took clean clothes from her saddlebag. She hadn't spoken to Gil since the night he and Van had argued, and Gil had made no attempt to speak to her. Surprisingly, she turned to Van with a request she once would have asked of Gil.

"Van, I am going down the river to take a bath. Please see that no one comes that way."

Mariposa and Estanzio had the horse herd half a mile upriver, and while Rosa's request was simple, Gil thought it unnecessary. This was her way of further antagonizing him. He said nothing, but the furious look he directed at the girl wasn't lost on Kate Donnegan.

"I have nothing better to do," said Kate. "I'll go with you."

All eyes were on Rosa, but she said nothing. Van started to speak, found Gil watching him, and kept his silence. Van had no idea what might take place between these two, but he believed Rosa could and would stand up to her. Once the two had disappeared into the chaparral, the rest of the outfit sat looking after them. Judge Donnegan cleared his throat but did not speak.

Rosa followed the river until she came to a place where the bank was clear enough for her to reach the water. There was a flat, mossed-over rock shelf that offered a place to sit, but Rosa remained standing. Kate laughed.

"Go ahead and strip, chili pepper. Or do you think your parts are different from mine?"

"I know they are," said Rosa, turning to face her. "Mine have not been used."

It was a direct insult, and so intended, but Kate only laughed. Then she threw a taunt of her own.

"Sure they've been used, you little smartmouth, and they'll be used again. I'm used to hooking what I want, and my bait's better than yours."

"We shall see," said Rosa. "I have no interest in anything you have to say. Please go away. I wish to be alone, to take my bath."

"Maybe I want a bath myself."

"There is plenty of river," said Rosa. "Please find your own place and leave me alone."

"Oh, I couldn't do that," said the arrogant Kate. "I like it here."

"Then you may have it all to yourself," said Rosa.

Cat-quick, she backed away from the river, giving Kate a violent shove. With a shriek like a gut-shot panther, the redheaded woman hit the water flat on her back. Rosa took the clothes she had brought with her and walked back upriver. Kate's scream had them all on their feet, and Gil looked murderous.

"Quick bath," Van said, a twinkle in his eyes.

"There was none," Rosa said calmly. "Kate fell in and muddied the water."

June 28, 1850. Northwest, along the Salinas River

Gil estimated they'd traveled only a little more than twenty miles, after five days on the Salinas. The outfit was up well before first light, and by the time it was light enough to see, they were pushing the herd toward what he hoped would be a better day than the last five. Kate kept well behind the drag riders, and didn't smile as often, but the judge spent more and more time in quiet conversation with Gil.

July 2, 1850. Soledad

Soledad proved to be a sleepy little village with nothing of prominence except the standing walls of an old Spanish mission.*

"In the morning," Gil told them, "we travel due north fifteen miles, to the San Benito River. We'll follow it for about thirty miles, and when we leave it, we'll be less than twenty miles from Coyote Lake."

"Some lakes have names, and some do not," said Pedro, looking at the map Gil had spread out.

"I reckon the government surveyors who drew this map wrote down names when they could," Gil said, "and when they couldn't, they just put a lake there without a name. There's one, unnamed, maybe fifty miles

---

* Soledad Mission was built by the Spanish in 1791.

north of Coyote lake, and I'm thinking it'll be a good place to settle down the herd while we visit San Francisco."

"How far is that from San Francisco?" Judge Donnegan asked, taking interest.

"Six or seven miles from the eastern shore of San Francisco Bay," Gil replied. "According to this map, there's little villages scattered all along the bay. Once we reach this lake, I can't see moving the herd again until we're ready to leave for the goldfields."

"Of course not," Judge Donnegan hastily agreed. "That should be convenient to any part of the city."

July 3, 1850. San Benito River

Once they left the Salinas River at Soledad, it was dry country all the way to the San Benito. East of the river there was a mountain range that stretched as far south as they could see. On these and other mountains, as they traveled farther north, there was more and more yellow pine. Their first night on the San Benito was peaceful enough, but the second night, a few minutes into the second watch, Mariposa and Estanzio became uneasy. Mariposa greeted Gil quietly before approaching in the darkness.

"Trouble?" Gil asked.

"Mebbe so," said Mariposa. "Hombres come. Back trail. Mebbe dawn."

How the Indian knew, Gil had no idea, but not for a moment did he doubt Mariposa's judgment. When one or both his Indian riders sensed danger, he prepared for it, as he did now.

"Before dawn," said Gil, "spread your blankets where they can be seen at first light. Then take some limbs and brush and elevate them enough so it'll look like you're sleeping. It won't fool them in daylight, but I'm not lookin' for them to wait for that. I'll warn the rest of the outfit."

Actually, he had only to talk to the five riders who had nighthawked the first watch. The second watch would be with the herd, mounted and ready.

"That sounds like the bunch that was after Murrietta," Van said. "What bothers me is, maybe they *are* the law. You give any thought to what might be the penalty for gunnin' down a sheriff's posse?"

"No," said Gil, "and when a bunch comes after me with guns in their hands, killing on their minds, and without cause, then I purely don't give a damn *who* they are. It was you that said I should have asked them jaybirds where they was from, so we could avoid them. A lawman will identify himself. I have no respect for men who travel in packs, like cur dogs."

"All we have done," said Ramon, "is stop them from killing this young hombre we did not know."

"It's just built up to a hell of a misunderstanding," Van said, "and on the frontier, that can get a man's neck stretched. But I'm with the outfit; if they come in shootin', I'll shoot back."

"If they're the kind I think they are," said Gil, "you won't have anything to shoot at. They'll likely bring more men, and they'll be shooting from cover. We'll all have the herd between us and the river, and with the chaparral and poor light, we'll let them open the ball."

"You're almighty certain they're goin' to cut down on us from across the river," Van said. "They could come at us from the west, and catch us totally off guard."

"No chance of that," Gil said. "Mariposa and Estanzio heard them as they came down our back trail. They're ahead of us. Those of you from the first watch, unroll your blankets near the river. Using grass, leaves, and brush, rig those blankets so that in poor light they look like sleeping men."

Satisfied they understood and agreed, Gil went to awaken the Donnegans. He would send them well into the chaparral, beyond the grazing herd. Then he would return to the herd and prepare the nighthawks on the second watch.

* * *

Not a sound broke the stillness of the night except the occasional cry of a coyote. Once, as though in answer to the coyotes, a steer bawled, but except for that, the herd was quiet. Since time immemorial, the most trying time for men was not the battle itself, but waiting for it to begin. When the sky finally began to gray to the east, Gil's eyes were on the far side of the river. The western slope of the foothills beyond the river would be out of range for the attackers. Gil didn't know how many men they might be facing, so he dared not split his force. Otherwise, he thought, he could have circled some men into those foothills and set up a cross fire. He hoped they could end this foolish running fight. Life on the trail was difficult enough without having to be forever anticipating an ambush. He longed for the day when there would be a repeating rifle, providing a man the firepower he now enjoyed with the Colt six-shooter. Finally, from across the river, the rifles cut loose, and in the wake of the thunder, there was a shout in a familiar voice.

"Told you we'd meet again. Now, send out that coyote, Joaquin Murrietta, an' maybe we'll call it even."

"Joaquin Murrietta is behind you," shouted a voice from the ridge beyond the attackers, "and this time, you cowardly dogs, he is not alone!"

It was all the warning the attackers had. Behind them more than a dozen rifles roared, and the silence that followed seemed all the more profound. Gil's eyes searched the terrain from the farthest bank of the river to the foothills beyond, and saw no movement.

"Madre de Dios!" Rosa cried. "They are all dead!"

"Nobody move," said Gil. "We'll give it a few more minutes."

The silence remained unbroken until the Donnegans arrived.

"So much noise," said Kate, "we couldn't sleep."

"We are so sorry," said Rosa.

"We're movin' out," said Gil. "Let's get with it."

"Must we go without breakfast?" Kate asked.

"The rest of us aren't hungry," Van said. "There's a bunch of dead men in the brush across the river."

"How . . . who . . . killed them?"

"Not us," Gil said, "but they may have friends who won't know that. I want us as far from here as we can get, before the buzzards gather."

July 5, 1850. Twenty miles south of Coyote lake

At the end of that day, following the shooting at dawn, the drive had reached the point where it had to leave the San Benito River. There, Gil had them bed down the herd, and at first light the following morning they set out for Coyote lake.

"The map shows no water nearer than Coyote lake," Gil said, "but there might be a spring or water hole. Once we reach the lake, we'll be just three days from the stop I aim to make near San Francisco."

"Ride ahead, then," Van said, "and let's try and make that twenty miles before dark. Not that I'm all that anxious to get to Coyote lake. I just want to be as far away as possible when somebody discovers that buzzard bait south of here."

So Gil rode out, hoping for a decent terrain the last few miles before they reached Coyote lake. He had a gloomy premonition that if the longhorns had water by sundown, they were going to have to rattle their hocks and run for it.

24

Gil reached Coyote lake without difficulty, and saw nobody along the way. He judged the distance at more than the expected twenty miles, but saw no reason the cattle couldn't run, if that's what it took to get them to water before dark. With that assurance, he watered his horse and rode back to meet his companions. It was still early in the day, and the herd was trailing well. Their orneriness and bunch quitting would increase as their thirst intensified. Gil had only waved to Mariposa and Estanzio, but he paused as Ramon rode to meet him.

"Good trail?" the point rider asked.

"All the way," Gil assured him. "We'll continue to trail them as hard as we can, but if they have to run to reach water before dark, there's no problem I can see."

Gil rode back and joined the drag riders, and was not at all surprised to find Kate Donnegan lagging as far behind as she safely could. She had distanced herself from them all, since that evening she'd left the camp with Rosa, only to return sopping wet from a dunking in the river. At this point, having no choice, both women had to bide their time. But something had to happen, and Gil could see just two possible conclusions. If Judge Donnegan and Kate *did* go to Texas, Rosa would make good her threat to remain in California. On the other hand, Rosa would demand a commitment from him that would destroy any possible relationship with the Donne-gans. However he viewed the volatile situation, he could be sure of only one thing: they were building up to a showdown, and it would come in San Francisco. Van was riding alongside him, and interrupted his gloomy meditation with a question.

"How does it look from here to Coyote lake?"

"No canyons or other pitfalls," Gil said. "We can run them if we have to. I'll send the horses on ahead, a couple of hours before sundown."

It was a strategy that had worked well before, and it did this time. The wind changed direction in the late afternoon, bringing the thirsty herd the scent of water, and all the riders had to do was get out of the way. Once they had settled down for the night and supper was done, Gil studied the map and announced their position.

"We're fifty miles from this unnamed lake, which is as near to San Francisco as we'll be takin' the herd. I figure three more days. There's no water marked on this map, but as near as we are to the coast, I figure there'll be creeks and springs along the way. I'll scout ahead for water."

July 9, 1850. San Francisco

As Gil had expected, there had been springs and creeks, and the three days' journey from Coyote lake had been without incident. At sundown of the 144th day on the trail, they bedded down the herd near the un-named lake that appeared to be only six or seven miles from San Francisco Bay.*

"We'll be here long enough for everybody to have a turn in town," Gil said, "but let's wait until morning."

* * *

* Lake Chabot, near present-day San Leandro

The night before, Gil had spent several hours in conversation with Judge Donnegan, so his announcement
the following morning came as no surprise.

"I have some business to take care of, and until that's
done, I'd like for most of you to remain with the herd. A
couple of you can go with me, and when we return,
some more of you can ride in."

"I wish to go," said Rosa.

"So do I," Van said.

The rest of the riders remained silent. They all knew
Gil was about to undertake something that would
change his life, and perhaps, in ways unknown to them,
their own. But this strange obsession of Gil's was hurting Van and Rosa the most, and it was their right to
keep whatever rein on the situation they could.

As expected, the eastern shore of San Francisco Bay
was but a short ride from the area where the longhorns
had been bedded down. The Donnegans and Gil rode
ahead, while Van and Rosa followed. Their first look at
this widespread town spawned by the discovery of gold
took their breath away. There seemed an unending ar-
ray of stores, shops, theaters, saloons, and bawdy houses
strung out along the shores of the bay. Eventually they
came to an enormous hotel, three stories high, and it
was before this magnificent structure that Gil and the
Donnegans reined up. The hotel had balconies on the
second and third floors, and above the third-floor bal-
cony was its name: THE PALACE HOTEL. The letters were
black, outlined in gold, and three feet high. The hotel
even had its own adjoining saloon and café, either of
which could be entered from the hotel lobby. To the left
was the Mother Lode saloon, and to the right, the Nugget Café. Gil and the Donnegans dismounted. Gil
looked at Van and Rosa as though he expected them to
wait outside, but they didn't. The five of them entered
the hotel, walking on plush red carpet, Judge Donnegan
approaching the registration desk like he owned the
place.

"We shall be needing rooms for several days, sir,"

said the judge in his most pompous manner. "I am Judge Lionel Donnegan, recently retired from the New York bench, and this is my daughter Kate. A two-bedroom suite for us, and a single for Gil Austin, my associate. Mr. Austin has a herd of Texas steers bound for the goldfields."

"Twenty-five dollars a day for the suite," said the clerk, unimpressed, "and ten dollars for the single. In advance."

"We will settle when we depart," said the judge.

The desk clerk looked as though he'd heard all this before, and before he could refuse, Gil spoke.

"I'll stand good for the rooms," he said shortly. "I have four thousand steers, and I won't be leaving in the middle of the night."

That got them a little respect and the keys to their rooms, and as Judge Donnegan and Gil signed the register, Van took Rosa's arm and guided her to the desk.

"A room for the lady," Van said. "She's with the Austin herd. I'm Van Austin."

Gil just glared at them while Rosa signed the hotel register. Van took the key to her room. It was on the second floor, and he and Rosa followed Gil and the Donnegans up the fancy carpeted stairs. The Donnegan suite was across the hall from Gil's room, while Rosa's room was two doors away. Van gave Rosa the key and they remained in the hall while Gil and the Donnegans entered their rooms.

"Gil does not like this," Rosa said.

"There may be a hell of a lot of things he won't like before we're out of this town," Van replied. "One of us needs to be close by all the time. I can't, but you can."

It was a brilliant move, and before the ordeal ended, Rosa would fully appreciate Van's fast thinking. Gil came out, locked his door, and without a word knocked on the Donnegans' door.

"Judge," Gil said when Donnegan opened the door, "I'm ready when you are."

Donnegan closed the door and they waited. Gil was

impatient and nervous, well aware that Van and Rosa watched him. Finally the door opened again and the judge came out. Kate wasn't with him. The four of them left the hotel, mounted their horses and rode toward the bay. The judge seemed to know exactly what he was looking for, and eventually they reined up before a squat flat-roofed building that proved to be the Bank of San Francisco Bay. Its name, in black, had been lettered in fancy old English on the glass door through which they entered. An elderly woman arose from her desk to greet them.

"I am Judge Lionel Donnegan, formerly of New York," said Donnegan smoothly. "We wish to meet for a few minutes with your president or head cashier."

"Our president, Mr. Rawlins, is out at the moment, but he should be returning soon. However, there's someone waiting for him in his office . . ."

"We won't need privacy," said the judge. "What I have in mind won't take a minute. We'll be doing some business with him, but not today. I just want him to know who we are. I can introduce myself when he comes in, and be on my way. Won't take a minute."

So they sat on hard-bottomed oak chairs and waited. When Rawlins came in, the secretary spoke to him first. He was a short, fat man in a neat blue suit, a flaming red tie over his boiled white shirt. He turned to meet Donnegan, who was already on his feet.

"I am Augustus Rawlins."

"Judge Lionel Donnegan, recently retired from the New York bench. I am receiving funds from New York, once my holdings there are liquidated. Also, we have a substantial herd of Texas steers to be sold in the gold-fields. We will soon be doing business with you, and I wanted you to be expecting us."

"Delighted," said Rawlins. "Come in when you're ready."

He went on into his office. Donnegan thanked the secretary and they left the bank.

"Now," said the judge, "I must go to the docks area,

find the mail facility, and see if my funds have arrived. You need not accompany me unless you wish to."

"I'll ride along," Gil said. "I've never seen the ocean up close."

"Rosa and me are goin' too," Van said.

Judge Donnegan said nothing, but Van thought the judge would have very much liked to be rid of his companions. Reaching the waterfront, they rode along the docks until they found the warehouse in which there was an office that handled incoming and outgoing mail. Gil, Van, and Rosa remained on the dock while the judge entered the building.

"Madre de Dios," Rosa cried, "so much water! It goes on and on, until the blue of it meets the blue of the sky!"

Gil laughed, and for a moment he was the Gil whom Rosa used to know. Ships lined the docks, most of them flying flags of lands unknown to the Texans. Only two or three flew the stars and stripes of the United States. When Judge Donnegan returned, he was empty-handed.

"Nothing yet," he said.

The four of them rode back the way they had come. Nobody spoke, but the same question was strong in the minds of Gil, Van, and Rosa. How long must they remain here, awaiting this mysterious letter Donnegan expected? When they reached the hotel, Kate was waiting in the lobby. Plainly, she didn't want Gil to escape.

"Gil, you simply *must* take me to the theater tonight," she cried. "It's Shakespeare's *Hamlet,* and Nicholas Bonner's playing the lead."

"I have to get back to the herd," Gil replied. "I promised the others a trip to town."

"The play doesn't start until eight o'clock tonight," she said, pouting. "You have a room here, don't you?"

"I reckon," Gil said, and seemed embarrassed. "I'll spend the rest of the day with the herd, and ride in after supper."

Gil reached the door before he seemed to remember Van. When he turned, it was to Van he spoke.

"You goin' with me?"

"I'll be along," Van said. "I know the way."

Without another word, Gil left the hotel and rode away. Rosa walked with Van to his horse. She could see the anxiety in his eyes, and when he spoke, it was in his voice.

"Rosa, we're building up to somethin', and I'm not sure just what it is. I can see Gil's goin' to be in town more than he's with the herd. I don't want our riders to think we're taking advantage of them, so I'll stay with the herd as much as I can. It'll be up to you to keep an eye on these Donnegans. I purely can't figure what this so-called judge is up to. Gil won't have any money until we sell the herd, and we can't do that as long as Donnegan keeps us sittin' here."

"I do not believe anything is coming from New York," Rosa said.

"Neither do I," Van replied, "and that means he's countin' on some slick dealing here. I'll try to see you tomorrow."

Rosa watched him ride away, feeling alone, uncertain as to what the future might hold. Not wishing to spend the rest of the day in her room, she began to walk along the bay. Even in her moccasins, man's shirt and trousers, and flop hat, she didn't seem out of place. San Francisco had become the melting pot of the new world, as men from South America, Europe, and even China were drawn to California with the discovery of gold. Rosa walked on, eventually coming to the theater of which Kate Donnegan had spoken. It stood out like a longhorn bull in a flock of sheep, painted a brilliant blue, with playbills pasted to its outer walls. Among the remnants of old bills and past attractions were new ones announcing the presentation of Shakespeare's *Hamlet*. While Rosa had read some of Shakespeare's works that Gil had inherited from his uncle, she hadn't understood them all that well, and she had never thought of them as plays involving live people. Now, here was this young man, Nicholas Bonner, who was going to recite the lines of *Hamlet*. Rosa had little doubt that Kate Donnegan would have her way, and that she and Gil would attend this theater. Rosa quickly decided that she, too, would be there. Never had she been to such a place in her life, and it would be a welcome diversion from Gil's foolish obsession with the Donnegans.

Rosa walked only a little farther before returning to the hotel. The lobby was deserted. From the saloon there was the clink of glasses, and from the café, the rattle of dishes. There came the sound of voices, of laughter, and her loneliness seemed all the more profound. She climbed the stairs to her room, let herself in, and locked the door behind her. The room was large and elaborate enough. There was a high-backed bed piled high with comforters, a magnificent oak dresser with filigreed mirror, and an overstuffed parlor chair. The carpet was a deep maroon plush. In one corner stood a solid oak commode and upon it sat a white porcelain pitcher with matching wash basin. Curiously Rosa opened the door in the lower part of the commode and smiled, for there was a white porcelain chamber pot. She hung her hat on the commode's harp, next to a set of fine linen towels. She then stretched out on the bed, fully dressed.* Her window was open, facing the west, and a gentle breeze brought her the salt smell of the Pacific. Never in her life had she felt so lost and lonely. She recalled the happy times on Bandera Range in Texas, which now seemed so long ago and far away. She thought of the lonely grave on the hill above the Rio Colorado, where they had left Bo. Finally she thought of the critically wounded Long John. Did he now rest beside Bo, or would he be waiting at Fort

---

* The harp is an elaborate towel rack mounted above the oak commode. It is so named because of the shape of the harp hand-carved into the wood.

Yuma? More and more it seemed she would not be with the outfit to greet him, as they returned to Texas.

Desperately, Rosa sought something or somebody to which she might cling, to draw strength. She took the old locket, the size of a two-bit piece, all she had that had belonged to her mother, and for a moment held it to her heart. Seldom had she thought of the old locket, for it brought painful memories of that day when her parents had been murdered and mutilated. Now she held it up to the light from the window, running her thumbnail around the groove in the edge. Dirt had collected there, and she tried to remove it. Suddenly the locket divided, and the startled girl was looking at a very old photograph of herself when she had been very young. But the other half of the locket startled her the most, for there was some very fine engraving. Rosa got up, went to the window, and in the better light, she read: *Rosa Onate   June 2, 1830.*

Slowly, she turned to the bed and sat down. Had it been only seven years since Gil had found her hiding from Mexican soldiers, after her parents had been murdered? Beyond a doubt, it was her own childish face in the locket, and June 2, 1830, must have been her birthdate. That meant she had been thirteen when Gil had found her, and she was now past twenty! Once it would have excited her, for it would have made her a woman in Gil's eyes. Now, unless something changed him, it wouldn't matter.

Restless, Rosa got up, stepped out into the hall and locked her door. For a moment she paused before the door of the Donnegans' suite, listening, but heard nothing. She walked down the stairs, and finding the lobby still deserted, paused before the double doors that opened into the saloon. The doors were propped back, and while she couldn't enter, she could see into the dim interior. Two of the poker tables were occupied, and there was the slap of cards as hands were dealt. She could hear a soft whirr and a clatter, and her eyes followed the sound to the far end of the room, to what she would eventually learn was a roulette wheel. A lone man sat at the bar, oblivious to it all. Judge Donnegan had three bottles on the bar before him, and a multitude of glasses. So he spent his free time in the saloon, and Rosa decided such information might be useful. Hungry, she went into the café. She still had sixty dollars of the money Gil had given her at Tucson, and the $550 in gold she'd found in the outlaw cabin, back in New Mexico.

"Come eat with us, Rosa!" cried a familiar voice.

Juan Padillo sat at a corner table, and with him was Ramon, Vicente, and Pedro. Ramon got an extra chair, and Rosa gladly joined them.

"Van said you stay in town," Juan Padillo grinned, "and there be nobody to cook for us but us. We come in so we don't have to eat our own cooking."

"I will be here as long as the Donnegans are," Rosa said.

"Is good," said Ramon. "We do not trust them, but it is not for us to say. We fear that Senor Gil be in trouble."

Rosa spent an enjoyable hour with them, but they all turned somber when it came time to pay the bill. For the five of them, it was twenty-five dollars!

"Por Dios," said Vicente, "mebbe our own cooking not be so bad after all."

When Rosa left the café, Donnegan was still in the saloon. With these gold country prices, where was he getting the money to spend the day drinking? Rosa thought she knew. Having eaten, and having spent some time with part of the outfit, she felt a little better. As she ascended the stairs, the big clock near the registration desk struck three. Rosa stretched out on the bed and slept. When she awakened, it was to a knocking on her door, and the room was almost dark.

"Who is there?" she asked.

"The hotel has a lamp for you," said a voice in the hall.

Rosa opened the door to find a young man standing

beside a four-wheeled cart loaded with coal-oil lamps. He removed the white porcelain globe from one, lighted it and handed it to her.

"We do not leave them in the rooms in the daytime," he said.

Rosa placed the lamp on the dresser and closed the door. Then she sat on the bed, watching the flickering flame as it wrestled with the shadows in the small room. She could hear knocking on other doors, as more lamps were delivered. Finally there was silence, and it seemed a long time before there was another knock, and it wasn't on her door. She eased it open just enough to see out. Gil stood in the hall, and when the Donnegans' door was opened, he stepped inside. Rosa sat down on the bed, tears creeping down her cheeks. She had hoped he might at least see how she was, and speak to her. With a sigh, she got up, poured water from the pitcher into the pan, and washed her face. She then slipped out her door into the hall, and down the stairs. She would reach the theater ahead of Gil and Kate.

"Where's the judge?" Gil asked, as Kate closed the door behind him.

"In his room asleep," Kate said. "He's not feeling well."

"How long is this thing—this play—goin' to last?" Gil asked.

"I don't know," Kate replied, "but what do you care? The theater's within walking distance, and you have a room across the hall."

"I also have a herd of steers out yonder by the lake, and an outfit that likely wonders why the hell I'm in town, sleepin' in a hotel."

Kate laughed. "You're a big boy. You don't have to answer to a bunch of cowboys. Besides, your brother left the chili pepper here, to see that I don't take advantage of you."

Gil didn't laugh. His face flushed, and she knew she'd gone too far. Hastily she tried to undo the damage.

"I'm sorry. I understand your concern for your herd and your men. You can ride out early in the morning, and you're only a few minutes away."

Slowly the fire in Gil's eyes faded and his anger died. He straddled a chair, keeping his silence, and Kate wisely did the same.

Rosa was one of the first to reach the old theater. Admission was two dollars. The stage was a half circle, with the seating curved around it. There were three sections of hard benches, facing left, right, and center stage. Being early, she took a seat at the very front, center stage. She didn't care if Gil and Kate saw her. There were coal-oil lamps along the walls, lamps at stage right and stage left, and one on the wall at center stage, which would light the area behind the actors. Still, the interior of the place was almost dark.

When the play began, the theater was less than a third full. While Rosa was fascinated by all the actors, she was especially impressed by Nicholas Bonner. He was maybe twenty-five, with dark eyes and dark, curly hair. There was an intermission following the second act, and since there was no curtain, some of the women from the audience approached Nicholas Bonner before he could leave the stage. One of the women was Kate, and Rosa wondered what Gil thought about that.

As Rosa observed Kate's fascination with the actor, she was struck with an idea so powerful, she missed the rest of the play as she thought about it. She must meet this actor, Nicholas Bonner, and she must do it tonight. But it wasn't as difficult as she had imagined. The audience departed quickly when the play ended, for it was late. Rosa remained where she was, until the little man who had collected admissions began blowing out the theater lamps.

"You'll have to leave, ma'am," he said. "We're closing."

"I wish to see Nicholas Bonner," Rosa said.

"You should of done that durin' intermission. He'll

leave by the stage door. If he ain't already gone, you can catch him there."

The actor was coming down the back steps as Rosa rounded the building. He paused, and she halted, out of breath.

"Well," he laughed, "the later it gets, the prettier the girls, and here I have only the moonlight by which to observe."

"I wish to meet with you tomorrow," Rosa said. "In private. I must hire an actor for several days. I can pay."

"Beautiful lady, I'm sure it would be more lucrative than what I'm doing, but I'm sorry to say that I am already committed. I will be stuck here every night for the rest of the week."

"I will not need you at night," Rosa said. "Only in the mornings and afternoons. Please, will you meet with me in the morning, where we can talk?"

"I have a key to this back door," he said. "It will be unlocked. Be here at nine o'clock."

"I will be here," Rosa said, and before he could say more, she was gone.

Far into the night Rosa lay awake, thinking, planning. The "play" she had in mind would depend almost entirely on Nicholas Bonner, and only he would be acting. The rest of the players—Gil Austin and the Donnegans —would be unaware of their roles, for their parts would be very, very real.

July 10, 1850. San Francisco

Van rode in the next morning, and when he didn't find Rosa in her room, waited for her in the lobby. At that moment Rosa was seated on a hard bench in Nicholas Bonner's dressing room.

"I wish you to convince a woman you are madly in love with her," Rosa said. "I will pay you five hundred dollars. Can you do it?"

"I have done that a few times," the young actor

laughed, "but never with five hundred dollars to sweeten the pot. Who is she, and what am I to do with her once she is smitten?"

"You met her last night. The one with the falsely colored red hair. Now here is what I wish you to do with her . . ."

Rosa worried all the way back to the hotel. Could she make it work? She had to! Van was right. This Judge Donnegan had some nefarious scheme in mind, and even as he discussed it, he was accumulating an enormous hotel bill—perhaps hundreds of dollars, at San Francisco prices—that Gil Austin might have to pay. She was startled but pleased to find Van waiting in the lobby, but so shaky was her plan, she dared not reveal it, even to him.

"I did not wish to sit in the room alone," Rosa said. "I have been walking."

"Has anything happened?"

"When you and Gil left yesterday," said Rosa, "the judge spent the rest of the day in the saloon drinking. Gil may have to sell the herd to pay the hotel. A meal in the café costs five dollars."

"My God," said Van, "no wonder Gil brought the Donnegans' horses back to camp. I'd better get yours out of the livery and take him with me."

"Did either of the Donnegans come down while you waited for me?"

"No," Van said, "I reckon his honor is sleepin' off his drunk. He'll be down later in the day to load up again. Just wait'll I get back to camp! I'll come down on Gil like a brick wall, allowin' this old bastard to use our money to keep himself in whiskey!"

"No, please," Rosa begged, "leave him in the saloon. I need him there for the next two or three days, and I will need you to take a message to Gil. Whatever you must do, ride in every day at noon. With you away, Gil must remain with the herd. Then when I am ready for him, you will take him an important message."

"You have a plan, then?"

"Yes," said Rosa, "but I cannot tell you more until I am more sure of it. Will you trust me?"

"Every step of the way," he said. "Tell me what to do, and when."

25

*O*nce Van had ridden away, Rosa went to her room.
She counted heavily on Judge Donnegan heading
for the saloon as soon as he was physically able. While
she waited, she read and reread the note Nicholas Bonner had written for delivery to Kate Donnegan. It
suggested a time and place for their meeting that afternoon, and extended to Kate an invitation to attend tonight's performance of *Hamlet* as Bonner's guest. It was
her strongest move, Rosa thought dismally, and her *only*
one. It was almost noon before she heard a door open
and close. She eased her own door open, and to her
relief, saw Donnegan walking unsteadily toward the
stairs. She gave him a few minutes, and once the hall
was clear, crept to the Donnegans' door. Under it she
slipped Nicholas Bonner's note, returned quickly to her
own room and closed the door. The time Bonner had
suggested was two o'clock, in his dressing room at the
theater. Rosa wondered how often the young romeo
had done this. She felt foolish, having paid him for what
he might have done for nothing, but she couldn't gamble on that. When again she heard the Donnegans' door
open and close, she watched Kate hurry down the hall
toward the stairs. She smiled as she recalled Van's de-
scription of Kate Donnegan from the rear. Van had said
there was more activity than two bobcats fighting in a
sack. Rosa stretched out on the bed, satisfied the bait

was more than adequate. Tonight Gil Austin was in for a surprise, which might just be the first of many.

Kate hurried across the lobby, not caring if the judge happened to see her from the saloon. The old fool was becoming overconfident, she decided. Without her to lead him on, how long could this dumb cowboy be kept at bay, while the judge drank himself into a daily stupor? Judging by the café, saloon prices must be staggering. With food and drink being charged to their room, the hotel would soon demand an accounting. This was Thursday, and Nicholas Bonner's last performance of *Hamlet* would be Saturday night. She could do, and had done, worse than this young actor, and the timing was right. Once she pulled out, and Gil Austin took his eyes off her curvy behind, he would divert all his attention to the portly judge. She smiled grimly to herself, contemplating the furor, and hurried toward the anticipated rendezvous.

Without telling Gil, Van had begun inquiring about life—and prices—in the goldfields. Gold, in any form, was going for sixteen dollars an ounce. Potatoes, when they could be had, were three dollars a pound; pork—fatback—was fifty cents a pound; flour, forty cents a pound; and sugar, sixty-two cents a pound. A good mule sold for two hundred dollars. Van spent some time on the waterfront, talking to miners who had a stake and were getting out.

"Our first day at Coloma," a pair of grizzled men told Van, "we went to this tent store an' bought us a meal. We got two tins of sardines, maybe half a pound of cheese, a pound of butter, a packet of hard bread, an' two bottles of ale, an' my God, it was forty-five dollars!"

Van laughed. "I'll stay away from there. What's the name of the place?"

"Sam Brannan's. We heard that he saw all this acomin', and he bought ever' damn tin pan in Californy. Then when we all showed up, a-needin' them tin pans, he was gettin' sixteen dollars apiece. That's an ounce of gold."*

Van was astounded at the number of ships around which there was no activity. Finally he was able to talk to a man who looked as though he might be an officer from one of the vessels.

"Lad," said the seafaring man, "a goodly number of them vessels has been abandoned. The minute they dropped anchor, their crews jumped ship an' lit out for the goldfields. I brought in the *Comet,* an' by God, I had to unload her myself, an' I was the captain. I'm told that since July 1848, out of thirteen hundred men, the United States Army has lost more than seven hundred. Deserted, taking their arms and horses, an' them sent to force the deserters back to duty didn't come back neither. The pursuers an' the pursued went off to dig for gold t'gether."†

Van visited a few of the shops, asking about the prices of beef.

"Name your own price," he was told. "Meat's scarce."

"Why?" Van asked. "There must be game in the mountains."

"The Sierra Nevadas? Damn right they is," said a shop owner. "They's deer, antelope, jackrabbits, quail, an' flocks of ducks an' geese. But nobody's got time to hunt. Men are half starved, livin' on beans, sufferin' from land scurvy, and workin' sixteen-hour days. They ain't no cure for gold fever, 'cept gold or starvation, whichever comes first."

Gil reached the hotel after dark, and when he knocked on the door to the Donnegans' room, there was no response. At the desk he learned that Kate had

* Prior to the Gold Rush, the tin pans sold for twenty cents apiece.
† So many sailors jumped ship that the Pacific Squadron's commander advised the Secretary of the Navy, "For the present and I fear for years to come, it will be impossible for the United States to maintain any naval establishment in California."

gone out in the early afternoon, but that Judge Donnegan was in. Gil went back upstairs and pounded on the door until he began to draw unwelcome attention. He even tried his own key, unsuccessfully. Finally he took his knife, slipped the blade between the edge of the door and the jamb, and forced the latch. While there was no lamp, there was enough light from the window for him to see that the sitting room was deserted. He was between the two bedrooms, and he knew the one on the left was Kate's. He found the door unlocked and the room deserted. In the other bedroom he could see the judge sprawled across the bed, fully dressed.

"Judge?"

The only response was a loud snore. When Gil moved closer, he could smell the whiskey. His honor was dead drunk.

"Damn," he said.

Kate unlocked the door, wondering where Gil was and what he might be thinking. When he suddenly spoke from the darkness, she almost dropped the lamp she'd picked up at the registration desk.

"This is a hell of a time of night for you to come driftin' in alone."

"Next time, I'll bring somebody with me. You're not my daddy."

"Speakin' of your daddy, he's piled on his bed, out cold as a dead trout, and smellin' like he's been dunked in a barrel of forty-rod whiskey."

"He's entitled to a few drinks."

"Few, hell," Gil snorted. "Am I entitled to know where you've been for most of the afternoon and half the night?"

"Not necessarily," she said, "but I don't care. I've been to the theater. The one we attended last night. The way you fidgeted through it, I didn't think you'd want to go again."

"It's the same damn play," Gil said, "and I can't see

why you'd want to go again. Maybe it wasn't the play you went to see."

"Maybe it wasn't," she said. "I'm tired. I'll see you tomorrow, but don't bother riding in until after six. I have plans for the afternoon."

"I have plans for tomorrow night," said Gil. "After your daddy's sober enough to talk, I have some questions, and he'd sure as hell better have some answers. You might want to listen in."

Without another word he stalked to the door, swung it open, stepped into the hall, and closed the door behind him. Just for a moment he paused before Rosa's door, before entering his own room.

Rosa knelt behind the door, her heart pounding. She had been near enough to the door of the Donnegans' suite to hear most of the conversation between Gil and Kate, and had barely gotten her own door closed before Gil came stalking out. She was elated, certain that Kate's plans for the following afternoon included Nicholas Bonner. There was only one loose end. Suppose Kate said something to the judge, and Donnegan stayed out of the saloon? But Rosa had one thing in her favor. The judge would be severely hung over, and his need for a drink should overcome everything else.

July 11, 1850. San Francisco

Rosa left the hotel at half past eight and found the theater's back door unlocked. Bonner sat with his chair kicked back against the wall, waiting for her.

He grinned. "It was almost too easy."

"She was gone all afternoon," Rosa said. "Did you . . ."

"No," said the actor, "we're saving *that* for *this* afternoon. At least, she thinks we are. She tried to lure me to her hotel room, but I persuaded her to wait until this afternoon. I'm meeting her there sometime around one, or as soon as she can hustle her old man off somewhere.

She doesn't strike me as the kind who travels with her daddy."

"I do not think they are related," Rosa said. "How is she to tell you when it is safe for you to go to her room?"

"I'll be in the café by one o'clock," said Bonner. "She'll signal me by coming down to the lobby. When I leave the café, I'll go up the hotel's back stairs. Maybe you ought to be in the café, so you'll know when I go to meet her. Give me fifteen minutes, but no more. There's a limit to how far I'll go with this one, even for money."

Rosa left the theater, taking a roundabout way back to the hotel. She must stay out of sight, lest Kate become suspicious. Rosa hoped Gil didn't ride in early, perhaps curious as to Kate's plans for the afternoon. But he knew the judge had been dead drunk and would need time to sober up.

Shortly before noon Van saddled his horse. Already saddled and waiting were Ramon, Pedro, Juan, and Vicente. Van didn't know what Rosa had planned, but he wanted to be prepared.

"You raised hell about stoppin' here," Gil said, "and you spend more time in town than I do."

"I have my reasons," said Van, "and one of them is to learn what I can about the goldfields. What have you learned?"

"That there's a need for beef," Gil said shortly. "That's enough."

Van and his four companions dismounted before the hotel.

"All of you stick together," Van said, "in case I need you. I'm going in the restaurant for a while."

"We be in the saloon," Ramon said. "First roulette wheel I see since Mexico City."

Van found Rosa already in the café, and hooking a chair with the toe of his boot, sat down across the table from her.

"How is Gil?" Rosa asked.

"About as sociable as a sore-tailed grizzly," Van said. "Did you have anything to do with that?"

"He is upset with Kate and the judge," Rosa said, evading his question. "When Gil rode in, Kate was gone, and did not return until late. Gil went into their rooms and found the judge very drunk. When Kate came in, Gil was angry and they had hard words."

"How did you happen to learn all this?"

"I happened to be in the hall, outside the door," Rosa said.

Rosa sat so that she could see through the open double doors and into the hotel lobby. She and Van had just finished eating when she saw the judge coming unsteadily down the stairs. She waited until he entered the saloon before she spoke to Van.

"It is time for you to take Gil a message. Tell him the judge wishes to see him as quickly as he can get here. Upstairs, in the judge's room."

"I'll get him," Van said, "and I'll be right behind him. I wouldn't miss this for anything in the world."

Rosa had avoided looking at Nicholas Bonner while Van was there. Now she nodded to him, and then toward the hotel lobby. Rosa gripped the sides of her chair to stay the trembling of her hands. If Gil arrived too quickly, the plot would be ruined. But the judge had been in the saloon only a few minutes when Kate came down the stairs. She went to the front door, looked out, and then hurried back up the stairs. Nicholas winked at Rosa, paid his bill and departed.

Rosa walked into the hotel lobby, where she could see the big clock, and it was then five minutes past one. When Gil and Van rode in, she could stand by the plate-glass window and see them long before they got to the hotel. By having Van ride out as soon as the judge had entered the saloon, she believed Van would have reached the camp by the time Nicholas Bonner had departed for his rendezvous with Kate. The lobby clock said it was twenty past one when Rosa saw Gil and Van coming at a fast gallop. She quickly crossed the hotel lobby to the open double doors of the saloon. At the far end of the room, Ramon, Vicente, Juan, and Pedro had gathered around one of the tables. The place was crowded, and ignoring the surprised looks of some of the saloon patrons, Rosa entered and went directly to Donnegan.

"Judge," she whispered, "something terrible is happening. Kate has a strange man in her room."

Donnegan slammed his glass down so hard, most of its contents sloshed out on the bar. He slipped off the stool, almost ran from the saloon, and headed for the stairs. When Gil and Van came in, Rosa was sitting in the lobby. Gil ignored her, but Van looked at her questioningly, and she nodded. Hurriedly they followed Gil as he mounted the stairs. By the time they got to the head of the stairs, they could hear the uproar. They were just in time to see the door open and Nicholas Bonner emerge, carrying his shoes. He closed the door and made haste down the hall, toward the back stairs. By the time they reached the Donnegans' door, they could hear the judge and Kate shouting at one another. Gil was about to pound on the door when their words froze him in mid-motion, and he just stood there listening.

"Damn it," the judge roared, "all I asked you to do was dazzle Austin until I could figure a way to get my hands on the money. You're nothing but a two-dollar New Orleans whore, and that's all you'll ever be!"

"Don't blame *me* for things going sour, you drunken old coot. Austin was here last night, and he's no fool. Anyway, I'm sick of nuzzling up to a man who smells like cows and horses, while you sit in a saloon. As for me being a whore, my money was good enough to buy you passage to California, and I'm more honest than you. At least I give a man something for his money, which is a hell of a lot more than you can say!"

"Get your clothes on, damn it. Maybe we can salvage this yet. Austin still sees me as an authority on the law."

"You?" she cackled. "An authority on the law? All you know about the law, you learned on the wrong side of the bars, and all you got comin' from New York is a bundle of wanted posters. Suppose gullible Gil knew you're in California only because the law's looking for you everywhere else?"

Gil had heard enough. He opened the door and stepped into the room.

"Gullible Gil *does* know," he said.

He left the door open, so Van and Rosa saw it all. Kate's clothes were on the floor, and except for her stockings, she was stark naked. Nicholas Bonner had played his role well. The judge recovered first.

"Gil," he cried desperately, "there's been a damnable mistake."

"There sure as hell has," Gil snarled, "and I made it."

He turned and stalked off toward the stairs, Van following. But Rosa wasn't finished. Her words were to Kate.

"Gil is *so* disappointed," she said sweetly. "He believed your hair was naturally red. You should have colored the rest of it."

With that, she turned away and headed for the stairs. She reached the head of them just in time to hear a fight erupt in the saloon. First there were angry voices, then a shot, followed by the sound of breaking glass. On hands and knees, Juan Padillo crawled out the door, blood dripping from a horrible head wound. He collapsed facedown in the hotel lobby. Using their Colts as clubs, Gil and Van waded into the fight. The barkeep came up with a sawed-off shotgun, and it blew a gaping hole in the ceiling when somebody slugged him with a three-legged stool. Bottles and glasses were flung with abandon, and the big mirror behind the bar shattered with a tinkling crash. Slugged from behind, Van went to his knees, and somebody kicked him in the head. One man was on Gil's back, an arm around his throat, choking the wind out of him. Somebody kneed him in the groin, and then they set out to rearrange his face. It was a drunken brawl, where men fought for the sheer hell of it.

"Knock it off!" a bull voice roared. "This is the law!"

His name was Burr Conklin, and he had two deputies with him. In all, he took fourteen men to jail. Eight of them were miners. Gil, Van, Ramon, Vicente, Pedro, and Juan Padillo were the others. There were four cells. The Texas outfit occupied one, and the miners a second.

"There'll be court in the morning," the sheriff said. "Nine o'clock. You gents just make yourselves comfortable."

Some of the miners began cursing bitterly.

"Quiet!" bawled the sheriff. "Any more mouthin', and I'll see that ever' damn man in that cell gets thirty days!"

That silenced them. The sheriff allowed Rosa to come in briefly.

"Por Dios," she cried, "what are we to do?"

Gil lay on the floor facing the wall and said nothing. It was Van who spoke to her.

"We'll sit here until nine o'clock tomorrow, I reckon, and then if I've got anything to say about it, we're gettin' the hell out of this town. For now, take my horse and tell the rest of the outfit what's happened. When you get back, round up the rest of our mounts and take them to the nearest livery."

When Rosa had gone, they sprawled on the stone floor in glum silence. They bled from countless cuts, their heads hurt, blood still dripped from smashed mouths and noses, and both Juan Padillo's eyes were swelled shut.

"I yet say," Juan Padillo declared defiantly, "that damn roulette wheel, it be crooked. I yet go back and prove it."

"You do, by God," Gil grunted, "and I'll leave you sit here in this miserable *juzgado* until you moss over."

Drawn by the sound of gunfire, Judge Donnegan had witnessed the tag end of the fight from the head of the stairs. He had no idea why the Austins had been sucked into the brawl, but he counted his good fortune, and watched with some satisfaction as Sheriff Conklin led Van and Gil away. It was seldom the law or its minions ever did him a good turn, but having firsthand familiarity with jails and lawmen, he believed he had at least until ten o'clock the following morning before the Austins could get at him. He had the rest of the day, a banker who expected him, and Gil Austin's reputation going for him. If he worked fast, by the time the Austins got out of jail tomorrow, he would be on a steamer bound for parts unknown. He returned to the suite to find Kate gone. Down the back stairs, of course, but where and why no longer mattered. She *had* paid his fare to California, but he no longer had need of her. He was on his own.

As Van had requested, Rosa rode out and told the rest of the outfit about the trouble in town. Once she had returned, she took Van's horse, along with the other five, to the nearest livery. That done, she returned to her room in the hotel, emotionally exhausted. The strain upon her had been terrible, and she hadn't realized its impact until it was so suddenly removed. Half the outfit being in jail was only a temporary inconvenience, and tomorrow they would be released. But now that the Donnegans had been discredited, where did she stand with Gil? Certainly he would be bitter, but for how long? Sooner or later he would conclude that she had been responsible for this tragedy in which he'd unknowingly had the leading role. There had been just too much coincidence. And their troubles in town were far from over, despite Van's determination to leave immediately. The hotel would have an enormous bill someone would be expected to pay, nearly all of it accumulated by the Donnegans. But that, as she later discovered, was the very least of their problems. . . .

* * *

From his small bundle of belongings, Judge Donnegan took a thick packet of papers wrapped in oilskin. From it he took a number of checks, each of which had been imprinted with the names and account numbers of some of the most prestigious law firms in New York. Each check had, apparently, been properly signed and countersigned. Donnegan dragged a chair over near the window where there was more light. He removed the cork from a small vial of ink, dipped in his quill and began to write. In the hand of one of the senior partners, he wrote the check to himself for fifty thousand dollars. Then from the oilskin packet he took the two written pages Gil Austin had given him. In a hand startlingly close to Gil's own, he wrote and signed two bills of sale.

26

July 12, 1850. San Francisco

Sheriff Conklin was at the jail promptly at nine o'clock. He stood in the aisle between the cell rows and looked at the disheveled men awaiting their day in court.

"Listen up, gents," he said, "because I'm only gonna say it once. The saloon has agreed not to press charges if each of you will post twenty-five dollars to pay for the damage. Now that's fair, and if there's any one of you that's too broke, too cheap, or just too damn ornery to settle, then I can arrange some jail time. Pay up, and you can go. Not you, Austin. There's some folks in the office with complaints and claims against you."

The miners paid and were released. Gil paid $150 for himself and his outfit, and the six of them followed Sheriff Conklin to the office. Rosa was there, but she looked worried. Waiting with her was the clerk from the hotel who had checked in Gil and the Donnegans, and Augustus Rawlins, the president of the San Francisco Bay bank.

"Now," said Sheriff Conklin, "let's get to the bottom of this dispute. You first, Bettinger," he said, pointing to the hotel man.

"Mr. Austin owes the hotel money," said Bettinger.

"His friends, the Donnegans, are gone, and he guaranteed their rooms."

The sheriff looked at Gil.

"I'll pay for the rooms," Gil said. "How much?"

"Thirty dollars for you, thirty dollars for Rosa Onate, and $925 for the Donnegans."

The panic in Rosa's eyes matched the anger in Gil's. When he spoke, his voice was dangerously low.

"Mister, you said the Donnegans' rooms would be twenty-five dollars a night. I figure three nights at seventy-five dollars, and that's all I aim to pay."

"The difference is food and drink," the clerk cried desperately. "It's customary to charge it to the room. . . ."

"I purely don't give a damn *how* customary it is," Gil roared. "I said I'd pay for the rooms, and I will, but that's all."

The hotel man looked pleadingly at the sheriff.

"I can't see he owes for anything but the rooms," said the sheriff. "You didn't tell him he'd be stuck for whatever was charged to the rooms?"

"No," said the clerk, "I thought it was understood."

"Next time, don't 'think,' be sure. Pay him $135, Austin, and before you leave, go to the hotel and get your receipt. I don't want to hear any more about this. Now, Rawlins, what's your problem?"

The banker stood up, nervously wringing his hands. He seemed extremely embarrassed, and swallowed hard a time or two before he spoke.

"Mr. Austin, yesterday afternoon, your associate, Mr. Donnegan, brought a check to me. A large check, payable to him, written on a New York bank. I saw nothing wrong with it, and based on your combined assets, I cashed it for him."

Gil knew what was coming. He caught a fistful of shirt and necktie, and the frightened banker found himself on tiptoe, struggling to breathe.

"Turn him loose, Austin," said the sheriff, "and let him finish."

"I told him," gasped Rawlins, "I needed something to guarantee the check until it cleared the bank in New York, and he insisted I take this."

Gil took the sheet of paper and couldn't believe his eyes. It was an unconditional bill of sale, giving the bearer rights to four thousand Texas steers, and it was signed by Gil Austin! The handwriting was so similar to Gil's own, it was uncanny. Furious, he turned to the sheriff.

"I never wrote or signed this," he shouted. "These steers don't belong to Donnegan, and he had no right to do this!"

"Rawlins," said the sheriff, exasperated, "when you took his check, you knew it might be months before it got back to that New York bank. Why did you do it, and not even twenty-four hours later, come whinin' to me?"

"Because," cried Rawlins, "the herd of cattle promised me in this bill of sale has been sold to some speculator in Coloma, and they're being driven to the goldfields."

"Damn you, Rawlins," Gil shouted, "that's a lie! I no more sold to some speculator in Coloma than I made out that bill of sale to you!"

"I can't stand a loss like this," Rawlins whined. "I'll be ruined."

"Tough," said Sheriff Conklin, "but I can't see Austin bein' responsible for any of this. He's been in jail since two o'clock yesterday afternoon, and he seems as much a victim as you. All I can do is look for this slick-dealin' Donnegan, and he may already be gone."

"My God," groaned Rawlins, "a steamer left at seven this morning!"

Gil heard no more. He was out the door on the run, his outfit right behind him. The hotel was almost a mile up the bay, and the livery beyond that.

"Van," Rosa cried, "I do not have a horse! You took him back to camp!"

"You can double with me," Van panted, "until we

reach camp. I just hope his honor didn't sell our horse remuda along with the herd."

The question foremost in all their minds was, what had happened to the rest of their riders? There was Mariposa, Estanzio, Juan Alamonte, Manuel Armijo, and Domingo Chavez. None of them would have allowed the herd to be taken without a fight. Unless there was another fraudulent bill of sale. Nearing the lake, they could see that the herd was indeed gone, but they all breathed a sigh of relief at the sight of the grazing horses. At least they had fresh mounts for the pursuit of the herd. But where were their riders?

"We are here," shouted a voice.

Juan Alamonte had heard their horses and cried out. The five riders were in a stand of sycamores, every man bound securely to a tree.

"Por Dios," Rosa cried, "they have been hurt!"

Each of them had been severely beaten. Estanzio and Mariposa seemed unconscious, on their feet only because the trees to which they were bound supported them. The riders left their saddles on the run, knives in their hands and anger strong in their minds.

"Water, please," Domingo croaked. "We have been here since dawn. I fear that Estanzio and Mariposa are very much hurt. They fought even when there was no hope."

"I'm goin' after a doc," said Van. "Estanzio and Mariposa need more help than we can give."

"Good idea," Gil said, "and have him bring a buckboard or wagon. We may have to send them back to town."

Carefully Gil cut the Indian riders loose from the sycamores to which they'd been bound and stretched them out on blankets. They looked as though they might have been unconscious since the beatings. Neither of them had spoken more than a dozen words to Rosa in her seven years with the outfit, but she thought of them as part of her family. She wept for them, even as she washed the dried blood from their battered faces. Of the three vaqueros, Juan Alamonte was the least battered about the mouth and more able to talk. It was he who told the story of their beating and the taking of the herd.

"Ten hombres," said Juan. "They ride in before first light. One of them whose name is Scanlon, he say they have bought the herd for a store in Coloma. He show us the bill of sale which has your name. *Ayer tarde,* Rosa tell us you are locked in the *juzgado.* We believe she would have told us if you sell the herd, so we do not believe these men. We say we will not give up the cows until we hear from you, but there are ten of them and but five of us, so we have not the chance. Mariposa and Estanzio, they fight with *cuchillo.* Some hombres cut bad."

That explained the savage beating of the Indian duo. They had been bound and made to pay for the hurt inflicted on the thieves. When Van returned, he brought with him Dr. Finch, who drove a buckboard. Finch was tall, thin, and three-quarters bald. He attended Mariposa and Estanzio first, for their condition was the most serious.

"For a certainty," said the doctor, "they have broken collarbones, and probably concussions. Some of their wounds need stitches, and they ought to have at least a week of bed rest."

"That's a problem," Gil said. "We have some hard ridin' ahead of us, and we need to leave them where they can get the care they need. But leave them among strangers, and they'll be like a pair of catamounts when they heal some."

"There's . . . ah, another problem," said Dr. Finch. "They're Indian, and Indians aren't well thought of in San Francisco."

"They're respected in Texas," Gil said grimly, "and this pair is mighty well thought of by my outfit. Now you make a place for 'em in a hospital, or wherever you have to, and see that they're treated like human beings."

"I can provide the beds and medical care," said the doctor, "but I can't promise nursing. San Francisco is short of women in general, nurses in particular, and all the men are looking for gold. You'll have to leave someone with them."

"I will stay with them," said Rosa. "They do not speak much English, and I do not wish them to be left among strangers."

"I'll feel a lot better about them if you do," Gil said. "I'm going to need every fighting man. We'll be gone maybe two weeks, Doctor. Do you need payment before we go?"

"No," said Dr. Finch. "You may settle with me when you return."

"Here," said Gil gruffly, and he handed Rosa five double eagles. "High as everything is around here, you'll need this, just to eat decent."

He turned away before she could speak, but he needn't have worried. Just having him speak kindly to her choked her up so that she couldn't have uttered a word. Quickly, Gil and Van carried Mariposa to the buckboard, while Ramon and Vicente brought Estanzio. Van helped Rosa up beside the doctor, and he flicked the reins, heading the horses for town. Gil looked around him. He had nine men, but only if his three badly beaten vaqueros could ride. They understood his dilemma.

"I hurt," said Domingo, "but my anger is greater than my hurt. Let us ride after the cows."

"Si," said Juan Alamonte and Manuel Chavez, in one voice.

"Bueno," said Gil. "Mount up, and let's show this bunch of *pelados* what Texans think of cattle rustlers."

The herd had been driven northeast, which would take them to the San Joaquin River, about thirty miles away. The rustlers could then follow the San Joaquin north another forty miles, until it forked into the Sacramento. Two days' drive along the Sacramento should get them to the Coloma diggings, in the very heart of the goldfields.

"Accordin' to our map," said Van as they rode, "there'll be good water all the way, once they reach the San Joaquin. From where they took the herd, I'd say it's a little over a hundred miles to the goldfields. A seven-day drive."

"Not for this bunch of thieves," Gil said. "They've got maybe six or seven hours' start on us, but they're not used to trailin' Texas longhorns. They won't make ten miles today, and I don't see any water on our map between here and the San Joaquin. With ten riders, they'll have one hell of a day, and unless they find a spring, a dry camp tonight."

"They are well-armed," said Domingo.

"So are we," Gil said, "and I don't aim for us to catch up to them in daylight. We'll let them wrestle with the longhorns all day and all night, and then we'll make our play at first light tomorrow."

By early afternoon Gil and his riders were near enough to the herd to see and smell the dust of its passing.

"We'll back off until after dark," Gil said. "Better for us if they think there's no pursuit."

But there were other factors—dangerous elements of which Gil was unaware. Scanlon, the speculator to whom Donnegan had fraudulently sold the herd, had been on his way to Los Angeles. He and nine men had ridden to San Francisco for supplies, and in a saloon, the speculator had heard Donnegan asking for offers. Scanlon, seeing the windfall for what it was, had made Donnegan an offer, and it had been accepted. Scanlon had put aside his other plans and was taking the newly acquired herd back to his store at Coloma. When darkness caught up with them, their first hard day's drive had covered less than ten miles. Scanlon sent a rider ahead to the San Joaquin River, to fetch the dozen men he'd left there. At dawn the herd of Texas longhorns would take the trail with twenty-two riders. . . .

* * *

July 13, 1850. Twenty miles west of the San Joaquin River

"Let's ride," said Gil an hour before first light. "If they're lookin' for pursuit, they'll expect it from the west, so we'll circle around and take them from the east."

They crossed a stream, evidence that the herd had reached water before dark. They smelled smoke, and they rode into the camp during breakfast, with their guns drawn. Three men went for their guns. Gil shot one, Van the second, and Juan Padillo the third.

"Which of you coyotes is Scanlon?" Gil demanded.

"I'm Scanlon," said a tall man in black hat, store-bought suit, and black polished boots. He wore a tied-down pistol on his right hip.

"These are my steers," said Gil, "and we've come for them."

"I paid eight thousand for them, and I have a bill of sale, so I consider them mine."

"You thieving bastard," Van shouted, "that's just two dollars a head!"

"Once I pay for something," said Scanlon, "it's mine, and when you gun down some of my men, you have to answer to me. Now three of you are going to hang. A miner's court will see to that."

"I reckon not," Gil said. "We've got the drop, and there's only seven of you. That's five short of a jury."

"The jury's behind you," said Scanlon with a smirk.

"Nobody move, an' nobody turn around," said a voice behind Gil and his men. "There's twelve of us. Drop them guns, or we'll drop you."

One false move and the Texans would die in a hail of lead.

"Drop your guns," Gil said as he released his own.

"Boys," Scanlon said, "I bought these steers, paid for them, and have a bill of sale. These hombres rode in, called me a thief, and killed three men. Now as I see it, we got no choice but to hold miner's court and try these killers before we hang 'em."

"They're all ridin' in the same pack," somebody shouted. "I say we hang the whole damn bunch!"

There were shouts of approval. The Texans were forced to mount their horses and ride ahead of their captors. Van looked at Gil, and Gil shook his head. A break was out of the question; they'd be blasted out of their saddles before they'd ridden twenty yards. Their captors had in mind a secluded place for the hangings. It was a box canyon, and toward the far end there were huge oaks with sturdy limbs.

"Ride to the trees and rein up," Scanlon ordered.

There was nothing else to do. The Texans waited beneath the oaks as Scanlon's men began knotting the nooses.

"This miner's court's in session," said Scanlon. "These gents knows what they're bein' accused of, and the jury knows what they're guilty of. Has the jury reached a verdict?"

"Hang the bastards," somebody shouted, and his comrades sided him with their own shouts of approval.

"Drop them ropes," said a voice from the canyon rim, "an' then yer irons. I'll kill the firs' man what even *looks* like he aims t' do otherwise."

Long John Coons stood on the canyon rim, a Colt rock steady in each hand, and he wasn't alone. Other men sided him, every one armed, and there were more on the opposite canyon rim.

"We're within the law," Scanlon bawled. "These bastards rode into my camp, shot three of my men—"

"They had cause," Long John said. "The tale's all over town, how you bought the herd, knowin' it was a crooked deal. You Tejanos, take up their irons an' cover them coyotes till we git down there."

When they rode into the canyon, Long John had twenty-five men with him.

"Long John," Juan Padillo shouted, "I kiss you, if you not so damn ugly."

"Now," said Long John, as he and his companions dismounted, "we're gonna have us a little talk. I rid into San Francisco, an' the firs' thing I see is Rosa in a buckboard with a gent that turns out t' be a doc. Estanzio an' Mariposa looks near daid, an' I begin t' fin' out what's took place. 'Fore Rosa's done talkin', these boys I got wi' me has gathered 'round. I reckon they got somethin' t' say about this Scanlon coyote."

"Damn right we have," said one of the men who had accompanied Long John. "We're from the diggings, and we don't aim to let Scanlon do what he's done b'fore. There was a herd come in from Oregon, and 'fore we knowed it was here, Scanlon and others like him had grabbed it. They robbed us, chargin' us seventy-five cents a pound for beef. It's wrong to take advantage of a man when he's hungry, bleedin' him dry, and that's what's been done to us. Right, boys?"

There was a thundering chorus of agreement from his companions.

"I reckoned I'd need some help," Long John said, "an' I made these boys a promise. I tol' 'em we wouldn't sell them steers t' nobody that was goin' t' resell 'em by the pound. I said we'd sell t' the miners, not t' the greedy coyotes like Scanlon."

"We ain't expectin' nothin' fer free," said one of the miners. "All we're lookin' fer is a fair price, so's it don't take all our dust just t' keep us fed."

"What's your idea of a fair price?" Gil asked.

"Four ounces of gold for a cow. That's sixty-four dollars."

"You got a deal," said Gil, "on two conditions. First, that you send somebody ahead and spread the word that we're comin', and second, that some of you will throw in with us for the rest of the drive. We're just a mite short-handed, and I don't trust Scanlon and his coyotes not to do a little back-shootin', given the chance. Every man ridin' the rest of the way with us gets a steer at the end of the drive."

When the shouting, cheering, and backslapping was over, Gil had a question for them.

"You gents know Mr. Scanlon, what he's done in the past, and what he's tried to do today. What do you reckon we ought to do with him?"

"We ought t' hang the greedy son," said a miner, "but that'd be too quick. Turn him an' his coyotes loose, an' we'll spread the word from one end of the diggings to the other about his thievery."

"I'll go along with that," Gil said, "on one condition. That we shoot this bunch on sight if they get within hollerin' distance of the herd."

When all the shouting was done, Gil turned to Scanlon.

"I reckon you heard," Gil said. "Send one man back to get the riders you left with the herd, and then the lot of you get the hell out of here."

"I won't forget this," Scanlon snarled. "You cost me eight thousand dollars!"

"Take it out of your profits on that seventy-five-cent beef sale," Gil said. "Now mount up and ride. Any of your men we find with the herd will leave here tied over their saddles."

Two of the miners rode out for the goldfields to spread the word, and Gil promised each of them a steer for their help.

"Those two, and the twenty-three ridin' with us," Van said, "that's twenty-five steers. At sixty-four dollars apiece, that's sixteen hundred dollars."

"If Long John hadn't brought these hombres, and showed up when he did, we'd be buzzard and coyote bait. Don't you think your Tejano hide's worth sixteen hundred dollars?"

Van grinned. "Ten seconds before Long John and his boys showed up, I'd have swapped the whole damn herd for a fast horse and a fifty-yard start."

* * *

July 20, 1850. In the diggings

Gil's final tally of the herd was 3850 steers. First they cut out the twenty-five steers he had promised the miners who had assisted them. The rest were sold, one or two at a time, to individual miners or groups of miners. One of the miners brought a scale to weigh the dust, and Gil was confronted with a problem none of them had considered. When they were done, there would be 956 pounds of gold dust, and they had no containers. Again the miners came to their aid, supplying old tobacco sacks, leather pouches, envelopes of letters from home, and a variety of other containers. They had the horse remuda, so they had packhorses, but no pack saddles or saddlebags. Gil went to one of the stores and paid $150 apiece for two tents, and from them fashioned ten huge double bags. A strap from each of the bags met under the horse's belly, and an equal amount of gold rode in each of the bags. Five months and six days after leaving Bandera Range, they rode away from the goldfields, bound for San Francisco.

"We have $244,000 in gold," Van said. "Once we get to San Francisco, we'd better find a bank and convert it to something easier and less obvious to carry."

"I aim to," Gil said, "but it won't be the Bank of San Francisco Bay."

July 23, 1850. San Francisco

Gil and the riders found Rosa, Estanzio, and Mariposa lodged in a six-bed hospital. Rosa had slept on one of the beds, while the Indian duo had preferred the floor, without even a pillow. They were as restless as a pair of caged cougars, and had remained there only because Rosa had managed to talk them into it. Once Gil had deposited the gold in the Miner's Bank of San Francisco, he allowed Mariposa and Estanzio to take the entire horse remuda back to the lake where the herd had been bedded down.

"I reckon we gon' be here a day er two, ain't we?" Long John asked. "I got me some business to 'tend to."

"I think so," Gil said. "Do you need some money?"

"Not fer a while," said the Cajun. "The cap'n at Fort Yuma got word t' the law in San Diego, got me the reeward fer them outlaws, six thousand dollars worth."

Gil avoided the Palace Hotel, taking rooms for them all in the Mariner's Inn, a less elegant place, where they could see the Pacific Ocean. Exhausted after holding Mariposa and Estanzio at bay for two weeks, Rosa was in her room resting. She answered a knock on her door, and found Long John standing there. On his lean face there was a grin, and under his arm, a parcel that was wrapped in brown paper.

"I got somethin' t' show ye," he said.

Rosa stepped aside and he came in. He placed the package on the bed and untied the string. It was a granite slab, two inches thick and a foot square. In the very center was a perfect star, and within the star, a single word: Bo.

"It is beautiful," said Rosa. "He would be pleased to know that you have remembered him in this way."

"But fer you," Long John said, "I wouldn't of been here t' do this. I want you t' put it on his grave."

"I am not sure I will be returning to Texas."

"Van tole me 'bout that redheaded wh—woman," Long John said. "Don't you reckon Gil's learnt his lesson? Ye cain't hold it agin a man ferever, jist 'cause he's made a fool of hisself."

"It is not that, Long John. Just because he no longer wants her does not mean he wants me, and if he is to become a lawyer, I do not want him."

Long John took the package from the bed and put on his hat, but he paused at the door.

"My mama's a conjurin' woman," he said, "an' she tells what's goin' t' happen. I git a notion m'sef, sometimes, an' this ye can be sure of. I aimed fer ye t' lay this slab on ol' Bo's grave at Fort Yuma, an' ye will."

Rosa closed the door and sat down on the bed. It was late afternoon, and the uncertainty was getting to her. Long John meant well, but he had no control over Gil Austin or his pride.

Long John had been out all day, so he didn't know whether Gil was in or not, but he knocked on the door. To his surprise, Gil was there.

"Got somethin' t' show ye," he said, stepping in without an invitation.

Long John placed his parcel on the bed and again opened it.

"It's nice, Long John," Gil said. His words had an air of finality, and sounded like an invitation to leave, but Long John didn't go.

"I aimed fer Rosa t' put this on Bo's grave," said the Cajun, "but she says she ain't goin' back wi' us t' Texas."

"Oh, hell," Gil groaned, "I heard that all the way from El Paso. Does she want me to whine and beg?"

"I reckon she don't like bein' took fer granted," said Long John. "If she felt fer me like she does fer you, I'd whine an' beg, if that's what it took."

"How in hell do *you* know what she feels for me?" Gil demanded.

"I asked her," Long John lied.

The Cajun stood looking out the window into the twilight. Gil grabbed him by the shoulder and whirled him around until they were facing.

"You lanky, meddling bastard." Gil grinned. "Thanks."

Long John stood there until he heard a knocking on the door down the hall. Carefully, he rewrapped the granite marker, tied the string, and stepped out into the gathering darkness.

Rosa's heart almost stopped when she opened the door and found Gil standing there. He stepped in and closed the door.

"I've had enough of this talk about you stayin' in California," he said.

"Do you have one good reason why I should not?"

"Because I don't want you to," he growled.

"That is not good enough," she said.

"Then, by God," he shouted, "try this. I want you with me, on Bandera Range. I aim to raise cows, horses, chickens, and kids. I aim to put my brand on you, and I don't give a damn if you're just sixteen and I'm a hundred and sixteen!"

"I am twenty years old," she said.

Gil looked at her as though she had betrayed him. "Then why the hell have you strung me along, having me believe you were a child?" he shouted.

"I have not misled you," Rosa said, "for I have known my true birth date for only a little while. I found it within the old locket that belonged to my madre. I am much like her, small in size, but a woman in my heart. It was you who called me a child."

"So I'm the cause of all my troubles," said Gil. "Do you aim to tell me to go to hell, shoot me, or just keep me in sackcloth and ashes for the rest of my life?"

"None of those things," Rosa said, with the half-smile that had always irked him. "I think having Gil Austin admit to being mortal will be enough."

"You purely know how to humble a man," said Gil, "but I'm glad we finally know how old you are. I'll feel better about marrying you."

"I will not marry a man who leaves me on the ranch and rides away to town to become a lawyer," Rosa said.

"I've always been a cowboy," he said, "and that's all I'll ever be. Do you reckon there's a lawyer anywhere in the world that's made two hundred forty-four thousand dollars in less than six months?"

"I do not wish to talk about money. I have waited a long time for you. Must I wait until we return to Texas?"

"No way, my little chili pepper."

She slapped him. Hard. He backed away, unbelieving.

"Do not *ever* call me that again," she hissed, "or I will tear your hair out by the roots!"

He seized her, and when their kiss ended, they were lying across the bed. Her face was flushed and her eyes were closed. Suddenly he laughed and sat up. She opened one eye.

"Remember that night," he said, "when you came into my room jaybird naked? I thought you were going to get into bed with me."

"I got no encouragement," she said, "but you *did* see me."

"I reckon," he said. "I may be old, but I'm still alive in some places. Let's go somewhere, find a preacher, and take up where we left off."

"But it is late."

"Not as late as it's gonna be. Tonight you have a bed. Tomorrow night, we'll be on our way to Texas. You'll be on hard ground, rocks pokin' you in the backside, and a dozen men listenin' for all they're worth."

"Let us find this preacher, then."

They found one, and while they wouldn't have a ring until the next day, they *did* have a best man. Long John Coons was glad to oblige.

July 24, 1850. San Francisco

Gil bought Rosa the ring she hadn't had when they'd stood before the preacher the night before. Since it was their last night in San Francisco, the outfit had made an event of it. Even Van went out and had a few drinks to celebrate a wedding he had thought would never come to pass. Everybody was at the hotel in time for breakfast except Long John.

"Damn it," said Gil, "he knows we're pullin' out to-day. If I can be up and ready at daylight, why can't he?"

"Perhaps he has a good reason," said Rosa.

As it turned out, Long John did. He finally showed up at ten o'clock, with a girl who was no older than Rosa.

She had dark eyes, long black hair, and curves that would have made Kate Donnegan envious.

"This is Suzanne," said Long John. "She's from New Orleans, an' don't much like Californy. She's goin' t' Texas wi' me."

Suzanne looked at Long John in a way that said the lanky Cajun was in deep water.

"Long John does not just play with fire," Vicente observed. "He takes a keg of powder with him and lights the fuse."

They had ridden the California Trail to the end, and on the day they departed for Texas came the news. The ship on which Lionel Donnegan had escaped had been lost at sea. There were no survivors.

EPILOGUE

~~~W~~~

*T*exas Ranger Captain Benjamin McCulloch was born in Rutherford County, Tennessee, on November 11, 1811. A friend of David Crockett, McCulloch went to Texas and fought under General Sam Houston in the battle of San Jacinto. He served as scout for Ranger Captain John Coffee (Jack) Hays in 1842, and in 1846, led a spy company of Rangers into Mexico, during the Mexican war.

W. A. A. (Bigfoot) Wallace was born in Lexington, Virginia, on April 3, 1817. In 1836, after a brother and a cousin died in the Goliad Massacre, Wallace set out for Texas to "square the account." He joined the Rangers under Captain John Coffee (Jack) Hays, and was active with the Rangers all through the war with Mexico.

N. H. (Old Man) Clanton and his gang of outlaws settled in southern New Mexico and Arizona, after being run out of Texas by the Rangers. Clanton's four sons —Isaac, Ike, Phineas, and Bill—were gunslingers, sidewinder mean. The Clantons moved into Tombstone following a silver strike there, and rose to power through payoffs to Sheriff Johnny Behan, staunch opponent of Wyatt Earp. After Bill Clanton died at the OK Corral, things were never the same. A year later, in 1882, Curly Bill, John Ringo, Old Man Clanton and the rest of his boys ambushed a mule-train in Skeleton Canyon, slaughtering nineteen muleteers and taking seventy-five thousand dollars in silver bullion. But relatives of the men slain in the bullion-train massacre got their revenge. While Clanton and some of his gang drove stolen cattle through Guadalupe Canyon, they were shot dead, ending the Clanton reign.

Joaquin Murrietta's young wife was raped by California miners, and his 1849 gold claim was forgotten, as Murrietta organized a band of eighty gun-slinging desperados and terrorized the mining camps of the High Sierra. He was finally ambushed in 1853, by a Los Angeles gunfighter and twenty men. His head was severed and sold for thirty-five dollars. He was twenty-three.

Here is an excerpt from

The Shawnee Trail

The next title in Ralph Compton's
exciting Western series:

"Come on, gents," Long John said. "Let's rope this
critter an' move her acrost the water."

Sky Pilot, foreseeing the need, had installed iron rings
on both sides along the bottom of the wagon box. Long
John tied his rope to a ring near the front of the wagon,
while Quando Miller tied to a ring nearest the back. Dent
Briano took his place in the middle, and they were ready.
Stoney swam his horse across, and as they clambered up
the opposite bank, the slack went out of the rope, and the
wagon lurched toward the rushing brown water of the
Pecos. The trio of riders kept pace, and when the wagon
left solid ground, the current took hold. When the wagon
hit the ends of the steadying lines, Long John's horse
staggered. Little by little they gained on the river, and
Stoney sighed with relief as his horse drew the wagon to
safety. Long John, Stoney, Dent, and Quando quickly
freed the wagon from the cottonwood logs, as Sky Pilot
began harnessing the teams. Seeing the wagon had safely
crossed, *Malo* Coyote and Naked Horse had driven the
horse remuda into position. Long John, Dent, and
Quando rode downstream to assist in crossing the horses.
Curiously, the Indians didn't drive the horses into the
river, but rode in ahead, leading them. The remuda followed willingly, as the rest of the riders already were
moving the longhorns toward the river. Llano was at
drag, and Stoney noted with satisfaction that Suzanne

was with him. Once the horses were safely across, Long John, Dent, and Quando rode out to meet the oncoming herd. The Kid, Stoney, and Bandy Darden were at right flank, on the downriver side. Long John, Dent, and Quando had ridden to left flank, while Deuce Gitano had joined Llano and Suzanne at drag.

"Let's hit 'em hard!" Llano shouted.

Deuce and Suzanne followed his lead, swinging doubled lariats against dusty flanks and screeching like Comanches. The lead steers plunged into the swirling water without hesitation, and it looked good. But it all changed in an instant, and Stoney saw the trouble coming. A broken cottonwood branch had been submerged, but when the butt end hit some obstruction, the leafy end of the branch reared up out of the water directly in front of the lead steers. It sprang out of the river like some green apparition, and while it hung there by a few seconds, it was enough to spook the leaders. With the rush of the current to their left and the rest of the herd behind, the lead steers turned downstream, seeking to circle back to the river bank they'd just left. In doing so they were about to engulf the three flank riders in the resulting turmoil.

"Ride," Stoney shouted. "Get out of their way!"

Bandy Darden broke free and rode downstream ahead of the longhorns, but the Kid wasn't so lucky. His horse screamed, trying to buck as a flailing horn raked its flank. Even then the Kid might have made it, but another horn ripped into his left side. The force of it drove him out of the saddle, and he disappeared beneath the swirling brown water of the Pecos.

Dodging flailing horns, Stoney fought his way to the Kid's frightened horse, to the offside where the young rider had left the saddle. The Kid, had he been trampled beneath the hooves of the milling herd, was finished. There was one chance in a thousand he was hurt but alive. A slashing horn tore a burning gash across Stoney's right thigh as he leaned out of the saddle, seeking the offside stirrup of the Kid's horse. While Stoney could hear someone shouting, he couldn't distinguish the words.

Suddenly his frantic fingers touched the toe of a boot. The Kid's foot was caught in the offside stirrup! Taking a firm grip on the horn with his right hand, Stoney leaned far out of the saddle, his left hand grasping the Kid's pistol belt. The Kid was a dead weight, almost more than Stoney could handle. When he came up, the first person he saw was Llano Dupree, as he was about to rope Stoney's horse. With Llano's help, the horse fought its way free of the longhorns. Stoney shook his head, trying to clear his eyes and ears of the muddy water. He had been lucky, but he wasn't so sure about the young rider. The Kid looked dead, or close to it . . . .

The Shawnee Trail—

Another exciting addition

to Ralph Compton's Trail Drive

series—Look for it soon!